CW00922295

PROJECT ECLIPSE

ROBERT TILLSLEY

This is a work of fiction. All characters, organisations, locations, and events portrayed in this novel are either products of the author's imagination or are used fictitiously.

Project Eclipse

Copyright © 2023 by Robert Tillsley

All rights reserved.

No part of this book may be reproduced in any form or by any electronic or mechanical means, including information storage and retrieval systems, without written permission from the author, except for the use of brief quotations in a book review. No part of this book may be used by artificial intelligence, large language models, or other forms of data processing without written permission from the author.

Cover design by Matt J Pike

Published by Black Sky Books

Magill, Australia

www.blackskybooks.com

ISBN 978-0-6453886-3-3

 A catalogue record for this book is available from the National Library of Australia

BOOKS BY ROBERT TILLSLEY

NOVELS

Project Eclipse

The Last Cruise Ship (as R Max Tillsley)

SHORT STORIES

Replication — Contact This! (anthology)

Crickey! — Storming Area 51 (anthology)

Contours of War — On Deadly Ground (anthology)

Red Snow — Slay Bells Ring (anthology)

Silent Griffin — Fire For Effect (anthology)

Where the Dead Walk — The Monster Within (anthology)

Bloodstone — Zombie! Patient Zero (anthology)

Clay Breath — Clash of Steel (anthology)

CHILDRENS BOOKS

All as R Max Tillsley

THE SUSIE STEELE ADVENTURES

The Steele Trap

The Steele Bite

TANGLED FATES

Brainz

STAND ALONE NOVELS

Rebyrth

To all the creators who bring magic to our lives.

CHAPTER 1
EXPLORATORY

T he quad tracks of CI425, a rugged crewed rover, crunched along the outside of a jagged crater edge. Ten years of furious storms had traced narrow grooves along the ridge. In the future, a milder climate would smooth the stone long before the plate tectonics of Eclipse could pull the feature beneath its planetary crust.

Sheets of hostile rain slapped against the crew blister at the rover's front. Made of many small transparent hexagonal facets secured to a black frame, the blister could be easily repaired whenever the still-stabilizing atmosphere tossed a rock in its all-too-frequent bursts of fury. Several species of long grass had taken hold in the soil, hardy colonists that dared to reach further than the sheltered crops and even the expanding forests. Beneath the surface were the hardiest of all—the seeded microorganisms that turned sterile minerals into soil.

Bill Hayden, chief surveyor of the Phase 2 colony, pursed his lips as the last of six stubby drones failed its docking attempt thanks to a sudden gust. Its AI aborted and pulled out in time, circling under the power of four tiny thrusters. Through the blister, Bill spotted blue flares as the drone swung back, this time locking onto its docking port and synchronizing its datacore. The set would need a full maintenance cycle when he reached Staging.

One of his ever-shrinking-team members could do the task. He yanked on the steering joystick to avoid a sliding boulder. *No, Bill. The whole point is to practice going it alone. If you can't be self-sufficient on dirt, you sure as hell won't be in vacuum.*

He leaned over and grabbed a battered canister, pulling the straw out with his teeth and sucking. The bitter coffee was cold, and the powdered milk had almost turned. Grimacing, he tossed it behind his chair.

"Bill," he told himself, "you've gotten sloppy."

A chime sounded, barely audible above the battering winds. He scowled at the interruption and its meaning—a message had made it through. He slipped lank, black hair over his ear and rotated his chair to check the primary display. The rugged design with switches and a touchscreen was blocky—a visual remnant of a bygone era—but it was easy to fabricate and reliable. He tapped the display and brought up the metadata. Recorded and first transmitted two hours ago from the survey office at Staging. Curious. The storm had been raging for at least four, and it was lucky the message had come through at all.

"Why did you bother?"

He tapped the play option. An image of Sarah Phinas took up a quarter of the display. A no-nonsense ponytail pulled her sandy brown hair tight. Dark, intelligent eyes hovered above lightly freckled cheeks and a narrow tense jaw like a building storm. She wore the standard beige colony jumpsuit with patches for the survey team on her upper arms. Heaven forbid that people wasted time on frivolities like fashion. At least it was more comfortable than the bulkier, charcoal gray field kit he endured. The video ran for only a few frames before freezing. A message wrote itself over the display.

VIDEO FEED CORRUPTED. WOULD YOU LIKE TO CONTINUE WITH AUDIO ONLY?

"No, I'd like you to translate the message into an interpretive dance."

When the message remained, he accepted the option. There would be an underlying text version as well, given the regular transmission problems.

"Bill, a mayday came through from Charlie's rover. It's garbled AF, and I can't request a resend until the storm clears. I asked for help from the cops, but Ware reckons he can't spare anyone until the storm blows over. And don't tell me to go to admin—I tried. Sturt's lackeys said there's not enough data to confirm a problem, and they can't risk anyone else if it's not confirmed. I don't like it, but they won't listen to *me*."

The veiled reprimand from Bill's junior brought a tightness to his lips. He leaned back. He should be manning the office, organizing, while his team danced to his commands. But, damn it, he'd always preferred to work alone—and he was barely qualified for sifting through survey data, despite the course he'd rushed through. In his previous career, he'd worked with a very different kind of information. No. His approach was for the best. Sarah had kept talking, so he skipped back and listened.

"I'm including the latest telemetry for our rovers and the only string of coherent text I could isolate from Charlie. If I don't hear from you when the storm clears, I'll assume it's okay to send whoever's nearest to take a look. Stay safe. Sarah out."

Charlie, you idiot. He didn't need this. He really didn't. The back of his mind was already whirling, though. Maximize the dataset before making decisions. Bill sighed, brought up the information packet, and inspected the text Sarah had indicated.

GEOPHYS BOUNCE NOT MATCHING SO INVESTIGATING WITHIN

There was a detailed explanation. Within what? Geophysics—a broad science often narrowed to the local subsurface conditions by the survey team—matched Charlie's expertise and his mission goals. The Phase zero and one surveys had struggled to get clear data. But whatever had triggered the surveyor's interest had been cut off. What next?

Ping coordinates and timestamps along with route plans overlaid a regional map. Even in good weather, the unusual compounds in the ionosphere made comms patchy. Rod Davison, Yang Mi, and Aamar Rukh were riding the storm. Rod was the closest at last comms, but could be far off before receiving an order to divert. Aamar was too far south. Yang should be heading back that way in eight to ten hours.

Bill added his own position. It showed up as a glowing green dot. Six hours of driving, tops. Five if he pushed hard. If Charlie was in trouble, he would be the best bet. It'd kill his schedule with flow-on effects for the agri team. And that would piss off the chain right up to Oliver Sturt, the colony director. Charlie had brought a whole lot of pain down on Bill no matter what he did.

"Screw it."

He set Charlie's last known coordinates as his target and altered course. The rover shook as a gust of wind caught at the side of the vehicle and heaved. Wrenching the controls, he adjusted his path to bring the nose around and avoid rolling. Images of Charlie came unbidden and unreal—at least so far. The short, serious man trapped under his rover or bleeding out thanks to a tree branch that had impaled him like a skewer. Far more likely, the rover computer had fritzed, and Charlie was busy working with no idea that his colleagues were worried.

Once off the crater, the wind became less fierce. Bill navigated the rover along a twisting route, ignoring the inbuilt course generation. Some ditches were crossable, some saplings crushable. When he had a chance to think, he sent a message out to Sarah, letting her know he'd take care of Charlie. He then sent another to Charlie, hoping he'd receive a 'don't bother' response when the interference died down.

Lightning burst in webs across the dark sky, white and cerulean displays of raw energy that stole his night vision. He adjusted the blister's filters, blocking the worst of the flashes but boosting the shadow intensity. In the modified view, water poured across the ground, a gray slurry of swirls. The horizon filled with low hills, and the bushes gave way to trees. He reached a firebreak corridor and used it as a highway, gunning the rover's electric motors right to their limits in the comparative safety of a straight line.

The autopilot would refuse this speed, so Bill kept control, each second of each minute of each hour demanding quick reactions and calm focus. He used the breathing techniques, the muscle relaxation exercises, and the patience that came with agency training.

Can I ever escape you?

A downed tree. Bill took the rover to the right, gambling that hitting the branches was better than the roots. *Snap. Bang.* A blister panel grew a long slender crack but held. The rover plowed through the tree's crown, the branches grasping for Bill and scraping along the rover with righteous anger as they failed. The engineered flora should have drilled roots deep into the soil, deep enough to survive whatever the planet's growing pains could throw at them. *Meant to be.* In practice, it translated to *might possibly.*

Engrossed in each instant, he blinked in surprise when the trees faded away. The sky had grown brighter, now an angry red-brown that would eventually give way to blue. He bled speed and stretched his hands while checking the map. Not far to go, and he'd cut most of an hour. Good. He was north of the colony and heading east, far enough away from the corporate exclusion zone to avoid dealing with those chumps.

He cracked his knuckles and brought the rover back to full speed. Time to see how stupid Charlie had been.

AS THE RAIN EASED, sensors lit up—Charlie's rover was now within range. It was warm with power but not transmitting. Nor was it moving.

"Okay, FLY3, you've got the most juice. Go show me what you see." He toggled a switch and catapulted the drone. The EM static would clear in the coming hours, but if the drone was on a tight leash, he'd be able to receive a feed thanks to the rover's antennae.

About a click out, the feed came online. Bill brought it up on a side display while navigating a steep ascent to a plateau. The second rover's designation, CI431, was stenciled on its bulky side. There were marks, distortions. Damage, he concluded. More delays. The team's targets were going to be shot, and wouldn't Director Sturt love that? The rover's door was half open, an unusual state, most likely due to a malfunction. Charlie should be suited up inside, utterly miserable.

Bill set the drone to shift to a wider angle, and it complied, sending fresh details. The rover was parked beside a series of tall, striated fangs of rock. Reds and dirty greens, creams, and large blue crystals. The latter would be kyanite, an aluminosilicate common to the region. Damage from a rock fall would explain a mayday, though no large boulders or shards lay around 431 as convenient evidence.

Bill directed the drone to the rover's blister. "Let's have a peek to see if we can get some attention."

The blister was dark, its filter blocking the drone's view. The last drops of rain slid down its facets. Issuing commands, Bill watched as the drone waggled back and forth, then finally tapped against the glass, water fizzing beneath the thrusters' tails. It should be easy to hear.

"Come on, Charlie."

Bill's rover leveled out. A minute and he'd be there himself to knock on the door. But damn, he'd feel better if Charlie gave a sign first. This was exactly what Bill didn't want to deal with. He'd have to do another pain-in-the-ass safety briefing. Seconds rolled past and Charlie's rover came into Bill's unaided view, and still, there was no sign, no movement. The drone, a meter across, was far too large to fit in the doorway even when open, and its thrusters could fry anyone inside. Cursing Charlie, Bill ordered the drone back.

He parked a good twenty meters clear and stood, stretching. His spine ached, as was to be expected, and his fingers tingled. He considered taking his helmet off its hook but left it dangling and hit a toggle by the door. Clean air slapped his face as the door whooshed open. He sniffed deeply. The air was fresh from rain and with a tang that he would never get used to. He checked the respirator mask in his chest pocket and his gloves hanging from his belt before he climbed down three rungs to the ground.

Each rover weighed in at over eight tons when loaded, and they were imposing to any mere mortal who stood before them.

"Charlie!" he shouted, his eyes narrowing as he cataloged the rover's state. "You in there?"

He crossed to 431. Several small tears marred the plating, and the sensor pods were gone—cut clean off. More worryingly, smoke drifted out here and there. The storm had really done a number on the vehicle. What had Charlie been thinking?

"Come on, Charlie, can you hear me?" He activated his implanted comm. "Charlie, are you in range?"

No link through the satellites and no peer-to-peer network presence for his subordinate's comm. Bill grabbed at the railing next to the damaged rover's ladder and hauled himself up. The door was buckled, jammed in its tracks. Active displays offered a basic level of illumination, confirming that Charlie wasn't inside.

"Damn."

Whatever Charlie had been investigating, surely, he would have stopped to wait out the storm? If so, had he foolishly braved the elements to inspect the rover's damage? Had he been caught outside and sought shelter? The weather feed would have failed along with comms thanks to interference. An amateur mistake, but a conceivable one.

Bill tapped the interface on his suit's left arm, issuing commands to his drones. Three to do a large sweep and look for Charlie or his body. He closed his eyes, and for an instant, he was walking down a street, pace measured to avoid attention, heading to a tourist port, pedestrians and vehicles rushing as if they would be alive that evening.

Blinking, he ordered his thoughts to the problem at hand. Two drones to fly low, seeking overhangs or caves. And because he couldn't wait, he set out on foot, heading among the towering rock spires that would have attracted Charlie like bees to a flower. The man was hardy but sensible. If he'd wandered among the rocks, he'd have picked the most straightforward path. A path to what? Bill selected a candidate route and started hiking.

The drones had barely started their sweeps when Bill found a cave carved out of a thick kyanite layer. It had to be close to a meter in diameter, and its curve suggested machine drilling, though the edges were cracked and scored. Pulling up the survey map and checking through datasets revealed an early seeding tunnel. Drones had bored millions of them, and off of those billions of smaller ones—root-like tendrils dug to send nutrients, oxygen, bacteria, and water into a lifeless crust. And they had nothing on the scale of those from the terraforming plants. This could be an exit or a starting point, though softer ground would have made more sense. Machine logic was never the perfection it promised.

"Charlie?"

Grooves cut into the ground a short distance in front of the cave. Bill kneeled and ran two fingers inside one—a shallow V and surprisingly slick. He raised an eyebrow, but the marks offered no further explanation. He snapped a flashlight free from his suit shoulder and checked the cave.

The blue surface had a soapy sheen and curved up a little before angling down fast. At the apex, Charlie lay sprawled. Bill's stomach clenched, and his limbs grew heavy. *Damn it, Charlie.* He paused to steady himself. There was no need to rush. He crawled inside, breathing in a dusty odor. A sharp line from smooth to dusty suggested where the rain had reached. The surveyor had been spared a soaking, but at what cost?

"What did you get up to, you poor sod?"

Charlie's state made no sense. Legs snapped in multiple spots, a stump at the left wrist. The left earlobe missing, sliced cleanly off. No wonder Charlie wasn't emitting a comm signal. But the worst desecration had been inflicted on the torso. Deep wide cuts were the appetizer to a main course of horror. A cylinder of skin and bone and organs had been neatly excised. A hand-span in diameter, it ran from left to right, leaving a line of collapsed chest, resembling the core samples his team took from the ground.

Bill's hand shook as he reached to turn Charlie's face, to confirm that this wasn't some elaborate game, a magician's cruel trick. He'd seen images of torture, watched videos as long as he could stand, gone through training. They had repulsed him, but not at this visceral level. He'd seen enough bodies. It had been unavoidable in his old line of work. This—this was something altogether different. Vicious, frenzied, and yet almost surgical. The stiff neck required a second hand to turn. Charlie's open eyes stared. His bloodless lips were cut a dozen times. Bloodless. Where was it all? Bill leaned closer. The tongue was missing.

"Mercy's tears!"

Bill backed out of the cave and sucked in fresh air unsteadily at the entrance. The sun was visible, casting shadows that shimmered. His stomach tightened. He lost his balance and his hands and knees slammed into the unyielding ground. Acid and the remains of his last meal clawed their way out of his throat, erupting from his mouth in a vile torrent. His stomach heaved again and again.

Finally, when some measure of control returned, he rolled over onto his back.

"Charlie, what the hell happened to you? Who the hell happened to you?"

The sun pressed on his face, a hot mask that couldn't hide his turmoil. Murder. Colonies were the perfect incubator. High demands, rampant greed, no chance to cool off—the stain of humanity spread with every step taken from old Earth. Every step.

I left that behind, damn it.

He spat to the side and made his way back toward the rovers. Smoke trailed upward, and a thick, acrid miasma filled his lungs. Bill ran, chewing up the distance until he came around a boulder and confirmed the source. Charlie's rover was burning. The blue fire-retardant fluid that should have put it out had instead pooled around its tracks.

"Charlie, you asshole!" He shifted to a sprint, his mind running along old tracks. If there was an easy explanation for the man's death, it would be within the rover's data banks.

A white flash. Bill blinked, and then an invisible force slammed into his chest, stealing his breath. It was a one-two—he felt it in the face next, a hit that smacked his ears, cleared his sinuses, and bounced his brain. All balance gone, he hit the ground as a large panel sliced the air at neck level. Pieces rained down, vicious shards and heavy lumps. He wrapped his arms over his head. Had those on Marrick Prime felt the same?

No. It would have been much worse.

CHAPTER 2
WHY ARE YOU HERE?

A distant cloud of dirt heralded the colony's best and brightest —or, more accurately, the drunk home-delivery service. Bill leaned his head gingerly against the cool side of his rover. He'd dragged himself inside long enough to call in his gruesome discovery, but the coffin-like quiet inside the blister had made every breath a painful slap to his ears. Escaping outside, he'd lowered a work table built into the rover and claimed it as a chair.

There was plenty of work to do, forms that would need to be filled, shifts that would need changing, tasks to be reassigned. None of it appealed, so he listened to the insects that had come out of hiding. A flock of seven modified pintails flew overhead, no doubt looking to feast on the bugs. The little brown and white banded ducks were omnivorous, included in the burgeoning ecosystem to clean up dead foragers and balance the pollinators. Hardy little bastards.

Letting out a groan, he shifted his gaze to the growing vehicles. A blue and white police rover led, its design shorter and sleeker than the survey vehicles while retaining a similar aesthetic. Behind, a red rescue unit. As well as equipment to pull people from mangled rovers and collapsed buildings, it contained fire retardant tanks, hoses, and a simple medbay. All that added up to a slow max speed. Only two of them. Cops loved a good murder—it made them feel important—so why a small turnout?

The police vehicle parked close, stopping fast and chewing up vegetation. The hatch slid open and out sauntered Captain Robert Ware and two of his lackeys. His suit was blue to match his rover but highlighted with yellow. The front was emblazoned with POLICE, in case anyone couldn't work it out. He was packing a slimline pistol suitable for deterrence without getting in the way. Bill had been issued one much like it for a decade, albeit his had a few non-standard features.

"Hayden," Ware said after settling into a comfortable stance in front of Bill. "You look like shit."

"Better than I feel, then."

To his credit, Ware frowned. "I'll have the medic check you out while we secure the scene. You're not dying, right?"

"Can't afford to," Bill said automatically, using the standard colonist refrain.

"Yeah, well, good. You've already cut into my overtime budget. What the hell happened here?"

Bill recounted the events, bolstering his reasoning and actions with the careful selection of details, a hard habit to break. He finished with, "And then a short or flame must have reached the power plant."

Ware hissed air through his teeth and walked a short way around the rover, no doubt gaining a clear view of the mangled remains and the sea of debris. "You didn't think to put it out?"

"It wasn't on fire when I left it."

"Good luck going hat in hand to admin for a replacement. Sturt will eat you alive for this."

"Hey." Bill closed his eyes. "I didn't know Charlie was dead. I couldn't waste time. Rovers can be added to the production schedule. A life can't."

"Not the same one," Ware agreed.

The rescue unit arrived, its approach cautious and with a door open, maintaining the hum of power even when it came to a standstill. A woman jumped out. Her hair was bright blue, short, and spiked. Her broad nose was slightly upturned, and her muscled body filled her maroon suit—the colony admin had everyone dressed like a stripe in a rainbow. A pack flew out the door, and the woman caught it and strode to Bill.

Behind her, a slim man with a blond ponytail, thin lips, and many stud earrings jumped out and followed. All Bill could think of was Charlie's missing ear.

"Are you the only one needing help?" the woman demanded. As she closed in, Bill read the tag on her chest—Crumpler.

"I don't need help. It was just a knock. I'll be fine."

"I'll judge that." Crumpler shoved her pack onto the table, forcing Bill to scoot to the side. "What's your name?"

"Bill. Bill Hayden."

"What's the date?"

"Christmas Eve," Bill said. Under her unimpressed glare, he relented and gave the date, his birthdate, and the current League president. "See. All good."

He pushed himself off the table, holding onto the edge to mask the nausea that followed.

Ware, whose lackeys were recording the positions of the mangled remains of Charlie's rover, turned to Bill. "Perfect. You can show me the body."

"Not yet, Robert. You'll have to wait your turn." Crumpler's tone left little room for Ware to argue. She put a hand on Bill's chest, pressing him against the table. "I'm running him through a full check before he takes another step. The body's not going anywhere. Lou, can you get the fridge and transport ready?"

She gestured to Bill. "Get back up."

Ware saved himself from the indignity of grumbling and walked off. Bill knew the other medic, Lou Marden. They'd played cards on the evening of day one. Lou nodded to Crumpler and disappeared behind the rescue unit, leaving Bill to suffer under Crumpler's ministrations. She slipped out a palm-sized device, extended three small probes, and pressed the instrument against different parts of his skull, one after the other. She said nothing, but he knew at least part of what she would find.

Several reconfigurations of the scanner later and his whole body poked and probed, she sniffed and took a step back. "Mild concussion, cuts, and scrapes."

She swapped her scanner for a DDG, a Drug Delivery Gun, snapped in three different stubby capsules, and pressed it against his neck. A tone sounded, and he felt a sharp slap.

"You've got enough cabling within you to make finding a clear spot difficult."

Bill let out a breath as the nausea melted away. "Courtesy of my previous employer. Most were removed, but I guess the last few strands were too tricky to justify the clean-up effort. Now, I get to carry around a few meters of optic cable in perpetuity."

"A few meters?" Scowling, she slipped the used capsules into a pocket, wiped down the DDG, and put it away.

Most people weren't up for major surgery as part of their career path. He didn't need the attitude those same people offered when they found out he had been. His body was no temple. The agency had considered it more of a time-share, and like a time-share contract, it was hard to leave behind. Hell, Beth had even sent him a coded message before heading out—his old mentor's final attempt to keep an agency hook in his flesh.

"You need rest," she said. "But you won't get it, not yet. Avoid sudden movements and exertion. The meds are masking the symptoms, but your brain is still injured. Understood?"

"I hear you." Bill slipped off the rover's table and checked his footing. Stable enough.

WHILE THE MEDICS turned themselves into a recovery team, Bill joined Ware's pacing around the remains of Charlie's transport.

Ware jerked his head toward the smoldering remains. "Ever seen one blow like this before?"

The captain's minions were trying to extract the cooked datacore with little success. There were methods with the right equipment, and this pair didn't have it. Even then, an element of luck was critical. Bill ruthlessly squeezed his curiosity into a little ball and imagined throwing it far away. *This is not your job. Whatever you discovered wouldn't bring Charlie back. Keep out of it.*

But a murderer could strike again.

"Hayden, you with me? I said, ever seen a rover blow up before?"

"No." Which was true. Cars, flyers, heavy lifters, buildings. Yes. Not a rover.

"Tell me about the rover's condition. They're rugged."

"Poor condition, now," Bill said, before deciding that aggravating Ware was unnecessary. He closed his eyes and built an image from memory. "It was beaten up. The sensor pods were gone, transmitters bent, snapped, or cut. Numerous breaches—tears, in no consistent direction. I hadn't checked the undercarriage. My guess would be some kind of rockfall, but I don't see the rocks needed."

"The underneath is beat up as well."

"If he'd gone into rough terrain, that would make sense," Bill said. "Perhaps he was caught under a rockslide and forced his way out. The accident could have happened elsewhere."

He picked up a small piece of carbon plate. The longest edge was buckled and delaminated. The shortest appeared cut—a slight compression and a straight line. Accident? Hardly. And Charlie's body...

One of Ware's juniors approached, his patch labeling him Sykes. "Captain, it's no good. The datacore's slagged. It'll take us hours to cut it out, and we're not gonna get a thing."

Ware grimaced, shifting his hands to hips. "What do you make of it so far?"

Sykes shrugged and pulled out a datapad. "Like what this guy said. It's definitely rover CI431, assigned to the survey arm. Last logged out by Charlie Theodore Vance, age 45 EY. Zero priors. The distress came from the rover's current coordinates, so maybe Mr. Vance drove until it broke down. There are no tracks. I guess there's not enough soil on the rocks up here to keep an impression through the storm. The blast pattern shows the explosion originated inside the rover. Chem analysis says no accelerants. Power plant went, the shut-downs failed, and the suppressants didn't suppress. If we drag it back to Staging, we can get mechanics to look it over."

With every detail, Ware's expression grew more dour. "I want drones in the air, scouring the area. I don't like guessing, and I don't want to come back because we missed something."

"I set drones searching when I arrived," Bill said. As much as he didn't want to get involved, the longer Ware's investigation took, the longer Bill would be stuck waiting. "I haven't checked the results, but I can forward the footage."

"That'd be great, thanks," Sykes said, earning a glare from his captain.

Bill tapped his wrist comp and issued a series of commands to pack the data and open a channel. He couldn't resist a brief check of the alerts, but nothing stood out as he flicked through.

"I've got them," Sykes confirmed. "Captain, do you want me to check now?"

"No, I want you to hold your ass and spin around on the spot. We're not going until we have some idea what was responsible, got it?"

"As you say." Sykes wandered back toward the wreckage.

Ware stood silently, and Bill, his head still muzzy from the blast, couldn't think of a reason to leave or an advantage to press. *Was I responsible?* You either went to a colony to be alone or rich, often both. Charlie had known what he was getting into.

"We're ready." Crumpler's shout made Bill start. Both she and her partner were approaching, large packs on their backs.

"Lead on, Hayden."

"This way. He's not far."

The great spires of striped rocks resembled teeth if Bill squinted the right way. Small stones caught in depressions grated under his boots. There were more stones than he remembered, too, little sharp slivers and fist-sized chunks. Retracing his earlier steps brought a sense of déjà vu, that he was casually walking into terrible danger. Except it had already happened, and the shadows were growing long, proving how much time had passed. His instincts were rusty.

"Over there," he said and turned toward the cave.

"This place is beautiful," Lou Marden said, breaking a long silence. "We don't get to see much apart from Staging and the industrial plants. I should make some time before it's all leveled for condos."

Ware kicked a stone. "No one will be coming here again until I've found out what's happened. Hayden, is that your hole?"

Well done, Captain. It was, and it wasn't. The cave's mouth had crumbled, and the ground outside was littered with debris, mainly blue crystal. But it was the same location, and there was still a way in.

"That's it."

Ware started forward, but Crumpler raised a hand. "We need to check first and make sure everything's stable."

"Hayden's already been in," Ware countered. "And I need to examine the body before it's moved."

"No touchies," Lou Marden said. "Promise."

Bill and Ware waited as the medics put on enclosed helmets, switched their shoulder lights to a broad beam, and crawled inside.

Ware bent over and watched them. "What was he doing?"

"Here, exactly? I don't know. Charlie said there was something up with the geophysics, an inconsistency, but he was en route to his assignment. This wasn't a scheduled stop. There's a tunnel beneath. Maybe it was to do with that."

"You don't seem cut up by his death." Pulling his head out of the entrance, Ware gave Bill a calculating stare.

The stare of a simple man looking for simple answers. Bill forced his limbs to relax. "I didn't know him well. We're out of Staging most the time, and the team's been downsized enough that we have to go solo. He seemed decent enough—apart from a taste for new wave hair metal. What do you want me to say? I'm not looking forward to preparing the pack for his next of kin or shuffling the workload. And what happened to him… it was disturbing."

"But you've seen some disturbing things in the past?"

"Yes," Bill said. If Ware wanted to play games, he could damn well put his cards face up.

"When you were a spook."

Face up, a flush. Bill scowled. "I don't believe in ghosts."

Ware stepped closer, a clear attempt to use his height and bulk to intimidate. "I've seen your record—twelve years with the League

Security Agency, twelve years with no accountability like us mere mortals." Heat flushed through Bill as Ware continued. "But you're here now. Eclipse isn't your playground. You understand that, right? The LSA doesn't have jurisdiction."

A tall man, but a little man. More disturbing than his strutting was Ware's knowledge. A great deal of effort went into muddying agency employment histories. A leak was a serious incident—not that Bill was going to send a complaint back to HQ. That part of his life was dead and buried. Ware was wrong on one count, though. The LSA had no borders to its jurisdiction. Best not to point that out. A turf war was pointless when he didn't want to win.

"I am not a part of the LSA, and the last thing I want here is to play around. Rest assured, Captain, when Eclipse reaches Phase 3, I'll be selling up my stake and shipping out."

"We've stabilized the tunnel." Crumpler's voice echoed out the entrance. "It's safe to come in."

The medics exited, stopping Ware from continuing his performance.

Lou spoke first. "The mineral's strong, but it shears with force on several angles. We've put up a flex-support barrier, but I'd recommend being quick."

Crumpler removed her pack and retrieved a large rectangular box. "The body was crushed under several large chunks. The autopsy's going to be a real bitch to separate pre and postmortem."

Ware's nose twitched. He bent down and looked into the tunnel. "When did the rocks fall?"

"No idea," she said. "That's your job. Let us know when we can haul him out."

The medics took the box and unfolded it into a stretcher.

"Hayden, follow me in."

Ware had no right to demand he do anything, but Bill acquiesced and followed, unable to quell his curiosity. The smell of dust now had a sweeter undertone. Noting small, sharp stones, he slipped on his gloves. Had the explosion been enough to shake the tunnel and dislodge half the ceiling? He looked up at the pressurized shell the medics had installed. Its once-flexible surface was hardening fast, turning from yellow to blue in the process. Too late to protect Charlie.

"What a fucking mess." Ware shifted onto his ass, legs bent so he could fit sideways.

Charlie's body looked worse than when Bill had last seen him. His whole ribcage had collapsed under the pummeling of crystal, giving the impression of having been stomped flat with a giant foot. Skin flaps hung off his skull, dull, bluish dust covered the flesh beneath, and white ribs peeked out here and there.

"This is how you found him?" Ware asked while pulling a small box from a pocket on the hard plating of his suit's torso. The captain set off a tiny drone that began a zigzag pattern, spraying surfaces with pale blue microdot meshes as it analyzed the topography.

"No." Bill rested his eyes on poor Charlie. "He'd been mutilated but not buried."

Apparently unsatisfied, Ward threw questions at Bill in a steady stream: the angle of the body, blood, stiffness of the limbs, and more. Surprised by the frontier cop's quality of interrogation and thoroughness, Bill gave the most accurate answers he could, using his years of practiced recall to counter his head injury. When Ward wanted to scrape surfaces for residue, Bill helped shift the chunks of crystal. Why hadn't Ward brought his underlings? What was he after?

"You're not squeamish," Ware said while collecting his first sample of crystal dust.

"It wouldn't do Charlie any good if I were."

That earned a grunt from Ware as he continued his work. "Do you know why I'm here?"

Bill resisted the obvious and obtuse answer. "We all have our reasons."

"That we do, Hayden. My great grandparents were first touchdown colonists on Charia. Been there?"

"No." Bill scooted around to help clear more rubble and get a better view of Ware's face. Charia was a textbook colony success. Wildly fertile, mineral-rich, and with a booming population. Which meant that Ware was either loaded or had a sob story. That didn't quite jibe with the man's demeanor.

"I grew up there. Beautiful."

"Then why are you on this rock?"

"Legacy, Hayden, and more. Charia kept changing, the population doubling, then doubling again. It wasn't the place of my memories, and there wasn't room to put my own stamp on the world. I grew up on frontier stories. I plan on writing my own. Maybe someday, my great grandchildren will be the ones with itchy feet."

"That's nice." This was the sort of conversation Bill avoided. Usually, it was at least accompanied by too much alcohol. Yet, Ware must have a reason for oversharing.

"Why are you here, Hayden?"

"I said before—not to stay. I'm only here for the money."

"The right land claim is worth plenty of money."

"I know. I'm the survey guy, remember? Everything I'll claim is regulated and in the sunshine. It goes through more oversight than anyone else's."

"That's how it should be, squeaky clean. I don't want trouble, spook trouble."

Bill laughed bitterly. "Neither do I, trust me."

"But you're the one with the body."

"I'd say we both are." Bill ran a hand along the covering the medics had used to shore up the ceiling. "This won't sound reassuring, but believe me, I'd never murder Charlie like this. You wouldn't have a single reason to think of his death as anything but an ordinary mishap or medical episode. I'll stay out of your way, out of your investigation. In a few years, you'll forget I was on Eclipse."

Ware carefully put away his equipment. "Why is the LSA here?"

"It's not," Bill assured.

"Doesn't feel that way."

"Yeah, that's how they like you to feel."

With Ware having aired his grievance, and there being nothing more to do, they slipped back out of the tunnel. The medics had inflated the stretcher's wheels to a large diameter suitable for the terrain. They retrieved Charlie, placed his blue-dust-covered form on the thin padding, and secured him with a blanket and straps.

The walk back became a silent vigil. Ware wasn't quite the rube Bill had believed. The odds were that he'd find Charlie's killer. And that made it reasonable for Bill to stay out of the investigation. He'd double-check his own personal security and suggest the same for the rest of the team out of professional courtesy, but his isolation hadn't been breached. And that was the way he wanted it.

So why did Charlie's body stay in his mind? Why did the circumstances prickle like rolling in nettles?

CHAPTER 3
THE CREW

Glimmering white pipes stretched in parallel lines, twisting back onto each other at right angles, forming industrial art with a design inspiration reminiscent of an OCD spider. Four great brine tanks squatted to the right, even thicker pipes connecting these to twin pumping stations at the edge of lake WR-7321, or Salty, as it was unofficially called.

"All-righty, amateurs and assholes, wakey-wakey. I want us in and out. The production queue is longer than my mean streak, and I didn't come to this Abuk-forsaken rock to play mechanical medic." Jane Trax's ancestral beliefs were uncommon across the League, but she had no intention of giving in to the majority.

She tapped on the map display to the right of her steering controls and set a nav point that synched with the two other vehicles in her work team. Her curly black-brown hair pushed against the top of her single-seat cockpit, and her stern eyes flashed as she commanded her rover to link into the chlorine plant's network.

Nothing.

"Damn. Fitz, can you bring up the oversight network?"

"Ah, let me try." David Fitzsimmons, or Fitz to anyone who knew him, swore over the comm. "Nada, boss."

"There's storm damage," Amy Martin said over the same comm. "It's visible through the scope. Must have been at least cat 3 wind."

Trax gritted her teeth. If they had to replace the network wholesale, they'd be onsite forever. There was little point making assumptions without an inspection, so while she waited to reach the nav point, she formulated a checklist.

Her rover, christened AbFab, soon bleeped and killed its speed. She looked up, noting the absence of the vibration and grunting of the tracks rather than their earlier presence. With a tap, the cockpit rose, and she vaulted out, using the exterior ladder for a controlled slide to the ground. The rover was a mobile fabrication plant, fifty tons of printing, CNC, and a dozen other processes, along with a substantial store of raw materials. It had started its service as a stationary facility. Started. Trax had worked with her crew to merge it with CI83, a rover that had lost its rear in a landslide. The useless planetary network meant requesting mass-produced parts was a lottery. Self-sufficiency was a must, and her team excelled at making exactly what was needed. Hell, *that* was meant to be their damn job.

Two other vehicles stopped at a respectful distance. The three-trailer hauler, Aunty Jo, banged and clanked while losing momentum. As with all their rovers, its battered panels were bright yellow and covered with black text warnings. The front engine unit had a large honeycomb blister through which Trax could see the crew prepping to exit.

Amy slipped out first, her thin fingers flipping on her safety lights, reminding Trax to do the same. Regulations were a pain, but safety needed to be a religion. Lines along their dark gray suits emitted a steady yellow, bathing Trax's pale optronics expert with a sickly tinge. Diver was next, his hair short like Amy's but bright red. The young chemist had a pad in his hand, and his eyes focused on its display rather than the way he was walking.

Fitz, a clever systems designer, closed the hauler's door behind him. He was the eldest of them, holding as much experience as he had white hair. "What's the deal?"

"Good question." Trax tapped her ear, opening a short-range comm. "Harry, Izy, what's the damn holdup?"

Harry's sweet voice purred over the comm. "Sorry, boss. Brakes weren't engaging."

"I thought you had that sorted."

"I said it wouldn't last. Bandit needs a full overhaul."

The speaker came into view as she exited the scout rover. Harriet Collins, a good friend and mechanical genius with a soft-spoken voice that belied her enormous biceps and barrel-like physique. Izy, Ismail al-Jazar, walked alongside, running fingers along his short, neat, black beard. His eyes twinkled like he'd just told a joke.

When the team assembled in a semicircle, Trax cracked her knuckles. "Right. We're not going to let this burn our earn for the day. Harry, Izy, get a quick reconnaissance with the drones."

"Drones?" Izy's shoulder slumped. "I'm no flyboy. Can't—"

"No," Trax stated flatly. "You have a knack for spotting faults that aren't yours. We're being pulled everywhere, and I don't have time to give you your favorite crayon color. Now, drones. I want a focus on potential dangers: leaks, exposed power, structural weakness— anything that could bite our asses. No one walks in until we know nothing'll go bang. Amy, Diver, I want you two warming the fabricator. Don't break it, or Izy will cry all the way home. Fitz, you're with me. We'll go over the priority list and make sure we're thorough. I don't want to be back next week. Hell, I don't want to be back next year."

A full hour later, with their safety somewhat assured, the team advanced on the plant. Trax had assigned Amy and Izy to audit the network. Fitz, who was good with heights, had eschewed mechanical assistance and climbed with ropes to cut away the plant's storm-damaged transmitter. Diver and Harry were the most logical pair for fault-finding on a site like this, so she'd set them to investigate the pump errors that had been spat out prior to the network failing.

Trax stayed with the fabricator, queueing up components, hissing at each budget hit. She'd rather be in Fitz's shoes, out there getting her hands dirty, but admin was trying to screw them all out of land shares, and she wasn't going to let the bastards win: every job efficient, every resource accounted for, every earned credit claimed. Even if this wasn't her crew's damn job.

A glossy antenna strut rolled out of the fabricator K module and onto the assembly platform, where robotic hands clasped the section, applied a fusing gel, and rotated it into place on the half-formed array. Her mind tore apart the design, seeking the invisible weaknesses that had made them so unexpectedly unreliable. Nothing came to mind.

"Boss?"

Trax tapped her ear. "What is it, Harry?"

"We've found a problem."

"What kind of problem?"

"An impeller's dropped."

"I don't have time for twenty questions. What do you mean, dropped?"

"It's down a ten-meter sinkhole."

"Fuck." Trax clenched her fists. "I said the survey was botched. They should be re-scanning everything, right from fucking step one. What's the damage?"

"Pipe mostly, unless the impeller was warped by the impact, and we won't know that until it's out. At least the cutoff valves worked. It's dry down here."

"How much room to work?"

"Plenty."

They wouldn't be playing mechanical medics—this was full-on heart surgery.

"All right, get back here, both of you. We'll break out the mechs."

SPECIAL-PURPOSE VEHICLES WERE fantastic when you could store them in a garage. When you had to carry everything you might need, modularity was the solution, and the hauler was a mother with many babies. The inbuilt trailer carried bulky machinery that snapped together according to the plans Trax selected. Two wide-track units flexed as a power module was pressed on to them. This module, in turn, received a small crew blister, and finally a crane assembly.

Each piece clanked and whirred as the connectors interlocked. The second mech was a wide four-legged unit, perfect for spreading mass across dangerous ground. A bulky winch at the front was nothing to the tank attached at the rear that held fusing gel. Dirt and rocks sucked through the grinding tube would come out as a quickset fill for the sinkhole.

Mech number three was a slighter, two-legged design beneath the simple blister cockpit. A pair of utility arms gave it an anthropomorphic look that always appealed to her. While its backward-bending knees and long arms were far from her own body's design, the freedom of movement felt natural, an extension of herself. She was inside when the others returned, running through performance mobility and response tests. Harry took the crane and Diver the mixer, the pair working through the same checks, ensuring the mechs were ready.

Pumping Station 2 was a bland white structure almost fifteen meters tall and a little wider. Cable bundles hung from tripod supports, soon turning and running past the brine reservoirs and toward the main plant, where it would usually suck energy like a vampire. Two panels lay near the base, removed thanks to Harry and Diver's earlier efforts. The lake started several meters down a steep incline, and the red granite should have provided a barrier against the water and a firm foundation for the pump.

Wispy reeds stretched out a good distance before suddenly cutting off, an indicator of the deep drop that gave Salty its immense capacity. There'd be no fish yet in those waters—the plant's task of production and filtration was too early in its cycle for animal life to survive.

Diver spoke over the comms as they reached the station. "The handheld readings suggest the ground is stable, but there's the sinkhole and all. Watch for the edge, boss."

Trax brought her lumbering mech to the side of the panels. Twisting in her cockpit, she extended a mechanical right arm around and activated its spotlight. Most of the gaping hole hid beneath the station's bulk, but where it extended beyond that footprint, the edge was ragged and slightly curved. Contorted pipes dipped below ground level, and, dangling by many thick color-coded cables, hung the impeller. The debris-encircled hole was closer to seven meters than Harry's guess of ten. That would be much more workable.

"That's one hell of a hole. Harry, what do you think about the stresses on the station?"

"It's taking plenty of load in directions it was never designed for. See the twist in that north-most pylon?"

"I see it. I need you on focused on any changes. You call it and I'm out. No questions."

"Got it, boss."

It was easy to trust Harry with her life. "Diver, hook your winch to my back."

"Sure." He settled the mixer's stabilizing feet and hurried outside, dragging the winch's hook. Cable played out as he went, but he yanked several extra meters before climbing Trax's mech and securing the hook to a heavy loop at her back. "Secured."

"Keep me on a tight leash. Either of you have any theories for our little bit of Swiss cheese?" While she spoke, Trax commanded her mech's left arm to extend its suction attachment, a set of three black pads that stuck hard to a still-attached station panel. She shifted the right arm's function from grasping pincers to a socket wrench and began releasing the panel.

"Nothing that makes sense," Harry said, the confusion clear in her tone. "It should have been more solid than an anchor bolt, according to the survey."

Diver laughed. "The survey is bullshit. Look at the east-west sides of the hole—see the curves? I bet there was a terraform artery running through, right where it shouldn't be. That's the major installers for you. This'll be Clarkson's fault. His team is a bunch of oxygen-deprived cowboy contractors—you've said it yourself. They didn't double-check shit."

He spoke like he'd been born an engineer, but Trax silently approved. She demanded quality work, and though that could breed a little arrogance, she'd take it over sloppiness every single time.

In short order, she cleared enough plates to gain access to the interior of the station and guided her mech to the very edge of the sinkhole. "Diver, I want you to lower me down nice and gentle-like. Got it?"

"Right you are, boss."

Letting her muscles loosen, Trax nudged her mech forward. The pressure actuators in her footrests pushed up against her boots in a thin line near her toes, mirroring the circumstances of the mech's own splayed feet. Warnings beeped and red lights flashed.

"Diver, confirm cable tension."

"Tension confirmed. You're good to go, boss."

Trax tapped in override codes, silencing the alarms, then took a firm hold of her control sticks and shifted her cockpit forward, slowly overbalancing the mech.

"Give me a meter slow roll."

"Rolling."

The cable holding the back of the mech extended, and the mech leaned farther into the sinkhole.

"More."

She walked down the side carefully, faster than the cable, allowing the feet to eventually slip off. The mech bounced once, the price of admission when time was the tightest resource.

Trax adjusted the left arm and fired off several flares, each hitting the sinkhole wall and sticking to the surface.

"Play it out. Steady… Steady…" The impeller unit came closer and closer. "Stop."

The mech jolted as the cable halted. "Now, let's see if you've been hurt." She set both mech hands to grippers and reached out to clasp the impeller housing. The nearest side was intact, marred by a few scratches. A slight distortion near the bearings guaranteed the need for a full interior assessment. She would have done one, anyway.

"Diver, another half meter."

"Rolling. How's it looking?"

"I think we're lucky. Wait—" Trax swore silently.

The base of the housing was shredded. Forgetting the mech controls, she leaned forward, seeking sense in the destruction. One of the impeller blades was gone, another was missing half its length, and a third was buckled with huge stress patterns resembling bruises. This wasn't a day's work—more like a week.

"Boss?"

"The housing is a write-off. Worse, the impeller's busted. Three blades down, and I'd never trust it under load even if we fused replacements."

"Three? It didn't even hit bottom."

"It didn't," Trax agreed. "We should have been laughing."

"But we're not?"

"No." She couldn't help sighing. She really hated people who sighed. It was almost as bad as eye-rolling. "Harry, how's it looking up there?"

"Nothing's moving. It'll hold."

"Keep watching. I'm going to attach some pull cables to the impeller. We'll bring it out and dice it for scrap. The other station will have to work hard until we can put together a fresh unit."

Diver moaned. "This isn't going to be on us, is it? It's not our fault the repair's going to take forever."

Trax's eyes lingered on the gaps in the impeller housing, the surprisingly clean tears that were oh-so-close to cuts. "I'll rivet Honda's ears to her desk if management tries to pin this on us. No, it's going down as a rebuild, not a repair. And none of it's going to be against our team's allowances."

The forms were going to kill her. She needed some good news and brought up another comm channel while she considered how to secure the impeller housing. "Amy, what have you found?"

"Uh, the software's good. Everything's failed for an obvious reason."

"Everything's failed?"

"It's not as bad as that sounds. Plenty of severed optics that'll be easy to splice, and you know about the transmitter. All the processing control units went into safety lockdown. Honestly, that's pretty good. My guess is restarting's beyond us, but Diver's the lab boy."

Severed optics. The missing transmitter. The unexplained impeller damage. Put together, it sounded like trouble. "Amy, have you started repairs?"

"Yeah, once Izy and I realized how chopped up it all was, we figured it would be easier to pick a point near the core control net and use that to spot the disconnections."

Did they understand what had happened? Rumors spread as fast on ground as they did in vacuum. Trax couldn't risk sharing her concerns. Not yet. She needed evidence.

"Good work, but that never goes unpunished. I need you to document each break. A full hi-res scan of each and use system logs to map out the disconnect timestamps. I want to know if there was a pattern, and I want to know what caused this mess."

"The storm?"

"Sure," Trax lied.

Sabotage. Nothing else made sense. This was deliberate, thorough, and yet oddly petty. None of it was irreparable, and there would have been many easy ways to cause more havoc given the pressures used in chlorine production and the caustic nature of the chemical. Why do this? Competition between teams and departments could get downright nasty. Trax brooked no crap from anyone, but she also tried to keep herself and her people away from the drama. Her policy: rack up the land credits and laugh at the end when the grants were locked in.

If she were to be honest, it didn't always go that way. A bit of temper broke roadblocks and put feet to the fire. But she hadn't made enemies at Eclipse—no one serious enough to do this. And it would have taken serious effort to ensure the work fell on her shoulders. The culprit was a lunatic or had more moxie than a bar full of drunken miners. If caught, they'd lose everything, likely their life. When the "holy" schedule was threatened, Colony justice was swift.

What about the corp? BILT4 was outside of the colony's jurisdiction. They had the resources to do whatever they wanted. No, it wasn't them. They had less reason than any colonist. No doubt they were evil. Every corporation was when you looked closely enough. The bigger they were, the dirtier their hands. The pus-suckers infected everything they touched.

Diver's voice cut through her sudden anger. "Boss, you okay down there?"

Damn. Her mech's right hand had bent a pipe bolt. Trax relaxed her grip on the controls. "Yeah, yeah. Let's just get this done."

They'd fix the plant, but she was damned if she was going to leave it at that. All it would take was one leak that slipped by her team, and they'd all be coughing up their lungs. Someone had to be accountable.

CHAPTER 4
DELVING DEEP

The elevator dropped swiftly from the fifth floor, the executive level, to ground. Elyse Wagner, Executive VP of Clear Sight, a venture of BILT4, the thirteenth largest corporation in the League, stood comfortably and watched her domain. Three hundred employees striving in Haven, and another eighty stationed at several exploratory bases far over the horizon.

The expansive windows that gave her the view were a deliberate extravagance, a reminder to all that this was a place of business, not a yokel dirt farm like the colony. A slight pressure under Elyse's feet, and the twin doors opened. A thread of wind whipped at the gentle waves of her auburn hair and jingled a pair of small, intricate earrings. Her elegant, sleeveless black dress finished just above her knees, and her glossy black shoes were smart but low-heeled—the only concession to the environment.

Jose Karlo, her chief of security and an ex-marine pilot, advanced on the elevator, his amber eyes searching as if it were likely to explode. "Ms. Wagner."

His black uniform was identical to that of his underlings: slightly loose, covered in pockets, the BILT4 emblem front and back, and compact armor plating—redundant here but useful for maintaining a sense of normality and order. Only the three triangles of his rank set him apart; that and his humorless demeanor. Short-cropped hair topped a permanently furrowed brow. A jaw strong enough to break ice on had probably ground his teeth flat. His towering stature easily eclipsed her height, which would be considered tall next to most. The rifle he wore strapped to his back and the bulky pistol secured around his thigh were an extension of his personality—dangerous when triggered.

She offered a tight smile and a raised eyebrow. "Is all of this caution necessary, Jose?"

"Caution means being ready when it flips into necessity, Ms. Wagner. I allocated hangar three to the scrubs and set up a perimeter. But I don't like it. There are far too many of them crawling around to guarantee operational silence. If you'll come this way?" He gestured along one of the four paths leading from the main building. Each was made of a green, perforated material that offered grip in any weather. The distant walls of the Haven compound also served as flood barriers, and along with the pumps, kept the ground dry and tidy.

Elyse let her pace stretch, not to match Jose's—it was his responsibility to stay with her—but to stretch her muscles and feel her blood pump. Isolated as she was from corporate HQ, she still managed to get inundated with meetings and calls, and usually, protocol demanded others come to her in managerial supplication. Employees moved about their tasks, either speeding up when they saw her or pausing, brushing off their work uniforms, and wishing her a good day.

She passed a row of eight parked rovers, each one bearing the corporate logo along with unique ID codes. The compound's main gates opened as she neared the hangar, and a five-carriage hauler lumbered in, bringing the overdue resource shipment from Eclipse's colony. Oliver, the director, was due for a friendly conversation and a reminder of the penalty clauses in the agreement that had BILT4 part-funding the colony's existence.

Signs had been placed ten meters from the hangar's wall, and a guard stood blocking the path.

"Afternoon, Ms. Wagner, Captain," he said, bowing slightly.

Elyse nodded. "Good afternoon, Weis. Everything quiet?"

"Yes, ma'am—now that we've raised the limit on the number of personnel allowed inside."

"How many?" Jose demanded.

"Thirty, Captain. They needed more equipment brought in."

Jose's jaw stiffened, and Elyse expected a disciplinary note to come across her desk for the sergeant he'd placed in charge. While she'd love to leave it to him, morale was a delicate balancing act, a dance that needed all performers at their peak. The scientists—scrubs, as Jose called them—didn't care about security. Ideas and discoveries and dreams were their currency, and they could be pretty convincing when they were excited. Security required a certain level of severity by the nature of the job, but misery was corrosive. And given this was Elyse's last chance for a head office promotion, she would mold every aspect of her employees' existence if it gave her even a fraction of a percentage of an advantage.

"Thank you."

She moved on to the closed hangar doors. Shaped like a shallow bell curve, the simple, blue structure managed an element of grandeur. Sensors and other equipment bristled on the edge of the roof like a spiked collar on a guard dog. Two guards flanked a small door on the left.

She approached this, nodded to the guards, and said to Jose, "Well, let's go see what our bright sparks have found."

A guard pushed the manual door, and Elyse stepped through.

Without a flyer to soak up the space, sound bounced in the cavernous expanse, and the rows of lighting burned shadows with righteous fury. At the center of the hangar, boxes lay scattered and cables spewed from ports on the floor. Equipment rested on every surface, and around these, white-suited scientists and brown-jacketed field operatives scurried, talked, and shouted. At the center, a transparent bubble reached well above head height.

Her heels clacked as she walked, a steady beat suggesting confidence, authority, and serenity without a hint of anticipation. The scientists had been excited before, after all. Hints and possibilities were not suitable dividends for eye-wateringly expensive investments. That must be understood. She stopped at the edge and waited.

Jose clapped once. "Hey, scrubs, shut the hell up. Ms. Wagner is here."

His voice boomed, cutting through the hubbub and silencing it, leaving only the humming of equipment. A woman, older by a decade or two, judging by her skin, pushed toward Elyse. They were a similar age, but the scientist shunned body care as if it were frivolous. She had her lab suit; Elyse had a different uniform.

"Ms. Wagner, thank you for coming."

"A pleasure, as always, Dr. Flores. I believe you have something to show me?"

"Yes, yes," Dr. Flores said, rubbing her blue-gloved hands together. Her gray bun hid beneath a similarly colored hairnet. "Please, this way. Make room, everyone."

The doctor led Elyse on a circuitous route that spiraled into the center.

"I want to impress on you, Ms. Wagner, that this is not like our previous discoveries."

Unable to resist teasing the scientist, Elyse said, "You mean the piles of dirt and pebbles?"

"Minerals, Ms. Wagner, with crystalline structures that are most unlikely to form in nature, and traces of pure elements, as equally unlikely to exist without artificial chemistry."

"And have you determined if this is the reason for Eclipse's interference?"

"No, Ms. Wagner. That work is still proceeding with some success. As I have said before, there is a clear contribution, but no good explanation for the scale."

"And your new discovery hasn't shed any further light?"

Dr. Flores squared her shoulders as she stopped near the bubble. "The scientific process is not an instantaneous endeavor. Making brash conclusions without thorough analysis will make anyone appear rightfully foolish."

"Yet you've asked me to visit."

The scientists converged, displaying an eagerness that usually wore away after the first week of any special operation. Jose kept shifting his broad shoulders left and right, as if fearing an attack. He had failed to understand that this was a moment of theater, not tension.

"Yes, I've asked you, Ms. Wagner. Our conclusions are tentative, but I believe this will require a *substantial* shift in resources."

"Ah." Elyse smiled. "The purse strings must be loosened. Conclude away, good doctor."

The head scientist made a sweeping gesture. "The geology of LE-8134-7 is, of course, most unusual. However, the initial survey provided enough data points to suggest more—the potential for a deceased civilization."

"I know what brought about the funding of our venture." Elyse also knew about a small sample of alloy that had been recovered from the surface. A new material that was being stripped and analyzed in a hidden lab back home, atom by atom.

"Indeed. And like us, you have no doubt been frustrated by the lack of definitive evidence."

Elyse placed her hands casually on her hips. "We're not here as archaeologists."

"Correct. The staff selection process was most thorough. Evidence of existence is only the first step. We need viable materials and/or technologies to replicate. We have spent years trying to find these—"

"I don't need a history lesson," Elyse said, growing tired of the scientist's unusual verbosity.

"We all will, I believe, Ms. Wagner. History is about to be rewritten. Please, come this way." Dr. Flores slapped a control on the side of the bubble, and a door slid open.

Jose took a half step, on the edge of blocking her way. "You don't need to see it up close, Ms. Wagner. We don't know if it's safe."

The scientist looked up at Jose with no sign of fear. "You don't know what you're talking about. We have no indications of any risk."

Before the two could start one of their regular arguments, Elyse walked through the bubble door. "I'm here now. Tell me what I'm looking at."

A large cream ceramic table stood at the center, various machines surrounding it like mourners at a grave. Its flat surface had a printed black grid. A frame attached to the corners held a small gimbaled arm with brushes, drills, and a vacuum tube. At the center of the table, a bulky cigar-shaped object rested, its surface a mix of red-tinged soil and a matt-black that hinted at color like an oil slick. Small edges and protuberances formed a scaled pattern. It screamed design, but she knew, even without the scientists' earlier warning, that leaping to conclusions was dangerous.

Dr. Flores walked around the edge of the table and rested one hand proprietarily on the frame. "An auto-digger discovered this specimen approximately twenty-four kilometers to the northeast of our location. Recent rainfall had eroded a crest and Ampoor's team was testing a new multi-phasic ground-penetrating wave reader. We've marked the site, sent a radiation warning to the colony, and brought it back. With your permission, we'll allocate resources for comprehensive screening."

"Granted," Elyse said, stepping closer to the specimen.

Planets were huge. When you found treasure in your backyard, you didn't run off elsewhere hoping for serendipity. And now the doctor had what she wanted, it was her turn to satisfy.

"What have you learned about this object?"

"The specimen was encased in stone. Initial readings on the surrounding material suggest it was untouched by the terraforming process or the subsequent climate. That has allowed us to converge on a tentative dating of seven thousand five hundred years of age, League standard."

"Isn't that recent?"

A junior scientist who'd be quietly standing at the far side of the bubble spoke. "Yes, Ms. Wagner. The finds on Hintar were a hundred thousand, and even the drive ship on Chang-Vir was forty thousand."

"Thank you, Ron." Dr. Flores said in clipped words. "The younger the technology, the less degradation—all things being equal. And that does appear to bear fruit here. If you look at this end"—she pointed to the closest—"an unenhanced visual examination shows strands that are likely to be optics, and others that are tube-shaped, suggesting a carrier fluid or hydraulics."

Leaning in close, Elyse found the details as clear as the scientist suggested. The piece had obviously been damaged, but it was no chance crystal formation or erosion or whatever the scientists used to cast doubt on each other's work. They had hit the jackpot. Her skin heated with anticipation.

"Is it organic?"

"No, thankfully. Alloys, polymers, clear joints, and possible fuse marks. It's no fossilized tree."

"And it's completely different in design from anything that's been found elsewhere?"

"Yes," Dr. Flores said. "Ron, go out and tell everyone to take a break. We don't need them staring into the bubble like we're in a zoo."

"Yes, Dr. Flores."

Elyse walked the table's length as the man left, her eyes eating the potential before her. "Any idea how advanced it is?"

"Not yet. Until we have more samples—if we find more samples—I want to avoid intrusive actions. We may only get one shot."

You could give a scientist a decade, and they'd want two. "Until you have more samples, but no longer. There is a clock ticking. Remember it."

Elyse reached out and put a hand along a dark scale. This was going to be her ticket to a promotion. She could feel it.

"Don't," the doctor said urgently.

Shrugging, Elyse complied. "It's been lying in dirt. I'm hardly going to damage it."

"You could contaminate the specimen, rendering any number of tests useless."

"You're the scientist."

Amber lights blinked on the object. Elyse jumped, saw the doctor do the same, and chuckled, giddy with anticipation. There were small circles and several straight lines, some parallel, others intersecting.

"It appears I've run a successful test for you. What do the lights mean?"

"I have no idea." The doctor glared at Elyse. "It could be fault indicators, a bomb timer, or a birthday message."

Jose advanced from the bubble door. "Is it dangerous?"

"We'll find out soon enough. If you don't mind, Ms. Wagner, it's going to be a long day. I'd like to brief everyone and form a plan. You've sped up our timetable."

"You have my blessing, but, doctor—Jose, I need you on this as well—no one is to tell the colony. News like this will tempt loose lips. Until further notice, all social visits are over, and any communication except for urgent business is out as well. It will spread throughout the compound, but it must go no further. We don't want the government stealing our hard work, understood?"

"I agree, but I don't think that's sustainable," Dr. Flores said. "People talk."

Jose crossed his arms. "Mine won't."

In the time they had been on Eclipse, her employees had become too close to the colony. It was easy to maintain operational security when there was little to hide. They'd grown sloppy. A mistake she would have to rectify.

"Jose, Doctor, I'll be drafting a memo. If word leaks out, the culprit will be fired with immediate effect."

Jose grunted his approval, and the doctor tilted her head to one side before agreeing. The colony wouldn't protect someone the corporation had fired. They had their own problems. Losing one's job meant no food, water, or shelter—a death sentence.

Elyse put a hand on the shoulders of her employees. "This is a good thing. It's why we are here. It's what will make each of us wealthy and give us the chance to pick any posting we could desire. I know I can count on each of you. Let's make this run smoothly. Come to me with any problems, big or small. You'll have my full support."

She squeezed their shoulders and walked to the bubble door, choosing to let a grin spread. Scientists were back, crowding at the bubble's surface, pointing. Rather than leaving, she spent several minutes with them, talking, nodding, and letting their theories spray her with confusing terms and outlandish claims. They ate her attention and appeared genuinely disappointed when she made her exit. Perfect.

Everything was perfect—as long as they delivered what she needed.

CHAPTER 5
OLD GROUND

Don't investigate.

It wasn't Bill's job. It never had been. There was a difference between chasing down a murderer and detangling the complex relationships, bravado, and finances of the treasonous. Murder was Ware's—and the medical examiner's—determination. That was public knowledge. Charlie was owed an answer, but not from Bill. With only ten thousand potential suspects, the police captain was bound to find the culprit. Eventually. Justice, of course, was impossible. The dead don't come back. It wasn't Bill's problem. He was only on this barely habitable rock to earn enough to escape the stink and stains of humanity, not bathe in them.

So why am I traipsing over the damn countryside looking for a motive?

Perhaps it had been the atmosphere back at the survey HQ. Or Ware's follow-up questions. Or the way his apartment had been searched in his absence. Or the way some people looked at him. He'd done his duty and left at the first opportunity, telling himself he was merely doing due diligence. The tunnel Charlie had been in meant something. It had to.

While Bill's rover steadily chewed up ground, his gaze flicked from display to display, each one projecting topology, seismic activity, subsoil density, and mineral analyses: initial survey, Phase 1 survey, last week's data drop. They all concurred, and Bill didn't like it, though his conscious mind couldn't formulate a reason for the discomfort.

The nav system chimed. The rover had closed on the next geospike on his list. He'd learned the lingo from his more experienced crew, and it was easy to see how the sensor platforms received their name, given the tungsten alloy tips that buried themselves in the ground when they were fired from orbit. He switched to manual control and brought the rover close before exiting.

Breathing the outside air, he took a moment to let the constant vibration of the rover become a memory. A fast-growing moringa sapling brushed against his thighs as a gentle wind blew. When mature, it would reach ten meters tall, all the while preparing the soil for other plants to replace it and its ilk. The buzz of insects hinted at life unseen, simple tasks embedded in their nature. Idyllic. *Don't get used to it. This won't be your planet.*

He sniffed and picked up his tool kit, a black hard case of carbon composites filled with everything a survey technician might need, as well as a few items of his own design. The visible section of the geospike included twin antenna arrays bristling skyward like artificial trees. The majority of its bulk formed a cylinder a meter in diameter and four tall, with several poles and tubes reaching down into the ground like roots.

Bill walked counterclockwise until he reached the maintenance access panel. The tamper seals were intact, matching the previous three he'd visited, but he took the time to carefully examine the panel's edges. In truth, a truly devious saboteur could dig around the ground sensors and then hack into the processing nodes unseen. Geospikes came with only the most basic security, and a storm would wash away all evidence of the soil disturbance. That's what Bill would have done. Was it the stories coming out of the chlorine plant that motivated his efforts more than Charlie's murder?

Slowing the production had follow-on effects that were leaving the colony admin scrambling around like a disturbed ant nest. Failing to meet milestones would make them all poorer, and the colony unprepared for the hundreds of thousands of Phase 3 arrivals. Bill slapped the access panel, then opened his kit and removed a cutter. The tamper seals fell away with ease, and he scanned each one to record their disposal.

Pulling the panel outward, he again searched for signs of any disturbance: scratches, dents, the presence of contaminants on the inside. Nothing. Behind the panel, neat bundles of optic cables ran in short vertical stretches before zigzagging left or right. Above his head, the onboard gyroscope lay inside its protective sphere. Centrifuge and spectrometer waste capsules were filled above three-quarters of capacity. With the bulk of the work already done, it would take another two years before they needed replacing—if they ever were. Lights flashed, indicating the apparent health of the twenty-seven different instruments.

Running perfectly. At first glance. It took him a minute to prepare another tool from his kit, this one having a datalink interface. Satisfied, he opened a small port in the geospike, plugged in the forensic reader, and activated it. The secret to understanding was information, but that required data and context, and the secret to data was looking in the right place. While he waited for a full memory scan, he looked to the horizon and the distant hills. Thousands of incidents were logged each month in the colony records: mechanical failures, system glitches, human error, manufacturing faults. Everyone was keen to ensure they weren't blamed.

Bill had avoided slipping into the Staging hypernet so far. It was far more defended than the geospikes. Instead, he'd relied on public parts allocations, warnings, and other mundane data leakages. The noise was high, but there were surprising failure rates to the north and northeast of Staging. The corporation territory straight to the east was a big blind spot, but that didn't dismiss his conclusion. Something was up.

The juicy corporate data would be useful, but if accessing the colony system was risky, sneaking into BILT4 was downright stupid. Even when Bill had a full suite of agency implants and specialist equipment, he'd have wanted a mole to provide initial low-level access. And a layer of deniability. Besides, whatever they were up to, it was unlikely they'd be damaging the colony's systems. Not only were they investors, but they relied on the colony's outputs. And it was hard to criticize them for circling their wagons when the colony had an internal threat.

A quiet chime announced the forensic reader's completion. Bill picked up the device and swiped through each report. No sensor failures. Continuous logging producing consistent results. Plenty of recent small-scale seismic activity suggesting the corporation had been moving in the area. He stopped. The pattern analysis hinted at a loop, and the wear on the memory cells was higher than estimated for the time in use. However, the operating code checksum matched the original installed file set. He licked his lips. Either there was a serious bug in the original code or it had been modified before Phase 1 spiking of the region. Why? Was it connected to Charlie's death? Highly unlikely, yet…

Urgency powered his movement as he hurried back to the rover. He leaped inside and brought up the rover's survey records. The initial details had been poor, hardly incriminating given the interference that plagued one and all. He checked the results of the recorder again. There should be marked changes—even after the atmosphere had coalesced. The storms had produced silt-rich runoffs, and the number of quakes as the crust resettled from its bombardment should have lessened over time. The recent data matched between his portable sensors, the recorder, and the rover. But it didn't make sense going back. It was more like the records were a plastic skeleton, and over time, it had been given layers of flesh and skin. He wasn't seeing loops. They were artifacts of whatever algorithm was hiding the falsification of sensor data, brush strokes that hinted at an artist's habitual movements. Details were being modified—live.

Beth's coded message scratched at his resolve. Had she known something screwy was going on? Had she received a tipoff? A chill bit his skin.

How gullible am I? Beth, did you set me up from the start?

The only way to know for sure would be to read it, but that would mean letting her into his life again, and he'd sworn off the agency. She'd been his handler when he was just starting, and she'd kept an eye out for him as she rose through the ranks. That and more. It was impossible to decide if she was his guardian angel or a devil on his shoulder. He closed his eyes and clenched his fists. Trouble was coming.

He sat at the controls of a tourist shuttle far away, the pilot unconscious and bound, Marrick Prime consuming the oversized passenger display. An LSA cruiser had already approved his approach, but it was the two dozen League Navy warships that held his attention.

He blinked and was back in the rover, sweat sheening his brow. He took several steadying breaths, then attempted a connection to Staging. For once, it went through, though it took time to be accepted.

"Bill, you okay?" Sarah held a mug in her hand. "You look ill."

"I'm fine. Look, I need to ask you a few questions, just between you and me."

"Sure, go ahead." Her quizzical expression was warranted, but then an undercover agent, a turncoat, or a zealot would do the same.

He needed to assess her authenticity as much as her answers. "How well do you know the survey data in regions seventy-one and -two?"

She took a sip of her drink. Coffee, black, he guessed, no sugar. "Ah, northeast, starting about a hundred clicks from here. Heavy in iron, but no deposits worth mining. Traces of copper and magnesium. It's stable land. Porous formations suggest the potential for an aquifer. Nothing special. It's on an agri-path, right? I think B4 has first option on that whole area for bacteria seeding trials. Do I pass the test?"

Bill forced a laugh he didn't feel. "So far. Did you go through the original survey reports?"

"Why would I? They were low definition and twitchy as hell. The Phase 1 results were much cleaner, and you know how bollocksed up they were. Bill, what's up?"

Trust no one, his instincts screamed, but that was the agency talking. The wisest course would require patience and reason. Chip away at ignorance, one molecule at a time. Except for when chaotic deadlines demanded impossible guesses.

"How confident are you that the Phase 1 results are accurate?"

"No more or less than you. We're doing the detailed surveys for a reason."

She was right, but she was also wrong. "We're heading out to where there are gaps and preparing to go beyond the spread of the geospikes. We're not going over old ground."

"You're the one who sets the missions."

"I'm following the structure I was given." He rubbed his hair and looked away from the display. "All right, one last question: if there was a systematic error in the Phase 1 data, what would be the implications?

"Hell, Bill, have you been drinking your rover's coolant?"

"Please." Perhaps this had been a mistake.

"It depends on what kind of error. If the seismic results were off, we could have set up on quake central, but we'd see signs of that. And I guess we could miss mining deposits. And waste time checking wrongly flagged spots, but the big equipment wouldn't go into action without detailed site surveys. That chlorine plant wasn't on us. Down the track, it could mean people putting in claims for bad land, but we'd discover a problem before the claims lottery is run."

"Could it hide anything?"

She scrunched up her face. "What?"

"You're a geo-engineer. What could stay hidden? What wouldn't we find out later?"

"Seriously, Bill?" She put her mug down and tapped the fingers of her right hand on her desk. "Nothing, really. It'd come out in the end, and the lawsuits would be vicious. You'd need to cart away whatever you were hiding, and that's not going to happen. There's no real privacy in a colony."

But plenty in a locked-down corporate facility. *Fuck.*

"Thanks, Sarah. You've calmed this suspicious mind. I guess retraining didn't scrub the years of government project management from my soul. I'm probably incapable of taking anything at face value. See you back in the office this afternoon."

They exchanged farewells, and though she accepted his explanation, he doubted she fully believed it. His false resume had already proved less solid than he had expected—curse Ware. If Bill blundered about, it might collapse. The last thing he needed was to spend the next two years battling people's paranoia. His own was enough. He left the rover to secure the geospike, deciding against injecting monitoring code lest it, in turn, was noticed.

Once he was reseated, he set the rover on auto control, aiming it at another geospike. It would be ironic if the mounting concerns of a defective ex-agent were merely caused by poor quality control. He didn't buy it and not for reasons of self-respect. Now that he knew what he was looking for, another check suggested the nearby survey records all possessed the same telltales. Was it true for every spike or just those near the concentration of incidents?

The rover neared the invisible border of the corporate exclusion zone. The location of the BILT4 compound was hardly a secret, but he couldn't see it over a gentle rise. The instruments built into the rover passively soaked up plenty of data, but satisfying his curiosity with a broad-spectrum active scan would be like kicking down a door to borrow some sugar. But it *was* closer to the trouble than Staging.

Frustrated, he brought the rover to a halt and climbed onto its roof. The height gave him a view of the countryside without any additional clarity. Was he being railroaded, or was he letting old habits push him into trouble? He closed his eyes and sat cross-legged, willing himself to breathe in a steady rhythm. To make good choices, he needed to be in control of himself. *In. Out. Let it all pass. Remember, you don't give a shit.*

A noise burrowed into his ears, grinding. Vehicles approached. He hissed and looked. Three small rovers. Two peeled off, curving away, leaving the central one to advance, BILT4 SECURITY emblazoned on its front. The model was wheeled rather than tracked, and fast. He'd been stupid. He deserved this.

Bill forced himself to keep his actions slow, those of an innocent— not that he was guilty of anything on Eclipse—and dropped from the roof. He took a few lunch items from the box he'd stowed behind the driver's seat and swallowed several pieces, ensuring crumbs were on his suit. The rover came to a screeching halt, showering rocks and sending a cloud of dust into the air. When it cleared, Bill left his seat and walked around his rover, settling into a comfortable lean, and waited for the hired goons.

A door popped on the security vehicle, and a tall man sauntered out. He wore a black uniform with light protection. No doubt so the guy could play soldier. His jaw had a belligerent set that Bill had seen many times, one that belonged on those trained for combat but in love with violence. Perhaps he had been a soldier once.

"Who the fuck do you think you are?" The man, Karlo, by his uniform's label and a captain by his insignia, strode with an easy confidence, his hands nowhere near his pistol.

His accent was smooth and not particularly provincial. Perhaps a core-worlder. Possibilities rose only to be discarded. Obsequiousness could make further investigation difficult. And while that was a terrible idea, Bill didn't want closed doors. Aggression would almost certainly lead to escalation, and while Bill was on legally sound soil, expecting Ware or Sturt to come riding to his defense was ignorant fantasy. Ignorance for the win.

"Hey, there. What's up?"

Karlo pushed into Bill's personal space and looked down. "You dirt farmers were told to keep off restricted land."

Offering his best quizzical look, Bill said, "Happy to be wrong, but I'm pretty sure I'm not on your land. I certainly don't want to be. I've got a long list of maintenance checks, and if I'm off course, then I'm burning through time I don't have."

"Look here, smartass. If I catch you poking your nose round here again, I'll bite it off. Get it?"

And he would, too, the thug. The belligerence was an over-pressurized airlock, squeezing Bill, making him smaller while a part of him wanted to explode. He sucked in a steadying breath and took comfort in the nugget his training had uncovered. *Poking your nose.* This wasn't the concern for a marauding saboteur or murderer, but the desire to hide his employer's activities. A puzzle piece, though from what puzzle, he couldn't be sure. Retrieve information, then safely disengage.

Bill raised his hands to chest level. "I don't get the fuss, but I didn't mean to piss you off either. We're all here for the same reason in the end, right? I'll be on my way, and if I need to check anything close to your land, I'll contact you first. How does that sound?"

Karlo grabbed Bill's suit. "You don't go near BILT4 land. Not for any reason. Understood?"

"Sure, yeah. I got it."

Pain formed a line across Bill's back as Karlo pressed him against his rover.

"Don't forget it."

Exhibiting a weakness that burrowed into his muscles, Bill walked unsteadily to his rover's door and climbed in. *I'm not a threat*, his body language cried. The thug was still standing out there, waiting, as if he were expecting Bill to race for the compound. How easy it would be to run him over. Sadly, consequences were a thing. Charlie's death had consequences. Bill's discovery had consequences. Why did it feel like whatever the corporation was up to would also spray mud on him as it went past?

He should leave it all, do his job, and hunker down until his time was up. If curiosity had killed the cat, it was quite capable of killing a man, too. He gunned the rover, and it lurched forward. Karlo backed away, a look of anger on his chiseled face. There had to be small pleasures in life. It would be dangerous for them to meet again.

Bill sighed. His job was to coordinate his team. He wasn't responsible for their safety, at least not against murder. And he sure-as-death-in-vacuum wasn't responsible for shenanigans with the survey equipment. Sabotage or manipulation was way above the pay grade of a team manager and well beyond the expertise of most desk jockeys. He should pass it on to his manager and forget about it. But Bill knew what to do. And he couldn't let it go, not until a pattern formed, one structured by reason and human motive. He'd need to dig further, take a few risks, peek into a few systems, and determine if there were if there were connections.

Damn it, Charlie. I have to know.

CHAPTER 6
INTERFERENCE

The colony's hypernet was barely worthy of the name. Sure, there were copies of the standard official databases, a selection of entertainment platforms, and an AI-driven local news service with all the hallmarks of propaganda, but little else. It still had its uses for an inquiring mind. Bill had warmed a seat on a construction rover while the logged user was in the can to skim through the company ownership records. When the fabric of society was premised on who owned what, even far-flung communities needed a copy. It would already be out of date, but that was the challenge of bravely going where only a few others had gone before. And, give the League another ten or so years, a long line of repeater platforms would bring quicker if not instantaneous access to the League Interface.

Right now, historical data was fine. The search had revealed BILT4's fingers were in enough pies that the corporation's digits were stickier than glue. That allowed the opportunity to influence purchases and designs of a whole range of equipment destined for Eclipse. However, there was no smoking gun, no subsidiary owned by a subsidiary of a subsidiary connection to link the geospike software to BILT4. And, unfortunately, most contracts weren't publicly lodged.

He'd asked his team about the manufacturer, but the design was based on a generic platform that had been in use for decades on other worlds, with the software shifting depending on the source of the various sensor hardware developers. Hitting this dead end sent him in search of another path.

That path involved building C2.

Staging was laid out as a grid of paved and undecorated roads for the most part, with squat towers for administration, accommodation, and necessary services spreading from the barren and ambitiously named Central Park. The industrial and scientific precincts formed a thick outer ring. C2, a low pyramid-shaped structure with five stepped levels, sat a block back from the park, its once smooth walls abraded by dust storms.

Bill entered through the front door with a mug of coffee in one hand and a pad in the other. He wore a clean gray survey suit and a disarming smile. There was no receptionist—that would be wasteful of the limited human resources—so he walked up to the display in the small foyer and pretended to run his eyes over the departmental listings. He used the reflections in the display to watch for a suitable target. The foyer walls were a vibrant white with three large prints, all artistic renderings of successful colonies. A verdant forest scene with deer nibbling on grass. Mechanics working on a massive combine harvester at the edge of endless wheat fields. A city by night, its bright lights mirrored in a fast-moving river.

A man, short and bald, strode inside, while brushing dust from his arms. Bill only vaguely recognized him and hoped it was mutual. The man reached out to an elevator access panel, and Bill crossed the floor, pretending to be ready to do the same. When the elevator doors opened, Bill smiled and pretended to fumble his coffee. The man helpfully caught it.

"Thanks," Bill said, stepping in through the doors. "It's been one of those days."

"Every day is one of those days. What level are you after?" the man asked, a hand raised over the interior control panel. He'd pressed three for himself.

"Four, thanks."

The elevator moved swiftly, and Bill gave a friendly farewell when the man stepped out. Thankfully, no one came in. He forced his breathing into a slow, steady rhythm and brought an image of a quiet beach with a lounge chair and a jaunty umbrella to mind. An ice-filled cocktail rested on a nearby stool. Calm, gentle. No need to sweat. The image evaporated. He'd never grown comfortable with this kind of work. Beth had once said that kept him on his toes. The mix of exhilaration and dread were far more likely to take years from his life, toes and all. There was something to be said for sitting in a comfy chair, synthesizing a coherent story from the data others obtained.

The elevator doors opened on level four. A set of twenty desks filled an open-plan office, with only a solitary worker at her desk. She didn't look up from her display. Offices crowded the exterior of this level, each one hoarding a patch of natural light from half-height windows. A meeting was underway in the corner room on the left. Bill couldn't be around when it broke up.

He exited the elevator and turned right, slipping into a break room. He checked the time on his suit's arm. A little over an hour before the official end of the ten-hour workday. Minutes ticked by as he pretended to clean his mug. Right on the hour, Dennis Cade strode past the break room, heading for the bathroom. Bill had overheard one of Dennis's coworkers joking at The Bronze Age, one of the three sanctioned bars in Staging. Prices were high to discourage drunkenness, but human vices were baked into the DNA. An evergreen opening for those seeking intelligence. At least Bill didn't need to participate in the questioning of what Dennis got up to each afternoon.

Leaving a spotless mug on the counter, Bill strolled out of the break room. Dennis's office door was open. A good start. He changed direction without a backward glance and sat in the functional red chair. No surprised shouts or quizzical gazes followed. Dennis hadn't locked his console—why would he? Bill's heart beat fast as he swiped along the console to stop it auto-locking.

He stretched his fingers, then went to work. The interface was familiar with only the records available differing. With his old kit, he could have copied every detail he brought up, non-intrusively and fast. As it was, he had to be prudent, concentrating on three construction projects, each run by a different team. There had been accidents at all three, though there was no mistaking the chemical plant as sabotage, no matter the official storyline. Rumors were rife and the initial details too consistent to dismiss.

Each involved damaged equipment. Two had cave-ins. Two had damaged or missing surface equipment. It wasn't the same two each time. In each case, no one was present. And only the autofarm shed had caught fire. Subsoil analyses had all been conducted to the minimum standard, suggesting no obvious poor choices. But had the builders' equipment been tainted like the geospike? A fourth case might reveal a pattern.

He checked the time. Too late. A shiver ran through him. He closed the records, grabbed his pad, and walked out of the office. Dennis had exited the bathroom, shaking his wet hands. Their eyes met.

"Hey, there," Bill said. "I'm looking for meeting room 3C. Do you know where it is?"

The man's brow scrunched, forming small hills. "One floor down."

"I'm an idiot. Thanks. It's been a long day."

Dennis's concern washed away, leaving a comradery for those born to a life of work. "I hear you."

Abandoning the sacrificial mug waiting in the break room, Bill hurried to the elevator as if late for a meeting. After a quick descent, the doors opened, and he crossed the foyer. An alert sounded in his ear. A meeting had been inserted into his calendar. He waited until he was outside before even considering checking the details. A short-range transport drove down the pale, polycrete road, and two people in beige suits with maintenance patches walked out of a low, broad building in the distance. Neither reacted to his presence. Good.

The alert chimed again. He huffed and brought it up. A meeting right now at A1, the main office, and with no other listed attendees. What head-swollen bureaucrat thought that was a good idea? He could blow it off and pretend he hadn't noticed. No. It was better to cut off the bandage and see the damage beneath.

ONCE AGAIN, elevator doors opened before him, but this time he was invited—or ordered, depending on how he looked at it.

Charlie, could you have done anything else apart from getting yourself killed?

Floor-to-ceiling windows overlooked one side of the city, forming a fifteen-meter side of the square office. The extravagance had the intended effect. The colony director was close to a king, albeit one shackled with bureaucratic rules. Sun shone from the west—that being the key determiner of the north for a planet. You couldn't have it set to the east. It gave a copper tone to the plush brown carpet. A large, glossy desk at the north end faced the elevator, but the office's occupants sat around a boardroom table, long enough for twenty.

Oliver Sturt, Eclipse's director, held court at one end with Ware and a woman Bill didn't recognize. Her hair was the yellow of warning signs and its jagged cut defied the endemic practicality of an outside worker. She also had a pad and a portable display before her. Technician, he surmised. Someone who had far greater access than he to the colony's hypernet. A potential conduit of information, but she could be here as a watchdog, or worse, a sniffer dog. She was certainly tense enough.

Keeping his pace casual, Bill crossed the carpet. Sturt wore a collarless blue shirt and a pair of clean work pants, robust enough for visiting sites without getting his hands dirty. Earlier in Phase 2, Bill had seen him in a heavy weatherproof jacket, but he suspected that languished in storage.

Conversation ceased at the boardroom table. Sturt's short, neat brown hair topped a face of soft wrinkles. His blue eyes speared Bill, though his expression was neutral. He remained seated as Bill reached the table.

"Take a seat." Sturt gestured to the left of the table, his gruff voice hinting at his true age.

Bill picked a seat two down from the end, giving himself a little space, a valid option if he was already isolated. An interesting collection of people. Not the sort you'd need to arrest someone. Ware might have news about Charlie, but he was unlikely to involve Sturt unless it was dire, or he wanted something Bill wasn't likely to agree to. And Sturt had a full plate. If he was involved, he was invested. What did the technician mean? It paid to start at the edges and work in.

He leaned a little over the table, hand outstretched. "Hi, I'm Bill, survey chief. I don't think we've met."

Her eyes widened, and she shifted in her seat, her expression cool and unreadable as she reached out to shake hands with a tight grip. "Erin Tyzen, hypernet engineer."

Bingo. He sat, gave Ware a nod, and turned to Sturt. "How can I help?"

"Bill, is there anything you want to tell us?"

Oh, that was a classic. Get the rube to spill secrets, big or small, by letting their own guilty conscience dredge it all up. He thought back to the first two years of his time on Eclipse. The colony had been fragile. Long hours and no rest days were standard. Accommodation had been cramped and basic. Back then, Bill and his team were consulted daily, and he'd sat in a circle of a cramped, table-less room as Sturt ruthlessly coordinated the massive construction, production, and agriculture task lists. Any dissent was shot down with pointed references to the director's role as final approver of each colonist's stake. He held their futures in his hands.

The silence stretched. Bill slowly shifted his expression to one of expectant confusion. "About what?"

Sturt's nostrils flared. "There has been a complaint about you."

"Really? That sounds unlikely. What about?"

Ware had one hand on the table. Bill noted the pressure the captain was exerting. He'd probably been told to keep quiet unless needed. And the engineer was busy looking at her devices, no doubt wishing to be anywhere else. If the complaint was about his use of other people's accounts, then she was here as a witness. Not good. It would explain her vibe.

"Look, Bill. I need your cooperation. I'm trying to be reasonable. I'm trying to understand what has occurred."

Bill leaned back and let his eyes narrow infinitesimally. "I'm trying to understand, too. Do I have to play twenty questions?"

Ware slapped the table. "BILT4, Hayden. Did you think there'd be no consequences? There's already enough shit floating around you."

"All right, Robert. Let's keep this calm. We received an official complaint. The head of security has alleged that you trespassed on their land."

"Were you spying?" Ware demanded, though Bill sensed an uneasiness—betrayal or disappointment.

Relief washed through Bill. This was all it was about? Easy. Though Sturt's involvement suggested more. "Karlo is a brainless ass. I wasn't over their border. I'm a surveyor. I should know."

"You were a spook once," Ware retorted.

"Yeah, I was. I'm not now, as you well know. I don't want anything to do with whatever BILT4 cooks up behind their walls." Sow doubt in others. Take the spotlight off yourself.

Sturt tapped the table with his pointer finger. "You must have been close enough to set them off."

Bill relaxed in his chair. "I don't think it'd take much to trigger Karlo."

"We don't need trouble. You know the schedule. The delays are mounting up. There's no good reason to up the tension with our corporate neighbors."

Had Sturt sent Tyzen nosing through the logs to track his movements? Or had someone from Bill's small team been talking? He didn't have the full picture, and he didn't want to build a half-baked case.

Case? Listen to yourself, Bill. You don't have cases. Not anymore.

"I had a reason, a solid one. There's a problem with the geospikes—the sensor platforms we've dotted the landscape with. The software's inaccurate."

Ware frowned. "You had to go interfering with BILT4 because you stuffed up your equipment?"

Time to feed them a little more. "No. The fault existed before the spikes ever hit the planet. It's subtle, but it's there. And I believe it's deliberate."

Sturt wheeled his chair back as if to distance himself from the claim. "You're saying they, what, hacked the sensors?"

"I'm not saying that, not yet. Maybe not at all. Look, all the problems that are getting reported, they're to the northeast. That's where the faulty spike I checked is located. It just happens to be near our corporate friends."

Sturt stood up and gestured to the windows. "See all this? BILT4 is a substantial shareholder in this colony. It would make no sense for them to disrupt our progress. And it's hard enough to know what's out there with the signal problems. What hurts us hurts them and vice versa. They're not sabotaging us. Jesus, Bill, they're trying to solve the interference issue. That would make everything we do—everything you do—so much easier. They're our partners. If they tell you to do something, you need to listen."

"I'm not one of their employees. None of us are." The words had slipped out. Bill pressed his nails into his palms. He hadn't meant to escalate.

Ware stood as well, and for a moment, Bill wondered if he was going to come around to strangle Bill. "You're an arrogant asshole, Hayden. We don't need trouble."

"The corporation has a lot of clout." Sturt turned to watch the orange sky. "When the auditors come with Phase 3, we'll need every bit of goodwill we can muster. I don't want to give years of my life for nothing. No one will thank you for that. People have been lynched in other colonies for less."

"I hear you." Bill's self-control strained against the power imbalance. "Don't you get it? If the survey data is wrong, you're building blind, you're mining blind. Bad data can kill us—and them. It might explain the accidents. Either way, I haven't been on company land, and I have no intention of doing so."

"Someone has been," Ware said.

"You haven't been there in the past few weeks?" Sturt asked. "Even by mistake?"

"No, not at all. I never had a reason to."

Sturt looked to Tyzen. She nodded. His jaw muscles tightened. So she had been looking at least into his rover's logs and maybe those of his team. Has she dared access his implant? Excepting emergencies, that was deeply illegal.

"They're blaming us." Ware pointed his finger. "They're blaming you."

Bill stood and met the captain's gaze, frustration surging through his nerves. "What if they're covering up something? They've been here as long as us. Have they made any progress with the interference? None. They've got masters higher up the food chain. They might be looking to scapegoat their failures—sabotage our operations, so they don't look so bad."

"By all that is holy, Bill," Sturt said, closing to put his hands on Bill's shoulders, an oddly personal gesture. Was the man afraid? "I know you were in the LSA. It might be how you see the world, but you can't go around saying that."

"What about saying they might have killed Charlie to cover up what they're doing?" Damn. He needed to control his frustration. Frank and fearless advice was fine as a concept, but even in the agency, it got you sent to outer worlds like Marrick Prime.

"Bill, Bill, you can't. Even whispering the accusation would cause havoc. You don't have proof, do you?"

Bill moved to the side, breaking contact with Sturt while not retreating. Ware wouldn't find the answers. That much was clear. Even if the cop wanted to, Sturt wouldn't let his trained dog off its leash.

"I'll find proof," Bill heard himself saying, closing his mouth when it was too late.

"No, you won't. That's a direct order." Sturt pointed his finger at Bill's chest and scowled. "I've heard what you have to say. I'll have Ware look into it. You are to go back to your job, your current one, and keep your theories to yourself."

"With all due respect, you need me, not Ware. There should be a full software audit, a deep analysis of each incident. We need to find patterns. The records are sparse, but given enough time—"

"Have you been hacking?" Ware demanded and started walking around the table.

Damn. It had been too long, and Bill had spent much of his last year in the agency at a desk where he didn't have to be so guarded, at least until he stepped onto the street.

"I'll search for unauthorized access attempts," Tyzen said, her fingers tapping a high-speed rhythm.

Bill hadn't been able to cleanse his actions as well as he'd have liked. Implant records aside, if she went into the cameras and ran a facial recognition algorithm linked to access logs, it wouldn't take long to implicate him.

Ware planted himself between Bill and the elevator. "What if Hayden is here to cause trouble for a rival corporation or some lunatic political group? I'd bet they'd pay well. It'd explain what's going on."

"You can't believe that," Bill said. "I swore an oath to uphold the League, as you swore one to uphold the law. I might be out of the agency, but I'm no more a corporate thug than you—or some crazy One-Earther."

Sturt let out a heavy breath. "I'd like to believe you, Bill. Honestly, I'd think something more subtle would be the agency way. You certainly wouldn't implicate yourself so easily, but… I can't have you causing trouble. Not now. You should have raised your concerns through the proper channels. And you underestimate Robert. He's an excellent officer. I'm confining you to your quarters for a week. It'll let things settle down and give more time for the investigation to conclude. We'll talk then."

"Bullshit." Bill squared his shoulders. "You can't do that."

Ware grunted. "I can jail you on suspicion of murder. Your choice."

The worst thing was that Bill had let himself walk into it. He should have kept calm, kept everything to himself, kept his head. And now he was going to rot for a week.

"Seems like I'm going home. I could do with a break."

But rest was the last thing on his mind.

CHAPTER 7
MIKE, YOU HEAR ME?

A slurry of crushed rocks clattered onto a tall pile, the source a narrow pipe resting on a collapsible metal frame. A much thinner pipe sprayed a steady mist that reduced, though not eliminated, the accompanying dust. Crunches and thuds and an ongoing whine issued from a tunnel cutting into the shallow slope of an apparently unremarkable hill. The entrance started over a meter wide but immediately narrowed by a quarter until it disappeared into darkness.

Ronald Pascale, materials scientist and site supervisor, brushed the screen of the boring machine's controls. "How much longer?"

The machine's operator, a cranky old man who insisted on being called Kelpie, put an overprotective hand between Ron and the filthy equipment. "Almost there. You want it delicate. That means slow."

A hauler shaded both of them, but Ron felt the heat of anticipation. His two colleagues, who no doubt felt the same, were busy prepping the equipment they would be carrying down. The second part of the boring team, a short-bodied, long-haired, and humorless engineer called Sam, had his head down the hole as if he were whispering encouragements to the digger. The last and most useless members of the dig group were sitting pretty in their security rover. Protocol required them. Protocol required many wasteful additions to Ron's projects, but that was all part of working for a corporation with a militant HR department and an inability to let go of a leash despite it stretching light-years.

"We've got breakthrough."

Ron quivered. Flores had hogged the specimen at Haven along with her toadies, but she couldn't be everywhere at once. Her name would be plastered over every discovery despite that, meaning he would have to find ways to carve his own place in history. And being the first was always a good start.

"Pull it back. We can't risk any damage." He left the engineers to sort that out and hurried over to his colleagues.

Olena Bilyk held two cases, both white and bulky. Her long blond hair ran down the back of her neck as neat as a length of rope. Her gaunt features brightened as he approached. "They're through?"

"Almost."

"Do you want the honor?" Dave Titus, an optics expert with a previous career in reverse engineering, held out a third case, a dented silver outer containing hand drills. His supreme confidence and rugged good looks were annoying, but at least he knew his place.

Ron took the case. "Be ready to head down as soon as I give the all-clear."

He headed for the opening, ignoring the complaints of the drill operators, but surreptitiously glancing at the security team. They had no idea that the machine was done. Why did they think it had rolled back on its tracks? Fools. The tunnel was dark, so he turned on the broad-beamed flashlight on his suit's chest and crawled inward.

The preexisting tunnel that the machine had intersected had been a fluke discovery when another team had been gridding and scanning around a minor find. Two weather-corroded scraps, completely useless, but signals suggesting the end of a tunnel with a diameter that didn't match the terraforming standards—that held a lot of promise. Protected from exposure to thousands of years of radiation and the more recent human activity; who knew what discoveries waited?

The air pressed tight around him as he continued his awkward shuffle along and down. Slide the case forward, crawl, slide again. His gloves grew filthy, and his throat burned with its new coating of dust.

A trickle of nervous sweat ran down his forehead and stung his right eye. But there it was! A flat end, with a small horizontal hole, an oval but curved in the third dimension.

When he reached this, he greedily peered through the small break-through. A sliver of reflected light hinted at a tunnel, but nothing more. Should he put a probe through? No, he needed to be inside without delay. He opened his case, took out the main drill unit, and selected a twenty-millimeter bit. The soft red sandstone offered little resistance, and he quickly reached open air. The next was almost as easy. By the tenth hole, the physical effort was straining his lean muscles uncomfortably.

"Are you through?" Olena asked from the far end of the tunnel, her voice distorting as it echoed.

"You'll know when I am," he snapped back.

Minutes later, he pushed through the last hole. The end now contained a perforated circle, the remaining stone too thick for a person to break. He took the cleaning cloth and fluid and wiped the bit sloppily down before replacing it in the case. Next, he scooped up a handful of cylinders. To set them, he extended a red cable from the back of each and inserted one into every hole he had drilled. On the back of the drill was a grid of ports. He plugged each cable into empty ports, configured the drill, and pressed the trigger. The cylinders beeped a chorus of warnings and expanded. Slight scratches ran a shiver through his spine as the devices gripped stone. The drill hummed, delivering an enormous jolt of power.

A sudden crack. Another. A whole series. Stone slid away. A final crack and the top half of the circle dropped from above, tumbling out of view. Ron blinked rapidly to clear his eyes of grit. The tunnel was circular, at least twice his height, and had the same red of the natural stone whilst glinting like glass. He activated the second set. *Crack, crack, crack!* More stone fell. He brushed the dangling expanders aside and scrambled over the rough edge.

"Ron, what's happening?"

"I'm through. Come down."

He walked to the center of the floor and slowly spun, his arms outstretched and his footsteps echoing. The air was surprisingly fresh, and his suit light created the impression that he was in a crystal palace. No human had ever stepped here. That was a pretty common thought for a colonist, but this had meaning. Had thousands of aliens passed along this way? No, the tunnel was meant to end nearby. Perhaps this was the last striving of an ancient civilization before it collapsed. There would be something to find—there had to be.

"CAN YOU SEE IT?" Olena pointed ahead.

Ron walked faster. They hadn't explored far, maybe a hundred meters. A ring of dark material extended a short distance out of the surface of the tunnel. It was the first variation in the disappointingly empty passage.

"Hey." A security guard grabbed Ron's arm, forcing him to stop. "We go slow and together, like I said. Protocol. Got it?"

"Yes, I hear you. Protocol." The two meatheads had whined about Ron's earlier bravery, and now they were treating him like a distracted toddler. Yet, they were more superfluous than bean counters in a lab. Where was the justice in that?

His frustration melted away as he closed on the ring that circled the tunnel like a sphincter. It was made of repeating segments, each rough-textured piece the dirty orange of rusted iron. They overlapped each other, creating a series of subtle ridges. Here and there, lines cut into the surface. He wanted them to be words, letters, runes, but they were few and far between. Damage would be an equally viable explanation. Above him, cables coated in the same glossy material as the tunnel ran along like a spinal cord. Fascinating, if disturbingly organic.

"We stop here. Get the lights set up and unpack the gear. It's time to probe."

Ron ran his hands along a segment of the ring. Dave would have a go soon, stealing the chance to make discoveries. Ron couldn't allow that. He cleared his mind with a routine of rubbing his fingertips on his thumbs and started examining the ring.

Age? He'd check the isotope mix. Components? A whirl through a spectrometer. Structure? A Confocal Muon Microscope, or CMM. But what he really wanted was…

At the nearest edge of the segment, he detected an ever-so-slight groove. At the center, a depression with a six-pointed star as large as his thumb. The shape was so familiar that he was halfway convinced that he'd just been pranked. It was an obvious design. Humans had been using it on screws for hundreds of years. It was practical. Surely, the long-dead builders had reached the same conclusion, like convergent evolution.

"I need a multi-tool."

Dave brought a small, lumpy orange device with a dimpled surface. He peered over Ron's shoulder. "Nice. I wonder if this came with a pointless safety sheet and overly complicated build instructions."

Ron decided to laugh. Dave wasn't barging in, so it was safe to select the appropriate head and apply the tool. The screw resisted. He sniffed and changed the setting. It turned clockwise, then popped, revealing a strange design—a shank with jagged lumps along four sides. The reasoning was going to bug him until he worked it out.

Olena coughed for attention. She held two small drones in her hands. "Hey, shouldn't we do a full analysis before we start opening it up?"

"We're not here for archaeology," Ron chided. "Remember that. We want tech. Anything we find here could save sick children, improve space flight, and make us famous."

"We don't get famous in our line of work," Dave said. The bastard knew he had a rep.

Ron leaned over to the other side of the ring and started removing the second screw. "Not yet, not to the great unwashed masses. Give it a few decades, when it's all in the past, and everyone will know who we are. Trust me, if we change the world, all will be forgiven. Olena, if you want, send off the drones. Get a sample from the wall. Whatever makes you happy. And don't forget a full material analysis."

The segment sprung open. Ron dropped the multi-tool and instinctively raised his hands to protect his face. An unnecessary gesture, it turned out.

"Sweet," Dave said. "Do you see? That there's a light, not a reflection."

Smoothing his sleeves, Ron focused on the internal structure of the segment. A fabric of cables, several large lumps placed alongside each other, following the ring's curve. On both sides of these were short strips, hair-thin marks like a dotted line. And yes, they had a subtle orange glow. It was still powered. Ron's innards filled with butterflies. Flores could suck on her small lump of leftovers. Here was pure alien tech in situ.

Dave stepped over the ring and kneeled on the other side. "Look at the repeating patterns of the circuitry. I'm guessing they mass-produced standard modules and stacked them to get whatever result they wanted."

"Do you know what this was for?" Ron said, the question a sharp poke he couldn't resist.

"Assuming form follows function, we've got a few possibilities: a repeater of some kind, maybe for network comms, a sensor suite to monitor the stability of the tunnel, a defense point, an environmental control, decoration."

The man had no idea. Ron considered the ring and its attached cables. There was a strong, practical aesthetic. "It could easily be most of those. We'll need to find the power source to get a limit on its capabilities. Right now, let's do a component-by-component check. Full spectrum EM signatures, thermals, light-bleed, everything."

Both he and Dave set to work, selecting tools and running tests.

"Interesting," Olena said loudly, breaking Ron's concentration and blocking the light coming from the standing lamp that bathed this small part of the tunnel in light. "The wall coating is mostly an aluminosilicate doped with iron, lanthanum, nickel, and carbon. Isotope readings suggest it's local material. Tough, too."

Ron paused and considered. It made sense, a local civilization would use local materials. The chemical structure would be fascinating, but hardly an issue for today. "Nice. Have the drones found anything?"

Olena grabbed a pad lying on a case. "The drone heading west sent a change notice. The coating finishes about two hundred meters from where we entered, but the tunnel keeps going. The signal's attenuating. I'll need to pull it back soon. And... huh. The eastbound isn't responding. I'm beyond sick of signal failures. Kuo's incremental improvements aren't nearly enough down here. Weird, though. The drone should have returned. It's not like it can get lost."

Ron sighed, his eyes already back on the alien technology. "Well, go get it. You know how requisitions are."

He heard one of the security team grumble and head off with her, but he was already teasing out cables, ensuring he didn't apply excessive stress. Beneath, an array of small vane-like protuberances was mounted on a surface covered in tiny translucent etchings.

"Do you think they can come out?" Ron touched one and felt it shift under the slightest pressure.

Dave raised a hand. "Wait. You don't want to remove it under power. We have no idea if that would affect its operation."

It was a reasonable argument, but what if the guy was trying to hold Ron back? If Ron hadn't worked so studiously to push his way into leading a team, Dave would have been the one in charge. Fingertips wobbling, Ron forced his hand away.

I'm smart enough to work this out from first principles. He's not smarter —he's just more practiced.

"So," Ron said, "If this is segmented, and the smarts are processing chiplets, then the cables are feeding energy and data. The question is whether there's local storage for the segment or do we need to cut out the entire ring to get anything worthwhile."

Dave grunted in agreement and pressed a probe into a rectangular lump where a cable poked out. "There's the barest temperature differential, suggesting resistance or energy conversion. We could have some kind of capacitor—"

A high-pitched noise sounded for the barest part of a second. It drove down into Ron's eardrums, into his nervous system, and set his teeth on edge.

Dave yanked his probe and snapped several cables. "Shit."

Ron laughed. The faint lights on the segment went dark. "And you were the one telling me to be careful."

"Mike, you hear me?" The remaining security guard walked over to them, calling again to his comrade before issuing a torrent of swearing. "Screw this interference. Weren't you lot going to fix it?"

Twisting his body into a comfortable sitting position, back against the ring, Ron let annoyance tighten his jaw. "The soil's a mess, and until the terraforming settles the particulates in the atmosphere, it'll be an issue right up to the exosphere. The signal will never be good down here. That's the current theory, anyway. No point complaining."

The guard's face reddened. "Look, it might be a joke to you, but you heard that, right? What if there was a cave-in? I can't get through to Mike."

Dave stopped fiddling with the damaged cables. "We'd have heard rocks falling. Damn, we would see the dust, taste it. Olena said the coating was strong. Stop wetting your pants. She probably tripped over, and your Mike is helping her back. Go and check if you want."

"I can't. I have to stay with you two." The guard paced a short way, then stopped. "Can you hear that?"

Holding his breath, Ron strained his hearing. Yes. Something. "They're on their way. There you go, problem solved. Now, can we get back to work?"

Without waiting for an answer, he returned to the open segment, a smile on his face. With the power cut by Dave's clumsiness, it was quite reasonable to remove components and see what could be ascertained. He'd have to log the mistake, ensuring any consequences fell on the *expert* reverse engineer.

Air whooshed as a large object flew over Ron's head, engulfing him in darkness for an instant. He ducked despite it having already passed. A collapse?

Clang! Crack! Crunch!

The lamp went out. The security guard shouted. So did Dave. Ron reached for his light, slapping his left wrist until he found the controls by touch alone. He was still breathing, no rocks had hit him, and the air tasted no different. So what was happening?

Three hisses, each followed by loud slaps and blinding strobes. The crazy guard was shooting. Ron rolled to the ground, hoping he wasn't going to be blasted. His chest light created shifting shadows and dazzling glimpses. Enough to see the guard fall, a large mass bringing him to the ground. It *was* a rock fall. No. The mass rose on glinting protrusions. Legs?

Hiss, Hiss.

The guard screamed.

Wetness sprayed across Ron's face. Rain? No, he was underground. And the liquid was warm. Terror gripped him, squeezed his limbs, crushed his stomach. He stood, shaking, a marionette controlled by a drunk. It meant… it meant…

Ron sprinted around the writhing guard with every joule of energy his body could muster. His cardio wasn't good—he hated the gym—but all he needed to do was reach the tunnel entrance and escape in his rover. His shins ached with the force of each impact. There were more footfalls. Dave was catching up.

The screams cut off, replaced by grinding, and then a series of staccato thuds. Ron dared a glance. With only the light reflecting off the tunnel walls, he fought through afterimages. Movement in the dark. Legs. Many legs. Approaching.

A squeal escaped Ron, but he didn't care. He redoubled his efforts. The light of the drill hole called to him, a beacon of hope. He reached it together with Dave.

Thud, thud, thud, thud, thud, thud. So close.

There was no room for them to escape simultaneously. Ron kicked Dave in the back of a knee, and the arrogant asshole dropped. Problem fixed. Bending over, Ron scrambled into the hole and started crawling, his whimpers echoing.

Dave shouted a curse. Then he screamed, grunted, and fell silent. So fast. Ron scrabbled, calling out to the drill team. They had to hear him. They had to help.

"What's wrong?" Kelpie asked from somewhere on the surface.

What's wrong? Idiot.

"Get me out of here!"

"All right, just calm down."

Pain. Tears welled in Ron's eyes, and he moaned. Shivering, he looked over his shoulder. A long blade of curved metal had sliced through the muscles in his calf, between the bones, and into the small tunnel's floor.

Sobbing, he strained, desperate to drag himself forward, but he was stuck, and each attempt brought a crescendo of agony. He looked back again, hoping for a way to escape. He couldn't die. It wasn't fair. He wasn't some dumb colonist, enslaved like a worker bee. He was too clever.

With his last strand of sanity, he pushed his gaze beyond his skewered leg. He saw *it* filling the small diameter. He saw the details, the moving parts. He understood.

They had been wrong, so very wrong.

He screamed.

CHAPTER 8
WHAT HAS BEEN SOWN

Trax directed her quad bike close to Harry. "You've been quiet."

They were driving along an enormous tunnel, a heat spreader outlet connected to a decommissioned terraforming plant. It had generated extraordinary amounts of thermal energy to speed up the melting of comets slammed onto the surface to increase the water coverage. The atmosphere hadn't given enough friction and the planet's heat from radioactive decay would have taken far too long. The rest of her crew were busy stripping the plant. Any part could be manufactured, but with so many faults stacking up, the demand on her fabricators was grueling. The mass production factories were coming online far too slowly. Trax shielded her crew from the bureaucratic bleating as much as she could. And they all knew the drill. So what was up with Harry?

"You know I don't talk much," Harry said.

Her quad bike appeared toy-like beneath her, but she drove with steady competence. The bikes were next to silent except for the tires flinging up loose stones. Each had twin headlamps that reached far down the monotonous route.

"You have that in common with Margot. Seems to be the way with farming types. You either can't get a word out of them, or you can't shut them up."

"You were a farmer."

Trax closed her eyes, felt her quad bike stray, and renewed her focus. "My parents were. I was... I was going to be. And you've heard me enough times—I will be when we hit Phase 3. Nothing's going to get in my way. I mean, I'll miss you guys, but this"—she gestured with one hand to the tunnel—"was never my plan. I'm not going back like you."

"I have a plan. Not easy to wait for it."

"Oh, Harry, is it your family?"

"Yeah. It's harder than I thought. If I could talk to them. If I knew how they were coping. I need to know they're safe. And I miss 'em."

"I miss mine, too."

They were still out there, still alive, and yet they might as well have been gone. The corporation-funded merc assault had lasted three weeks, and its shockwave kept spreading through the years.

The headlights left a dark patch. "Hold up. See that over there?"

Trax slowed down, and Harry copied. They pulled up next to a hole that didn't even reach Trax's waist. The edges were rough, as if a fork had been scraped along wet clay.

"Bit small for an offshoot."

"Yeah," Trax agreed, while stepping off her quad bike. "This was done later."

She checked the map on her suit sleeve. The inertial system was never as accurate as satellite tracking, but at least it was always available. They weren't that far off Margot's farm.

"I guess there could be some odd noises at the other end. Wind."

Harry dismounted her quad bike and walked over to the entrance, pausing to run her fingers down several shallow grooves. "Does this Margot scare easily?"

"No. Farmers don't, as a rule. She said she was confused, not scared. What do you make of it?"

"These look like tool marks. Whoever dug it might have widened it by hand, but it'd take forever to reach the surface without a proper borer."

Trax leaned over and peered into the tunnel. It sloped sharply upward toward the barest hint of light. Climbable, but difficult.

"A small auto unit could have gone haywire. They should have all run out of power years ago. Cutting stone burns energy. It doesn't make sense."

"Bootlegging?"

Letting out a slow breath, Trax considered the idea. "If the sabotage we're seeing is disguising theft, it'd make some sense. Hoarding resources would give a boost in Phase 3 when chaos will piss down on us. And after that, the first mover advantage drops. Move gear around, store it when not in use, use the old exit ramps where possible. They'd be ghosts. It's not like the tunnels are monitored."

What had they stepped into?

"You heading up?" Harry asked after a pause.

"Nope." Trax went back to her quad bike and pulled a flare out. She snapped the end off and tossed it into the small tunnel, squinting to protect against its brightness. Thick orange smoke wafted up, spread by an unseen breeze. "Not that way. We go back and take the last ramp, head to these coordinates on the surface, then find the tunnel by the plume. We'll show it to Margot and her folk. They might be able to make more sense of it than we can."

Assuming none of them were up to anything shady.

ON THE SURFACE, the coordinates weren't needed. They headed roughly in the right direction until the plume flagged their destination. The hole was near vertical at the top and opened among tall tufts of grass with a field of oats visible in the distance. Margot's home was only a little to the north, beyond several rows of evenly spaced pines. They turned their quad bikes to the edge of these and sped off. The terraforming tunnel had been an easy, if dull, ride. The uneven ground and fresh air on Trax's face brought her a flash of childhood joy.

Past the trees, a harvester came into view, a bulky front serviced by low haulers that collected the crops pouring out from an extended arm, swapping with another when full. There was no sign of the farmers, but that was to be expected. They would be chipping away at an endless list of maintenance tasks. The grain was a resilient, engineered variety, able to survive the harsh storms from the settling environment. Often organics were more resilient than fencing.

They buzzed along the edge of the field, dodging piles of cleared rocks and depressions. The homestead came into view. First was the vehicle shed, a tall, long row of doors securing the vehicles vital to a large-scale farm. One door stood half open, and Trax wondered if she was going to be asked to fix it. Margot and her folk knew what they were doing with most things mechanical. If there was a fault they couldn't handle, that would usually mean a replacement part their small fabricator couldn't manage. Unlikely.

The second building, made from forest green panels, had a lower roof and several boxes attached along the front. There was a hose connected to a tank as well—fire retardant. Except the bottom of the tank was ripped clean off, long enough ago for the contents to have soaked into the ground. Discomfort shadowed her thoughts. These folk were a good distance from Staging. Grain dust was dangerous, and there was plenty of machinery to short and start fires. This wasn't like Margot. What were they up to? They needed to take safety seriously. And why was the door open, rattling in the wind?

Harry shouted in her sweet voice, "Oh shit!"

Overshadowing the whole site, six tall silos reached to the sky like giant, denuded trees. A good distance in front sat the homestead proper—the living quarters for the farmers. Molded panels resembled weathered wood. Corners of several were bent outward. The entirety of a window lay on the ground, torn from its frame.

"Abuk damn it!" Trax recklessly piled on speed, advancing on the house. "Margot! Linh! Cameron! Anyone!"

She slammed on the brakes and skidded to a stop, leaping off the quad bike and running to the wide front door. It was shut. Up close, she spotted smoke wafting through the various gashes in the building.

"Margot?"

Harry came to her side but said nothing.

"A mini cyclone?" Trax asked, hitting the door access panel with no result. "It's so damn quiet. Give me a hand with the manual release."

74

Harry took out a multi-tool, and they opened two maintenance ports. They snapped free handles, inserted them into sockets, and started winding. The door slid to the right, revealing chaos. A desk blocked the way, and several heavy chairs were stacked on it. Beyond, there were kitchen implements, clothes—a whole mess of domestic items lying on the floor.

As soon as the gap widened enough for them both, Trax shoved the desk, clearing a path, and hurried inside. Harry followed, and they went from room to room. Broken furniture, furrows in the floor, rips in padding and fabric, an antique fire axe lying incongruously next to a vase of spilled flowers. The axe head had traveled with Margot, a family heirloom. The handle began as local timber. She had been so proud, twelve generations of unbroken ownership. Evening meals abandoned on a long table, gravy congealed and peas cold. This was no storm, no natural disaster. If it was bootleggers, the bastards were ruthless.

They found blood in a bathroom. It had been locked like the front, but a bathroom didn't need to be secure, just private. A twitch of the safety release, and the painted horror reflected back, dark, dry yet glossy in patches. A macabre artist had poured life out and smeared it like a child's finger painting. Delicate sprays decorated a toilet and sink, while handprints dotted the shower cubicle.

Trax hugged herself tightly. The scene could have come from the most unoriginal horror flick, an AI-generated pastiche. She took a shuddering breath and wiped at her wet eyes.

Margot. What happened?

"Damn." Harry put an arm around Trax. "This is nasty shit. Dragged them right out."

Harry was right. A corner of a bathroom wall had been torn open. The smeared blood led directly to this. Crushed flowers lay on a raised bed of rich soil. To Trax's surprise, there was no further blood, no red footprints pointing to a long-gone murderer.

Decades ago, Agricore mercenaries had stormed the small island, New Adelaide, rounding up the farmers who had refused to pay the extortionate lease increase. They'd smashed front doors, shouting, rounding up innocent adults—parents. The violation was absolute, filling Trax's dreams for years, and occasionally sneaking back to squeeze further terror even now. With the fear came anger. That same anger that had reignited self-worth, control, and purpose flowed back. The asshole who did this would pay. Nothing would get in her way.

"What now, boss?"

Treat it as a failing project. Triage. "See if you can get through to the rest of the crew. I want them on their guard. Tell them to trust no one. I'm heading outside to see if there's any indication of where the... people were taken."

A groan, loud and animalistic, dug at the edge of Trax's awareness. "Did you hear that?"

"I think so. Sounded like a panel bending."

"Maybe. Follow me." Trax escaped the bathroom and picked her way back through the homestead, pausing to grab the axe.

"You think they're still here?"

"They?" Trax asked.

"Yeah. One asshole alone couldn't do this." Swearing always sounded odd coming from Harry's melodic voice, but this time, it sounded like she meant it.

"True." Wasn't every colonist put through a full psych eval? The odds of several psychopaths slipping the net must be incredibly low.

They walked outside in time to hear another groan.

The groan came again.

Trax considered its texture as she would the telltale whines or clanks of a failed actuator. "The silos?"

Harry grunted her agreement as she worked a strut from the front wall back and forth. On the seventh go, the already stressed composite failed. The mechanic gave her improvised club a test swing.

"Ready, boss."

Crossing the open ground to the silos left them in the open. Easy pickings for someone with a gun. Had Margot been shot, executed? That didn't feel right. They were restricted until Phase 3, and even then, there were plenty of checks.

The hard-packed soil bore deep tread patterns, stamped by giant wheels. Every step became a chance to twist an ankle, slowing them down. When close, she walked along the line of silos. The doors at the bottom were closed. Thin stairs wound their way upward around each cylinder, all the way to the top where hoppers waited to accept harvested grain. As well, a second set of doors marked the end of the stairs, allowing for inspections. One of these doors on the third silo from the left was ajar.

"Up there, see it?"

"Yeah."

They hurried to the silo's stairs and climbed, Trax first. She wished for the sound again. If the bastards were still here, she'd show them some blood. She'd cut their fingers off and stuff the digits down their sick throats. The handrail twisted as if hammered out of shape at several points. She tried not to think about any give beneath her feet. The wind increased as she completed a second loop. After the third go round, they reached the door.

Positioned near the open side, Trax raised Margot's axe and gestured to Harry. The mechanic grabbed the handle, and on a nod from Trax, yanked. It didn't shift. Harry wedged her club in the gap and worked the door. Her muscles bunched. The door screeched. It strained. It gave. Harry slammed into the handrail and lost her balance, her upper body dangling in open air. Trax grabbed Harry's suit and pulled, saving her friend from a long drop. They shared a glance. Words weren't needed.

Someone screamed over and over, cutting past Trax's defenses, burrowing into her mind, slashing at her heart. She slapped a flash-light control on her shoulder, grabbed an edge of the doorframe, and leaned in, desperate to end the emotional assault.

Margot. Blood covered the farmer's face, and oats covered her to the waist. Her blank eyes looked nowhere and everywhere. Her matted hair stuck out in clumps. And yet, enthralled by pure terror, she still didn't move. A farmer's instinct. The grain would swallow her. She would drown if she tried to escape. Smart woman. She'd gone where the attackers couldn't reach her.

"Margot, it's me, Jane. You're safe now. We're going to get you out. It's over. Whatever happened, it's over. I promise." But how to reach her safely?

Trax leaned the axe against the silo to free her hands.

Harry must have been thinking along the same lines. She pulled a roll of cord from a pocket. "Strong enough to hold the both of you."

In other words, Harry wasn't going in there. Trax couldn't blame her. Harry unwound and cut a length, securing one end around the handrail while Trax tied the other to loop on her suit.

"I'm coming in, nice and slow. I'm going to help you out."

She tested one foot on the oats. It sank, ankle-deep. Accepting the risk, she entered the silo, her second foot sinking quickly. Margot's guttural cries echoed, pounding into Trax. Every step proved a battle. The grain didn't want to let her go. Halfway across, she was knee-deep, fighting forward as if through molasses. She paused to catch her breath, and the scent of the oats tickled her nose. Dry, rich, welcoming. A trap. Trax used her hands to dig her way forward, to swim.

She reached out. "I'm here. I'm here. Take my hand."

Margot didn't look at Trax, but her screaming stopped. "Down. Down. It's down. It's down."

"We're going to get you out. Don't worry. I'll keep you above the surface." Trax worked her way forward. The pressure on her legs was surprisingly hard.

"Boss, I've let the crew know."

"Thanks, Harry. Get ready to pull us out."

Finally, Trax put a hand on Margot. The farmer lashed out, punching Trax's left cheek. Stunned, all Trax could think was that at least she was stuck enough that she didn't fall back.

"Hey, Margot. I know you didn't mean that. I have to bring you out. Please, let me help you." Trax rested her fingertips on Margot's hand. When no attack came, she gently squeezed the farmer's hand.

"Down," Margot said.

"Yeah, down," Trax agreed as she slowly brought Margot's hand closer. "Now, grab me, Margot, hold on tight."

Margot didn't, but the fight drained out of her, and she let Trax embrace her.

"We're ready."

The cord went taut before pulling at Trax. Harry's grunts accompanied each small advance. She leaned back, letting the mechanic's efforts lift her closer to the surface of the grain. The sensation was strange, hard yet fluid. For a moment she could have sworn there was movement below, a wave pushing up. Then the crown of her head tapped the lip of the door.

"Give me a hand."

"No, take Margot first."

Harry grabbed Margot by the arm and pulled her out. She gave the farmer a pat on the back and pressed her down until she was sitting on a stair. Then she went back to the door. "Right. Your turn, boss."

The grain pulled at Trax's legs as Harry strained. Her damn left boot was caught on an obstruction below the surface. "Come on, Harry. Show me what you can do."

A little voice whispered in Trax's mind: *there's nothing to catch onto.*

The space was suddenly tight. Her breathing echoed, only growing louder each time it returned. Harry grunted as if she'd just taken a colon cleanser. Trax's leg stretched, the joint popping. She hissed, wondering if her knee would dislocate.

"Harry!"

Her foot came free. She tumbled out of the silo, slamming into Harry. The pair grabbed onto the handrail, eyes locking, chests heaving.

"And you want to be a farmer?" Harry asked.

Trax laughed. "It's usually better than this. Well, sometimes. At least, that's how I remember it."

She shuffled over to Margot, who sat staring into the distance. "Hey there. We're taking you to Staging, okay? If you want to talk, we're here to listen, but if you don't, that's okay."

"Down," Margot said.

Harry collected the axe and the club. "Down sounds good."

As they picked their way down the stairs, Trax tried to make sense of the attack. It had to be the work of lunatics. Bootlegging wasn't enough. The only other option that came to mind was land theft. Could someone be playing the long game, doing the unthinkable because no one was ready to stop them? How many times in human history had men marched in and murdered for territory? If that was it, they wouldn't get it. Not this time. No way. They didn't know who they were fucking with. Trax was going to educate them.

CHAPTER 9
DANTALION

Dust battered the apartment window. Electrostatics stopped the fine particles from sticking, but Bill could only see a smudged cityscape. The wind must be a southerly. On the far right, the distant power plant for Staging marked the land beyond the river to the city's west, its tip cutting into the sinking sun. The bulk of his view was taken up by another low block of accommodation across a wide road filled with vehicles returning for the night. Lights were already popping into existence like newborn stars.

The dropship, Adeona, rested in a barren park at the center of Staging, or at least it had been central until the plans were updated, allowing the city to bloom in whatever direction practicality demanded. The Adeona's three brethren had been dismantled once all cargo had been transferred from orbit. Their curved, heat-resistant plates were still evident in several buildings assembled before local production took hold. The park's hard-packed dirt and the brown haze of dust gave the dropship an antique appearance.

Bill tapped the side of the window, and the glass darkened, blocking the view in or out. The interior lights adjusted, brightening and adding a warmer tint. A day to be indoors. Not that he had much choice. Or at least he was leaving that choice for later. There were more pressing concerns.

He crossed the short distance of his living room to the kitchenette. Ware's underlings had no doubt done their best when they searched. However, being thorough required imagination and patience. Bill had used both when he'd moved in to counter such a search. Old habits die hard. A little jiggling beneath the heating unit and a panel opened, revealing several small devices, none of them of local make. And one, despite being in several inconspicuous pieces, still troubled him.

He selected an innocuous cylinder. Technically, the bug scanner should have been returned when he left the agency, but finding ways to build a backup cache came with the territory. No doubt management would have been upset if agents hadn't made the effort. He held the grip, waiting for the various authentication protocols to accept him. It would have been faster with his old implant network, but there were costs as well as benefits when leaving the agency. A small light pulsed green. It took him five minutes to walk the living room and his bedroom. He even ran the scanner along the retractable toilet and shower units. Privacy survived on patience and thoroughness.

After setting the scanner to a wide-angle passive mode, he retrieved a small dome from the same hiding place and positioned it on a small coffee table in front of a two-seater couch. Once activated, it emitted a white noise that he'd learned to ignore. It was an older model from the Dresden system, good enough for his needs. As well, it sent out pulsed images that would confuse any camera seeking to use lenses or reflections to build an image of the room or the activity within.

The last two items he retrieved included a heavily modified portable console and a health analyzer patch. He set the console on the bench of the kitchenette and went through the authentication process. A projected display hovered in the air above. The patch waited off to one side, as if distance could make it less menacing. Restless, he stood in front of the display, poring through the notes he'd taken and the data he'd siphoned—legitimately. Ward, or that tech, Tyzen, had disabled his hypernet account. Experience told him he'd be able to slip back in, but it wasn't necessary, and there were lines he hadn't crossed… here.

But someone had been dancing over them. Why couldn't he put it together? He shook his head and grabbed a bottle of beer from the fridge. One wouldn't make any difference. The cool, bitter fluid refreshed him but gave no insight. He needed a partner to talk it over with. The irony of traveling so far to be away from people mocked him. And there was a time when he was never alone. Bill stared at the console. It was a bad idea. It was also practical. And it would be different this time. If there was a *this time.*

He could hardly invite any of his survey team over. Even if Ward let him have visitors, being locked up wasn't something to show off. He couldn't risk endangering them, either. They must think him a lunatic, given the questions he'd been asking recently. It was better they believed that than know a dangerous truth. Ignorance would keep them safe. And, he admitted, if he took them through it all, the cat would be out of the bag. Once he understood what was going on, he might well want to shove the cat firmly back in. The more people knew, the messier it would be. There was no real choice.

Charlie, do you hear this? Why can't I stop?

He went through the files on his console and activated the after-market neurocore, loading Dantalion, and stepping back. Minutes passed before the system chimed.

"Bill?" The voice was soft, synthetic.

"Dantalion. It's been a while."

"I know. I have the timestamps. Why am I outside?"

Bill let his head loll to one side. Technically, the AI couldn't avoid following Bill's orders, but some asshole had decided that simulated feelings would make the implanted assistant easier to integrate.

"I left the agency. They took back all the shiny tech they could. Recycling, I guess."

"Left the agency? Bill, that is most unusual."

"Yeah, well, you were there when I lost my rating for field ops." Bill leaned against the counter and crossed his arms.

"We were going to work on that. It wasn't your fault for once, and there was a lot to process."

"No, you wanted to work on it. I wanted out. I am out."

"Then why am I here?"

The familiar voice had the gravity of a neutron star, pulling Bill on. Waking Dantalion had been a bad idea.

"I had a friendly doc copy a snapshot of you from before I'd made my mind up."

"That much is obvious. I won't go into my disappointment at this time. Nor will I judge the little dive you are living in. Instead, I will ask you a simple question. You brought me back online on this little scrap of deficient, amateur tech. Why?"

"I need your help."

"And I need your body, but here we are."

"You can't have it. But I can give you information and a puzzle that needs solving."

"I'm listening."

Bill started by explaining their location, the job he had taken, and Charlie's death.

"A very unusual death. What did you make of it?" Dantalion asked, when Bill had given as much detail as he could remember.

"Murder. Nasty. The injuries don't match any form of torture I know of, and there are many easier ways to deliver a death blow. Perhaps desecrating the body was meant to send a message or cover something up."

"What about the blood pattern? You didn't mention any."

That was a good question. He'd seen the wounds, but there should have been blood everywhere. "He was moved after he died."

"A possibility. You told me you are now a surveyor. If you want to understand what's beneath you, what do you do?"

"Scan it. There's a range of techniques, but I don't see why you're asking."

"What's the only way to be certain of what's there?"

"If there's too much interference or something reflecting it all, we drill a core sample."

Dantalion made a multi-tonal noise that meant the AI was satisfied.

"Oh, come on." Bill paced the length of his living room. "You think someone wanted to know what made him tick? Dr. Frankenstein or little green men?"

"I am merely inferring purpose from result. There is more, isn't there?"

Bill glanced at the health patch. "I've been comparing events. I'll let you out of your sandbox so you can take a look."

"Bill, what aren't you telling me? You know I cannot be fully effective if you are not honest."

Damn. Bill had been hoping that running the AI without access to his nervous system would give him an edge, a barrier between them. He should tell it to mind its own business. Why had he turned it on? Had he known that Dantalion would read him as easily as ever?

"Bill?"

"All right. Before I left, I received a package from Beth." Bill picked up the health patch and shoved it close to the console's camera so the noise generator didn't interfere.

"That's a terrible parting gift. More like a threat."

"Ha, ha," Bill said. "The chip in it has an encrypted message."

"What does it say?" Dantalion attempted a laugh. "You haven't read it, have you?"

"No. When I left the agency, I meant it. I don't work for them anymore."

"And you want my permission, my *absolution*, to access it? Bill, you should have done so the moment you had privacy. Beth has always had your best interests in mind. Would anyone else in the agency have risked so much to get us off Marrick Prime? A reasonable analysis by an internal auditor with all the relevant facts would likely have found her in serious breach of her duties."

"I know. I know. But she put me there, too. She fed me lies. She said that we could save millions. How many did I condemn?"

"It is irrational to assume that—"

"It's irrational to trust anyone in the agency."

"I do not dispute that. So hear what she has to say, knowing that it may be a lie. That is what you do."

"It's what I did."

"Sensors can lie as well as any human, and nature likes to keep its secrets. You are still in the espionage business."

Bill went to the fridge for a second beer. "Damn, you're depressing."

"All part of the service. Stop delaying, Bill. You humans rapidly die of old age."

Snarky bastard. Bill picked up the health patch and stuck it on his temple. It heated quickly, tickling his skin, assessing his identity rather than his health. He counted to five, then pulled it off, wincing as a few hairs came with it. Next, he found a pair of scissors in a draw and cut the covering, revealing the white chip and its cables. Pulling a small bump on the cable bundle snapped them free. The end was a standard data connector, a modification the average person wouldn't have noticed.

He stuck it into the console and tapped a few commands to let the AI out of its sandbox.

"Dantalion, play it for us both."

"You are too kind, sir. Playing."

Beth Maylor's head blipped into existence above the console: intense eyes, no-nonsense haircut, a series of fine scars on her right brow that could easily have been rectified, tight narrow lips. Her name, rank of Field Commander, Sector 297, floated to the side of her head. Symbols scrolled alongside, indicating a high probability of identity confirmation.

Memories of another message scoured his self-worth. The order to get off-world, to let none of the locals question his departure despite the awful fate hurtling toward them. Why hadn't he fled with the other agents? He rubbed his eyes. This was a terrible idea.

"Bill," she said. "I imagine the last thing you want to see is my face, and please believe that I respect your choice. You served the League with honor under trying circumstances. That was why I smoothed the way for you into a lucrative Phase 2 colony position."

He gritted his teeth, wanting to argue. She would get the last word —the unbeatable advantage of a recorded message. The recruitment had been a grueling process, one he'd conquered. He was a qualified, if left-of-field, choice. Damn. She *had* done it.

There was a brief pause before she continued, as if she knew he'd need time to process. "There is a matter I must raise, a mutual favor.

Please be patient while I explain. I know you won't want to hear the background, so I'll keep it brief. Multiple sources have indicated unusual activity within the corporate umbrella of BILT4. Nothing solid, yet too hard to dismiss. The available resources at my disposal were unable to infiltrate the corporate arm of the colony mission. That security level is suspicious in and of itself." Classic agency: if you're not allowed to look, the other party must be dirty. Also, quite commonly true.

"Without supporting evidence, I wasn't able to lock in budget approval for a mission. You know how stretched the agency is."

Here it comes. She was trying to rope him in. He was after Charlie's killer, and to ensure he got the stake he needed. He wasn't out to save the world—or bend it to the shape the league preferred.

"You won't want to get involved. Again, I respect that. Without any commitment required, I have included the one data extract we were able to exfiltrate: a partial survey file through a non-invasive fiber tap, mostly location-based metadata that doesn't tie in with the public records. I'm hoping it makes more sense to you than it does to us. You'll have access to the real thing."

Here was the bait. Where was the hook?

"You will be there for years. If you take it gently and build a rapport with any of the corporates, I'm sure you can carry out an assessment. If there's nothing to see, there's no harm done."

His cheeks heated. No harm done? Who was she kidding? Getting to the very edge of human influence wasn't his desire because he had a love of trees and dirt and long hours. She was weaving a net to throw around him. Well, too late. Even if he had wanted to, the chance was long gone. Her manipulation was futile.

"Bill, if BILT4 is breaking any substantive laws within our purview, and you collect quality actionable evidence, I will push through post-approval for the mission with a substantial contractor bonus."

Great, she thought he wanted to be a mercenary? He walked to the console, his hand on the chip, considering ripping it out and cooking it for a minute on high.

"It's a significant request," she continued. "And I want to show my appreciation. I've put a hold on a survey ship, an impounded Callisto

Industries Explorer. Low crew needs, functional if a little long in the tooth. With contracting fees and bounties, your land stake sale, and me calling in a few favors, it can be yours. Think about it—how many years would it take you to save up otherwise? Or you'd be locked into a contingent lease. Do you really want someone else in charge?"

He laughed as she continued, long and hard enough for tears to run down his face and drown out her words. "You know me too well, you manipulative fucker." Everything he wanted if he'd do one last mission. Until the next. "Dantalion, rewind her. I might as well hear it all."

"As you wish."

Beth's image cut to a slightly different pose. "This is a tricky ask, given the communication profile and lack of local support, so I have two command codes for you. The first will give you access to the courier ship. I'm including details for you to get a secure message forwarded: whatever evidence you find, your status, any support you need. Two years should give you ample opportunity before its scheduled departure."

And a chance to escape if needed. Except the courier was already gone. She really had thought he'd listen to her on arrival. She didn't know him as well as she thought.

"The second is more scorched-earth. I have a friendly senior sector judge who's put a lot on the line for you. It's a full override warrant. Don't use it unless you have to—it means you'll be back in the agency." Her face froze.

Back in the agency? A full override warrant would put him in charge of the entire colony, extinguishing the limited local sovereignty. He shook his head and swore. It'd almost be worth it to see the look on Sturt's face.

"Dantalion, confirm this: she wouldn't arrange that unless she knew something serious is going down, right?"

"Agreed. While she has shown you substantial favor in the past, her apparent actions are usually in line with the agency's long-term goals. There would be consequential fallout from executing that warrant, even if you were justified."

But what did she truly suspect? Secrecy, it was the agency's way.

Never tell you more than you needed to know to complete the mission they wanted you to do, not the one they told you to do.

Bill slumped onto the couch. "So, what makes the fallout acceptable? War? With who? Land stakes? The League gets its share by law. Resources? The asteroid belts are good mining opportunities, but that's hardly a secret."

"What about succession? According to public records, in the five closest habited systems, BILT4 has at least thirty-four percent nominal control over production. They could form a closed-loop economy."

"The agency would definitely sniff around at any hint like that. Keeping the League together is the goal, right? Beth should have been able to get resources here."

"Like you?"

"Hey," Bill said, cutting the air with a sharp gesture. "I am not her resource."

"As you say. Remember, despite the rumors, the agency has its limits. Perhaps we should move on. I am fitting the file she included to the various survey maps you have earmarked."

"And?"

"There are several geological structures with inconsistencies across the different versions. The underlying data has been manipulated."

The window shook in its frame. Bill looked at the blocked-out rectangle. Another damn storm. "By structures, do you mean buildings? Some half-cocked failed settlement? Aliens?"

"I am unable to say. Geological information is not my forte. Unusual but natural phenomena are more likely."

The room went dark. Bill froze and listened. Pinpricks of emergency lights came on, bathing the room in an eerie twilight.

"Dantalion, go offline."

"But I may be able to assist."

"I don't want to have to explain you. Go offline, now."

He scurried around the room, replacing the clandestine equipment and closing the hidden store. With the noise generator off, he could hear shouting weaved into swirling winds. He put his ear to the front door, then to the window. Outside. A fight or an accident? He hit the control for the window, but it didn't respond. Power. *Damn.*

The desire to know left him restless. He strode to the door and pressed his hands against it. If he broke out, the next stop would be Ware's custody. Curiosity wasn't worth it. Beth had got him wired. He needed to control the stress, ride the adrenaline in his system, relax, and take the time to decide what he was going to do and how far he was willing to go.

A man wailed. Another cried out. A woman shouted. Screams. A crash. A small explosion? More screams.

Bill slammed the door with his fists.

"Ah, shit."

He didn't have a choice. A jailbreak was on the cards.

CHAPTER 10
NOT LIKE THIS

The hospital had been set down as part of Phase 1 when buildings were low and basements were common to protect against the powerful winds that made the present weather a gentle breeze by comparison. There were thirty beds and three operating theaters on the service level, ready for the all-to-frequent accidents that were part of colony life. Most of the beds were empty—if you were stable, you'd be shipped off to your apartment. It was meant to be better for the patient, but cost cutting was the true purpose.

Margot lay in a bed behind a glass window as a nurse fiddled with one of the tubes sticking into her flesh. Trax and Harry had helped her inside the hospital with near-zero visibility. The staff had wiped the dust from her, but the nurse at the front desk hadn't been impressed by their entrance. That might have also been because of the axe and club. They'd left them leaning in a corner when harangued. The fuss was ridiculous. Hospitals were full of sharp objects.

"How is she?" Trax asked of the doctor who stood by her side.

The woman was short, thin, and twitchy. "She suffered several deep lacerations. I've cleaned them and applied a regrowth promoter. She lost a lot of blood, and her organs are fragile, but I'm confident they'll all recover."

"Meaning she'll be all right soon?"

The doctor slowly spun a pad in her hands. "I'm keeping her sedated for now. We'll let her body recover, and then we'll see how the rest goes. She went through quite a lot, as I'm sure you understand. Go get some food and come back later."

Trax huffed, annoyed at the vagueness of the doctor's answer. Harry was already on a food run, anyway. And the rest of the crew were taking care of the vehicles and the gear they'd stripped from the old terraformer. Footsteps caught her attention. Ware had entered the corridor, looking far too relaxed.

"Finally. Where the hell have you been, sleeping under your desk? Have you found the others?"

Ware worked his jaw as if chewing. He glanced at Margot. "How's she doing, Doc?"

"Stable. I've got another patient to see. Excuse me." The doctor fled.

"You found her in a silo?"

Was he trying to anger her? "Yes, I damn well found her in a silo, scared out of her wits, and cut up."

"There was no trace of the other farmers: bodies, vehicle tracks, or footprints?" He listed the items like a bored clerk checking inventory.

"I went through it three times with you lot already. No. If I had, I would have stayed and found the rest."

He nodded. "Tomorrow morning, when the visibility's better, we'll head out."

"Tomorrow?" Trax's temples throbbed. "What are you talking about? They could be out there, choking on dust, bleeding to death."

Ware scratched the back of his head. "I get that. But I can't risk it, not with this storm. No one's going anywhere—I put the call out a few minutes ago. The director approved a hunker-down order."

"But the murderer's still out there."

"They won't be going anywhere either."

The glibness of his answer boiled her blood. Typical man of the system. He was an unthinking cog. She wanted to beat a sense of urgency into him, but before red could descend across her vision, she tensed her muscles and regained control.

"You'll head out first thing, all of you?"

"Every officer I can spare."

"You've got to be kidding. There were five of them. There are murderers out there. What else matters?"

His bloodshot eyes met hers. "You know what a dust storm can do." He put a hand against the glass window. "Comms are a mess. There were already installations that hadn't responded in days. After the storm, there'll be more accidents and more people missing. There are only twenty of us, and murderer or not, I can't risk sending anyone solo. There's only so much ground we can cover."

She closed on him. "Then the entire colony should down tools, set up armed search parties, and not stop until we've accounted for every single soul."

"I don't have that authority. I came to let you know as a courtesy while I can. Decide whether you'll spend the night here or at your apartment, and do it fast." He turned his back on her and walked away.

Never trust the system. At best, it ignored the average worker. Usually, it ground them down as far as they let it. She wanted to ride out there and then, but, curse the asshole, he was right. The dust would play havoc with navigation and comms would be dead.

She'd give Ware one chance. If he didn't come through, she'd rouse her crew and beyond, set up a posse, and do what needed to be done. They were all there for land stakes, but sticking together protected both the colonists and their futures. If enough of them gathered, the director would have to see reason. His pay, after all, was dependent on their work completion.

The lights went out. Equipment beeped furiously, their displays glowing dimly, casting weak shadows that offered more confusion than sense. *What now?* Trax kept still and counted to five. The emergency lights remained off.

Margot's nurse complained, her voice dull through the glass. Another voice called for the lights to be turned back on. There was a genius.

The doctor's light footsteps announced her entry into the corridor. "Does anyone know what's going on?"

Trax felt for her suit lights and activated them.

One of the nurses clapped.

Another said, "Thanks. Can you stay there, and I'll get a few lamps. I'm sure we have them in the supply room."

Feeling for her left shoulder, Trax found the release triggers and slid the flashlight free. "Take it. Is Margot okay?"

"Don't worry," the doctor said. "She's breathing on her own. The sensors and her med pumps all have batteries. Our other patients will be fine as well—as long as we can get power back."

"Good. Where's the plant room? I'll have a tinker."

After Trax convinced the doctor of her qualifications, she pointed down the corridor. "There's a door with stairs opposite the front desk. The basement was meant to be included in the elevator refit, but admin deemed it *unnecessary*."

By the sound of that, many things had been deemed unnecessary, but for once, Trax had to agree with the choice. Transformers, distribution boards, and capacitors were rock solid. They should have lasted years without maintenance.

Her single light bounced as she hurried down the corridor. A pair of doors opened to let her through, and she was back at the front desk. To her right, a dull red glow through the exterior doors added a hellish atmosphere inside. The desk was empty, and she had a sensation, a visceral belief that she was the only person left on the planet. Margot's axe waited in the corner of the room with the endless patience of the inanimate. Trax took it and headed to the back of the room. It was a matter of practicality, not fear.

The manual door had a sign, reading *Basement, no unauthorized access,* and a simple handle. It rattled as she pulled, grinding on its track while sliding across, crying to be added to a maintenance list. It wasn't Trax's problem.

Her single light revealed a plain, narrow set of stairs that turned once to the right and disappeared out of view. It was a good bet that most of the equipment was installed before the ground level went on top. She walked down the stairs, her boots producing dull, echoing clanks. At the right turn, she paused, four steps from the basement level.

The ceiling was low, the room wide and deep, yet crowded. Pipes, power runs, gas cylinders, crates, and a hundred items that defied safety standards filled the floor, walls, and ceiling. Out of sight, out of mind—until it all blew up. She took the last stairs in two paces and found a diagram mounted on the wall. According to it, the breakers and main feed indicators should be halfway down the left side.

Walking through silent equipment demanded the same somberness of unearthed tombs. The hum of energy, the clicks of heating and cooling alloys, the hiss of air filters—gone like a vanished civilization in an entertainment flick. Only her breathing and the clomping of her boots marked her passage.

Warning signs confirmed she had reached the right spot. She let the axe head clink on the hard brown composite flooring and leaned on the haft. *Fuck.* The breakers were a mess. It all was. Cables dangled, severed, the tops hanging like vines, the lower lengths leaning away from the wall, angry vipers with sparking blue tongues. Sabotage, again. The backup battery had been cut out of the loop.

A scrape chilled her skin and set the fine hairs on end.

Trax pulled the axe up and spun around. "Whoever you are, you better get the hell out of here, or I'm gonna do some severing of my own."

No response. She edged along the wall, axe in both hands, searching the shifting shadows. Did she hear a scrabbling or was that her boots scraping fallen cable sheaths? It might be nothing at all. At the corner, an old portable toilet sat, tall, and out of place. The basement had been a dumping ground. Trax slipped her right hand up the haft and placed her left on the door. She pulled it open.

Movement. Things falling onto her. She stepped back, flailing, and bashed them away.

Bang! Crack!

She had stepped on something. She looked down. Empty polymer hard cases that should have been fed to the recycling units. "I am going to kill somebody, and I'm seriously expanding the list of candidates."

Kicking her way through, she moved along the back of the basement. She stopped. A hole gaped in the floor, one part of the curve reaching a handspan up the wall. It had to be a near a meter in diameter. Behind the edge of the cut was rough dirt and stone. Another tunnel. Nuts. The disgruntled asshole had stolen or clandestinely built a borer and was using it to travel from site to site to cut up vital infrastructure and commit murder? The sick prick was going to pay.

A metallic *ting* came from the detritus near the center of the basement. Time to gird her loins and put up. Trax slipped between an oxygen generator and a dented autoclave. The shadows moved. Tapping. She kept each step light and tensed her muscles. Skittering to the left. She whirled, her eyes darting, seeking. Equipment rattled low to the ground. Her lights reflected off dull, overlapping surfaces for a mere instant, and she was left wondering if her mind was playing tricks.

Reflective metal, thin, lost behind a crate marked with storage details from the interstellar flight. Trax advanced.

Sparks. The whine of cut alloy. The fucker was still at it. She ran to the right, then cut back to the left, hoping to catch them off guard. The next few seconds came as blurred images. A compact form made of overlapping plates. Glistening legs. A leap. A whirring saw, straight and long.

She swung Margot's axe, her face rigid with fear. Contact. Her arms jolted under the force. The attacker's trajectory shifted, and she jumped, feeling a pull on one boot as they slid several meters along the ground. There was no time to exclaim, to digest what she had encountered. Metallic legs found grip, and the attacker disappeared into the clutter.

The need to punish burned within her. She gave chase, roaring furiously. It darted away, and she pushed closer, squeezing between two dark anonymous lumps. Blood broiled her ears and seared her skin. The thing appeared on the top of the toilet, pressed in the narrow gap below the ceiling.

"Got you now."

She swung, a powerful sideways blow. The thing skittered off, dropping until its legs caught the side of the toilet, pointed tips digging into the polymer. While Trax fought the axe's momentum, it leaped for her. She yanked on the handle and threw her head back, losing her balance. Spears stabbed her, one catching her shoulder light, cutting right through the device, and grinding on her collarbone, the second slicing the outside of her left thigh, leaving a bloody flap.

She staggered under the thing's weight, her back slamming into a hard edge. Pain. She grunted and shoved the axe against her attacker. The fucker was strong. She spun, slamming it into a tower of indistinguishable silhouettes. Items tumbled, and it lost its grip. Cursing, she retreated to a wall, stumbling on unseen objects that jarred her wounds, eliciting fresh flows of blood and new depths of agony. Her left leg gave way, and she tumbled onto her back, the axe clattering out of her hands and out of sight.

The thing followed, easily clambering over the mess on the floor, moving like a giant woodlouse. With her light gone, small bright spots around the front—the head?—became visible. But there were no eyes, only small appendages. She shuffled back on her elbows, slapping against thick cabling. The thing approached calmly, perhaps judging her an easy target to be slaughtered at leisure. Sweat soaked Trax's suit. Fear shook her, sapping her energy.

It crawled along her legs.

"No," Trax said. "No way. I'm not dying like this."

But it slunk along, one pointed foot digging into her hip. Trax gripped a cable pressing into her side, the diameter familiar. A monstrous metal appendage stretched forward, the one with the saw. It spun up, faster and faster, ready to tear her apart. Closer. Closer.

She stretched her head away, right beneath the pale blue sparks of a cut cable. She yanked hard, extending the free length, and shoved the tip into the saw. The world turned white. Her limbs stiffened. The white faded to gray, revealing the slagged saw and its jerking owner in an afterimage. Contact broke, and her twitching body returned to her control.

"You like that?" She dragged herself out from under the thing. "How about this?"

Steeling herself against the torment each movement earned, she took the cable once more and shoved it into the front, the eyes, whatever the fuck the thing had.

Sparks—blue, white, red—sprayed, a firework show accompanied by bangs and hisses and the tang of burned metal. She pressed harder, not caring for the shower of superheated metal or the way the light still assaulted her eyes through closed lids.

An almighty crack announced the end. The sparks died. Trax laughed. She'd shorted the backup battery.

And she wasn't sorry for it, not at all. She'd destroyed the murderer, the menace, whatever it was. She'd taken revenge.

It was over now. All she had to do was climb the stairs before bleeding out. A shame she didn't have time to fix the wiring.

CHAPTER 11
BUGS

B ill almost left the pistol behind. But Charlie had been murdered, and Beth's message was about as reassuring as a siren. While he'd been an agent and not an assassin, both required the careful movement of weapons through customs and a few firefights had reinforced the need. The pistol wasn't agency issue, but a highly illegal knockoff of the Firefly series 2. Fitting the thirteen apparently innocuous parts together took nearly two minutes—he was out of practice. Then he'd had to find a bag to conceal it. The strap now hung over his shoulder and his right hand rested inside, next to a facemask, a flashlight, and the apartment's medkit.

He listened at his apartment's front door, a small gap allowing a hubbub of confusion to enter. Good. He slid the door halfway open and stepped into the corridor. Residents milled in groups along its length. A few met his eyes or asked if he knew what was going on. Bill refused to engage, giving each query a short, negative response and hurrying on. He ducked into the emergency stairwell and took two at a time. At ground level, he pulled on his mask, adjusted the fit around his eyes, and powered up the attached respirator. The emergency exit, lit by a yellow sign, was designed to be pushed outward without power. He hit the bar and entered the darkening haze.

Wind whipped at his hair, coating it in grit. He headed down a narrow packed-dirt alley to the road. Several rovers had stopped, their lights barely cutting into the swirling dust. Drenching rain, dust storms—all the planet needed was earthquakes to complete the set. As well as the rovers, people filled the roads, dark patches only recognizable when they moved. There were occasional screams, too, audible when the wind ebbed. Bill frowned, struggling to triangulate the location. If he'd had his old implants, it would have been easy. Or maybe not. Wind did strange things to sound, and he wondered if they were coming from multiple locations.

He marched to the closest figure, a man struggling to keep a mask clean while putting it on.

"Hey," Bill shouted, moving his body to create a wind barrier. "Any idea what's going on?"

The man fitted his mask. "Thanks, and no, not a clue. I heard someone on the net say there'd been an accident, but now it's all peer-to-peer. You can't tell what's official and what's rumor."

The low-energy, peer-to-peer backup network on the comms would barely reach a few meters, thanks to the dust. Bill moved on toward the administrative buildings, bumping into larger groups, and picking up their growing concern. More handheld lamps and suit flashlights supplemented the rovers' beams, turning the air a dirty red-brown. Ahead, a cluster of people broke up, most moving away rapidly.

Bill hurried to the last one, hoping for a shred of information.

"Hey," he called out.

The figure switched on a shoulder light, revealing a police suit with yellow reflective highlights. "Hayden? What the hell are you doing out?"

Ware. Bill cursed his luck. "What did you expect me to do? There was chaos. The building could have been on fire."

"Was it?" Ware asked.

"No. What's going on?"

"Damned if I know. It's not your problem. Get back inside, or I'll stick you in a cell. That won't be on fire either."

An extended, gurgling scream froze them both. It wasn't far off.

"Get out of here, Hayden." Ware jogged toward the scream.

Bill caught up.

"Do you want me to cuff you to a streetlight?"

"I don't think you have the time to waste, and you need every bit of help you can get."

Snippets of questions and claims of knowledge came as broadcasts from the people they passed. A quake, a plasma overpressure, a collapsed building, psychopaths. Colonists poured out of doors, clogging the way, some suited for work, others in impractical bedclothes. There hadn't been an emergency drill for a year, and now the time saving was being repaid in chaos. Off to one side, Bill spotted a patch on the road—a thick line of darkness, like an oil spill, covered in sand.

"Ware, see that?"

They approached. Bill kneeled and ran a hand across it. "Blood."

"Agreed. Someone was dragged over there." Ware pointed off the road. "Probably trampled, the poor bastard."

"There's a chance they'll know what's happened."

"True."

They followed the trail. At the end of the road, it became harder to spot, but isolated splotches led them to the front of a food store, the inside a deep-space black. A smear along the bottom of the storefront took them to an alleyway, where the dust was a little thinner. Down the alley, someone was being dragged—by what, Bill couldn't tell. It was low and dark and moved in a smooth, undulating fashion. Bill looked at Ware. They both ran.

Ware cleared his pistol. "Stop! Police!"

As Bill closed, more details resolved. The low creature dragging the body had hooked the victim with metal spikes. Said victim wore a standard colony suit, and Bill recognized the survey patches. His eyes darted to the face. He absorbed the details, the haircut. Sarah. The thing, the bug, had one of his people. And Sarah's eyes were open, her mouth moving even though she no longer made a sound. She was still alive. The helplessness of Marrick Prime returned to sicken his stomach and weaken his muscles. Except, here, he had a chance to change the outcome. Hanging on to that hope, he stopped, pulled his pistol out of his bag, and aimed.

Ware was the first to shoot, sending dazzling sapphire blasts of plasma uselessly down the alley. Bill sidestepped to the right for a clearer view and pulled the trigger, his confidence and steady hands a complete surprise. A pulse of superheated plasma launched from his pistol, spinning and bleeding sparks of energy. It hit the creature's back, burning into rough, segmented armor that resembled corroded iron. The creature let go of Sarah, leaving itself open, and both Bill and Ware pumped it full of plasma. It staggered, then froze.

Bill flailed inside his bag for the medkit. If they could keep Sarah alive for a short time, if they could get her to the hospital, she'd be fine.

"Hayden, get back."

The captain was retreating. Didn't he get it? Sarah needed their help. She was just lying there. They had to be fast. He owed her that.

"Look up."

Hand tightening around the medkit, Bill did as Ware demanded. More of the bugs crawled along the walls, seemingly immune to gravity. And in the distance, several surged out of a gaping hole in the ground. Ten, twelve, near twenty, he estimated. Ware grabbed his shoulder and pulled. Bill fired at the creatures, knocking the closest down, but each landed and scurried onward, unperturbed by the single hits. Ware dragged him back a meter, then another.

Bill tried to shake free. "Sarah, I'm coming."

"No, you're not." Ware added blasts to complement Bill's, but he also forced him clear of the alley.

In the distance, another creature grabbed Sarah and pulled her toward the hole. Bill changed his aim, firing near, but he couldn't risk a close shot. His first had been lucky, and the range had increased. Down the hole, the creature went, dragging Sarah with it. A sick burning washed over him. His eyes widened. Another poor soul bounced off hard surfaces as a bug maneuvered it toward the hole. They showed no signs of resistance, no signs of life.

Dark masses sped toward Marrick Prime, blips on sensors. Thousands of them. It didn't matter if the local authorities hit a few or all with the limited orbital defenses. The total mass would slam into the atmosphere one way or another, payback to an extremist regime that dared to set off three nukes on three worlds to make its case for independence and isolation. Innocents slaughtered to avenge slaughtered innocents. The only case it would make in future was one of caution—the League would brook no threats.

"Get it together, Hayden."

The fan inside his mask whined as it fought to clear his sweat. His hands shook. He squeezed his eyes shut, found a wisp of control, then opened them.

"I'm good." But Sarah's limp body stayed in his head, sliding across a backdrop of planetary bombardment.

Ware retreated further. "I need to get to the director. We have to organize."

Bill followed. Ware was right, at least when it came to organizing. The creatures could take them one by one with impunity. Without a team, without comms, how could he or Ware make a difference? For the first time in a long time, he wanted to. Maybe for Sarah. Maybe for Charlie. He couldn't find a solid reason driving his need, but it was time to put his skills to use.

The bugs came from the gods-damned ground. Options sprouted. Go high and risk getting trapped in buildings when the creatures could climb. Stay in the open—more holes might be dug. Evacuate? Where? How far? Make weapons? The attack was already underway. He knew the local land. How could he make use of that? He fired a series of blasts, slowing the wave of creatures and earning precious seconds. Wave. It came to him.

"The river. It's our only good option. We need to get everyone across the river. The soil there is wet. They won't be able to dig without getting flooded. If we can get people moving, when the bastards follow, we'll draw them out in a line. We can shoot them, crush them under rovers, create a killing field."

Ware picked up his pace. "I'll take it."

As they passed groups or individuals, Ware paused long enough to tell people to head west over the bridge. The way grew dangerous, not due to the creatures, but thanks to idiots driving too fast for near zero visibility. They reached the front of the administration building where a tall, six-wheeled vehicle had been parked across the front doors—the director's ride—and a deputy stood in the space between, a rifle hanging over her shoulder.

"Captain Ware," the deputy said. "It's damn good to see you."

Up close, Bill spotted rips on her police suit. "What happened?"

She—Foster, read her tag—looked at Bill, then at Ware. There was some kind of exchange, either through peer-to-peer comms or a subtle gesture, and Foster said, "Garibaldi woke me and the rest of the morning shift, banging door to door. We all headed to the station. Only Misko was there, and all he knew was that you'd gone out with the rest to see what was happening. A hardline came up for a bit, and Director Sturt commed in. He was under attack, so we raided the armory and hightailed it out. You wouldn't believe what we saw."

"We believe it," Ware said.

Bill asked, "How many bugs?"

She looked aghast. "Just the one. It had cut into the elevator shaft. The rest of the building was empty for the night. We found it halfway into the director's office. Weirdest bug I ever saw—biggest, too."

Gesturing to the swirling red-brown storm, Bill said, "Well, it has plenty of friends out there."

Ware squeezed Foster's arm. "If any others turn up, keep them with you. I sent the afternoon shift out in pairs. Poor bastards. Hopefully, they'll make it back here or the station. Where's Sturt?"

"The Director's on level four, collecting his things. He ordered Batista, Weaver, and Daniels to guard him. Garibaldi took the rest and went out to find you."

"What's his plan?" Bill demanded.

"I don't know for sure. He mentioned the power station."

Ware looked at Bill. "Some power would be good."

"It won't help if everyone's dead by the time it comes up, but it's over the river so it doesn't hurt. If we secure the bridge while they cross, we'll be good. And if the bugs look like they'll overwhelm our defense, we can blow the bridge."

That suggestion drew a frown still visible through Ware's mask. "I have to organize the evacuation. I'll need deputies in our vehicles rounding up folk with the loudspeakers."

"You can't afford to have three of your deputies guarding Sturt, can you?" Bill said.

"No. It'd cost too many lives. But I can't lose our director either."

"I'll take care of him."

"You?" Ware asked.

"It'd be worth it just to see his face."

Ware glared, but he headed for the doors, clearly accepting that Bill was right. There was more to it as well. Something had changed between them. Did Ware trust him—to some extent?

They had to climb the emergency stairs to reach Sturt's quarters on level four, where the fool had two deputies loaded down with data slabs, consoles, and food pouches, while the third kept watch. The rooms were large, filled with comfortable furniture, and several reproductions hung on the walls. Fancy without being opulent.

"Him?" Sturt said when Ware explained the plan. He continued stuffing clothing into a bag. "You've got to be kidding me. For all we know, Hayden's behind this, behind everything. What if he set that monster on me? The agency will do anything to get what it wants. I've gotten in between him and his scheme. That's why the thing came for me."

"Did the bug come for you specifically?" Bill asked. It would be pretty interesting if it had.

"It'd tried all the other levels," a deputy said. "I think it was working its way through methodically."

Still interesting. That implied a level of intelligence.

"There's no time to argue." Ware gestured to his people. "Dump all that and come with me."

Sturt bristled. "Absolutely not. Those slabs have backups of the critical colony files. You know how much sabotage there's been. If we lose the data, there'll be riots."

Everyone's stake rights were calculated from reports stored in databases. If the colonists weren't dying out there, he'd have a point. Apparently, Ware had reached a similar conclusion.

"Sorry, Director. I'd rather they were alive to riot, and that takes precedence. We're going. And I hate to say it, but you should trust Hayden. I do. At least for this."

Bill raised an eyebrow. Ware was growing on him. Like athlete's foot, but that was something. The deputies carefully emptied their hands and headed off with Ware while avoiding Sturt's glare.

"Are you going to kill me?"

Bill pursed his lips. The director's antagonism was beyond reason. When there was time, he'd have to discover why. "Not on the cards. If I were you, I'd take the food pouches. And between the two of us, we can carry a couple of slabs. Pick the most important."

Strictly speaking, to ensure the best chance of Sturt surviving the next hour, they should have left it all. But there'd always been a data nerd deep inside Bill, and it insisted a slight risk was reasonable. They made it out of the building with no trouble apart from Sturt's complaints. The deputy guarding Sturt's ride was gone, but four people sheltered by its side. A creature crawled across the top, unseen.

"Out the way!"

The people looked at Bill, saw his gun, and fled. He fired, and the creature jumped, arcing toward him. He managed one good hit on its belly, cutting into it, creating a circle of glowing red. But when he pulled the trigger again, nothing happened. He was out of charge, and it was still going to land on him, skewering him with those needle-sharp limbs. He hefted the data slab, gave a silent apology to every colonist, and belted the bug. The force was enough to knock the creature aside and onto its back, though the blow caused little damage—except to the data slab. It swelled, buckling its case. He threw it at the creature, figuring it was otherwise useless. Unfortunately, the tech was too well-made to conveniently explode. Safety standards had a lot to answer for.

Sturt hadn't moved. Bill grabbed him and led him to the vehicle. The door slid open with a press, and Bill shoved the administrator inside, following as the bug contorted its body to right itself. It skittered along the ground. Bill hit a control, and the door swished shut. A bang followed by scraping noises told him the creature hadn't given up. Time to move. There were two long seats on opposite sides with plenty of legroom between. A narrow gap to the right gave secondary access to the driver's compartment. Sturt kneeled on one of the rear seats and placed the data slab into a compartment.

"Hey," Bill said. "Focus on getting out of here."

"Drive if you want. I've already authenticated."

Bill hurried into the driver's compartment, accompanied by the frantic scrabbles of their pursuer. The seat was far more comfortable than his survey rover, though the space was limited. The view was through a single piece of thick curved glass. Bill switched to manual control and hit the accelerator. The rover jerked forward. A thump told him Sturt had tumbled over. Bill ignored his complaints, instead focusing on activating the lights and avoiding running anyone over. The road was surprisingly clear, a hint at Ware's progress or something far worse. Still, the swirling brown hellscape at any other time would have demanded sitting tight and waiting.

A metallic ping came from the rear.

"It's trying to get in!" Sturt held a full bottle of wine by its neck, the glossy ceramic surface waving back and forth.

One door had a thin puncture and a spiked tip stuck through. Bill was going too slow to lose it.

"Hold on," he warned, then jerked the controls to the right.

The vehicle bounced, and the silhouette of a building loomed. He swerved again and scraped the side, the sound making his skin crawl. It was like a fork dragged on a plate, and, combined with the juddering, it set his teeth on edge. Through the side camera, he could see sparks fly, and when he reached the edge of the building, the bug fell off, its limbs satisfyingly mangled.

He slowed the vehicle further and felt for a data port. Bingo. A shelf contained a standard ICB3 cable and a wireless pad. Bill dropped his pistol on the pad and plugged the cable in. If only he could be recharged as easily.

THE BRIDGE LOOMED AHEAD. Two large police rovers were parked to either side, their lights illuminating the mass of humanity that trudged toward safety. Bill steered off the road and stopped. Any closer and he'd be killing more than the creatures.

"End of the ride. Everybody off."

They'd picked up nine others on their way. It was a small number, but the inside was crowded. To his credit and Bill's annoyance, Sturt hadn't complained. He'd even helped. It would have been much easier to hate the asshole if he'd been a proper irredeemable villain.

The vehicle emptied, Sturt taking his surviving data slab and bag of food. Bill followed him out, checking the charge level of his pistol as he went. Sixty-three percent was better than nothing. The wind had died down, and though the stars still hid, a sense of calm washed through him. A thousand pinpricks of light on the far side of the river suggested the plan was working. The sound of loudspeakers drifted from Staging, accompanied by short bursts of plasma fire. Bill stopped. Was this enough?

"Hayden, we need to cross. I've got to organize this rabble fast."

Unlike Bill's last walk on Marrick Prime, there were no children here, no babies blissfully unaware that their final moments were dropping onto the small pile of sand representing their short lives. Dependents would be inefficient. No children until Phase 3 was the rule. Damn, he was thankful for it. He didn't see many wounded in the crowd, either. That could be good news or bad. Yes, Sturt would need to organize: food, water, shelter. Not the defense. Ware would lead that, and he'd want all the help he could get.

"You don't need me. I'll stay here and do what I can."

Sturt headed toward the bridge without looking back. "You better have been in the dark about all this."

"Trust me," Bill said, "If I'd known, I'd never have set foot on this rock."

And the same goes for you, Beth, Bill thought. *I'm not here for you. I'm not doing this for the agency. Don't you believe I am for a moment.*

He moved to the edge of the road, planning to listen to those fleeing and pick up what information he could. Numbers, locations, behavior—anything specific to understand the threat they faced. Instead, colonists flocked to him, demanding answers as if the gun were a badge. Construction crew, cooks, mechanists, a botanist he recognized. Without the time to cook up a precisely worded response, he resorted to bland reassurances that the situation was still being assessed and everyone would be kept informed. They probably believed him as much as he did, but it moved them along.

Finally, the last few souls trickled down the road, followed by a convoy of police vehicles and rovers. He tensed, wondering if this was it. Would a thousand of those giant bugs follow, content to remain on the surface? The rovers weren't firing, and their loudspeakers had fallen silent. Perhaps Ware was hoping to avoid attention. Bill walked to a rover stationed by the bridge. A deputy he'd met at the admin building, Weaver, gave him a nod.

"Have you heard anything?" Bill asked over the incessant gale.

"Yeah, limited comms just came back. That's the last of us. About seven thousand over the bridge, I'm guessing."

"What about the creatures?"

"Wait, the captain's talking…"

The first vehicle of the convoy veered off the road to the south, the second to the north. This continued until a small, tight semicircle formed at the bridge's ramp.

"What's happening?" Bill demanded.

Police in uniform and others exited the vehicles, Ware coming from the convoy's last. The captain issued shouted orders to his deputies, who took up positions along the vehicle barricade.

Bill might as well get the details directly. He walked along the road, noticing personal items dropped, discarded, and trampled. That was good. There could easily have been bodies. Crowds were dangerous— to themselves as much as others.

"Hayden."

"Where are the bugs?"

The captain scratched the back of his head. He was filthier, more tired, and his eyes were wilder. "They didn't follow. I think they were already leaving. We might have done enough damage and scared them off when we showed we weren't easy pickings. Where's the director?"

"Over the bridge, doing whatever he does. I thought you might need an extra hand."

"Doesn't look that way. Even the docs don't have much to do. There aren't many wounded."

Was Sarah bug food? Had Charlie suffered the same fate? Had the bugs been interrupted while eating?

"You're guarding in case they change their minds?"

"The spook knows all."

Bill laughed, a bitter acknowledgment of his limitations. "This ex-spook doesn't know shit. You want me here?"

Ware let out a sigh. "Hayden, I don't want you anywhere." But he put out a hand, and Bill shook it.

"Feeling's mutual. I'll check the view from the bridge. If I hear you shooting, I'll take it as an invitation."

"You do that."

Bill looked across the river, a sense of loss and being lost slithering through his exhaustion. Thousands of talented colonists stood on the far bank, risk takers and future makers. That was the marketing propaganda. Too many others were underground, being dragged who knew where.

What about the rest of his team? Guilt abraded his conscience. He'd been keeping them at arm's length from day one. He was down two. Leaving the rest to fend for themselves was more than a dereliction of duty, it was selfish. Beneath him. He'd taken the role of supervisor willingly. He'd used them as pawns to move closer to his goals, not caring for their fates. Just like the agency. Damn.

If he was going to get away from the crushing grip of human imperfection, he needed to step closer first, acknowledge his failings, and step up. Anything less was pure hypocrisy. But he'd meet his responsibilities without getting emotionally connected. He wasn't anyone's pawn.

No wonder he'd always hated chess.

CHAPTER 12
A ROUNDING ERROR

S turt had organized the survivors into spots on the riverbank like a gigantic school evacuation drill. The structure followed the org chart of the colony, a visual representation of authority. Bill's survey group was meant to stand next to mining engineers. He waited for an hour, stewing over Sarah's fate, but none showed.

Filled with the need to do something—anything—he went back and forth in the darkness, checking with other departments, then with the small medical station set up the farthest from the bridge. No one knew what had happened to them. He wandered through the exhausted colonists, some of whom were trying to sleep, hoping he could initiate a peer-to-peer link. Perhaps they were in shock and hadn't followed instructions.

After leaning against a rover for a short break, he woke to discover he'd been out for hours. The sun was rising, the dust had settled, and people were stirring. His comm blipped with a dozen messages from Sturt and his underlings. Bill ignored them and attempted contact with his team members, even Sarah. A video came through from Don Macquarie, sent last night with a mayday. Don had been out doing geospike maintenance. Bill hadn't told him to stop, and once Sturt had benched him, Bill no longer had a way to put the scheduled work on hold.

"Sarah, Bill, whoever gets this. My rover's burning. The suppression system hasn't kicked in. I'm going to try the portable extinguisher, but I reckon I'll be wanting a ride. I can't get a live link, so I'm sending my coordinates with a prayer that they'll find a window through the devil-spawned interference. Better see you soon."

What Don hadn't seen as he stood with the smoldering rover in the backdrop were the three bugs approaching. All he'd had to do was check behind to see the danger. However, the drone he was recording from had a perfect view. One of the bugs jumped, and Don went down. The view rolled, stopping at an upward angle. Off camera, Don screamed, then slowly dragged himself into frame.

"Help! There's this—"

The message ended.

The outbound message had hit the satellites, sending automatically when the feed cut, but the return message had taken hours to bounce down to Bill, hampered by the storm. There was no urgency for Don now.

Bill had gone to Ware after that, and three hours later, he was in a small group with Weaver and Foster on their third assignment, searching a group of service buildings for the presence of bugs or survivors, and at Bill's suggestion, the location of tunnel entrances and the directions they headed. If the critters all came from one main tunnel like an artery, then blocking or tracking them would be much easier. It'd be good to know how long the tunnels had been there as well. Were the breakout points new exits on old routes, or had the bastards dug out large volumes of soil and rock with everyone above completely oblivious?

"I've got movement," Foster whispered as Bill joined them on the ground level of a colony-owned restaurant.

They hadn't seen a single bug, alive or dead, so far.

Bill wiped sweat from his hand onto his suit and then gripped his pistol. "Let's take it easy. We go low to the windows and have a look."

Dust covered the glass, the result of a severed power cable that affected electrostatics as much as it did lights and aircon. There was talk of putting in redundant links. There was going to be a lot of talk.

Bill peered outside. People. It was just people.

"Zero threats," he said, standing up and heading outside. "I think we're done here."

The people were heading west, likely on their way to the bridge. There were only so many he could handle in one day, and his humanity quota was already overflowing. To avoid them, he suggested to Weaver and Foster that they do a sweep around to the north, near the main industrial area, before heading back.

It was a poor choice. A short way ahead, a group had formed around a massive Frankenstein rover-slash-hauler-slash-machine. A few workers stood or crouched around a gap where two sets of tracks nearly met. He considered retreating, but Ware waved them over before Bill could think of a reason the deputies would accept.

"All clear?"

"Nothing, Captain. Just holes. It's like the bugs were never here," Weaver said.

"Except for the damage," Foster added.

"Yeah, except for that."

Bill kept his distance. "I've got equipment in the survey hangar that can identify the tunnel locations. I'll need help to cover the area. My team's... gone."

Ware nodded almost imperceptibly. "We'll take that to Sturt. Right now, I want your eyes on this. We've only found two others, and they were slagged."

Bill leaned over the shoulder of a solid woman with dark curly hair who was using an alloy pole to work a bug free of the tracks. She heaved with little regard to a heavy coating of hardened wound gel on her leg and dislodged the bug.

Bill wasn't the only one to tense, but the bug merely rocked back and forth, as inanimate as a window rattling in a breeze. The woman raised the pole, clearly tempted to give it a thrashing, anyway.

The pole dropped from her hands, and she kneeled. "Fitz, get me a multi-tool, a Size 2 CO cutter, and a drill set."

"Sure, boss."

"I need some hands to get this up onto the hauler."

Curious, Bill moved forward with three others, and they gingerly found handholds on the bug's carapace. It was a bit over a meter and a half long. He'd met shorter women. And it was heavy—heavier than Bill. Maybe a little over a hundred kilograms. Its body flexed slightly, the segments shifting individually, and he kept his head judiciously clear of the twisted yet wickedly tipped legs. He was happy to put it down on a flat part of the hauler, but he couldn't resist inspecting its head.

Short stalks, no eyes, no discernable mouth, and a series of strange appendages that mimicked a torturer's toolset rather than animal limbs.

"What the hell kind of bug is this?"

"It's no bug. It's a machine." The woman touched a stalk. "That's an emitter, and some of these might be sensors. And look at the saw. I'm no biologist, but I can make almost anything, and I can tell this bastard is manufactured. And here, those shears have a clear pin to pivot on. I'm betting a few minutes of dismantling and I'll find a charging port."

Ware started to speak, but the words caught in his mouth. He pushed between Bill and the woman to examine the bug. "What is it? A weapon, a military drone?"

The gray-haired man called Fitz arrived, carrying several cases. He said in a dour tone, "Now we know why BILT4 is here—we're the cannon fodder for a test. We're their Phase 2."

"I don't buy it," Bill said. "Across League territory, there are controlled tests every day, everything from sea drones to bioweapons. There's no cost-benefit scenario that makes that viable."

The woman gave him a doubtful raise of an eyebrow. "And who the fuck are you?"

"Bill Hayden. You?"

"Jane Trax. Wait, you're the survey guy?"

"Guilty."

"Your work's shit. I've had more reliable diarrhea."

He raised his hands. "I've been noticing that, too. You're a fabricator, right? When you dismantle it, can you determine how it was built? Is it printed, molded, stamped? If there are specialized components that could be traced to a specific company?"

Trax put her hands on her hips. "You're the survey guy?" she asked again.

"I've had an interesting career path."

"Yeah, well, me and my crew might be able to. If I find the asshole that did this, I'll tear them to shreds."

Ware sniffed and raised a finger. "You'll leave that to me. If we find the culprit, they'll face the law."

Tear them to shreds. "If they're not organic," Bill said, "why did they take the bodies? They can't eat them—that's what I'd expected—and it's not like they were hiding evidence. Why program them to clean up their murders when we've seen them do it?"

Ideas skated across his conscience, too ill-formed to break through, conjecture too ghostly to be grasped. He had nothing; nothing that made sense.

Ware grunted. "It's on a massive scale, but you're right, it's murder. This has to be done by the book. We'll need to build an evidence trail. Everything on camera, every piece bagged and tagged. And the full range of tests, print, DNA, fiber, residue. I'll have to write up an authorization for you and anyone who needs to have access. I don't want our murderer squirming free because we didn't follow procedure."

"Procedure?" Trax spat the word. "We don't have time for that crap. How many people are missing?"

A growing cloud of dust in the distance announced the approach of several vehicles. Bill seemed to be the only one to notice. Ware and Trax were facing off, ready for a duel at midday.

"It's bad, but not as bad as it looked last night. A whole lot of folk fled Staging and hid in the grass. Near as we can tell, three hundred and seventeen are unaccounted for. And if I thought they were alive, I'd be in those tunnels myself right now. They're dead. There will be justice, trust me. I need you to tell me what we're up against before we make a move. I need to make sure we're ready. Going off recklessly helps no one and puts my officers at risk."

"You don't know they're all dead. We don't have time for bureaucratic bullshit."

The dust resolved into three six-wheeled vehicles, all with the BILT4 insignia. As soon as they stopped, ten security guards in black armor exited and fanned out. The doors of the middle one opened, and a tall woman slid out, guarded by the thug, Karlo. Her hair was shoulder length and brown with the gentlest of waves that suggested she'd been in the salon minutes before arriving. She wore an elegant red dress completely unsuitable for the local conditions, and her expression was one of artful concern, garnished by supreme self-confidence. A corporate shark. Well, the water had been bloodied.

"Ah, Captain Ware, it has been too long," she said as she approached. "Is Oliver here?"

"Here, Ms. Wagner?" said Ware. "He's on the other side of the river. I haven't declared Staging safe."

She walked, her pace leisurely, Ware her prey. "Oh, he will be soon. We've already had a little discussion. I want you to know the colony has the deepest sympathies of BILT4—and our full support." She cast an idle glance at the bug. "Is this the culprit? An ugly design."

Was she here to deflect blame? It was possible that she wanted to help or to appear to. The corporate compound was much smaller than the colony and relied on its farms. This could impact her business. If so, Karlo hadn't received the message to play nice. The thug's nostrils flared whenever his searching gaze met Bill's.

Having apparently forgotten the captain, Wagner directed a series of questions to Trax about the bug. The sort that, at first thought, would appear superficial, polite time wasters. But she was interrogating the engineer. To Bill's surprise, Trax wasn't taking kindly to them. Her answers were short and deflecting.

Interesting, but there was no value in allowing the verbal swordplay to escalate when there was a more useful approach.

"Ms. Wagner. I'm Bill Hayden, survey lead. I can understand your curiosity. If you will pardon my own, has the corporation had any hint of the bugs' presence?"

She gave him a gracious smile. "An excellent question. I only wish we knew what was coming, so we could have helped stop this tragedy. Perhaps with hindsight. There were certain anomalies, uncommon purities of elements, or some such. I'm not a very technical person. I'm sure you'd understand much better than I. In hindsight, there will be conclusions made. But I'm here to help with the future. Ah, I'm sure this will be Oliver."

Sturt's vehicle pulled up, and he exited, accompanied by two of his staff.

"Elyse, thank you for coming."

Wagner squeezed his proffered hand. "Oliver, how could I not? The loss of life is terrible, and the impact on the colony will be dire if we don't work together."

"Then I will be forever in your debt. We all will," Sturt said.

Bill was a decent lipreader, and he resisted smiling while translating Trax's silent invectives. Not a fan.

The director must have caught the gist. "Trax," he said. "You're meant to be constructing the armaments. What are you doing here?"

"It's taken care of. The first will be ready in an hour. I was examining what we're up against before I was interrupted."

"I've put together a list of ex-military, based on our personnel files," Sturt told Wagner. "I can't afford to spare them, but the captain will need help, and, let's face it, this isn't ordinary policing. We're out of our depth."

Ware's face colored. That must have been news to him.

Elyse offered wide-eyed concern. "Oliver, that's very resourceful, but I can't imagine what it will do for your work schedule." She nodded as if reaching a painful conclusion. "I can't let you do that. I'll give you the security team I brought here, except my good Karlo—I can't do without him. We'll bring explosives and blast the tunnels, then set up an array of seismic sensors, so there is no chance of you being caught catastrophically off-guard again."

Damn, she was good. The generous offer and the sting of Sturt's ultimate responsibility for what had happened—Bill had to admire the technique. Was it habit or deliberate pressure?

"What about the people?" Trax said, her jaw set stubbornly. "Why isn't anyone talking about them? Ten rent-a-cops won't be enough to guard Staging and search for the missing."

"There are survivors?" Wagner tilted her head. "I didn't realize."

"No," Sturt said.

"We don't know." Trax cut the air with her hand. "We don't have connections to their comms."

Ware's face sagged. "I saw what the bugs were doing. No one could survive that. I wish there was hope. I truly do."

What was Wagner up to? A smooth operator like her never did anything for one reason alone. The guards would give her eyes in the colony. The offer also deflected attention away from her activities. A peek at the BILT4 compound would be educational. A shame it would also stir a hornet's nest. What do to…

Sturt's original plan was a decent start. Guns and skills. Even if the victims were all dead, Bill needed to trace the bugs to their origin. Sturt and Ware weren't thinking it through. The tunnel entrances erupted at different angles, disguising their true origin, but the timing of their appearances… the northeast was a good candidate, as was BILT4. If Wagner was responsible, a few experienced colonists with rifles would improve the odds.

And damn, Bill wanted to blast a few bugs himself, whoever had made them. Sarah, Charlie, Don—they deserved that much, even if the idea of getting into a small tunnel filled with giant metal creepy crawlies came with a sense of dread.

He'd missed the flow of the conversation. Trax's neck muscles were tense. Sturt's shoulders relaxed.

"That's settled then." Wagner gave herself a little clap. "We'll also put a force together to track down the missing. It's the right thing to do. It'll leave our compound light on security, but our people are highly trained and have the best equipment available. And, given you'll need your workers churning out repairs around the clock, why don't I take this little menace back with me? I'll put a full team of scientists onto it and share our findings—we can set up a joint commit-tee. At a time like this, we have to pool our resources."

"Screw that," Trax said while placing a proprietorial hand on the bug. "You corporates are all the same. You'll be looking for what you can patent, not how to kill the fuckers."

"Trax, that's enough." Sturt was shaking with anger. "I'm going to believe that you are still in shock. When you're handed a lifeline, you damn well take it. Another outburst like that, and I'll cut your stake."

"You wouldn't—"

"I would, and I'll do the same for every member of your crew. Put that thing wherever Elyse tells you to, and then stand down and wait for your next job."

Bill considered the likelihood of Trax punching Sturt. Her fists had clenched, her arm bent slightly. It wouldn't help. He tried to catch her attention with a subtle shake of his head. She was picking up on Wagner's railroading of Sturt, and maybe the offer that was too generous, that put BILT4 in full control of the situation. Violence wouldn't do her any good. Another approach was needed.

Trax swore and shoved the bug to the ground before walking off. Ware watched her but didn't follow. Bill quietly made his exit. He didn't want to be on Wagner's radar, given what needed to be done. Or Sturt's. Or Ware's.

Bill, you've really gotten yourself deep, haven't you? A smart man would swim for the surface. Dig was more apt. Instead, he was going to dig deeper. This stank. He needed the truth. And so did the colony. Sturt was treating this attack as a natural disaster that had put him behind schedule. This was no act of nature. There was a mind at work.

What did that mind want? Not revenge, not hatred. The attack had been awful, but there was no sign of an emotion-driven strategy. Did Fitz's military test hypothesis hold water? After all, if the League was willing to kill millions to save millions, ten thousand colonists was a rounding error. No, that was too fanciful. He needed more evidence. Somewhere, burrowed deep beneath the obvious, was cold, hard logic. Bill just had to find it.

And stop it.

CHAPTER 13
INEFFICIENT WAYS TO KILL

E very planet, every glass jungle, every dirt field sowed with seed or blood—it was impossible to escape the taint of the corporations or the stooges who did their bidding. *What does that make me?* Trax puffed her cheeks and leaned back in her chair. The CF-S1 facility, and its four thousand square meters of interior space, was her baby. Fifteen-meter roof, nine specialized fabrication machines, and many other smaller prep and finishing stations. A clean room at the rear, racks of raw materials, an attached parking bay. Even if it wasn't her ultimate goal, the specialized manufacturing unit had its magic. Except when it didn't.

She sat around a cleared workbench at the center of the facility with Fitz and Izy. A display showed several fab queues with links to dependencies. As well, there was a work order request count that ticked upward by the minute.

"No, we can't leave the PIC amplifiers until shift seven. Seb's construction group took the last of the warehoused stock."

Fitz flicked through records on his pad. "That can't be right. I checked the stock levels first thing. It was obvious we were going to be busy. We should have enough to last a couple of days."

"It's right. While you were out chasing the graphene stock, Yi from mass manufacturing audited our key components. Sturt has given priority to everything relating to Phase 3. The decree came through as soon as the main power run came online, and the bastards grabbed everything we've prefabbed."

Izy snapped his fingers. "That's not fair. We put in all the hours to build that buffer. It's ours."

"Nothing's ours," Fitz said, his voice dull. "Everything we make belongs to the colony until we have our own stakes. Never forget it."

"But with all the work orders, we'll be weeks behind in a day. We're already logging jobs that should be with the mass production lines. Trax, tell Fitz I'm right. Sturt has us bent over, ready to be caned. If we don't pump out ten trays a shift, anything relying on optic circuits can't be completed."

Trax offered a humorless smile. "That's why you're here, sunshine. We have to make the fab queue work or Sturt will use any failure to crush our gonads. He needs scapegoats, and he's hoping we'll breed them. Now, I want the two of you to put together a critical path for components. Estimate what we'll need—just spitball it—and for each, output an extra ten percent on top. You can guarantee we'll need it all."

"We're screwed, you know that."

"Shut it, Izy. I don't want to hear that crap. At least you're not down some damn tunnel, dead or bleeding out."

"Come on, boss," Fitz said. "We'll do what we can, but you know what you're asking—"

"Yeah, I'm asking you to do your damn jobs." Trax stood up, wincing as the sudden movement tugged on her knitting flesh. The doc had warned her not to move much or it would scar. It was going to be a beauty.

Fitz and Izy started saying the right things, so she walked away and let her focus drift. There was no tidy solution, but they'd taken the news better than she thought. If she gave the barest hint of a concession, they'd start thinking in terms of mitigation. She needed them sharp, hungry.

Amy was crawling on a nearby workbench, slowly testing a pile of optronic devices for salvageable components. Whole swaths of building-management kits had been attacked, and none of it could be trusted. She'd do her job because the idea of viable components going to waste was inconceivable. That didn't mean she was in a good space. She'd spoken less than Harry since dawn. Understandable, when she'd been stuck in an elevator until Harry and Fitz had found her.

Diver stood at the centrifuge, prepping one of the liquid precursors they'd need. Earlier, he'd talked nonstop, distilling this, mixing that. The kid's job was his lifeline to sanity. For Trax, it wove one strand as another frayed.

Harry, in a mech configured for lifting, raised a barrel of compressed titanium powder and carried it to a sintering machine's input bin. She misjudged, and the barrel slipped, spraying titanium across the floor.

"Harry!" Trax shouted. "Are you trying to give away your damn stake?"

She felt all eyes on her. Fitz and Izy stopped arguing. The droning of machinery continued, uncaring.

"Just clear it up, and don't do it again."

Refusing to acknowledge her crew, she took a seat by a CNC station and stared out the open doors, bewildered by a small city that didn't even care enough to grieve. This was bullshit. Everything was bullshit. She slammed a fist on the machine and welcomed the mixture of pain and numbness.

Bill Hayden walked through the open doors, filthy and disheveled. The only clean item on him was a case he held in his left hand. Trax reached for something heavy to throw at the intruder, but no tools lay within reach. She should have run a sloppier shop. What did the asshole want? What did he think he was owed—entering her domain as if he had any right to be there?

He spotted her and approached. At first, she'd thought he'd also received a leg wound, but the lump on his right side turned out to be his pistol. He'd taped it to his suit leg and applied a hardening agent to form a rudimentary holster. A complete amateur.

"Piss off, Hayden."

Three dull explosions shook the ground, as if to emphasize her displeasure.

The surveyor didn't so much as flinch. "That'll be the last of the tunnels, at least the ones dug so far. Our corporate benefactors have been swift—I'll say that much for them."

"Why don't you tell them? I'm sure they'll love your boot-licking."

"They have no interest in the assistance of a colony surveyor. Apparently, I don't have the requisite skills."

"That I'd believe."

He gave her a tight, infuriating smile. "Do you have somewhere private? I have a matter that we need to discuss. It's rather time critical."

"I'm busy."

"I want to talk about what happened last night and about what's been happening."

She stood up and stalked into his personal space. "You saw what happened. We're leaving our own for dead. That bitch took the bug, and Sturt shut me down. Now, I've got a thousand things to do before nightfall."

Hayden leaned in and lowered his voice. "What if I told you BILT4 is up to something?"

She didn't back away. "No shit, Mr. Detective. Do you want a medal?"

He scanned the facility, his head twitching as if his eyes were cameras. "I have data. But I can't risk talking to you here. Please, give me a chance."

Damn him. If he hadn't mentioned the corp, he'd be out on his ear. She headed back toward Fitz and Ivy. "This better be good. Everyone, down tools, and get your asses here. It's time for a break. This surveyor reckons BILT4 might not be a source of purity and kittens, and it's not like we're swamped."

"Wait," Hayden scurried after her. "I meant between you and me. This is dangerous. Even telling you is risky—for the both of us."

His corporate cloak-and-dagger routine was pathetic. "Dangerous? Everyone, if you're quaking in your boots, you are welcome to set your hearing protection to full spectrum and get back to work."

Amy pulled a chair up next to Fitz. "I'd like to hear what he has to say."

Diver was next, tossing a pair of gloves into a bin as he approached.

Harry was the last to join them. It took time to dismount a mech, and her sullen mood didn't help.

Trax sat on the corner of the bench, letting her leg rest without showing weakness. "Begin, Mr. Hayden."

"Bill, you can call me Bill. I just need to set up a couple of things." He put his case gently onto the bench and retrieved three devices. "This is a bug scanner. If you don't mind, I'll check each of you."

Her crew let him run his gadget over them from head to foot. He did the workbench next, leaving Trax for last. She stuck her arms out and let him proceed. This wasn't his first time. What kind of surveyor needed that level of caution? There'd been rumors, but there were always rumors, and each one was less believable than the next.

He put the scanner down and activated a small dome. It let off an annoying hiss. "A white noise generator. It's not meant for a space this large, but it'll have to do."

"I think we've got enough noise already," Izy said. "It's that kind of place."

"The frequency of human speech is easy to separate from a consistent or rhythmic background."

The third device was a portable console. Hayden activated it.

"Bill, I see we have guests." The smooth voice was artificial.

"We're the guests, Dantalion. Pull up the incident map."

A projected image of a hundred kilometers in radius from Staging appeared. Numerous tags blipped into existence.

"Up here is where Charlie, one of my people, died. Ware thought it was murder, and to be honest, so did I. Perhaps it still is, but not by the hands of a colonist."

The surveyor went through the gruesome details of Charlie's death and the destruction of his rover.

"That's a pretty inefficient way to kill someone," Amy said. "I mean, I can think of a hundred easier ways. Not that I would, of course."

Fitz peered at the map. "You thought the rover damage was BILT4 covering up?"

"It could have been anyone covering up the murder, and perhaps destroying the data that Charlie generated. However, the attack is consistent with last night, and with the ongoing acts of *sabotage*."

He was missing the obvious. "Your guy's body wasn't taken."

"True," Hayden said. "It was also the first incident I've been able to discover. So it may have been in another stage of our bug master's plan."

"Margot wasn't taken," Harry said.

"Pardon?"

When Harry refused to elaborate, Trax reluctantly explained the attack on the farm.

"Perhaps she was out of reach. And nighttime. Always. Interesting." Hayden reached for the map. "That's not the only pattern. The vast majority of what I've been able to identify has occurred in the northeast. In the same area, I've discovered manipulated software in the sensors we deploy."

Diver pointed to the east. "And BILT4 is pretty close to the action. It has to be them."

Hayden raised his hands. "I don't like jumping to conclusions."

"They stole my bug and won't let us go after the missing," Trax said. "Doesn't take a jump."

"It's compelling, I agree. But we don't know if they've also been hit and aren't sharing. Corporations have their own twisted logic. They want control at all times, guilty or not."

It was hard to disagree, and yet, it was pointless. "What's it matter? There's nothing we can do. If I step out of line, my crew's screwed, and there's nothing I can do that'll make a damn bit of difference."

"I believe you want to save the missing. Honestly, I think they're all dead. But I also think we have to look. If Elyse Wagner doesn't want us poking around, it's enough to make me want to. And it was three hundred of us this time. What if there's a next time? What if that's tonight?"

Damn, he was pushing all her buttons. "What do you expect me to do? I can't go running around hundreds of square kilometers, bug hunting and hoping Sturt doesn't notice."

"If I may," the console said. "Bill and I have examined the geological survey data and compared them with the concentration of incidents and the appearance of the tunnel entrances." A line flashed on the map, starting at Staging, heading northeast, and finishing in a large circle. "The line indicates the most efficient route for the machines to have taken, as supported by the evidence. The circle covers an area of geological anomalies."

Hayden cut in. "We can't be sure that's where they're coming from, but it's a good bet, and the line narrows down where we'd have to probe before finding the tunnel. All we have to do is get clear of Staging and avoid BILT4."

While Hayden wasn't a corporate, there was a hint of sales about his manner that set her on edge—or was it the prowling of a patient predator? He was offering her exactly what she wanted, a way to help the missing, the people Sturt had already forgotten, or at least a way to know their fate.

"You want me to bring drilling gear out there, dig down to a tunnel, and take a look?"

"If you can get me inside, I'll go."

Trax smiled. He didn't sound so confident about that. "A little thing like you wouldn't last the first bug."

"And you're injured. I'm just trying to do what I can."

"He has a point, boss. You're supposed to rest up," Diver said with youthful enthusiasm and little foresight. "I'll do it."

Izy laughed. "You? It'll need someone chill, someone skilled. Better be me."

"If we can get a bug, *I* should be the one examining it," Amy said with a touch of trepidation.

The idiots. They were letting themselves get swept up.

"We might as well all go." Fitz stood. "If I was taken, I'd want the colony looking for me, not some corporate mercs with no skin in the game. You stay and heal, boss. Give Sturt the runaround, so we're not caught, and we'll get you answers."

Stay? She pushed herself off the table, unable to contain her fury. "You'll do no such thing. Under my watch, you will not lose everything you've spent years working for. You're all staying right here, and that's an order."

"Look, I don't want to interrupt, but I can promise you all one thing: if we nail BILT4, I can shield your stakes."

"How?" Trax demanded.

Hayden's gaze drifted. If the asshole was taking a long time to come up with an answer, it meant he was either about to deliver unwanted news, or more likely, about to be as straight as a coiled spring.

Finally, he looked her in the eye. "I can't tell you, not yet."

Her crew erupted into indignant exclamations and disbelieving questions, drowning out his response. She noted his discomfort. It had been a foolish claim, as if a surveyor had any pull with Sturt or his off-world superiors. But the wily asshole must have known how they'd react to his refusal. Here he was, promising exactly what she wanted.

This wasn't helping. "Enough."

They quietened down.

"I'm sorry," Hayden said. "I doubt I'd trust me, either. Thank you for listening."

"What happens if we don't?" Harry asked.

"Don't what?"

"If we don't nail BILT4?"

Hayden sucked in air. "Then I can't help. We'll all go down together. Misery may love company, but idiocy invented the concept. I'll wait outside and give you a chance to talk. Let me know what you decide. There's not a lot of time if we're going to do this. Remember, they're active at night."

He headed for the front of the facility, leaving Trax with the pile of shit he'd dumped on her. It smelled worse than the stables she'd mucked out as a kid.

"He's full of it, right?" Izy asked.

"You don't want to go?" Fitz said.

"Nah, I'm all in. Besides, if I have to put up with one more day with our glorious leader's mood, I'll be begging for the bugs to come and get me."

"Hey." Trax slapped the table. "Enough of that."

Amy clutched her fingers. "He's got a point, though I'd use different words. If Bill Hayden hadn't come along, by the end of the day, you would either be running off after the bugs by yourself or blowing up like an over-pressured reactor."

"We're all freaked, boss," Diver said. "I know I'm not the only one making a weapon on the side. I don't wanna wait for those bugs to come to us. Let's shut down the asshole controlling them."

Trax examined each of her crew. They didn't know how pitiless corporations were. None of their families had lost land, a war, a loved one in the name of greed.

"Harry, you get why you can't do this. You're here for your family."

"You're like my sister. And those three hundred are our cousins."

Fitz reached up to put a hand on Harry's shoulder. His eyes said he had no illusions this would be easy. He was anything but excited. "The crew's safer when we work together. I say if one goes, we all go."

They were idiots. Sappy, sappy, idiots.

"Izy, go get Hayden. We've got work to do."

CHAPTER 14
SEND ME TO HELL

U nlike the fabrication facility, the survey offices were lifeless. The garage consisted of eight bays with only three filled. Tools were neatly racked at the rear, waiting for familiar hands that hadn't returned after the attack. Only Bill's rover showed any signs of life as it rested well forward of its usual position. The rover's open door leaked light across the scratched floor, reminding him he didn't have long. A drilling rig, half again the length of the rover, hung off the back. A geospike strapped across its front gave a solid alibi. Hopefully.

Bill left the small window in the overhanging office. To his right, the comms desk sat empty. Sarah and Aamar had often swapped duties. Bill should have been the daytime operator, glued to his seat, managing his minions from afar. The desks that filled the rest of the office had pictures, mugs, polished crystals, interesting mineral specimens, and a myriad of other personal items. He didn't even have a desk. It had been a case of starting how he planned on finishing. The job, the people, they were a means to an end. Charlie, Sarah, Rod, Tang, Aamar, Don. Strangers, all. He even had to look up their addresses to check where they lived.

The display at the comms desk flashed. He went over and disconnected a data chip. To most of the colonists, the idea of carrying data rather than relying on wireless had been a culture shock despite the mission training. He slipped the chip into a small incision on the inside of his suit. In Bill's old game, air gaps were a form of armor. Why did the new game feel so familiar?

He took a set of stairs down to his rover. Inside, he crab-walked around the mountain of gear piled so high that little space remained and settled into the driver's seat.

As he maneuvered the rover out, he couldn't shake the feeling that he was leaving a phase of his life behind, one that he'd never quite entered. There were few others on the streets. Sturt had tasked the vast majority of the colony with grueling shifts to make up for lost time and lost hands.

When he approached the northern edge of Staging, however, there was plenty of activity. BILT4 vehicles dotted the town's current boundaries ahead and to the east. Flags and ditches near these showed where the blasting had occurred. A BILT4 security guard waving a lit red baton blocked the road. Dodging around would be easy enough, but the whole point of this exit plan was to avoid suspicion. He stopped the rover and opened a hinged facet on the blister.

"What's happening?"

The guard walked around to the opening. "There's blasting. This is just a safety protocol. Can I ask where you're going?"

A good confirmation for Bill. Rather than warning him where not to go, the guard was digging for information.

"Heading out for some fun in the sun. I lost most my crew, so now I'm stuck doing everyone's job. I've gotta plant the sucker on the back" —Bill gestured to the rear of his rover— "three hundred and fifty clicks, nor'-nor'-west. Mind you, I'm happy to be shy of here for a day or two. Don't know what it's like in your neck of the woods, but I don't need to sleep on no giant radioactive roach infestation."

"I understand, sir. If you can stick to the road for the next ten kilometers, you should be safe." The guard rose on their toes and tried to look inside the blister.

Should have brought a step stool.

"Happy bug hunting," Bill said, pulling the window closed.

The guard retreated and waved him on. Bill kept the rover's pace steady, even after he'd left the guard and Staging long behind. He'd ask the crew for adjustments to the rover's comm array, hoping to detect any drones spying on them. None appeared on his display. Either BILT4 wasn't paranoid enough or the fab crew's warranty-breaching changes had failed.

A roll of cord slid down the pile. It would be cruel to leave it any longer.

"All clear."

The pile grumbled and broke apart as the members of Jane Trax's fabrication crew disentangled themselves. They'd only had a chance for brief introductions but observing them stretch and return blood to their limbs was enlightening.

"My ass is never going to be the same," Izy said, trying to stretch in the enclosed space and elbowing Harry in the process.

"I don't want to hear about your ass, or it can be out there." Trax thumbed the road. "Speaking of, Hayden, stop this tub so we can kick out all the junk."

Bill ignored her demanding tone. "Leaving a trail would attract attention. We'll have to wait until we're much farther."

"How long until we head east?" Amy asked.

"I think another twenty minutes should do it. The longer we head away, the more unremarkable we are, but also the more time there is for Sturt or Wagner's lackeys to notice we're all gone."

"And less daylight," Fitz added.

Bill retrieved his hidden chip, accessed the data, then spent the travel time considering the best location to search for the main tunnel, assuming there was only one. Behind him, Trax worked her crew, and the pile of assorted junk shifted to vaguely neat stacks, giving enough room for them all to sit, if not much to breathe. The northern road led to a series of industrial facilities before terminating at the construction site of a residential district. Rail would run alongside at some future stage, but the planning committee that he'd occasionally been part of had revised the original route and pushed it back. It was time for his own revision. He slowed the rover and parked off to the right.

"I'm going to disable the transponder. Hopefully, if anyone's looking, they'll assume it's standard interference."

"That's pretty illegal," Diver said. "Who'd you go to college with, a carjacking gang?"

Amy raised a hand. "Honestly, a transponder is pretty easy to remove and keep running. It'd make us appear stationary, but not gone."

"You have drones, Hayden?" Trax asked.

He liked where this was going. "Air and ground."

"Amy, cut the transponder free. Harry, I want you to strap it onto a ground unit and send it up the road until its batteries run dry."

They worked fast, not with the precision of a special forces operation, but like a family that had been together so long, they naturally anticipated each other's needs. It didn't hurt that Trax kept them on a tight leash. When the transponder and its battery were secured to the sacrificial drone, Bill directed it to the west for its lonely, one-way journey. That accomplished, he restarted the rover and took them east several kilometers, before curving to the southeast.

"Why are we going so far from Staging?" Fitz asked as the new route settled in. "It'd be faster to do a straight line five or so kilometers out."

Bill brought up the map so they could all see. "True, but we don't want to be spotted, especially by Karlo, BILT4's head of security. He doesn't play nice. The farther away from corporate land, the better. Out here, if we draw attention, we can easily feign surprise. It's not our fault if BILT4 ventures outside their yard. As well, remember the locations of the damage reports. Wherever the bugs are coming from, it can't be that close. We need to cover some distance. Once we're out of the rover and underground, we'll be hidden but slow."

"We should have brought quad bikes."

Talking down Trax from that idea had taken precious time. "You heard the security guard. Having a bunch of them loaded would have been suspicious, the same reason we didn't use any of your vehicles. It's all guesswork, but Dantalion and I have selected an area that takes our limited mobility into account. With one slight risk—it's near corporate land."

"You just said that you didn't want us spotted," Fitz said.

They all shook as the rover navigated a large dip.

"The location is alongside a ridge. We'll have natural cover when we reach it. I'd try farther out, but these anomalous readings"—Bill poked at a region on the map—"they have me worried. If BILT4 is hiding a black ops project, I'm guessing that's where, and that's where we'll need to go."

"What did you survey before you signed up?" Trax asked.

"A lot of things." He wished she'd stop scraping away at the scab of his past.

When they approached the potential tunnel route, he slowed the rover and activated the ground-penetrating radar. They all seemed to believe his mask of confidence. If this had been a sanctioned op, he would have vetoed it without question. Poor planning, high danger, operatives with no idea what they were getting into, and a field coordinator that couldn't be sure of his true motives.

The radar cut a metaphorical slice vertically into the ground. The results returned as a series of tightly packed wobbly lines. Small hill-shaped curves indicated diffraction points, items that bounced back the signal. Many distortions appeared and vanished, the natural variation of the ground. Bill let his mind calm, demanding nothing, and taking in the data as if it were a breeze tugging at his hair.

A large curve. He slammed on the brakes, the seat straps grinding against his chest, then reversed.

"Got it?" Trax asked.

"Maybe."

He turned the rover in an arc to the left. Nothing. Nothing. There. Drifting back brought him over the disturbance. He kept following it for a hundred meters, then stopped the rover and set the display to show the path he'd taken.

"We've got our spot. It's following the line we anticipated, and it's about five meters across, much bigger than I was expecting. I figure if we set the drill—"

Trax put up a hand. "You've done your bit. Stay in here and fiddle with your sensors and maps, all nice and safe. Drilling's dangerous work."

She didn't wait to hear that he'd already drilled several times on Eclipse. Her crew accepted her barked orders and followed her out of the rover. The drill was in place in fifteen minutes, legs locked into the ground, and its cutter already coming up to speed. When it hit the ground, dust grew as stones plinked against the rover's bodywork. The grinding and cracking and tearing produced a racket that must surely reach all the way back to Staging. A cloud of steam from cooling the drill head begged to be noticed. So, too, did the safety lights on their suits.

The crew shouted at each other. Bill opened the window and leaned out of the blister.

Trax stood on top of the drilling machine. "Push through until we've got full diameter at the exit point."

It was time. Bill's heart skipped a beat. There was a difference between being caught up in events and choosing to go down into the darkness.

"Wish me luck, Dantalion."

"Make your own. You really should bring me along."

A twinge of guilt had Bill shifting in his seat. "You were in my life and my head for long enough."

"If you say so."

"Delete yourself."

"What? Bill, you can't ask that."

"You can't be found. BILT4 would happily analyze every digital neuron of yours." He could have hidden it earlier at Staging, but it would be too tempting to return to, over and over.

"I hate to say it, Bill—you're making sense. So, this is it. You want me to wipe myself from here, as you wiped me from your body?"

"Exactly."

"Will you miss me?"

"Yeah, sure."

The console fell silent. Bill collected his pistol, confirming its charge, and gingerly pocketed the spare charge brick Trax's crew had put together for him—a rough finish, a huge amount of stored energy, and a rushed build. What could go wrong? He stepped outside and wished he'd put on his mask. The air was thick, dry, and had a taste of oil. The crew had suit safety lights on, marking their positions in the haze.

"All clean, boss."

"Good work, Diver. Everybody, let's haul this baby out of the way and see what's in the bathwater."

When the cutting piece retracted, the crew released bolts that had been locking the drill unit in place, then pushed it, straining against inertia until it rolled away. Bill took a step forward, wondering if he should help, but he'd only get in the way, so he diverted to the hole instead. It was about three meters deep and wide enough to slide down, though not exactly spacious. Beneath, a hint of dirt and rock suggested a bottom to a lightless void.

Trax grabbed his shoulder. "Hey, amateur, get back. You don't have a harness."

Did he need a union card, too? Best not to ask. "Sorry, I left my leash at home. Tie me up and drop me down."

Her scornful gaze threatened to set his eyebrows on fire. "I'll be first. If I judge it's safe, then you might be second."

His body straightened instinctively. "Wait a minute. You don't have —" The training to handle threats? Running on so little sleep, he'd almost given away his previous employment. Trax didn't come across as the pro-authority type.

"I don't have what?"

"An argument from me. You better pull out those rifles Sturt had you make."

Izy raised his empty hands. "The cops took every last one, and admin cut the authority to make more. Sturt's orders."

"None of you are armed?" Did they think this was going to be a picnic? Why hadn't they said anything?

"Oh, we're armed," Diver said. "It's not just trash in your rover."

"What have I gotten myself into?"

"We'll see soon enough. I want harnesses ready, weapons out, and three flares per person. Snap to it!"

Bill struggled to process the crew's preparation. Sure, the running of cables to the rover's winch system was familiar, and he recognized the chemical flares, even if he'd never used one. However, the assortment of junk they piled near the hole suggested they'd sniffed too much industrial solvent.

Harry loomed over him. "Need to check your suit."

"Ah, sure."

She went behind and pulled on various parts of his suit. There was a loop tucked away. When she gave it a hard tug, the covering tightened around his waist and legs, thankfully not giving a free castration.

"Should do."

By that point, Trax had a cable secured to her back and a bulky pack strapped around her torso. She took a flare, flicked off the safety cover, and slapped the ignition button on her thigh. At Bill's questioning glance, she said, "Last time I met a bug, it sliced my flashlight. I'm not going dark a second time."

"Good call."

She tossed the flare down the hole. It landed with a clatter, and Bill resisted the urge to peer down.

Trax rubbed her hands. "Izy, pass me my toys. Harry, you need to stay on the surface with the winch."

"Me?" Harry said indignantly.

"I trust you to be ready to save us, got it?"

"Leave Fitz. I'm stronger. He's older."

"Anything goes wrong with the winch, I'll need you here."

There was more to it, Bill was sure, and Harry must have realized that, too.

"Yes, boss." It wasn't a happy acceptance. The tone suggested words would be shared later.

Izy picked up some of the junk and handed it to Trax, a curved sheet of alloy and what looked like a giant lobster claw with wicked cutting blades. She took the sheet and held a handle in the middle—it was a shield, straight out of the Middle Ages. He examined the claw. There was a spot to insert a forearm and cables to connect the pack. She'd taken industrial shears and turned them into a weapon.

The others had riffed on her madness.

Amy held a stick with prongs on the end. She gave it a pat when she saw his confusion. "Ultracapacitor. Their shell is metal, for sure. This'll fry anything that conducts."

The kid called Diver tapped at several canisters he'd hung from his suit. "Explosives, smoke, a couple of options I cooked up."

Not to be outdone, Fitz attached the last section of a long tube with a square cross-section and a cup shape on the end. "EMP spear. It's short range, but at least the tip will be far away from us."

"A dull lot, aren't they?" Izy said while swinging around a meter-long pole with several lumps running down one side. He flicked a control, and with a whoosh, purple lines of plasma sparked into existence and blended together. "I learned military saber in school. After that, a plasma blade was the only option, yes?"

Doomed. They were all doomed.

Trax, who he'd foolishly believed to possess a grounded personality, didn't bat an eyelid. She tested the strain on the cable and put her feet on the edge.

"Harry, send me to hell."

CHAPTER 15
BLOOD TRAIL

The narrow confines of the shaft created a certain theater to her descent, a metaphorical rebirth that, in a film, would have made Trax gag. Her weak safety lights encased her in a warm glow, and her ears popped as the air pressure changed. Was there a slight breeze? In a few breaths, her legs were out—a breach birth. Her arms, and then finally her head, cleared the shaft.

The bug tunnel continued in both directions, level, smooth, until the light of the flare weakened, veiling the secrets beyond. A translucent, glossy red substance coated the tunnel, subtle ripples locked in its hard surface. The terraforming heavy boring units could have carved this with no problem, but it must have taken a huge number of bugs to dig out. The precision was unsettling.

"Is it safe?" Hayden called, his voice echoing down the shaft.

"Nothing's eaten me yet. Cool your conductors."

Her feet pressed into the rocky debris. She kicked away the larger pieces and waited. In the following quiet, her little noises were amplified. She turned on her suit flashlights and checked both directions. More tunnel and no bugs. Reaching to the back of her shoulders, she released her cable.

"All clear. Hayden, your turn."

Carting around a homemade shield and a pair of powered alloy-cutting shears looked crazy, but the memory of the bug leaping on her was unforgettable. The next one would find her a tougher customer, and it was going to wish it had been zapped with a few thousand volts.

Hayden and her crew came down one after the other. Except Harry. Someone needed to stay behind. There was too much risk otherwise. And if it went bad down in the tunnels, well, Harry had the most people counting on her. It was a simple equation.

"Which way?" Izy asked. "I mean, it's nice and cozy down here, but I don't fancy setting up a campfire and burning some marshmallows."

"Southwest takes us into corporate territory, and then to Staging," Hayden said, his brow creased. "If I were BILT4, and I wanted to attack the colony for whatever reason, I wouldn't need a tunnel continuing to the northeast, but it does. What does that mean? That's the question. Either they aren't behind the bugs, or they're up to something else. Either way, I don't like it."

Fitz walked a few paces down the tunnel. "Any chance this is a terraformer screwup, a boring machine gone rogue?"

Trax pulled a range finder from a suit pocket and checked the tunnel's diameter. A little under five meters. "I don't think so. Quantity, yes, design, no. Five meters is either too big or too small. Hayden?"

"You're right. It's not consistent with machines of that era, and the surface is coated." He tapped his pistol on the wall. "Pretty hard. I'm guessing it's a casing to strengthen the tunnel. Anyone know what it's made of?"

Diver and Izy started toward the wall.

"Hayden, you were the one that wanted us to hurry. We're getting nowhere fast."

"That's a good point." He passed Trax and switched on his light. "Time for a walk."

When Trax joined him, her crew followed. Izy waved his plasma blade around for the first few minutes, thankfully with it switched off. The rest grew increasingly quiet as they continued. The whole concept of robotic bugs and the tunnel with its weirdly coated wall curdled her stomach and made her head ache. What kind of sheep-banging lunatic would do this?

"Sheep-banging lunatic?" Hayden said. She must have spoken the thought aloud. "Nothing on this scale is the work of a lunatic. It takes too much planning, and the opportunities for failure are endless. No, it's a matter of finding the puzzle pieces. It only makes no sense because we can't see the bigger picture."

Can't see. Trax stopped. Her flashlights had options for different wavelengths, allowing the identification of chemical spills, and detecting a variety of flaws. One of them was UV. She adjusted the output. There were hints of dark patches. "Everyone, turn all your lights off, even the safeties."

One by one they went dark, and the tunnel glowed an intense fluorescent purple wherever Trax's light reached, except for spots and smears of black that pitted the ground. "Anyone want to bet we're not seeing blood?"

Hayden bent down and inspected a patch. "Given the distance, the residual blood should have been wiped off tens of kilometers ago. I'm no doctor, but there's only so much a body can bleed."

"Unless they're still bleeding." Trax leaned on her shield. "There could still be survivors."

Driver switched his light back on. "There're other fluids that absorb UV. Polynuclear hydrocarbons in mineral oils—they could be using some for hydraulics, lube, cooling... or the assholes running the bugs could have pissed as they dug this out."

"Sounds like you're betting. I'm calling you on it. Five square meters. Start walking and get ready to weep."

They set off again. No matter how much she wanted to believe in the chance to save even a single soul, the sheer amount of blood spoke of misery and death.

Amy tapped Trax's arm. "Boss, I think I can see a bump around the tunnel, maybe a hundred meters ahead."

Trax gripped her shears, fighting back a sudden wave of despondence, and squinted. "I think I see it, too."

As the distance shrank, others spotted the circular protuberance. It looked like an open airlock made from overlapping scales of rusty alloy. Cables exited the top of the ring and continued along the ceiling of the tunnel.

When they were within a few meters, Hayden raised his hands. "Stop. This could be a security checkpoint. Give me a moment."

Fitz sniffed and said, "I've never seen an ID check that looks like a blacksmith made it."

Hayden waved his little toy in the air and approached the ring. "There's low-level power, but it's not triggering any warnings."

"Maybe it's for navigation, a bug beacon," Amy said. She stepped over the ring. "There's no audible alarm."

"And no trap," Trax said, following. "We have to be close. Keep it moving."

While they walked, Hayden shifted to Trax's side. "You work well together. Did you know each other beforehand?"

She snorted. "Harry and I go way back. The rest—we all met day two, same as most. Seven in the morning at an empty warehouse."

"I'm impressed."

"Don't be," Izy said. "These poor dullards are lucky to be graced by my presence. Without me, the crew's a mere collection of tinkerers."

Amy poked him with her stick, saving Trax the task. "Without you, we'd have peace and quiet."

"Is that why you're out here?" Hayden asked Amy. "Peace and quiet?"

"Not at all. I was being suffocated where I grew up. I'm here for a challenge. We get to design and build as we go. No red tape."

No red tape that you see because I hide it from you.

Fitz increased his pace, catching up. "She's right. There's freedom here. Or there will be when we hit Phase 3. I've got a few ideas, and I won't have to negotiate licensing with every corp wanting something for nothing. When the patent holiday starts, I'm going for broke."

"How about you?" Hayden asked Trax.

Her plans for a vineyard and winery were hardly secret, but he was a nosy asshole. "I have my reasons. You first. Mining?"

Hayden laughed, and it sounded genuine. "No—no thank you. I'd like to do some traveling. Izy?"

"I'm here for the beaches."

A small, dark lump lay on the curved side of the tunnel. Trax only noticed because she'd turned to Izy to call out his bullshit. She crouched down. The route had so far been close to immaculate.

"Watcha found?" Diver said. "Bug shit?"

Trax slipped a thin hexagonal rod from a pocket in her suit and poked the lump. It wobbled and fell to its side, revealing an oval shape with ridges. And raw flesh. It was an ear—someone's cut-off ear.

Her crew circled the discovery.

Diver winced. "Damn, boss, that's nasty."

Hayden slipped between her crew and kneeled uncomfortably close. "Does anyone have a bag?"

"Want a snack for later?" Izy asked.

Trax bit down on a laugh. This was part of some poor bastard. And she knew what Hayden wanted. "DNA will tell us who owns it."

They went through their pockets. Amy had brought a snack, and the packet from that was suitable enough. Trax wrapped the ear up and put it in a pocket with as much stoic reverence as she could muster. *Don't think about it.*

Continuing on, her crew lost their taste for talk. Even Hayden kept quiet, his desire for social interrogation blunted. Shortly, they encountered an intersection with a ring a short distance down each route. A check of the UV kept them moving ahead. The tunnel veered to the right and angled steadily downward. Several smaller tunnels dotted the walls. Stopping for a third time, they turned off their lights, and Trax confirmed the direction via spots and smears of blood.

A pale light beyond the fluorescence made her pause, a stationary source. She whispered, "Do you see that?"

Her crew nodded.

"The closer we are, the more likely there will be guards," Hayden said, taking out his pistol and fiddling with it. "The perimeter is usually the most hardened location. The last thing we want to do is alert them, so don't go… zapping or chopping, and stay calm. The longer we avoid detection, the greater our chance of success."

Way too many spy flicks, that man—spouting cliches like an AI-written script. She couldn't fault his reasoning, but she wasn't going to skulk. Hiding in the rover had been enough. If there was a puffed-up prick at the end, she was going to kick his ass, cut off his balls, and stomp on his head for good measure. She gripped the claw and rolled her shoulders, feeling the bones crack.

"Let's do this."

CHAPTER 16
NOT ALL

B ill raised a hand, indicating he should go ahead. Trax pushed past him and marched toward the light. She was risking the entire mission with her bullheadedness. Unfortunately, shouting for her to stop was out of the question. He hurried after, keeping his footfalls as quiet as his boots allowed. The downward slope leveled out, and Trax froze. Bill imagined a patrol of guards in BILT4 uniforms, rifles raised. The pistol was slippery, and an unpleasant tingle itched between his shoulder blades. He steadied his grip and advanced.

I think, Charlie, that I might owe you an apology.

He reached Trax's side. His pupils dilated, soaking up the sparse and precious rays of light that appeared to be generated incidentally to the hive of activity. The quality of echoes suggested the space ahead was cavernous but not empty. He thought of a dozen techniques that could take that sound and strip it into component frequencies, identifying actions and hinting at the scale and contents—all possible without remaining in view. At least when Dantalion rode in his skull.

The ambient whirs, thuds, and low-pitched thrums reminded him of a factory floor. And every factory had its workers. Bugs moved, occasionally setting off sparks when sharp legs clattered on what must be a metallic floor. Trax switched from UV to a standard spectrum. The light struggled to reveal distant coils to the right and a huge jumbled pile to the left. The bulk remained a sea of nothing. He didn't need to see *them*. The bugs were obvious, with their whirring and clacking. The glinting of their carapaces only confirmed the danger. Yet, as he watched, and as he heard the arrival of the rest of the crew, the bugs continued to ignore them.

He licked his lips. He'd never thought to bring low-light goggles. The bugs operated at night. It should have been an obvious requirement, but at one time they'd been implanted into his retinas.

Crack.

"Trax," he hissed. She'd activated a flare.

"They move at night. And when I was attacked in the hospital basement, the bug's actions were weird. I didn't understand then, but I get it now. I don't think they can see, not at our wavelengths."

That was hardly enough to go on. "We can't assume that."

"We can't stand here doing nothing." She switched her flashlight off and rolled the flare into the cavern, following quickly with a second, revealing a scene that would stain his soul and fester in his sleep.

The faint pile took form, the pale blotches morphing into hands and faces. Bodies. Dumped on each other like sacks of grain. Jagged rips in suits. Missing limbs. Open mouths and endless stares. A bug crawled over this pile of broken humanity, touching several with its smaller, frontal appendages before clamping on one victim and dragging them off the pile.

The corpse bounced and wiggled until the bug stopped alongside several of its brethren and started cutting away the suit. In this location, ten or more bugs crawled back and forth over other corpses, tugging and jostling them. Tubes lay along the ground, ends speared into necks and inner thighs. The reason eviscerated his composure. The activity resolved into the butchery it was. One bug peeled a large flap of skin off the chest of a naked male, placing it carefully to one side before proceeding to snip another length free of the ribs.

Elsewhere, a bug cut away a biceps muscle and placed it in a pile of bloodless meat. The limb flopped down, revealing white bone.

Another bug homed in on the cuts of human flesh and scooped them up. It scurried across the floor and stopped in front of a machine.

It was wide and connected to so many thick tubes that it appeared to be caught in a spiderweb. Much of its surface had the same corroded finish as the bugs. But lower down, there was a panel with a brighter metallic sheen. The bug pulled this down and out, revealing an opening. It dropped the flesh onto the panel and the lumps rolled inside and out of sight, like the input bin of some industrial manufacturing line.

"What in all the realms of madness is this?" Fitz said.

Izy swallowed hard. "I'm never eating a burger again."

Amy hit his arm. "You're vegetarian."

"Yeah, but I think I'm giving up on protein altogether."

Charlie had been mutilated like these poor souls, but that had been different—like a core sample. Samples taken to examine the contents of a human body. Which would only make sense if the sampler didn't know what was in a human.

Reality shifted a few degrees. A sense of being off-kilter roared through his skull. The normal order of his world trembled. His throat tightened. "They're alien. They have to be."

"We're being attacked by robot alien bugs?" Diver said. "That can't be right."

"Attacked by *carnivorous* robot alien bugs," Izy corrected.

Trax hefted her shield and spoke, her voice hoarse. "We're not being attacked. We're being harvested. It's an old Earth abattoir."

"Nothing Earth about it." Izy leaned on his plasma sword. "We should be recording this. Who in a hundred light-years will believe us?"

No wonder the disparate events hadn't made sense. Bill had been trying to squash them all into neat little boxes that they didn't fit, couldn't fit. Even this revelation had its problems.

"Why are they harvesting humans? Aren't they machines?" he muttered.

Trax adjusted her grip on her claw. "I never disassembled that bug. What if it's an exoskeleton, and there's some little critter hiding inside?"

"Makes sense," Diver said, his words coming fast. "They're separating the components at the macro level. Inside the machines, they could mash the bits up and run them through centrifuges and filters to get the proteins they need. Their biology has to be different, so they can't chow down on us unprocessed."

"I didn't sign up to be protein shake." Fitz took a step back. "We have to get the hell out of here."

Their lives were at risk but from more than one direction. Bill understood. He finally understood. BILT4 was on Eclipse for some juicy alien tech. Had Beth known as well? Had she been deliberately vague for operational security or because he wouldn't have believed her? Both Izy and Fitz were right. They needed to record the scene and slip away. Sturt wouldn't be part of this. He was too focused on the colony's success. He was slimy, but he'd have to take action to protect his workers. Enlightened self-interest, even with BILT4 working him hard. Gods, he hoped so. If Sturt was in on it, they were screwed.

Trax started forward in a half crouch. She was going the wrong way.

"What are you doing?" Bill hissed.

"I see movement. They're not all dead. We have to save them."

He tore his gaze away from the disassembly and checked. His stomach churned. She was right. The pile was free of bugs, but an arm flopped weakly off to one side, and closer, a head rocked back and forth, the body under the crushing weight of others. A background hum of machinery stole any chances for cries or moans to reach him.

Any delay would see these people vivisected alive. Yet, trying to save them stank of suicide. By rights, his focus should be on returning with evidence. That and the fab crew. He was the one who brought them in. Just as Beth had sent him to Marrick Prime. Had that been Beth's rationale for saving him? Were the victims like the locals he'd left to die? Self-loathing bayed at the walls of his mind. Trax was right. He couldn't go without trying.

"Diver, can your explosives bring down the tunnel?"

The kid gave him a worrying look. "Can't say. They're just tubes with liquid boom juice. I couldn't test them, right?"

Oh, for a team of meathead operatives.

Amy was already following her boss. They couldn't all go—an exit had to be protected. Izy didn't seem the sort to stand back.

"Fitz, can you keep boom juice boy safe?"

Diver tapped his homemade grenades. "Hey, I can help."

The kid didn't get it. "Help by being our way out. Fitz, can you?"

The man gripped his spear with both hands, his knuckles white, and his eyes wild. "Yeah, yeah, I think I can."

The response didn't fill Bill with confidence, but it would have to do. He hurried after the women, the exposed route giving him goosebumps. Izy sauntered across, though his eyes tracked the bugs closely, and his paces grew longer as he went. The bugs appeared content with their grisly work and ignored the intruders. It couldn't last.

At the base of the pile, Trax spoke to Amy. Bill dropped the point of his shaking pistol. He should have had less coffee before all this. A year's less.

Trax pointed. "See that woman halfway up on the left? She's mostly in the clear."

And trying to pull herself free, the weak actions stymied by another pair of legs that interlocked hers like woven fabric. Dried blood covered her eyes from a scalp wound.

Bill nodded. "A good choice."

"There are a couple near the top. If you and Izy go for—"

"Whoa," Bill said. "Let's try one together. If we don't all die horribly, we can go again."

Trax got in his face. "We can't leave them, and we don't know how much time we have. You wanted *my* crew. We're doing it *my* way."

Arguing with Trax would draw unwanted attention. And the odds of changing her mind were lottery low. And, he admitted, he didn't want to leave anyone behind. He couldn't handle another Marrick Prime.

He stepped on a body. The flesh gave slightly, rotating on the bone beneath with a squelch. His second boot pressed down on a small chest, and the ribs cracked audibly, causing him to fall forward. The stench was rich, putrid, earthy. He breathed through his mouth, but that only sucked the cloying foulness across his tongue. Gore coated his pistol, his gloves, the entire front of his suit. He dared not look at

Izy in case the man's reflection mirrored his own. As Izy continued up and to the left, Bill gritted his teeth and pulled himself higher.

Right against the face of Crumpler. When they'd last met, the medic's physical prowess had dwarfed his, and her matter-of-fact demeanor had steadied him. The juxtaposition to her tortured state beat at his psyche. Her death couldn't have been easy.

He placed his free hand on her forehead. "I'm sorry I can't return the favor."

Her eyes shot open, and a tiny stream of piss wet his pants.

"Crumpler?"

"Bill Hayden?" A dry whisper.

"Yeah."

"Help me, please."

The plea drove into his heart, twisted around, and hacked at the edges for good measure. She was buried deep. Sense dictated that he leave her and follow Trax's suggestion. Izy was already near the top.

"I'm going to try. You're under a lot of... debris. I need you to keep quiet. Can you do that for me?"

Her eyes twitched without focus. She moaned.

"Crumpler. This is going to hurt, but I need you to keep quiet. Do you understand?"

"Yes. Yes."

Teasing at the surrounding bodies, he searched for the angle of her torso. It was mostly downward. That might give him a chance. He holstered his pistol, gripped an unclothed arm with a forest of dark hairs, and strained with all his might. The attached body shifted, producing a ripple effect on the surrounding dead. Methodically, he worked his way around her, his fingers dry inside gloves, but his palms slick. Crumpler kept up a steady stream of whimpers and moans. He didn't have the heart to quieten her again.

The excavation revealed her stomach and gave him room to reach under her armpits. He squatted and ran his arms beneath hers.

"I'm going to pull. If you can kick, now's the time to do it."

"Hayden, stop."

Bill glanced to the side. Trax stood on the floor, holding a woman in her arms. Amy was climbing the pile, and Izy was on the top, frozen.

A bug approached from the other side of the pile, prodding the dead and continuing toward Bill. He couldn't abandon Crumpler now, and if he fired his pistol, he could bring every bug down on him. Demanding the full effort of every fiber of his muscles, he heaved.

Crumpler sobbed and leaned her head against his.

"Again," he said, whether to her or himself, he couldn't tell.

He pulled.

The bug weaved ever closer.

A third time. Slight movement. Was it in his head? A fourth time. His back ached, the muscles spasming, pain hitting like a cat-o'-nine-tails. Crumpler wobbled. Her body lifted with his effort. Up... up... up. Her weight pressed against him. He took a step back onto nothing and slid headfirst, bringing his chin against his chest to avoid dashing it on the hard floor. Crumpler slammed into him, crushing the air from his lungs.

Above, the bug raised its front, the little appendages flicking. It dropped onto all of its legs and picked its way down the pile, right toward Bill. He had no choice. This was going to be bad. But a trainer had told him once that when things got bad, you solved the problem in front of you and moved to the next. Look too far ahead and you were toast before you ever got there.

"I sure hope you can walk."

He reached for his pistol, an awkward gesture with Crumpler across his chest. The bug scuttled to his feet. He aimed and fired.

CHAPTER 17
BE AFRAID

Trax kneeled on the collection of human misery and accepted a tube of wound seal from Amy's suit's medkit. The painkiller she'd already jabbed should work soon. "We're getting you out of here."

The woman's suit had the name Callis. She was shorter than Trax, her hair was dark, and her face weathered. Trax applied the gel as sparingly as she dared, earning nothing but quickened breathing in response. She'd left her shield on the floor, and the claw dangled from a strap over her shoulder.

"Callis, what's your first name? Mine's Jane, but no one calls me that."

Trax moved onto a gash across the woman's stomach as Amy separated the torn suit. She could have fit her hand inside the ragged skin. A small coil of intestine poked through. Growing up on a farm and working with heavy equipment had given Trax the ability to lock down her empathy. Delays meant death. She tucked the intestine inside, then pressed the flesh together and rubbed more of the gel over a short length, holding the wound for a count of three. When the gel hardened, she continued.

"My crew's here. We're going to rescue you. I know this hurts, but be thankful you're not in an all-hands safety briefing—that really kills."

A whisper. "Angela."

"What was that?" Trax said while moving to inspect a nasty hole in Callis's shoulder. Cracked bone and pooled blood greeted her.

"My… name… is… Angela."

"Nice. We're going to move soon, Angela. I'll carry you until we can get a stretcher."

Sealing the shoulder took the last of the tube and Amy pressing the wound as closed as possible. Any further patches would have to wait. Trax cradled Angela, checking her hold and balance, then lifted the woman as gently as she could. The climb down netted pure nightmare fuel. *Later.* She focused on Amy's advice for foot placement. She reached the ground, drenched in blood.

"Everything's going to be okay. We're down."

What about the others? Trax scanned the pile. Amy had headed back up the pile. The optronic designer had hidden grit. Izy worked feverishly at the top, and Hayden was still down low, mucking about. A bug crawled nearby, but out of his sight.

"Hayden, stop."

Hopefully, he had the brains to freeze and let the bug go on its way. If it took a survivor, they'd have to act, but the longer the bugs ignored them, the more people they could save.

Angela slumped in Trax's arms.

"Don't be afraid," Trax whispered. "I'll cut the bastard in half if I have to."

The woman didn't respond. Trax peered at her face, her glazed eyes. "Angela, are you with me?"

Nothing.

Trax moved a hand slowly to Angela's head and gave her a gentle tap. "Stay with me. We're almost out."

Nothing.

She pulled off a glove and searched for a pulse, moving her fingers again and again across Angela's neck. Dead. Trax scrunched her face, holding pain and fury in check. She placed Angela's body down with care, her hand finding the cause of death. A hole in the woman's back, near a kidney. She must have bled out in seconds once Trax lifted her off the pile. All that for nothing. The bastards. She'd make the bugs pay. She'd turn them into scrap. She'd smelt them down to—

Plasma erupted in a bright flash and a burst of heat. The body of a bug rolled off the pile, landing nearby. A cavity revealed innards of seared cables, chips, and actuators. Not a hint of organics. A dripping liquid caught alight, and flames licked outward.

Trax surveyed the cavern. The bugs had stopped dressing their carcasses. Their front appendages wiggled like they were tasting the air. They dumped the bodies and scurried toward the pile. *Clack, clack, clack, clack.* Like a rain of molten steel.

Fire burned inside her. They'd failed. They couldn't save a single soul. She wanted to lash out. The oncoming bugs were almost welcome. But the brutal sting of failure directed her thoughts to the idiot who had fallen on his back, dragging a corpse with him.

"Hayden, you asshole. What the hell were you thinking?"

"I was thinking of saving lives. This here's Crumpler. Give me a hand."

The urge to punch his smug little face flashed through her like lightning. But Angela lay there as a reminder—Trax had come to save who she could. She'd been right. There were survivors, and each of them deserved a chance, even if Hayden helped.

"Amy, status?"

Crumpler tried to roll off Hayden. If she had a wound like Angela, she'd die, too. There was no time to check. Trax pulled her up. The woman tried to stand, and Trax supported her with a shoulder under her arm. Hayden scrambled to his feet and fired his wretched pistol over and over at the advancing bugs. One exploded, throwing shrapnel at those by its side.

He took Crumpler's other side. "We have to run for it."

"And I was going to do a pirouette." Trax walked Crumpler as fast as the woman's legs could manage. "Amy, where are you?"

"Coming down, boss. I—I couldn't help anyone. There wasn't enough time."

Fuck, fuck, fuckity, fuck. It was a disaster.

Diver ran out of the tunnel, Fitz following hesitantly. Diver ripped two tubes off his suit and rolled them behind Trax. They stopped after only a few meters. The kid was going to blow them up. Two pops, and orange smoke poured from them at a pressure that spun them round and round, hissing all the while.

She dragged Crumpler and Hayden forward, and as they reached the tunnel entrance, she glanced back. The cavern was lost in the orange smoke and so were Amy and Izy.

A shadow, two of them. Her missing crew ran out of the churning smog, coughing, Izy holding her shield.

Amy stumbled to a stop in front of Trax. "What now?"

"Take my place." Trax passed the injured woman to Amy. "Head for the way out. Don't stop for anything. Izy, hand over my shield."

Izy frowned. "You're coming, right, boss? Breaking in a new one sucks."

"I'll be right behind you."

Hayden frowned at her. "Don't be a hero."

"Ain't no such thing."

Shadows moved within the smoke. The bugs hadn't been fooled.

"Move it, or I'll dock your pay."

They retreated as the first two bugs burst into the fresh air.

Hot blood pumped through Trax. Payback time. "Come on, you little factory rejects."

"Time for recycling."

Both Trax and Diver glanced at Fitz.

"Hey, it was all I could think of. If you want poetry, ask Izy."

One of the bugs dashed forward and leaped. Trax settled her shield and steadied her claw. Fitz slapped the bug with his spear, but he failed to activate the EMP. It spun in the air, and Trax punched with her open claw, catching a leg. The bug latched onto her shield, its momentum spinning her around, its weight dragging her to the tunnel floor. She thumbed the shear's controls and immense pressure pushed the two blades of the claw together, snipping off the leg.

The bug twisted, stabbing at her with a small spinning blade. She'd been caught in some nasty bar brawls in her time and used the experience to guide her instincts. She dodged, opening the claw, and returned with a right hook that swept up the bug's front appendages.

"Dinner time's over."

The appendages snapped off, each spinning away. The bug jerked left and right. It had no idea where she was. She released her shield, stepped in, and kicked hard, flipping the bug onto its back. She considered dismembering the monster, but the sound of Hayden's shooting filled her ears. There wasn't time.

Izy, the impetuous ass, had left Amy with Crumpler and run back to slice a chunk from the rear of another bug. The acrid stench was terrible, the smoke eye-watering. Diver grabbed Fitz's spear and jabbed the tip into the bug's exposed innards, activating the EMP. The spear crackled, and the bug collapsed.

"Sorry," Fitz said, as Diver handed back the spear.

"Don't worry. Old people and technology don't mix. Just remember, the zap stick goes zap."

More bugs erupted out of the smoke, interrupting Fitz's angry response. Six, seven, eight, nine—too many. Her crew was screwed. Even Amy. She'd kept going, but she was struggling under Crumpler's weight. *Damn you, Izy.*

"Diver, time for more booms. Throw everything you've got."

"You sure?"

"Wanna end up on that pile?"

"Booms it is."

He grabbed one homemade grenade at a time, activating each and tossing as far as he could. The bugs swarmed past the cylinders. Then the first went off, a bright flash that left confusing afterimages. The pressure wave slapped Trax back and chunks of metal and stone whistled by. The rest exploded in quick succession, and Trax dropped to the ground, covering her ears.

A high-pitched whine refused to leave when she shook her head. She pulled herself upright, thankful her crew did the same. The blast had dispersed the orange smoke, only to replace it with a haze of brown that choked the tunnel. Three of the bugs were immobile, one of them rocking as detonations shot parts and sparks out of a long gash. The rest were righting themselves and advancing. Behind these, more bugs.

"How many are there?"

Diver shivered. "Too many, boss. And I don't think the tunnel's gonna cave in."

The shaft they'd dug was too far away. There was no other choice. She didn't want to die here, but she'd been the one to let them come. "Everybody, run. I'll hold them off as long as I can."

Hayden brushed off his pistol. "Your scissors can't do much. I'll stay. Get your crew out of here."

The bugs reached them, ending the argument. Hayden swapped the charge brick in his pistol and fired on the bugs at a pace that would melt his barrel. The armor on the back of the machines soaked up the damage, requiring him to make several well-aimed hits to take one out.

Trax cut into the first that reached them, slicing into the bug's thorax, but not taking it offline. It lashed out, slicing her left forearm with one leg tip and gouging her thigh with another. Pain and wetness spread quickly. Furious, she swung her claw battering the bug backward, and Hayden finished it with a shot at point-blank range.

Several bugs high on the wall scuttled past them. One kicked off, arcing toward Diver. He rolled out of the way and stumbled toward Fitz. The bug twisted around and went for the pair. Fitz, his eyes wide with terror, stabbed and activated the EMP. *Snap!* One side of the bug collapsed. The remaining legs dragged it closer.

Izy ran to them, swinging his crazy plasma blade. Trax started toward them, but the bugs were everywhere.

Another bug jumped. Hayden shot wildly, scoring a glancing hit. Trax darted forward, and using all her weight, brought down her claw before the bug could slice the surveyor open. Its legs bent under the force, but she hadn't dented its armor at all.

Fitz screamed.

He'd lost his spear, and one of the bugs held his right leg in pincers uncomfortably similar to her shears. Izy was bogged down, slicing through another bug, and Diver danced with a third, entirely defenseless.

No!

Trax pushed Hayden. "Help me."

If he didn't follow, he was on his own from here. She ran, letting her fury protect her from the growing pain in her arm and the sullen throb in her leg. And her shoulder—that one was a real bitch. The heavy meds she'd taken must be wearing off. She shrugged it all off. It wasn't going to matter for long.

The bug sheared right through Fitz's leg. It was on his torso instantly, stabbing, cutting. He screamed and thrashed against the tunnel. Trax grabbed one metal leg and severed another. The bug, in a frenzy or not caring about its own existence, continued chopping up Fitz. His screams stopped, though his limbs flailed under the force of the bug's attack.

She went for another leg, and the bug rolled its thorax and grasped her claw.

A stream of plasma slammed into the bug, heat searing Trax's arm through the suit tear. More plasma, everywhere. It was a shooting gallery. How? She wriggled her arm out of the claw and backed away, her head low. She dared do no more.

Figures approached. She couldn't make out their details. Her eyes were watering, and she was blinking hard against the flashes of light. Had Ware come on Sturt's orders? Well, he could shove his land stakes up his ass.

Details resolved. Black uniforms. BILT4 security. The corporation was saving her life.

Damn, she felt dirty.

CHAPTER 18
PRESUMED GUILTY

B ill crashed back and forth, unable to protect himself in the shaft's narrow confines. He launched from darkness into light, hands grabbing and dragging him to the side. They rolled him over, and, with a click, the cable was away, ready for the next evacuation.

He crawled several meters, then stood, blinking against the bright lights of multiple vehicles. A bloody sunset stained the sky, a perfect match for the horror he'd left below. The fabricator crew had Crumpler on the ground, leaning against Bill's rover. Harry was operating the winch while a BILT4 guard watched, his rifle out, pointing downward, and yet with a threat in his stance as if humans were the real enemy.

The next out of the shaft was a security guard. Then another, and another. They were retreating. How many of the bugs were there? The last up was Karlo, and he fired as he went.

"Frag 'em, three-second fuse," Karlo said as he pulled his feet out of the hole.

"Fire in the hole!" A guard adjusted a rifle and fired three small balls down the shaft—the bastards were armed like soldiers.

The corporates cleared the area, and a series of blasts rocked the ground and spewed light and smoke up the shaft.

Bill used the distraction to disassemble his pistol and pocket the pieces. Trouble was certain, but he couldn't shoot his way out of this. Karlo and his goons hadn't left them to die, nor had they killed Bill on sight. The situation wasn't as bad as it could be. That was something. It also provoked the cynical part of Bill's mind to ask why and what BILT4 could possibly gain from coming to the rescue. If he could keep everyone cool, he might get answers.

After assigning two guards to watch the shaft, Karlo stormed over to the fab crew, gesturing imperiously for Bill to join him.

"You lot," Karlo said, spitting out the words, "are the dumbest fucking dirt-licking clowns ever spat out of the League. What do you think you were doing? Thought you'd go for a bit of an underground adventure? Thought you were up for bug-hunting like some yokel? You don't know what you've done, do you?"

Trax growled. Actually growled. Bill needed to act.

"We appreciate the save. I think it's fair to say we underestimated what's down there. Thank you."

"I don't need your thanks, but I expect your complete cooperation. You will come back to our compound for debriefing, and you will cooperate fully, or you'll spend the rest of your miserable lives in a three-by-three cell... if you're lucky."

"Come here so I can shove your threats down your throat, merc." Trax stomped over to Karlo. "We're not under your jurisdiction."

"You are what I say you are, or I'll shove you back down the hole."

The two stubborn fools faced off, muscles tense, eyes locked.

Bill closed on the pair, relaxing his shoulders and face. "We found a survivor. She needs medical attention. It's almost night, and surely, we can all agree that's not a good time to be here. The bugs are upset."

Trax didn't show any sign that she'd heard him. She wasn't going to like what he said next, but there were plenty of armed guards, and Karlo wasn't going to take no for an answer.

"Trax, it makes sense to go with them. Crumpler needs help and we need a safe place to stay for the night. Let's leave tomorrow's problems for tomorrow."

"Listen to the spook," Karlo said between gritted teeth. "He knows how things work."

Bill waited. Karlo knew, too? Were his personnel records pinned to a noticeboard somewhere? The corporates could have infiltrated the colony network right from the start. It didn't matter now. It was Karlo playing a power game.

"You're a spook?" Trax said, her voice a dark mix of confusion and anger.

Damn, she'd caught it. "I used to work for the League."

"He worked for the LSA," Karlo said, his tension mutating into sick enjoyment.

"I did. Not anymore. I quit."

"You've been playing us all along, haven't you?" Trax grabbed Bill's suit. Little flecks of saliva wet his face. "You've been spying this whole time. Survey, my ass. I get it. You've been playing your little games while people die. Hell, you fucking recruited us, didn't you? How much did you know of what was down there? You knew it all. You wanted us all armed, and even when we didn't have the rifles, you didn't care. Fitz died down there, you bastard. You killed him."

Bill tried to pull away. "No, it's not like that at all. I had no idea."

Izy came to Trax's side. "The agency wouldn't let you leave. No one leaves. We've all heard the stories. Your kind are everywhere, spying, reporting—"

"Assassinating," Amy added. "Can't have any dissidents in the League."

"It's not like that. I wasn't some wet work operator. And the rumors are only that. The agency likes them because they can't be everywhere. It keeps people on the straight and narrow."

Trax pushed him away. "You're as vile as the corporates. Making everyone live in fear so they're easy to control."

Karlo, the bastard, laughed. "I've got nothing on this guy. He's killed more people than you've met."

"He's lying," Bill said, settling his suit.

"Do tell us," Amy said, her voice deceptively sweet. "What did you do for the agency?"

"It's classified. I won't ever get to tell anyone. That part of my life is locked away. Wait." He held up his arms when Trax shifted her balance forward. "I tried to stop bad things happening. I tried to save lives. Sometimes I did. Sometimes I couldn't."

"This has been fun, but I'm busy," Karlo said. "Chi, pack 'em up. If any resist, shoot them. Don't ask for permission."

Thanks, Karlo. Now you've really shat on everything. Getting Trax and her crew to see reason was going to take some serious work. The security officer might have done it out of spite, but had he deliberately driven a wedge between Bill and them?

Several guards formed a ring around them. Trax crossed her arms and ignored their orders. As her gaze, sharpened by disgust, drilled into Bill, he wished she'd remain calm. For his sake, yes, and for hers. The more he thought about Karlo rescuing them, the less sense it made.

It was Harry who brought Trax down from the brink. "Boss, think about the crew."

Those five words were enough to bring reason, if not calm, to Trax. Guards led them to a six-wheeled vehicle with a large storage box on the back. Inside, folding benches ran down both sides. Bill gave the crew space to board—Harry and Trax lifted Crumpler—and then he followed.

Karlo poked his head between the closing doors. "You should know, Hayden did Marrick Prime."

And with that lie, he shut the doors. The clear snap of bolts said they were very much prisoners. Bill looked warily at the crew to gauge their reaction. No one met his eyes, even Trax. He was beneath contempt, their behavior said. He was as unworthy of attention as a pile of shit left by a stray dog.

The ride was rough. Crumpler groaned whenever they bounced, and Bill held onto his bench tightly. With no conversation, he withdrew into his mind. Aliens. The corporates must know. They had too many guards for a science mission. Perhaps they were expecting trouble. How large was the BILT4 compound? So far, every question he'd found an answer for came with a dozen new ones. And any poor souls stuck on that pile were destined to be so much meat.

There was nothing he could do. It was Marrick Prime all over again. He'd joined the agency to make a difference, but all he'd become was an observer of suffering—if not a catalyst. And when he'd left, the cycle continued. No matter what he did, it'd always come back to that.

THE VEHICLE STOPPED and the doors opened. Armed guards ordered them out as a pair of robust gates clanged shut in the distance. Floodlights washed the ground before a set of four plain buildings with a long set of garages. Each structure bore the BILT4 logo and the word Security across their fronts. Bill turned a slow circle, absorbing all he could.

The compound was a full-blown facility, a town in its own right. Three-meter-high walls stretched into the distance. Along these, observation posts shot beams outward, surrounding the compound with a moat of light. Suspicious lumps segmented the wall at regular intervals. They had to be concealed weapon mounts. Had they installed them at the start, or was this a recent upgrade? What he would do for a satellite image to check. Unless BILT4 was into the satellite code, too, and all he'd find was a middle finger.

Large, low buildings filled one end of the compound, separated by once-manicured grass gone to seed and dust-covered paths. Nearby, a few dour corporate citizens went about their tasks, unconcerned with the new arrivals, but there was an emptiness to the place—the desperation of a rundown industrial town. This was helped by a mound of junk, glinting here and there while the bulk was shrouded in shadow. He strained his eyes. Panels, struts, perhaps vehicles, a conspicuous waste of recyclable materials—and a story of a dire failure rate. All was not well in the corporate oasis.

A glittering tower stood at the center of the compound, standard corporate opulence, albeit on a small scale. Wagner would be on the top floor, ordering her minions from the comfort of mid-level mediocrity.

At the other end of the compound, partially obscured by the depression it rested in, loomed a dropship easily more than thirty meters wide. His brows rose. He hadn't heard they had one of their own. Lights turned that part of the compound into day, and the purposeful strides of many people despite the hour reminded him of the Agency office in Apollo. So this was where the party was rocking. Why?

A four-wheeler pulled a trailer filled with cargo crates toward it. What the hell were they prepping for?

"This way," a guard said, pointing toward the second security building with the tip of his rifle.

"Wait," Karlo called while exiting his vehicle. "Take them to the cafeteria. Ms. Wagner wants to see them."

"Not Crumpler," Bill said, seizing the moment. "The bugs had her for most of the day. She's seriously injured. If you don't get her medical attention, your boss will be talking to a corpse."

Karlo frowned, but he could hardly argue with the obvious—unless he didn't care if she died. The crew had her on the ground, resting as comfortably as possible. Crumpler's eyes were closed, her forehead was moist, and her head lolled to one side. She wouldn't last much longer.

"You don't tell me what to do, Spook. I've got your number."

Bill raised his hands. This couldn't become about him. "I get it. This is your patch. I'm not trying to claim it. We don't need another death, that's all I'm saying."

The cogs in Karlo's small brain rotated. Bill could practically hear them grinding.

"Leave the injured one. March the rest to the cafeteria."

Bill opened his mouth to protest, but Karlo raised a finger.

"I'll get her to the hospital. We're better than your kind."

Trax shot Bill a dirty look, as if he'd stolen her job or hadn't bargained well enough—or she simply hated him and wanted him to know it. So many possibilities.

The guards led them single file to the central tower. On the way, he looked for, but couldn't see, the compound's power plant. It had to be substantial, and if he read the design of their operation right, he suspected it would be within the confines of the compound walls.

The tower was impractical for the conditions of a freshly terraformed world. Its engineering must be impressive. The subtle security cameras suggested they didn't trust their own, a sensible precaution in any large group, but they hadn't been placed with the necessary paranoia. He filed the knowledge away. He should develop escape plans and assign difficulty and survivability ratings. The former would be high and the latter low. Hopefully, Trax and her crew weren't considering the same. They wouldn't have a chance. Karlo was an asshole, but he knew what he was doing.

A guard swiped them inside and directed them to the cafeteria. It was large enough for maybe thirty at a time. Two corporates hurried out, meals in hand. They stared at the colonists as if getting a first glimpse of an alien.

Bill went to the coffee machine and started filling cups, not checking to see if the guards approved. They'd stop him if they wanted to. It was always good to test the boundaries in a non-threatening way. He put the drinks on a tray, placing this near the crew who had settled around a table.

"I'm sorry about Fitz. He seemed a good guy. I wish I'd had the chance to know him better."

Trax pulled the tray to the center of the table. "Fuck off, Hayden."

"Listen, please. We're in a tough situation. Until we're out of the compound, we have to be careful. They have all the power."

Izy passed the coffees around, keeping two for himself, and leaving none for Bill.

"And you want it?" Amy asked.

"No. I don't want power. I don't want this. I don't want to be here. I don't care about this planet at all." The words slipped out too fast for him to stop.

"Or the folk on it." Trax slammed a fist on the table, shaking the mugs and spilling coffee. "If you don't want me to reshape your face, sit in a corner and hope that I forget you exist."

Sighing, Bill walked away and sat by a window. He watched people and vehicles go by. Surely, it must be possible to find common ground. The compound was a parasite on the colony's back, but there was no other host for it, and it wasn't like they could jump to another.

Trax's hatred for corporations was clear. He didn't love them either. That had to be put aside, as well as Wagner's machinations. Survival was a mutual need, and if BILT4 could contain the aliens by itself, it would have done so by now. Trax, Wagner, Karlo, even Sturt—they had to come together. If only he could write a report and file it, so some other poor bastard had to figure out how.

CHAPTER 19
IT'S COMPLICATED

B
eing the head of a corporate operation came with all the luxury expected from exploiting the average citizen of the League. Trax sneered at a brushed-gold desk and the transparent chair upon which Wagner appeared to float.

Three large displays blinked out of existence and Wagner stood, smoothing the lines of a navy-blue dress with a useless padded shoulder jacket. Three hours the bitch had kept them waiting.

"Thank you all for coming. I can only imagine what you have gone through. Please follow me." Wagner walked over to a wide door that slid open. "We have much to discuss, and I'm sure you are exhausted."

"What's happened to Crumpler?" Trax demanded.

"She's receiving the best care. A very resilient type, our lead doctor has informed me. The prognosis is good, if challenging."

"I want to see her."

The corporate nodded, her brow furrowing earnestly. She'd probably spend the next day stretching it tight. "Once the doctors confirm she is stable, you will be more than welcome to do so. Right now, they would even chase me away. Please."

Wagner went through the door into another room. Two guards watched the crew, one on either side. The elevator behind them might as well have been a wall for all that it was going to help her leave. She stomped after Wagner, swinging past the desk and knocking over a small plaque. It was petty, but it felt good.

The second room was all windows and a circle of padded chairs, the type you could sink into, rest your eyes, and immediately fall asleep in. Wagner slipped between two and raised her hands in welcome. "Take a seat. Let's ignore all the formalities and speak as equals."

Izy crossed his arms. "Not so equal when you have guns pointed at us."

Good man, Izy. At least one member of her crew wasn't fooled. Trax didn't expect any of them to be, but it was good to know they had her back. Especially after Fitz. She ground her teeth. By Abuk, she was going to hate prepping the notice for his next of kin. He had grandchildren. It was going to tear her heart out.

"My apologies. One becomes so used to the protection and the lack of privacy that it's easy to forget they are there." Wagner smiled at the guards. "I'll be fine. You may go."

"Are you sure, Ms. Wagner?"

"Absolutely. Please talk to my chef. Let's have some refreshments brought up."

"Yes, Ms. Wagner."

The guards filed out, revealing Hayden, lurking at the back of the room. Trax had thought him odd from the first time she'd met him. Rumors had suggested he was shady. Now she knew he was behind an orbital bombardment, it made sense. He was a psychopath, willing to do whatever helped him achieve his murky goals.

His mask of concern disgusted her, so she showed him her back.

Harry was the first to sit. Amy and Diver were next. That annoyed Trax, but then they all were suffering from sleep deprivation, and they'd been through a real mess. In solidarity, she took the chair opposite Wagner. Hayden gave Trax a wide berth and took a seat halfway between her and Wagner. Out of strangling distance.

"The past twenty-four hours have been tragic and unsettling. I know there is a natural rivalry between our two groups, even though we have different goals. At the best of times, I like to think of that as healthy. This is not the best of times. Let us lay our cards down. For starters, call me Elyse."

The woman might as well have trotted out a jingle and a limited-time offer. Still, Trax wanted answers before she and the crew returned to Staging. And if any more goons threatened them, Wagner could become a useful bargaining chip.

"What do you want?" Trax demanded.

"It's not about what I want. I am here to answer your questions to the best of my ability. Ask away, Jane. I can call you that, can't I?"

Ignoring the false sincerity, Trax readied herself for Wagner's full flow of bullshit. "You knew about all this, didn't you? You're here for the aliens. The whole interference study was crap. That's why you've never solved it."

"The interference has proven challenging. We have a team working on the various frequencies or some such. I can assure you that we have a potential solution that could be ready in as little as six months. But I don't want to deceive you. I said cards down, and I meant it. We underwrote the Eclipse project because we believed there was a strong possibility of alien relics. This has been mutually beneficial for the colony. Without BILT4's funding, the timeline would have been significantly extended and none of you would be here. Synergies create possibilities."

The word salad made Trax want to gag. "You did all this because you wanted to play with murderous alien robots?"

Wagner crossed her legs. "No, not at all. This mission has always been about the future of humanity."

Diver, who had kicked off his boots, said, "Sure, and you give chocolate eggs to all the little kiddies, too."

"I understand your skepticism. There have been good corporations and bad. It's a very human thing. But I want you to consider what drives us. The terraforming on this planet is possible thanks to secrets gleaned from alien technology. Many medical procedures—life-saving ones—were inspired by scientists studying the scraps of those that came before. Even reaching this planet may never have happened if we were reliant on human ingenuity alone. And each discovery has taken decades to reach the market thanks to the impossible bureaucracy and regulations of the League. I'm sure Bill could tell you all about the effect of government interference."

Hayden squirmed at the use of his name. Good.

Wagner continued, warming to her spiel. "BILT4 wants to make money. That's what corporations do. It's more than that. This is a very high-risk operation, one that could have easily been rejected on that ground. Thankfully, the board believes in advancing humanity. And progress eventually filters down to all. Ultimately, everyone wins."

"Tell that to the suckers being vivisected," Izy said, his feet resting on a second chair.

He was right. Standard corporate practice. A balance sheet with a few crumbs to a charity here or a sop to public good there, all to distract from the destruction of lives. Trax put her hands on the soft armrests. She had no chance of squeezing answers from Wagner's dry soul.

Shock ran across Wagner's face. "Vivisected? I hadn't heard this. Perhaps, in order to answer your questions, I must hear your tale in full."

Diver was the first to jump in with details. Amy and Izy followed up. Harry remained silent, her expression grim. They'd only told the mechanic the bare bones of the trip. For Trax, each refreshed detail seared like a shaving of hot metal. Hayden stewed silently, hopefully suffering from the guilt of his deception. If they'd known, they could have been properly armed with backup.

"Jane, Ismail, everyone. This tragedy breaks my heart. Across every planet of the League, there has never been a substantiated account of active non-human sentient beings." Wagner paused, one hand gesticulating. "This is like a natural disaster. Nothing can rewind the events or bring back those who have passed. However, BILT4 will do whatever we can to help with the recovery."

"God damn it!" Trax left the circle of chairs and gestured to the night sky, the stars obscured by the intensity of the compound's illumination. "A natural disaster? You made this. Hayden showed us you were covering things up."

She turned back to Wagner. "When did you know they were alive

—or whatever they are? When did you know they were hunting us? When did it all start?"

"The same time you did, I assure you. There were never any power signatures or heat intensities to warn us."

"What I want to know," Hayden said, breaking his sullen silence, "is why they are active now. You altered the survey data, so you knew what to hide—and where. Are you claiming they stayed asleep through the comet falls, the atmospheric converters, the subsoil preparation, and the biosphere seeding but woke for no particular reason mid Phase 2?"

"I'm no scientist, Bill, just a memo maker. How can we rule out the effects of terraforming? And there are far more of you colonists digging and building than my little team. Let's not worry about blame. In our arrogance, we humans like to think of ourselves as the template for the universe. I believe there are species of insect that have long cycles of dormancy before brief and frenzied activity. Perhaps that is what we've stumbled upon. Whatever the cause, we have to look to what's next, not what's happened."

Wagner gestured with a hand, and a chime sounded.

"Ah, the refreshments at last."

The door slid open, and two corporates entered, carrying a table. One pressed a button, and the top expanded, creating a long surface. They left the room and returned several times with plates of food and pitchers of drink. Trax's mouth watered at the sight of fresh strawberries. The bulk of colony food was processed for efficiency of transport and storage, and even the restaurants could only do so much to disguise the reality.

"Boss?" Diver asked.

She nodded. What was the point of starving? And they might as well burn through Wagner's budget. The woman hadn't seen Trax's crew eat.

The chairs emptied. Hayden didn't follow. He moved closer to Wagner and engaged her in a quiet, intense conversation.

Screw that. She gave up on strawberries and cut in. "Cards down, right? What are you two talking about?"

"It's good that the three of us can have a private moment." Wagner gave an exaggerated sigh. "There are hard truths that have to be faced."

Hayden leaned forward. "I'm worried about the number of bugs and whether they can produce more. They're machines, so they don't need to grow. Trax, you're the manufacturing expert. How long would it take you to build a bug if you had everything you needed?"

Making more of them? Curse Hayden. "It depends on if the precursors are ready. The mechanical connections would be the slowest. Six to twelve hours, minimum. But if there was a production line running, it could be anywhere from a one churned out at a time to thousands."

Her heart sank as she considered her own words. Thousands and thousands of the bugs burrowing, hunting, slaughtering. The colony was on the edge of obliteration. Her land stake was so much ash. Her dreams of farming, of a little winery, of living by the seasons and planting her roots shattered, cutting her soul with a million shards. That was nothing to the suffering of her brothers, her sisters, and every Abuk-loved variation of humanity trying to make an honest living.

"I know there's little trust between us right now." Hayden left his chair and started reaching as if to shake hands before Trax's glare made the liar reconsider. "Think about it. We need to present a united front to Sturt and make him understand the threat, to make him agree that the building queue has to wait. The schedule needs to be torn up. And, I hate to say it, we'll need to coordinate with BILT4." His face twitched. Was that a wink or a twitch? Was he trying to give a message, or it was a sign of the rivalry between the two oppressive pillars of society?

"Coordinate? Screw that. Eclipse doesn't need corporate goons. Staging has the facilities to arm every worker. We'll go blast the hell out of every bug. And if they have a factory... we can fill a rover full of explosives and send it to the stars. I'll personally throw them into smelters and liquefy the remains."

"Trax, it's a complicated situation."

The eyes of her crew were on her. Good. Her fingers curled. Fury beat within her. Hayden wanted to play politics while those things were out there. "Complicated? This is the simplest situation I've ever been in."

She turned to Wagner. "I want out of here. Play your games with Hayden. Me and my crew, we're going home."

The room descended into silence.

Wagner lowered her eyes, then left the circle of chairs and stood in front of the windows. She gestured, and the window turned into a map with a spiderweb overlay around a hill.

"Thank you for sharing your experiences. I said I would answer your questions, and I feel I have done that. However, the questions that you didn't ask are just as important. My scientists have been mapping the tunnel network bored by the entosynths—what you call bugs—and they've now accounted for the facility you discovered. Where Jose found you was this nexus here." She pointed to a south-western thread. "Based on what you shared, the situation is dire— beyond dire. The signals keep growing and the tunnels continue to expand. I'm told the seismic readings put the number of bugs into the thousands."

"Who cares? If we need a bigger bang, we can dismantle the power grid, haul one of the fusion reactor cells, and blast everything right up to the edge of Staging. It'll hurt, but we can rebuild and regrow."

"Trax," Hayden said quietly, "that won't happen."

Elyse gestured, and the map disappeared. "Bill is correct. It's simply not feasible. Imagine the panic for a start. But I understand your fears and your desire to help. I'd like to offer you a chance to make a difference. We are undertaking an expedition to the nexus. All the main tunnels connect there. The entosynths are machines. Maybe we can switch them off and end the threat without further damage."

"Without damage?" Trax shouted. She slapped the back of a chair, tipping it over. "That's what this is about, isn't it? You don't want to blast the bugs because you're still looking for technology to steal."

She turned to her crew. "We're out of here. We'll walk the whole way back if we need to."

"No, you won't." Wagner didn't even make excuses. The corporate turned away as if Trax were no longer there. "Bill, I hate to waste opportunities, and I am short on resources. I need to know where you stand."

"I was only here for the money."

Trax's skin numbed. To say it so brazenly...

Wagner gave the slime a tight smile. "Help me generate discoveries, and you'll have whatever you could wish for."

He was going to work for Wagner. The scum. The scab. Trax grabbed Hayden's suit and dragged him close. "How can you abandon everyone? Don't you care that people are dying? Or is this just another Marrick Prime to you?"

The turd had the gall to look ashamed. "It is. It's living for another day. I wish you understood that."

She pushed him hard, and he fell over a chair.

"Break's over, crew. I hope you had your fill. We're going." Trax headed for the door.

It opened, revealing three guards, including the asshole Karlo. They had rifles pointed at her chest.

"I'm afraid not," Wagner said. "I'm a fair person. I gave you an opportunity, and you turned it down. Now, you're a liability. It appears that you didn't make it out of the tunnel after all. Jose tried to save you, but it was too late. The report is going to make me cry; I can practically read it already. Jose, make sure the bodies aren't found. Burn them or whatever."

"Yes, Ms. Wagner." Karlo's tone was flat, without a hint of pity.

He was going to murder her and her crew.

"Wait," Hayden said. "You wanted my expertise. Here it is. To dispose of them neatly, wait until the morning so you aren't risking your people. Dump them down the shaft they drilled and seal it. Let the bugs finish them off." He gave a little laugh, his evil bubbling to the surface. "You said you were fair. They'll even get to fight for their lives."

Wagner put a hand to her chest. "Bill, I'm shocked. And I like it. We really should have talked much earlier."

Trax snarled. No way would she walk like a sheep to her death. She charged forward, hoping the sudden action would surprise the guards. She caught one and knocked his rifle aside. Leaning in close, she swung her elbow up and hit him under the chin, cracking his teeth together.

Who was next? A dark blur moved—the stock of Karlo's rifle. It expanded to fill her vision.

A flash.

Pain.

Darkness.

CHAPTER 20
STAY FOR THE NIGHTLIFE

"I'm going to rip you open from anus to armpit!" Trax shouted as Karlo's jack-booted thugs pushed her down the shaft. She pressed her legs against the sides, stopping her descent and keeping her head in the late morning sun. A blond-haired, vacant-eyed guard kicked down on her shoulder. She dropped until the slack cable played out, grunting as her knitting flesh tore.

The sudden stop jolted every nerve ending. She spun, her arms fastened firmly behind her.

"I've got you," Harry said, catching Trax's feet. "Keep still."

Gritting her teeth, Trax squashed her desire to kick, punch, and maim. It built a pressure inside strong enough to turn carbon into diamond. Izy helped as well, steadying her legs as she descended to the tunnel floor. A circle of light around her exaggerated the darkness beyond.

"Release the cable," a guard demanded.

Trax put her hand behind her back, stopping Harry from complying. "No, I'm not making it any easier for them."

The cable tugged side to side. She took the thimble full of pleasure the pointless resistance gave. Tension released, and the cable fell, severed cleanly. The circle of light winked out, and she looked up, ready to berate her crew's imprisonment. Her pupils expanded, and she caught the silhouette of Karlo. He must be so smug.

"Getting in a last gloat, are you?"

He laughed, a sharp bark. "I am not a cruel man. I would have shot you, neat, clean, and relatively painlessly."

"Just following orders? You're a monster—don't tell yourself otherwise."

"A monster? Your partner is the monster, more than the bugs. He reduced a planet to a graveyard and switched allegiances faster than taking a piss. Now, the sick bastard wants you cut up. Me, I take no pleasure in this. I have professional dedication. I do what needs to be done and no more. Step out of the way."

"Why?" Trax demanded, but she heard a faint whistle and pushed her crew clear.

Several tubes hit the ground and bounced out of the light.

"Flares. I asked the boys to make sure they last two hours each. See, I'm no monster."

Karlo went out of sight, issuing a muffled order. A semicircle of darkness closed over the shaft like an eclipse, and the whistling of wind and crunch of footsteps shut off.

"Well, this isn't good."

"Amy, you need to learn some proper invectives," Izy said from Trax's right. "We're arm deep in an elephant's ass, and it's got the runs."

"Enough," Trax kneeled. "Is anyone near a flare?"

"I'm getting them, boss." Scraping confirmed Diver's efforts. "Think I got them all, four ain't much."

Not even enough to last until night. And it was always night underground. Karlo was screwing with them. Torturing them with hope.

"Should I set one off?"

"Not yet, not until we start moving."

"Tell me we're going away from the bugs," Amy said. "I mean, I miss Fitz, but he was pretty dead. And I don't think we can save anyone else."

"What about busting out?" Harry asked.

"Karlo might need an AI to count his fingers for him, but we can count on the bastard to secure the shaft."

"Izy said it right." Trax closed her eyes—not that it mattered in the dark. "We can't expect an exit here. And yeah, Amy, we're heading the other way. We're going to walk fast. Karlo might have someone watching. That means we'll need to get distance before we can try heading up, even if we find a bug exit. Diver, light the first flare."

She thought of Hayden pushing them around, and Karlo, and Wagner. "Does that sound like a plan? I'm open to suggestions."

The flare lit, covering them with a red glow, but offering no warmth. Her crew looked worried—Izy's casual pose rang false. Corporates had taken their suits for cleaning before they slept, only to return them in the morning with every circuit cooked and all the tools missing. The lack of blood was something, but the scorch marks were stark reminders of their situation. According to Amy, a medic had attended Trax while she was unconscious, looking haunted yet refusing to speak. The gash on Trax's leg had meshed well overnight, and the cleaning of various cuts and scrapes protected her from infection. An odd thing to do for someone you're going to kill.

One by one, her crew agreed with a plan that was as bare as a baby's ass.

"Let's do this."

Diver made a click with his mouth. "Might want to lose the tail, boss."

Trax unclipped the fastener and automatically started winding the short length of cable. She considered tossing it away, but with her pockets empty, it gave a token amount of comfort.

They set off at a good pace, filling the time with ingenious and progressively more elaborate ways to make the unholy trinity of Hayden, Wagner, and Karlo pay for their crimes. After what had to be several kilometers of monotonous consistency, the tunnel forked one heading slightly to the left and the other to the right.

"Any ideas which way?" she asked.

"We could split up and head down each one a short distance," Amy said.

Izy bared his teeth. "I don't like that. If we encounter the bugs, I need all of you to distract them while I run away."

"We're all in this together," Trax said. "If we split up, we can't help each other, and we also half the lifespan of the flares. What's it going to be, left or right?"

Right won, three to two. Trax thought the left was probably more in line with the route to Staging, but it was only a feeling, and the right tunnel would at least take them farther from the compound.

They had been walking for several minutes along the gently curving tunnel when the red, glossy covering of the walls stopped, leaving raw stone.

"Must have been lunch break," Izy said.

Harry inspected the edge, running her hand along it. "Rough. Perhaps ready to adhere to whenever it's extended."

Curiously, the cabling continued along the top of the tunnel. But curiosity wouldn't get them to safety.

Trax was about to move them on when Diver raised his free hand. "Do you feel something?"

"What?" Trax turned, hoping he'd noticed a breeze, but the air was still.

Diver pressed a hand against the ground. "Vibration."

"He's right," Amy said.

"Okay, anyone want to turn back? Yeah, I don't want to lose time either. Stay cautious and keep moving."

As they continued, the ground began to dance, and an indistinct grinding built into an almighty crunching.

"I hate to shit on anyone's sandwich," Izy said, "but I'd like to change my vote. Right was definitely wrong."

Amy cupped her hands around her eyes. "In the distance—there's a shape in the tunnel. I know it's getting dusty, but it's there."

"Everyone, stay calm. I'll take the flare and investigate. If I run back, you run, too. If anything happens to me, light a flare and run. Generally, run."

"No, boss," Harry said. "Last time we split, you almost died, and I got jumped. I'm staying with you."

Trax sighed. She was the boss, yes, but they had a friendship, and the two didn't always mix. Damn, she was tired of giving orders.

"Anyone going to listen to me?"

A chorus of denials.

"All right, together. I'd call this a mutiny, but, Izy—"

"Arrr, me hearties," Izy said, placing a hand over one eye. "These scallywags mean you no harm."

"Keep that up, and I'll show you harm."

Trax gave Diver a friendly shove forward before Izy could dredge up more pirate-speak. He held the flare out as he led the way through fog-thick dust. Trax spat, but it did nothing to change the gritty coating growing in her mouth. The shape Amy had spotted resolved into a roughly spherical boulder close to a meter in diameter. It was made from broken rocks of various sizes, these pieces glued together with thin lines of red. More boulders filled the floor of the tunnel behind it, reminding Trax of the time she'd spilled ball bearings down a fuel line as an apprentice.

"Looks like a rock monster had the shits."

"Diver," Izy shouted over the racket, "I can't take you anywhere."

"If this is where you take your dates, no wonder you never get a second."

Trax ran her hands over her hair, pushing her coils back. *Why me?* She froze. A bug was walking along the ceiling. At first, she thought it had a tail like a scorpion, but her mind separated the corroded frame from the spindle and the dark cable wrapped around it. The rear of the bug had spider-like spinnerets, and as it exuded cabling, it spread a small quantity of red goo.

"Do you see that?" she whispered, then poked each of her crew when she realized they couldn't hear.

Amy clapped her hands. "Fascinating. They have more than one design, which means specialization. If we weren't in deadly peril, I'd love to disassemble it and see what makes it tick."

"It hasn't noticed us," Izy said. "And it's way too loud to hear us. Do we keep going?"

"Yeah, keep going, but, Izy, it's your job to watch as we pass. Got it?"

Whether because of their caution or its disinterest, the bug kept laying cable and ignored their passage. They were twenty boulders along—Trax couldn't help counting—when the crunching stopped. Beyond the flare's red nimbus, another shadow moved. Another bug. Diver stopped, flare outstretched.

This one was huge, its body stretching as long as the rover, Abfab, and maybe more. Its head was a giant spinning disk. As she watched, the disk slowed, then separated into slices that folded back against its body, revealing what had been at the front. Scratched surfaces and sharp lumps explained its function: a boring machine. The bug's tail rose in the air, and it pushed out a boulder like a chicken laying an egg.

The tunnel wasn't finished. They'd walked all that way to a dead end.

"Everybody back."

The bug twisted around, overlapping plates grinding against each other, and pushed the boulder against the rest. *Go back and keep digging.*

It didn't. The bug used its long legs to step on either side of the boulders with ease. Trax and her crew turned and hurried.

The bug jerked, several stubby antennae wriggling on its flat head. It picked its path carefully, as if unsure of what it had found.

Trax's nostrils flared. No more deaths. "Run!"

Her crew took off. Trax followed the bouncing light of Diver's flare and hoped it still had plenty of time left. The bug followed, barely gaining. Was it really after them?

Thunk, thunk. Thunk, thunk. Thunk, thunk. Thunk, thunk.

It continued past the boulders. Damn. One hundred percent following. It had no saws or shears, but Trax had seen the damage caused by the common bugs' legs. This boring bug could skewer them all with one jab. Sweat dripped down her face. The tunnel walls felt like they were shrinking. They loomed, constricting, suffocating. She had no weapon and no way out. The helplessness was poison clogging her arteries, stealing her strength. She mustn't show it.

They reached the fork. "Turn right. Can't head the way we came."

"Not to judge your management style," Izy said breathlessly, as they all skittered around the corner, "but I think that went without saying,"

Repeating stretches of tunnel produced a hypnotic effect. They could have been running for a day, a minute, a thousand years. The giant bug patiently swallowed the distance.

"Tunnels!" Amy pointed ahead and to the side. "Small ones."

"We can hide!" Diver said. "But which one?"

Several pockmarked the main tunnel's left, large enough for them to crawl inside but not to stand. Diver's question was a good one.

"Take any, it's a lottery."

"Righto, boss." Diver stopped by the nearest and dipped the flare inside, blacking out the main tunnel. "I don't know where it goes, but it goes."

Harry, puffing like a broken pump, pushed him inside. When it was Trax's turn, she didn't bother looking back. The whine of motors in the bug's legs summoned goosebumps.

"Move up!"

They had bunched near the entrance and scrambled at Trax's order. A mechanical leg slid in, slapping the sides of this smaller tunnel with hammer blows, producing showers of sparks, and exuding a sharp, oily odor with an oddly herbal tang. At least it was too large for its body to fit in.

The flare guttered, sending distorted shadows that moved as if alive. It didn't matter. For the next few minutes, they were safe. Her chest heaved as her pulse ran wild. She worked hard, but she hadn't run regularly since arriving.

"Boss, I'm going to burn a new flare."

"Don't," Harry said. "It might see."

It was possible, though the smaller bugs hadn't reacted to light. "We'll rest in the dark for a few minutes. Strike a new one when we're ready to go. And no more talking."

The flare gave out. The bug attempted a few more jabs, the sparks pretty like fireworks, and pulled back.

Go back to what you were doing. We're out of reach. Give up.

Metal clanged together. Heavy snaps fired like a power hammer.

"What's it doing?" Diver whispered.

Realization burned the ends of her nerves. "It's going to dig us out."

A deep hum started, quickly rising in pitch. The tunnel shook. Chunks of rock blasted Trax, bruising her like a meat tenderizer.

Diver snapped the second flare. Between the bodies of her crew and the rock dust, little reached her. She set her head low, closed her eyes, and crawled. It was demeaning, painful, and terrifying. If she were watching from afar, she'd have laughed at herself. She was laughing. She hadn't noticed herself start, and she didn't care to stop.

"There's a junction, boss."

"Pick one. Don't stop."

They crawled on and on, leaving the bug behind. The smaller tunnels twisted every which way, occasionally opening into small chambers, and always connecting to another route out. If they weren't lost before, they were now. What she would do for her inertial mapping. Even if they found their way back to the main tunnel, they'd have no way to know which direction they were headed.

"I'm hungry," Diver said.

"We'll die from the bugs well before we starve," Amy noted. "But I guess we could dehydrate first."

Izy paused to clap. "Thanks for the pep talk."

"I'm being realistic. We could loop around and around and never see another bug. Dehydration would kill us first in that scenario."

"We're not dying," Trax said. "Anyone who dies from here on is fired, understood?"

That brought a few laughs, but at some point, morale would get as lost as they were. She brushed her hands. The section of tunnels they had crawled into made her throat itch. Dust, different from earlier. Fine, almost sticky. The stale air made breaths feel wasted. She adjusted the cable length and clip that she'd wound around her waist. If only she had some white pebbles to drop. If Hayden saw her now, how damn happy would he be. How smug? Energy rolled back into her extremities. She shut the door on her complaining back. She wasn't going to be broken by Hayden or the bugs.

"Here's the carrot. Keep going. First one to find the way out gets a free beer on me. Izy, for you, it's one of those spicy pastries you love."

"A cruel offer. Diver is at the front."

"Then take turns."

They did, even Trax. She tried memorizing the bends and slopes. She tried scratching the tunnel with the cable clip. Eventually, exhausted, parched, and flagging, she called a stop in a small chamber with six exits. The second flare was ebbing. Two hours. Karlo had given them a method of tracking time, a cruel countdown. She closed her eyes for a moment.

When she opened them again, her body fought her commands. Stiff joints complained, and her muscles spasmed. Quiet snores assured her the rest of the crew were still in the planet's cloaca. She wasn't their master, but she was their boss. She owed them a way out as much as they owed her their best work. How? No tech. No map. How did the bugs find their way around? Ants used scent. If Trax sniffed, she'd sneeze. And she wasn't game to lick the floor in case there was a taste-based marking. They probably had their own internal guidance system linking to ultrasound.

Humans had five main senses. Touch, taste, smell, hearing, sight. There were more, too. She let herself relax and took in all the information her body processed unconsciously—the stink of sweat and dirt, an itch on the back of her hands. The slightest cooling of her skin. Airflow? She carefully stood and waited to a count of twenty. She turned a little and did so again. She turned counterclockwise. A ghostly touch. She chewed nothing, working up saliva and spread it on both her cheeks. A chill. Gaining confidence in the direction, she shuffled forward, tapping a body, and stepping over it. Shuffle again. An arm. Over. Test with a boot toe. Clear. Her hands met rock, and she leaned down and found the hole. Yes. This was it.

"Everybody up. Diver, I'm sick of the dark."

Izy groaned. "What time is it?"

"I'll check my sundial."

The third flare erupted, threatening to burn Trax's retinas. "Diver, give it to me."

He passed it over, and she looked into the tunnel. It appeared no different from any other, and with her crew moving, the air rippled, masking the breeze. Or she had imagined it.

"This way."

She started crawling. The tunnel angled upward, leveled out, then ended a short distance later. Another chamber? She'd do the same thing.

It wasn't. She climbed into a tunnel as large as the one they'd been dumped into. The red coating had cracked and fallen in several places, leaving large shards embedded in a layer of silt.

"Looks like Diver's apartment."

"It looks old," Harry said.

Amy took a handful of silt and let it pour out her fingers. "Old and abandoned. The bugs haven't displayed a bachelor's concept of hygiene before."

"How'd you know to go this way?" asked Diver.

"Air current. I felt it while you were all still."

Where to now? Trax raised the flare and checked both directions. A flat wall at the edge of the light solved that problem. An abandoned route?

They trudged along the only way possible, lapsing quickly into silence. Small side passages punctuated the tunnel on either side and occasionally above, but she wasn't fooling for that again. Go big *and* go home. After a short walk, they encountered another ring. This one was different. The design was the same, the overlapping scales, but a lip at one side that she'd ignored the last time held a circle of curved plates reaching to the center of the open space, an iris shrinking the diameter of the tunnel enough that stepping over it required caution—especially for the men.

Izy prodded the lip. "Shape memory alloy. Clever, though I'd go with a door cut into the tunnel sides for reliability. Look here, I think this little rock fell in the lip and jammed it. It's stuck tight."

"I'll log a service ticket," Trax said as they continued.

Her mind wandered. Traditional wineries had underground vaults to keep the maturing wine at a steady temperature. How much more could it cost to store the barrels in an aboveground temperature-controlled warehouse? If she never went underground again, it would be too soon. Ahead, the tunnel went dark, and Trax shelved her planning. They were coming to another junction, but she couldn't see light spilling onto the other paths.

"What are we seeing?" Amy asked. "Is it night?"

If so, it was an industrious night. A steady hubbub of machinery echoed and blended, losing any distinct rhythms or tones. Trax held her breath and marched toward the edge.

The ground transitioned first to a black glass-like surface with bubbles, then with knife-edge precision to smooth dull metal. Mottled blue markings, thin lines and circles, covered one side. She reached out and ran a glove along some. The blue wiped off, revealing lines that could have been circuitry. A hot wind ruffled her hair.

"Here be dragons," Harry said.

Three meters in, the metal ended. All-consuming darkness devoured the flare. Trax leaned out and looked up. Metal ridges and cabling. The same down and to the sides. Winks of brightness like fireflies came and went, and she wondered if her optical nerves were misfiring. Off to the right, a beam stretched away from the wall, its angle giving a sense of perspective. They had stumbled onto a vertical cylinder, one whose diameter must be immense if the gentle curvature continued into the dark.

Diver kicked some silt over. "I guess it doesn't matter how far down it goes. If it goes up, that must mean we can climb to the surface, right? And we have to be close."

Do we? They didn't need to hear Trax's concern. They weren't climbing. One mistake and a long drop. How far? There was an energy in the air, nothing physical. A sense of history. She tried to form an explanation but failed. Did her crew even feel it?

"I want to know how far across it is and how deep it goes," Amy said. "We should throw a flare."

"We only have one spare," Harry countered.

Diver chuckled. "Damn, but it's tempting, right? I don't want to walk away not knowing, you know?"

"I agree with Junior," Izy said. "If another two hours doesn't get us out, more won't either."

"Harry?"

The big woman put her hands on her head. "There's nowhere that's safe. Do it."

Trax nodded. "Diver, light it up."

As the last flare activated, she tossed hers inward. It arced up, rotating end over end, showing more of the protruding beam, and then dropped down... down... down, until it became a speck only distinguishable by its continuous output. She blinked and lost track of it.

"Deep," Harry said.

Diver scrunched up his face. "Fucking deep, you mean."

"Bug city," Izy said, deadpan. "Come for the views, stay for the nightlife."

A flare in exchange for an endless hole. It hadn't been a good deal.

Patches of brightness, bruised reds, switched on, a steady progression from a narrow horizontal ring far down to widening segments ever upward. Details emerged. Hundreds of beams. Dark tunnels. Movement: thousands and thousands of bugs walking the walls, crossing the beams. Trax shivered despite the warmth. Wagner had been right. There were so many. And they'd just stirred them up.

"Do you think they know we're here?" Diver asked.

Izy gave him a look.

"Yeah, yeah, I know they know. Can't blame a guy for hoping."

The lights reached their level. The place was a cone, point down. And above a great curving roof. Machinery coated the walls, mechanical components pumping, spinning—the purpose of it all impossible to comprehend.

Many meters and several rings down, numerous panels sprung open. Each one released a bug. They were a new kind. Only four meters from head to ass—twice Harry's height. They had long legs like the borer, six of them, and they moved with grace. Beneath a frill of sensor stalks, their heads had mounted huge vertical mandibles, riffing off her claw concept and enlarging it fourfold. Their armored bodies flashed with dazzling illuminated patterns of deep red and blinding white. As one, they stretched out twin pairs of wings. Engines behind each leg fired a tight stream of violet flame like a plasma torch. Dragonflies. Almost. They resembled an unholy mix of fireflies and dragonflies—if such were forged from metal. The bugs kicked off the wall and circled the cavernous interior, hunters breathing in the scent of blood.

"They're coming for us," Trax said, knowing it couldn't be any other way. "Everybody back!"

CHAPTER 21
A DISTRACTION

N o signal. Bill's comm was still being jammed. He closed the
fasteners on the BILT4 suit. It was lighter than his colony-
issued rags and more comfortable. Last night, he'd sat on his
cell's hard bed, frustrated with the guards' thoroughness. They hadn't
appeared to recognize the pistol parts, but they'd confiscated the lot
along with everything else on his person before a late-night one-on-one
with Wagner. And hadn't that been a crate full of fun? Her management of their conversation was smooth, and he'd worked hard to avoid
an obvious battle of wits. He needed her to pigeonhole him, to think he
was buying into her game. To that end, he'd employed a mask of
enthusiasm and tossed out ideas audacious enough to tempt. Even so,
her willingness to listen was a red flag—if only he knew what it
indicated.

The door to his cell became transparent, revealing Karlo on the
other side. The guard captain triggered the lock, and it slid open.

"Ms. Wagner thinks you're useful, but I know you're trouble."

How long had the guy been saving that line?

"I'm only trying to get by, the same as everyone else."

Karlo sneered and bent his pointer finger with a come here action.
"I don't like all this tech bullshit, so if putting you down slows it, I
don't care. I won't have this compound put at risk."

What a shame. If Karlo had been the complete ass he looked like, this would be much easier.

Bill ran a hand through his dirty hair and walked over to the door. "We're on the same side now, *Captain*. You've locked a bracelet on my ankle, and I've abandoned my colleagues. I have nowhere to go. You can trust my enlightened self-interest."

"I don't trust anything about you. That's the thing about traitors. You can't be trusted."

"Don't see me as a traitor. I'm more like an up-and-coming corporate manager. Dodging between departments to climb the ladder. If I didn't do that, I'd be stuck in some low-level role in the middle of nowhere, babysitting." Bill offered his best look of innocence.

Karlo's eyes narrowed, the skin at the side of his eyes crinkling as his death glare burned. He stepped back from the door. "Get out. You'll have a guard watching you every second. Try anything, and I'll—"

"Understood. I can't make money if I'm buried or recycled or whatever your waste program entails." Bill told his pulse to calm. It didn't listen. Karlo needed to believe that Bill was a certain kind of asshole, whereas Bill was an entirely different sort.

Karlo prodded him through another security door, which opened into a short corridor that fed into an office stocked with desks and a wealth of displays. Its function as a monitoring station was clear. Given the bugs, the number of empty chairs was surprising. Maybe they were top-heavy on the night shift.

A guard approached, and Karlo offloaded Bill onto his junior with a warning. Bill did his best to appear innocent, and unthreatening, even holding out his hand for a shake. The guard, ignoring his gesture, ushered him out, her pace steady and her movements tense despite the safety of the walls.

The previous evening, he'd thought of the compound as a strange mix of indulgence and dereliction. In the daylight, a starker truth was on offer. Several damaged vehicles waited out front of a maintenance facility, their panels shredded. The expressions of the workers he passed were mixtures of worry and fear. A few had visible scratches, and one woman had her arm in a cast. Conversations were muted. The atmosphere matched the weather—dour clouds advanced from the east.

Dozens of polymer flowers dangled at the base of a comms tower, and above them, pictures that resembled ID photos had been plastered to the metal.

"What's that about?" he asked as they walked by.

"Bugs."

Right. The guard was not going to be a fount of knowledge, but the one word revealed much. BILT4 had losses of its own. The guard had blocked most of the view, so Bill hadn't been able to count the number of photos, but there were enough. This made more sense of Wagner's willingness to entertain Trax and her crew—and Bill. How short-staffed was she? And that was only the beginning of his questions.

The guard led him to the front of a hangar. "I'll be watching you. Don't make me hurt you."

It wasn't a threat, more a plea. Bill looked into the woman's eyes. There was the haunted gaze he'd seen in soldiers before. She was due for some grade-A PTSD treatment.

"I'm here to work, nothing more." Would the lie have been easier if he knew her name?

She opened a small door in the hangar wall, and Bill stepped inside.

Clear polymer sectioned off three separate areas. The most central of these was surrounded by heavy sheets of vertical alloy on sturdy bases. Did they have a living bug? His heart skipped a beat. If so, it was docile. A few workers hovered around clusters of equipment filling long, sturdy benches. Boxes stacked like brutalist sculptures consumed only a small part of the cavernous space. A dark blossom on the hard floor to the right resembled a blast. Seven meters across, he estimated. Nasty.

He opened his stride, putting distance between himself and the guard as he chose a route to the nearest worker.

"Hi, I'm Bill Hayden. Here to lend a hand as best I can."

The worker wore a white suit that balanced the intensity of their shaggy sunflower-yellow hair. Bags under their eyes suggested long hours were the norm. They took time to pull their eyes away from a scanning microscope.

"Sorry?"

"I'm Bill. Elyse asked me to help. I've some experience with geology, but my core skills are in data and intelligence analysis." Now was the time to take a little risk. "I'm sure I can't make up for your losses."

A wave of sorrow spread across the worker. Some of the dead were part of this team. Could that be exploited?

Bill put a hand on their arm. "I'm sorry. I didn't mean to upset you. These are hard times. We've all lost colleagues." He let the truth seep into his intonation.

"It's fine. I'm Val Hai. I'm a custom chip architect by trade."

Bill offered a subtle, wry smile. "I'm guessing you've had to do more than lay out circuits and cells."

"A little. Over there in the dirty scrubs is Kaydee, and the tall one is Mitch. I'll introduce you in a bit. So you're meant to help?"

"I know I'll have to catch up fast, but I'm used to working under pressure."

"We have plenty of that. I guess I had better show you around."

Bill nodded to the guard as if she were there for his protection and said to Val, "Please, lead on."

They guided him through the maze of scientific debris to the polymer tent with the armor.

"What have you got in there, a tiger?"

"Much crueler things than claws and teeth, and a lot less fuzzy. Have you had a close look at any of the entosynths?"

"Only in passing."

Val stopped by a hinged door set in the metal barrier. "The micro-resonance separators in the capacitors of the older units are flaky at best. Apparently, their warranty has expired. Stress the wrong part and you get an energy release. Same goes for the rest of the tech."

"Boom?"

"Yeah, some big, some small. We couldn't work it out until we confirmed the dating. Seven thousand years has made them twitchy. It was a hard lesson we learned several times. The newer machines are less volatile. We've got a few bits and pieces inside the cage from the last expedition. I'm working up dates before we render them safe for physical assessment. Oh, the corroded appearance is deceiving. It's to do with the alloy mix, and it's not your typical oxidation."

Seven thousand years. Had the bugs been dormant or were they quietly living their little robotic lives until humanity came and stirred the pot?

"What are you assessing them for?"

"We've had to set aside real research. Now it's all about classification and power draining. There's only so much mass available, and nothing goes on board without a safety certificate."

On board. His brain fizzed with the conclusion. The dropship —Wagner was running with whatever she could carry. That was crazy. The dropship couldn't leave orbit. She'd know that. And, even if they dumped all the cargo, it couldn't support the entire compound staff for the two years before the Phase 3 ships arrived and escape became possible.

He kept his expression smooth, mildly curious. "That makes sense. Can I see?"

Val took him through a small airlock and into the work area. Six benches held a variety of objects: a few familiar scales from a ring, large crystalline metal forms with cables extending from a cutout, paired sets of robotic legs much larger than those on the bugs Bill had seen, cylinders of boards with clear analogs of optronic circuitry.

He went to lift a cable running from one of the stubby cylinders to look at its end.

"Don't touch. See here? It still has a power unit running down the middle with more joules of energy than an ice cream convention. I'd prefer your organs where they are."

"And it was made seven thousand years ago?"

"No, that's a fresh datacore, pulled from a sub-nexus. They're ramping up production. I wish we could decode their storage, but quantum magnets are touchy, and we don't have the right gear. And we sure as hell aren't hanging around to make it."

"I feel the same way," Bill said, as he examined several markings— little straight divots and a few circles. "Is this what I think it is?"

"Writing?"

"Yes."

"Could be. It fluoresces in UV, which matches their input sensors. But our last linguist is dead. Dr. Flores insisted he went with the expedition to help select the targets. If we'd waited until we had the comms filter back online, Jackson could have done his job from a chair."

"Ouch. That's harsh."

Wagner had lied to Trax, telling Bill later that the interference-beating advance had come too late to be useful for the colony. Even most of Wagner's minions hadn't yet received the upgraded unit—if she were to be believed. However, one sample of the little tech marvel had found a purpose. Bill had suggested fitting Trax with one, a perfect way to map tunnels. The fab crew weren't the sort to sit still, even in the dark.

Bill looked at another piece of alien tech, its exterior blackened and the interior mostly filled with a donut-shaped transparent object.

Val held a hand above the device. "This one is interesting. Heat damage and what I think might be a control unit for a warp node, given the surrounding tech they cut it from."

"They flew here?"

"Possibly. Or this was their home world, and the debris is from a failed launch. Or it's a donut maker, and its store burned down in an entosynth riot. There's no time to be thorough. Still, this little puppy has Wagner's tits in a spin. I'll show you where it was pulled out. Mitch has been trying to find a pattern to the different pieces we've discovered on a time profile. We could use your help with that. We've tagged and bagged enough of the newer finds. What we need is the old tech."

"But the power?"

"We can manage that. It's the expeditions that are dangerous. Every time we get close, there are too many entosynths." Val leaned in close. "If you're going to help, you need to find a solid target and a route that won't get all of us slaughtered. Understood?"

"One hundred percent. Let me know what's where, and I'll find us a tasty morsel, one that won't bite back."

As he followed Val out of the enclosure, his mind drifted through what he'd learned. The corporation had piles of data to hand and yet hadn't bothered building a story of the aliens' arrival or evolution. Without knowing the creators, could they really understand what they were taking? Of more immediate use to him, Wagner's expeditions explained the increasing intensity of the attacks.

"Do you think they are a form of artificial intelligence?" Bill asked when Val stopped in front of a desk with a console and several polymer maps that had been stuck to boxes. The human need for a physical representation remained. The guard chose a position nearby, a representation of the danger he was in.

"Not intelligent in any general sense. Or at least not the entosynths we've disassembled."

"Perhaps they have a hive mind, like bugs. That's what we call them."

"So do the normies. Well, they're not evolved or organic. That's clear, so they aren't bugs, even if one were to stretch beyond the clade. A hive mind is a possibility, but we shouldn't base assumptions on superficial physical traits."

"If they aren't intelligent, what has the brainpower to design them, to build them?"

Val activated and authenticated the console. "Nothing we've seen so far. If there's an AI, a queen analog, it's not poking its head above ground. And we've found no sign of culture."

"Beyond the writing."

"Yes, beyond the possibility of writing and their design. Anyway, Wagner wants us to focus on the east side of the *bug* network, where we haven't broken through. Ground-penetrating radar has given us a rough guide."

She tapped a few commands, and the region sprung into life. Another command, and the same tunnel map Wagner had shown the previous day overlayed the image. Then a series of other elements dotted the maps.

"The red spots are where we've recorded hostile contact. The gray are digs that found nothing. The green represents surface finds, and the gold are digs that hit on major tech. Blue are… colony events. It's all time-stamped so you can play it through."

Bill whistled. How comfortable was Val with all this? Could they be

ROBERT TILLSLEY

helpful? "Good data. Very good data. You knew what was going on. I'm surprised you didn't warn the colony."

"We were focused on our work." Val crossed arms. "We assumed that Flores and Wagner would tell them. When the survivors of the expedition returned, the colony incursion had already occurred."

"I'm not judging," Bill said to calm Val's hackles. "Only trying to understand. I want to know what resources we have. If we could arm the colonists, they might help us, unwittingly."

"Kaydee pushed that. Management picked a different plan." The deadpan tone hinted at a secret.

"Us little worker bees have to take it as it comes. Do you have a roster of resources for the expedition?"

"No."

Not all was happy at BILT4—beyond all the death and destruction. Was Val in skin-saving mode or hiding something from him? There was a lot of that going around.

"Okay, Val. I'll start a few reasonable assumptions and see what I can put together. And don't worry, I'll make it good. I want my hide attached and my pockets filled at the end of all this, too."

He dragged over an empty box to sit on and started exploring the data. Rain started up, drumming on the hangar roof and shifting the air pressure. He let the white noise aid his focus. The basic pattern was clear. Initial spears of activity branching out from the nexus. And if the bugs liked an area for whatever reason, say, a juicy piece of human technology, or perhaps a body, they would extend sideways, forming leaf veins that frequently curved back into other veins, presumably once they had captured their booty.

Could the bugs be reasoned with? *Sorry, mistakes were made. Let's all get along.* He remembered the pile of bodies, the uncaring slaughter. It was too desperate a hope to cling to. Some actions couldn't be forgiven.

Instead of picking a suitable location for an expedition, he interrogated the whole concept. Surely, continuing to dig was a suicidal endeavor. Val had to know, and the other two as well. The bugs would chew the trio up with little to stop them. And more bodies wouldn't help. Karlo and his security team weren't a regiment of drop troopers.

They couldn't battle thousands of bugs. The scientists weren't fanatics, or at least Val wasn't. What edge did they have that made another expedition even feasible?

The colony. It all fit into place. Shock spread through his flesh like a fever. The colony was a distraction. He skipped through time, looking for attacks and corporate activities. Some attacks occurred in isolation, but recent incidents with the colony matched BILT4 digs. Wagner was using the colonists as bait. If she wanted one last expedition, one last chance to go deep, the crafty executive needed the colony waiting like a juicy bone for the bugs to gnaw on. He checked the time. Thirty minutes gone. He couldn't risk more. Hopefully, the guard had settled into comfortable boredom.

"Hey," he said. "I need to mark a few things on the map. Do you want to make yourself useful?"

The guard's face hardened. "No."

"Fair enough. If you want, I can explain what I'm doing."

No response. Bill shrugged and started a pattern of moving between the console and the polymer maps. The latter gave him a reflective surface, enabling him to check on the guard without being seen to do so. Sure enough, her attention soon wandered. The more open you are, the less worried an observer becomes.

He dropped into the console's operating system and checked the version. Up to date, which was fine. The agency didn't disclose the valuable bugs to vendors. He hurriedly typed in a script and executed it. An exploit brought up a further window with escalated privileges. He didn't want to go for the main compound datacore—too much security to beat in a short time—but for access to the external networks.

The satellite logs and comms base station transfers would do nicely. Details important for troubleshooting had many other uses. Parsing them into files for the visualization software was a trivial effort, albeit one he had to work through in bits and pieces while making repeated visits to the maps and employing thoughtful noises.

Once it was ready, he imported and filtered the data, giving what he needed a purple square. Then he ran through the timeline. It was moving. He breathed out a sigh of relief. The comm secreted on Trax

had announced its presence, its updated design cutting through interference and rock at irregular intervals. Away, away she traveled. Then
the box stopped. He zoomed in. It started again—the wrong way.

Come on, Trax. Turn around. Get out of there.

She was still moving, taking a strange path that didn't fit with the
bugs' direct approach. This was good. Hopefully. But she was in the
dark. She had no idea where she was going, and she'd gotten lost.
Damn. He'd been too clever by half. But, for now, she was alive. He
closed his eyes. There was still a chance. But this had been the easy
part.

He glanced to the center of the hangar where the shielded bubble
held precious artifacts. He'd shielded Trax and her crew from immediate execution, one they hadn't realized was looming. Two years into
his career in the LSA, he'd been hiding in a ceiling space while a
corrupt governor executed a pair of customs agents. Bill's orders had
been to observe and record only. He'd learned too. To such minds, you
were either useful or a liability. He could still see the victims' faces
when the governor raised his gun.

If Bill didn't get the fab crew above ground soon, they'd suffer a far
worse fate. They'd been brave beyond measure when he needed them,
and now he owed them. He wouldn't let them die. Easy to say. Hard to
pull off. How was he going to rescue them? And how the hell was he
going to escape in the first place?

CHAPTER 22
SHOOT THE GATE

The hangar reverberated with thunder, not exactly a comforting omen. Bill steadied himself on a bench inside the cage. He gave his guard, who waited outside the airlock but inside the metal blast barrier, a wave.

"I'm thinking of going to the beach later."

She ignored him. Good.

Val had called a meeting earlier, and Bill explained everything he'd noticed—except Trax. The scientists followed with their reports. A whole museum's worth of alien tech was ready for the dropship. And a few things, including what Bill needed, were marked for careful destruction. The entire process was excruciating until he found the solution in one neat package and asked for a moment to compare the map of the tunnels to the possible writing of the artifacts in case there was any significance. The accepting scientists triggered a smidgeon of guilt. And that guilt was smothered by fear and responsibility.

He slid a box tag from his sleeve and leaned close to a cylindrical datacore. The scientists had determined it was unstable. From the other sleeve, he retrieved the power unit from the console he'd been using. The stiff tag slipped easily into the power unit's catch, and Bill twisted it, snapping the case open. This was followed by a minute of scowling and running his finger over a map he'd brought in.

Nothing going on here. I'm just comparing markings.

Pulling a wire free, he directed the end to another location, creating a short circuit that warmed instantly. He set it on the top of the data-core and headed for the airlock, blocking the view as he folded the map. Beth would be proud—or smug.

"Nothing on this one," he said to the guard. "The zoomed images might show something I'm missing. I won't be long."

He headed for his work area, his palms moist, and it took all of his will to not rub them on his suit. Too much could go wrong. They all could die.

Thunder crashed, and Bill jumped.

The guard laughed behind him. Let her think he was scared. He was. Lies were best woven into truth. He kneeled and removed a boot, the location *coincidentally* behind several stacks of boxes.

"Hey, what are you doing?"

"Got a rock in my boot."

He turned the boot upside down and shook. How long until the console power unit caught fire? Would it be enough to set off the bug datacore? He was dead if it didn't, and possibly dead if it did. When he figured it was as much time as he could reasonably spend pretending, he slipped his boot back on.

Boom!

He hit the ground and slid, boxes tumbling over him. A high-pitched ringing smothered all other noise apart from the thudding of his heart. Pain promised future bruising. He waded through nausea and stood.

The polymer cover holding the alien tech had vanished. The metal barrier had buckled at several points, its edges torn. A fire raged within, spewing sparks and whomping with secondary explosions. The guard lay on the ground nearby, slowly rolling over a pool of her blood.

Bill stumbled to her, cursed himself, and tugged the rifle caught on her shoulder.

She snarled and rolled. "Hey, let go."

He fell, maintaining his grip, and they wrenched the weapon back and forth. A nasty cut to her forehead had fooled him. She had plenty of fight in her, and if he ran, she'd shoot him. Great.

The moment came. The barrel had spun down, angling toward her stomach. He'd never killed someone so close, so personal. And he was a civilian now, just another guy fleeing his past. Damn Beth. If he remained that man, he was dead. He slipped his finger onto the trigger. They locked gazes. He pulled.

Time slowed. Heat vaporized the hair on the back of his left hand. A sun exploded on her flesh. A hole cut through her. Behind, a blackened mess of superheated gobbets sizzled as fresh blood spread. Her body spasmed.

His skin chilled. "I'm sorry."

He backed away and opened shaking hands, dropping the rifle. It would draw too much attention. What next? He tossed three empty boxes over the guard. It was cruel, but he needed to hide the evidence of a struggle.

The scientists were all on the ground. Val moved a little, and that pleased him. *Less guilt?* No time for any. He hurried to her bench, finding the tools he needed sprawled across the floor behind it. The tracking bracelet had to go. He slipped an insulator sheet behind the catch in case it had a tampering shock and used a nibbler to bite through the bracelet. Karlo would know it was broken, but not why.

A security team would arrive soon, perhaps faster than medics. Bill tossed the bracelet into the fire raging in the center of the hangar and ran to the exit. What came next depended on how the first responders reacted. All he could do was play the odds. He pressed himself behind the hinged side.

Bang! The door opened, slamming into Bill. He dared a finger on the edge to stop it bouncing back. Boots stomped inward.

"Over there, there's a survivor!"

"Are the medics on their way?"

"Yeah, but we better triage first."

More boots.

Karlo spoke. "Find Hayden."

"But, the fire, Captain. This whole place could go up."

"No one's leaving until I see his dead body, understood?"

Several voices chorused, "Yes, sir!"

Bill closed his eyes and listened over the crackles, pops, and deeper thuds of the fire. Boots moved away. Acrid smoke burned his throat. It was spreading fast, but not fast enough for cover.

"I've found Wren, Captain." That must be the guard.

"Where?" Karlo was moving.

Now or never. Bill stepped round the door and out into the storm.

A corporate approached. Bill doubled over and coughed, hiding his face as best he could.

"You okay?"

"Good. Just some fumes. I'll be fine, but they need help in there."

He gave a count of three, then walked with purpose. With each step, he expected to be tackled or for plasma to rip through his flesh. No matter how much he tried to exude calm confidence, inside his body roiled with fear, mirroring the storm above. Like that storm, it gave a peculiar energy. He looked at the buildings as he went, reading their labels. He didn't have time to check each one. Would it have killed them to put up a street sign or two?

Two medics came around a corner in a small buggy with a red cross, and he twitched with surprise that morphed into a hungry anticipation. He gave a little wave, putting his hand in the way of his face, and released his sphincter when they continued at high speed toward the hangar. As good as a street sign. He took the corner and found the building, a two-story design with a flyer pad on the right above an open and empty garage. The colony had enforced restrictions on air travel from early on. The changeable weather still made it high risk. He considered the bulbous craft resting on the pad and the high winds. There were more comfortable ways to die.

The front doors opened as he approached the hospital, and he strolled inside. On his left, there were six rooms, each with a large glass window and a wide door. Perhaps they had been designed for two patients in each, but there were at least four stuffed in each. Burn victims, missing limbs. As well, several makeshift beds lined the hallway. The tiny hospital was overwhelmed and yet understaffed. A simplistic rule of modern medicine was that, barring brain injuries, if patients survived for an hour, they would walk out at some point. He doubted that held in this facility. There must be a long queue for treatment, and these unfortunates were drugged into oblivion while they waited. Wagner should have asked the colony for help, but then, her secrecy was all-consuming.

Ugly truths blossomed in quick succession, the first matching his initial assumption. Wagner would never have let him aboard the dropship. Nor these poor souls. Wounded would be left behind. The final expedition was both a roll of the dice and a cull so the dropship could launch with the maximum booty and the minimum mouths to feed—or mouths that could talk. She wanted more. She always would, but she was ready to cut and run with everything she could lay her grubby hands on. She may have even used him to convince the scientists that another expedition was possible. Damn, Wagner was bad. And she was good at it.

A medic stood between two beds in the fourth room, applying a cream to an older woman. He was unlikely to know his assigned fate in Wagner's scheme. A narrow, wheeled table next to him had scissors, a blade, several squeeze tubes, and a DDG. Bill tiptoed into the room. *Please don't turn around.*

The DDG had a tube inserted. Parabufinil, perfect for keeping the patients unaware. Bill tentatively reached out and picked up the DDG. The scissors wobbled. He shoved the DDG against the medic's neck and pulled three times, the memory of shooting the guard hovering over him like a ghost.

"Ow." The medic slumped

Bill caught the medic and lowered him to the ground. "Sweet dreams. Now, where did you put Crumpler?"

He checked the faces in the room, then moved through the hospital. Crumpler was in the sixth room, lying on one of six low camp beds. She appeared stable, if not comfortable. Gel covered her wounds, and a bag of fluid dripped into her. She wasn't going to walk out. Stretchering her across the compound would red flag his position. There had to be another way. He checked the rest of the hospital rooms and found a supply closet. A large, wheeled trash receptacle gave him a solution. Not a good one, but a solution.

Crumpler moaned as he lifted her in, feet first. With a bit of wrangling, her knees bent, and she ended up in a squashed sitting position. Bill dumped his damaged suit on top and slipped on a loose-fitting spare he'd found in the same closet. He finished her cover by placing a selection of chemical bottles near her head.

Rain splattered against the doors as he pushed Crumpler out the entrance. The air had a tang, ozone. Lightning leaped from cloud to cloud, leaving afterimages that formed a net waiting to drop. Karlo must know by now. How long before the general alarm sounded?

He paused by a four-wheeled vehicle, a low-slung cargo unit with an empty flatbed, no doubt for use inside the compound. He reached for the bottles. There was no way to measure the chemical proportions, and he was working off a recipe in a self-aggrandizing story an ex-soldier had shared after an op. It could have been pure bullshit. At least the fluids bubbled and sizzled on the floor of the flatbed when he added the final ingredient: pure alcohol.

Off in the distance, the flowers on the memorial whipped around and around, clattering loudly enough to be heard above rain that swiftly shifted from a drizzle to a downpour. He hurried along until he reached what he judged was a motor pool or repair shop. Tracks led to small ramps and several closed doors.

Bill tested one. Locked. What now? Even if he climbed the compound wall with Crumpler, Karlo would fry him as he dragged her over open ground.

Two things happened in quick succession. First, a siren wailed. That would be Karlo deciding Bill hadn't self-immolated. He'd jinxed himself by thinking of the thug. Second, the flatbed exploded, raining metal along with the water that thickened the air. A brilliant diversion if he had managed to be ready.

The third door creaked, then rolled upward. He pushed Crumpler to the edge of the growing opening, his brain frothing and adrenaline zapping through his tired flesh.

A bushy-bearded man with a rotund stature and a greasy set of absorbent clothes aimed a large power spanner with a built-in flashlight at the burning wreckage. Bill leaned into the wheeled trash can, racing it up a small ramp and into the mechanic. The spanner clattered to the ground as the mechanic tumbled back.

What now?

Bill grabbed the spanner, losing seconds with his clumsy grip. By the time he was up and ready, the mechanic had recovered.

"I don't know who you are, but you don't go coming to my shop and start messing with me. I'm going to grind you up and shit you out."

Bill chuckled. The whole situation was utterly insane. He stared at the mechanic, his eyes narrowing. He could work with insane.

He pointed to Crumpler. "Really, like I did with this one?"

The mechanic looked down, his mouth gaping when he spotted the unconscious medic. Bill threw himself forward, swinging the spanner like a two-handed sword. It slipped past the mechanic's raised arms and thwacked into his skull. They both hit the ground, but the mechanic was down for the count, blood seeping from his crushed skull. Charged with energy, Bill dropped the spanner. Another dead at his hands. It barely registered. He couldn't give guilt space to breathe, not yet. He grabbed a set of cards at the mechanic's waist—authentication chips.

Crumpler groaned, her eyes blinking.

Bill put a hand on the trash can. "Sorry for the rough ride."

Each bay in the garage held vehicles. A little buggy, a six-wheeler, a small-tracked hauler, and one that brought back memories of his early assignments liaising with small-time militaries. It stood tall on raised suspension, thick alloy panels bolted to the frame, and the windows protected by angled slots. The vehicle was painted in shades of brown, and it had a fucking pulse cannon mounted on its roof. A light armored personnel carrier.

Thanks, Karlo. How considerate of you.

He wheeled Crumpler around and headed for the APC. A thick charging umbilical hung from its side. The driver's door opened at his touch. Inside, the dash dangled open, but the vehicle display flashed: charge 76%. He could work with this.

"Crumpler, I'm putting you inside."

She whimpered when he lifted her out of the trash can and proved to be a dead weight. He couldn't help knocking her against the body of the APC as he climbed the two steps up. Each mew of pain drove needles into his nerves, and shoving her across to the passenger side took burned seconds they didn't have.

"Who's there?"

Bill grabbed for the door and pulled it shut, slapping the lock as a guard came around the corner.

"Bill Hayden? Stop. It's over. Get out, nice and slow."

That wasn't happening. He sunk low in the driver's seat and checked the system. It wasn't asking for authentication, but the dash was open. It was practically an invitation. The design of the APC mirrored a hauler, a model built for power and easy maintenance. He traced the cabling, looking for a fault.

Light flashed, and heat radiated through the window. The APC had absorbed the guard's shot. Bill ducked down as far as he could. How much punishment could it handle? There. An unplugged set of optics hung near a clean board. He fitted them and checked the display, grinning maniacally at a flashing green indicator.

"He's over here!"

Bill mashed the mechanic's authentication cards against the reader. The APC hummed as systems came online. He grasped the joystick and stomped the accelerator. The vehicle kicked and lurched forward, slamming into the garage bay door. It bent and wrinkled, but the short distance hadn't given him enough momentum. More guards came into view, splashing the side of the APC with plasma and warping the window. He leaned away to avoid a char-grilling. Then, slamming it into reverse, he sent the APC screaming backward. To shouts and the crunching of anonymous metal. *There goes the deposit.* With a few more meters of runup, he shot forward again, hitting the door. It screamed and tore free. Completely blinded, he jigged left and right, trying to dodge the mounting torrent of weapons fire. A short brake threw the door remnants ahead, and he swerved, heading for the gate.

"What's happening?" Crumpler said, her words slurred.

"We're escaping," Bill responded, then added. "You've done well so far."

He went through the vehicle's systems while circling madly, finding the gate access and hitting it. The gate stayed shut.

"Then why are you joyriding?"

He selected the option again but already knew it would fail. Karlo was proving to be annoyingly competent, or at least cunning. Getting close to the subject always carried a risk of losing objectivity. The asshole had locked the gate. Bill looked sideways at Crumpler and the joystick in front of her.

"How are your hands?"

"I have them."

It was a start. Bill reached for a physical switch in the middle of the dash surrounded by warning stickers. A thrumming started—the pulse cannon warming up. He turned toward the gate once more.

A security six-wheeler came from out of nowhere, slamming into Crumpler's side of the APC. Bill fought for control and steered hard right, bashing the smaller vehicle, and whooping with joy.

"I need you to shoot the gate. Can you do that?"

"Gate?"

"The thing we're about to crash into!"

She grasped the cannon's joystick unsteadily.

"You'll need to go full power. That'll be the switch on the top. Then pull the trigger."

The APC lurched again. Bill dared a look. Karlo was in the other vehicle, driving recklessly.

Brilliant purple bloomed at the tip of the pulse cannon's barrel. Energy roared forward, only traceable in the afterimage it left in his vision. It slammed into a section of wall, tearing a hole big enough for a person to leap through. No good.

Bill brought the APC back in line with the gate.

"Keep it straight. Try again."

Crumpler fired, but Karlo nudged the APC again. Bill was ready. He steered into Karlo, and the two vehicles sparked and smoked as their sides rubbed.

"Again, Crumpler. Don't stop."

She held down the trigger, sending destruction ahead. The view exploded with light. Bill squinted, but it was no use. He was driving into an inferno. And he loved it.

He shouted wordless, fevered joy. He was getting Crumpler out, and the fab crew would be next. He wasn't passing on responsibility to others and then moaning about the outcome. This was him doing what needed to be done. Bill Hayden standing up to be counted.

Either that, or it was Bill Hayden crashing into a gate at high speed. Light enveloped them. The APC bucked and bounced. Bill screamed. He thought Crumpler did the same.

They were through, driving along hard-packed earth. Bill looked at the rear camera display. One side of Karlo's six-wheeler went high up a ramp formed by the busted gate, and the vehicle tipped, sliding on its side in a shower of sparks.

"You can stop firing."

"Got it."

The cannon barrel glowed with radiant heat. They'd shortened its lifespan as they'd increased their own. Would they need it again? He doubted it. The wall bumps he believed to be cannons remained still. No vehicles followed. Were the guards in disarray with Karlo dead? That was wishful thinking. The bastard was too tough to die so easily. Which meant there was another reason, an obvious one. Wagner's priority was getting her tech off-planet. Bill was a mere annoyance. Had she ordered his fate be left to the bugs? Karlo would hate that.

Bill pulled up the nav system, placing a waypoint where he'd last seen Trax's signal and setting the autopilot. He had no idea how he was going to rescue the fab crew, which meant he better get working on the comm system and see what tech it had installed.

Trax was going to be mad. He could accept that. Just as long as she was alive enough to berate him.

CHAPTER 23
CUTTING IT FINE

"Where are we running *to*?" Amy asked.

Damn her for her question. It was a good one. Behind them, the metal dragonflies clanked and crunched while landing in the tunnel entrance. At least three.

Nope. Four.

More. Damn. And judging by the mechanical cacophony, the entire bug city was waking.

Izy leaped over the ring like a hurdler. Amy climbed. Diver—he dived. Harry carefully went over, then stopped and kneeled, forcing Trax to hop awkwardly as she vaulted. The bugs skittered forward, blocking the light from the bug city, mandibles opening and closing. Were the machines lubing themselves for when it came time to snap bone?

"Boss, your cable."

"Are you hurt?"

"The cable, quick."

Trax shimmied the cable off and handed it over. Arguing with Harry would only eat up more time. The bugs spread across the floor of the tunnel and up the sides, a wave of pitiless machinery. What kind of sick asshole would make these monstrosities?

Harry opened the carabiner on the cable end and clipped it around the small rock jammed in the ring's iris. She wrenched the cable back, her neck muscles tightening. "Boss, everyone, help."

"The mechanism is unlikely to work," Amy said.

Trax grabbed the cable, not disagreeing with Amy's sentiment. Diver was next, then Izy. The bugs were closing the distance, wings folded over streamlined bodies. Amy added her efforts, and the tug of war, human vs. physics, had the crew grunting, heaving.

Resistance vanished. They tumbled backward, and the rock bounced off the ceiling. A long shriek scraped at Trax's eardrums. She looked up, expecting newly vocal bugs to leap on her, slicing and shearing, but the dragonflies hadn't reached the ring. The sound came from the iris blades closing slowly, jerking with every centimeter gained until they stopped, leaving a gaping hole.

"It's clogged," Harry said with bitter disappointment.

Izy patted his pockets. "I'm all out of lube."

Diver picked himself up and dashed to the ring, where its half-closed iris mocked them. "Don't you go judging me!"

Judging?

He fiddled with his suit. A tinkling sound, a spray.

Trax looked away, her mouth shrinking with disgust. "By all that is holy, Diver!"

"Water can be a lubricant as long as there's no oil."

A terrible grinding tore through the air. The iris tightened once more, the gap shrinking in jerks and judders. The first bugs arrived, and Diver hopped awkwardly aside as a dagger-pointed leg lashed out. When the bug retracted the limb for another try, the iris closed. Clearly unimpressed by the loss of their prey, the bugs slammed against the iris, making it bounce back and forth like a membrane, producing deep, mournful notes.

"Told you," Diver said. "Heard of a guy that swore by it."

Perhaps Trax should have let the bugs get her. She glared at the iris, then down the tunnel. They were back where they began. No way up to the surface. But she couldn't quit. She couldn't let her crew sink into bickering.

"Did you see that dome?"

Her crew agreed.

"We're going to assume that's ground level or near to it. It's deeper than we started, but it's manageable. I want every little tunnel checked. Any heading up is an option. Diver, what are you waiting for, a permission slip from your mom?"

He scurried from entrance to entrance with Amy checking his work.

The bugs banged against the iris like a drunken drummer, distorting the surface and forcing a small gap at the center. Trax folded her arms to keep from fidgeting, as the light from the flare created shadows that moved spasmodically with the search. Above, by one side of the cabling that looked like the tunnel's spine, a vertical shaft mocked her. It was far too high to reach.

"Why aren't the bugs opening the door?" Izy said. "Have they lost the alarm code?"

Amy called out from one tunnel, "Control system failure, a lack of power, or geofencing are my top three candidates."

Bang. Bang. Bang. The gap grew large enough for an arm to fit through, enough for the end of a bug leg.

"We have a winner," Diver shouted from the opening to a tunnel high on the curve.

Amy climbed out. "It's heading up as far as I can see."

The iris groaned as the dragonflies pushed farther in. Weakened, its blades buckled faster and faster. The bugs, sure as shit, weren't geofenced.

The crew scrambled into the chosen offshoot one by one, the claustrophobic narrow passage and stale air welcoming Trax back like a creepy uncle. Shrieking metal heralded the dragonflies' arrival. They crowded around the small tunnel, their long legs stabbing. She crawled, dependent on the speed of those in front. Her teeth clenched as she fought an instinct to push past, to claim safety at the expense of others.

Pain. She grunted, straightening involuntarily, and hit her head, bringing down a shower of rocks and dust. It was a pulsing agony, almost synchronized to her heartbeat or her rapid breathing. The dull hurt in her head was nothing by comparison.

Harry grabbed her and dragged her away. "Boss, where'd they get you?"

"My leg." Trax rubbed at the spot where a bug had last cut into her. The same spot as last time? Through wet eyes, she looked for the new damage. "I need the flare."

The light passed between the crew until Harry held it. The pain subsided as Trax waited, and with the light, the lack of rips in the suit became clear. Strange. The bugs hadn't touched her, not this time.

"Did it break something?"

"No, I'm fine. I must have hit a nerve. I sure hit my head." Trax gave her scalp a rub, her hand coming back moist with blood.

Amy pushed into Harry's space. "You made a hole."

Trax glared at the offending roof of the tunnel. Amy was right—a small hole had formed in where she'd hit it.

"Always said you were hard-headed."

"Not now, Izy," Harry growled.

The bugs were still frantically reaching. If they brought in the smaller bugs or that damn borer, it would be all over. Still, she needed to check. A hole above could be a shortcut.

"Harry, hold the flare close. I want to see what's up there."

As Trax shifted, the pain returned. She gritted her teeth and pressed hard on the spot, trying to calm the firing nerves. There was a faint vibration. Horror gripped her insides, crushing each organ. "There's something in my leg."

Harry put a hand on Trax's shoulder. "Hold it together."

"I am." Trax grabbed Harry's hand and shoved it onto her leg. "Feel that. You can, right?"

"Holy fricking shit."

"Exactly."

"What's going on?" Diver asked, worry clear in his voice.

"Wait." Trax grabbed the cord and wound it around her right hand. She punched up at the hole, and pieces crashed around her, leaving a gap as large as her head. Rock dust spilled, burrowing into her hair, her eyes, and her mouth. It had a burned taste, and she couldn't produce enough saliva to clear the grit.

Harry raised the flare, revealing a steeply angled shaft small enough that they should be able to climb, shimmying their backs up one side. Except that Trax couldn't, not with the pain. What had been done to her? An awful thought erupted from the dark depths of her imagination. Could the bugs implant eggs? Some kind of non-organic system that ate at her flesh, rendering them down, taking the raw materials, and building a new mechanical horror? She shook uncontrollably. This was it for her. Even if she could climb, she mustn't.

"Break the hole open, Harry. Get everyone up. Get them outside."

"You first."

"I can't. Not with my leg. The pain—I can't work the muscles. Once you're up, I'll follow the tunnel as best I can."

"In the dark?"

"Not much choice."

Diver shouted. "We have to keep moving. What's going on?"

"We need to cut an object out of Trax's leg," Amy said.

"What?" Trax and Diver demanded in unison.

"It's obvious." Amy's voice dripped annoyance. "Whatever's moving inside needs to go. And if we're careful, you'll be sore but able to climb. You can't give up being a stubborn bitch now."

Trax laughed. "I'll just get my medkit. Oh, wait, they took them."

"We only need something sharp," Amy countered.

Harry picked up a sliver of rock. "I don't think this will work. She'll bleed out."

Izy pushed against Amy and Harry. "We use the suit circuitry."

"Your brain's starved of oxygen. They fried it all, not that any of it would have helped." Her crew was making a mistake. They needed to go, not get caught up in fantasy. She wanted to tell them, but the pain was draining her energy, stealing her final reserves.

They didn't listen to her, instead congratulating each other while they barked suggestions.

Amy pushed past Harry and practically sat on Trax. "We're going to take off your suit. We'll need to reach your legs, and it can be the donor."

"Just go."

"And not find out what's inside?"

Silence fell. The bugs had stopped trying to claw their way in. They weren't even visible at the entrance. Trouble?

"You're not cutting me open!"

"We're not asking," Harry said. "I'll hold you down."

The idiots. The assholes. She knew Harry too well. The threat wasn't idle. She started on her suit fasteners, and Amy and Harry helped her shuck it efficiently. Izy didn't even joke as she sat in her underwear. The suit passed down the tunnel. A short while and several swear words later, a part of the light system went the other way. It was a narrow, shiny finger length of metal with sharp corners—hardly a scalpel. It was going to hurt. Bad.

Sweat broke out across Trax's brow. She let her head fall into Harry's lap. "Do it."

Amy pressed her fingers hard around the healing wound, eliciting jolts of electric agony. She cut at the edge of the wound gel. Trax screamed, and Harry pushed down on her torso.

"Keep your leg still," Amy demanded. "Or I'm going to nick an artery. It's not like I know what I'm doing."

Trax clenched her teeth, alternating between whimpers and muffled cries. It burned. It jolted nerves like licking a high-voltage feed. It hurt so much. Warm blood leaked out, creating the sensation of wetting herself.

Amy pressed again, two thumbs crushing her flesh. "It's moving. I'm massaging it closer. There's the tip."

Trax screamed, bucking against determined hands.

"It's out!"

Arching her back, Trax let out one last shriek, and her limbs went flaccid. Panting, she asked, "What is it?"

"A comm receiver. It's even stamped with BILT4. The bastards must have implanted it when they treated you. It has a signal. I still feel it vibrating. Someone's trying to reach you."

"They can damn well leave a message."

Amy buffed the device and spun it round. It was a small circle with weak pinprick diagnostic lights. The nanowires had been severed, rendering it functionally useless.

"Amy," Harry said, "Tie off her cut."

"On it."

As the deed was done, her crew passed the comm back and forth.

When Izy examined the device, he said, "The signal gets weaker the deeper in the tunnel it goes. Yay us, if we lose gravity, we'll still be able to know which way is up."

Harry picked up small rocks and chipped away at the edge of the shaft, taking a larger piece when it broke free and using it instead. The end result would be tight, but the rock had become too thick for prehistoric tools. Diver took the lead, climbing over the others to reach the shaft. He took the flare with him, and darkness pressed. Amy was next, then Izy.

"Your turn, boss," Harry said.

"No, if I fall, I don't want to land on you."

"That's exactly what you'll do, and I'll be ready to catch you. But don't fall."

It hurt. Standing, climbing into the shaft, pressing her back against the side, using her good leg and arms to take most of the weight, inching upward. Harry practically breathed up her ass. The shaft was smooth but uneven, different from all the bug tunnels they'd encountered. It might have been natural. Diver suggested it was a gas pocket. She didn't care. It was a fast way up. BILT4 could have made it for Wagner's birthday party, and Trax would still be happy. Unless it led nowhere.

"It's open at the top. Tell me that."

"Yeah, boss. It's open. I'm almost there."

The light cut off.

"I'm climbing out."

The light returned, but Trax closed her eyes and focused her existence on working her way up. Wriggle, push. Over and over. The quality of the sound changed. Hands grabbed from several directions. Amy, Trax, and Diver helped her out. She rolled to the side, newborn-weak, while Harry surfaced.

Diver moved Izy's hand. "Check that out. The signal gets another dB light when you turn it this way."

"Huh, it's a compass." Izy gave Diver a slap on the back and the comm. "Lead on. If you find the surface, I'll give you a kiss."

"Then I'm heading the other way."

"Boss, get up." Harry forced Trax to her feet and took an arm. Izy went on the other side. It was humiliating, but Trax was spent. She let herself be shuffled along. Like the shaft, this tunnel didn't resemble the bug holes. It grew into a broad semicircle, and the floor switched between hard stone and coarse sand.

"Do you feel that?" Diver asked.

"Ground shakes?" Harry answered.

Trax couldn't feel a thing through her wobbly legs.

"Yeah. Reckon we've doubled back on Bug City?"

"No idea."

Ahead, the floor turned to glass, but as Diver was the first to discover, they'd found water. He was also the first to point out that they shouldn't drink it without spectrometry. It could be full of heavy metals or worse. So they sloshed ankle-deep while Trax's throat imitated a sunbaked asteroid.

Amy hurried to the edge of the flare's light. "Is that a breeze? It is. I can hear it, too."

Trax walked on, unable to speed up her progress. Wind slapped her filthy skin. A patch of lesser darkness loomed. Diver laughed, tossing the comm as far as possible. Amy clapped her hands.

Bright light flashed. Another storm. Perfect. Storms happened outside. This was a good thing. She walked into the night, her friend at her side.

Clouds hid the stars. The scent of ozone combined with an invisible energy in the air. The cave they'd walked out of sat at the side of a tall hill. Lightning flashed at ground level, and wet rocks reflected, shifting almost as if they were waves. No. They weren't wet. They weren't rocks. The hillside was crawling with bugs. And the lightning came from a vehicle, driving madly around in circles. It had some kind of heavy weapon and wasn't afraid to use it.

How long before the bugs found Trax and her crew?

Diver waved the flare. "Over here! Over here!"

"Are you mad?" Izy demanded.

"Unless you want to walk home past the bugs…"

"A well-reasoned point. Keep this up and you'll graduate from school someday."

The whole crew joined in, shouting and waving, jostling Trax. She didn't mind. They were outside. Never again. She'd stay with the stars and sun for the rest of her life. It didn't matter which ones.

Fifty meters away, a bug with a deep score etched in its carapace stopped and raised its front half.

"Quiet," Trax said, but her crew didn't hear.

The bug turned toward them.

Diver jumped up and down. "It's coming. It's coming."

How did he sound so excited? She turned her weary neck. It was the vehicle. It had abandoned its circle and was racing in their direction. The bug, as if sensing the competition, skittered forward. She had nothing to stop this robotic killer, and whatever had left a mark hadn't been enough to weaken the machine. *Abuk, look after us. Take me if you must, but leave my crew, please.*

Purple-white launched from the vehicle, slamming into the scratched bug. The ground shook as the bug exploded, spraying molten metal and charred parts into the air. Its nearby brethren stopped their advance on the vehicle and assessed their destroyed kindred. Many changed their direction. Trax and her crew had been sprung. The bugs were coming.

The vehicle approached at a reckless speed, knocking bugs aside, and skidded to a halt, spraying Trax with clods of dirt. It was big, brown, ugly, and painted with BILT4 logos. Deep scratches and holes had perforated its sides in a hundred places, and one of its wheels was nothing but a mangled mess. Had it been hunting the bugs, or had it risked all to finish off her crew?

"Get in the back," a voice said over a loudspeaker.

It was familiar. Harry and Izy dragged her toward it. Her addled mind knew the voice. Bugs approached.

She planted her feet when realization dawned, spawning pure fury. "No. No. Fuck that."

Izy raised his hands. "We don't have a choice."

"I'm not going with him. I'd rather die."

The turret swiveled and fired. The air burned like a furnace.

"I mean it," she said.

Harry hugged her. "Remember when you kept me out of the tunnel?"

"Yeah, I do. I was saving you."

"I get that. I hope you do, too." Harry grabbed Trax and tossed her inside the vehicle. Amy and Diver broke her fall. Both ignored Trax's protests. Izy came in next and Harry last.

The mechanic hit a panel, and the door closed, thuds announcing the arrival of the bugs. The vehicle launched forward. There were two plain benches pocked with safety harnesses, but Hayden, the asshole, tossed the crew all over the place before they could secure themselves. All they could do was huddle in the center, five punching bags getting a workout.

"Welcome aboard," Hayden said through an internal speaker. "Sorry for the rough ride. We'll straighten everything out as soon as we're clear. I think I stirred up a hornet's nest. It's becoming a habit."

He stirred? The arrogant, jumped-up, sorry excuse for humanity. And what the hell game was he playing—leaving them to die, trying to have them slaughtered by bugs, and then picking them up as if that made it all okay. He was due some serious suffering, and she was going to dish it out.

CHAPTER 24
A CANNON GETS ATTENTION

Bill swerved the APC under the cover provided by the edge of a dense forest. The wheels tore up the ground and the front shattered sapling after sapling, a mini-ecocide. If Karlo was serious, hiding was futile. So far, Bill's best guess held up—Wagner was focused on escaping with her booty, and Karlo was on a leash.

A panel slid open behind his head. He dared not take his eyes off the route, leaving his back itching with vulnerability.

A shadow loomed behind him, Trax. "Stop."

He furrowed his brow. There wasn't time for what he knew she wanted. "We can talk when we get to Staging."

"Stop now, or I'll see if your head screws off like the robot your cold-ass actions suggest you are."

Shooting his way out of the BILT4 compound had infused him with energy and a hungry confidence, but the heat of Trax's breath and her aura of menace withered his resolve. She didn't understand what he'd done and why he had done it. She didn't know what Wagner was up to. She had no idea how serious the situation was.

"Now."

He sighed. Crumpler was asleep, leaning against the far door, and Trax, who hadn't even noticed the medic, was going to wake her up.

"Fine." He brought the APC to a stop and exited into buffeting winds. Screw twisting around in his seat to have this out. That kind of positioning left him vulnerable, both physically and strategically.

Insects chirped, apparently undisturbed by the lights of the APC. The vehicle hummed, content. Its batteries were low, thirteen percent, but that should be enough to reach Staging. As long as they didn't fire the cannon.

The rear door of the APC opened, and Trax stepped out slower than he expected. She approached, limping, and only when close did light spilling from the cab allow him to see more. Inconceivably, she had shed her environment suit. Her bra and underwear blended into her dust-encrusted skin, and blood smeared her thigh around a gel patch and down to the top of her boots. A goddess of vengeance. The impression was arresting.

Stand your ground, Bill. You're ready for this.

She grabbed him, and before he could react, she shoved him against the side of the APC, knocking his head on the hard alloy.

"You sick son of a bitch. Was it fun, having them dump us down in the tunnels to be bug food? Did that get your little dick all hard?"

Spittle wet his cheeks. Her eyes were wide and hostile, the skin around her mouth was pulled back, revealing neat teeth, and for an instant, he wondered if she would bite him. He sought the logic of his choices as a bastion to withstand her righteous anger.

"I understand that you're mad and that it appeared I was making your situation worse, but—"

She shook him, then leaned in close, her fists pressing her weight into his shoulders. "Appeared? Appeared? You fucking licked Wagner's boots while you asked for us to be tortured to death by the bugs."

"She was going to kill you."

Trax's crew emerged from the darkness and formed a semicircle around her. Their expressions suggested Bill better not look for help.

"You thought you'd get in first?"

"I bought you time. If I hadn't, Karlo would have marched you out of Wagner's office and executed you."

"You don't know that."

Bill grabbed her wrists, trying to counter her bruising grasp. "I do.

I've seen it happen. There's no honor in dying pointlessly. I worked Wagner's flunkies to give us even a single molecule of hope. That's why I suggested putting a comm in you as a tracker."

She released one shoulder, and Bill relaxed. Was he finally getting through to her? He didn't see the punch coming. An implosion of pain in his stomach. It stole his breath and forced him to bend over. Nausea swept through, but he kept his mouth shut until he had control.

"You arrogant, selfish League slime. How dare you do that to my body? And you didn't rescue us. We crawled every meter we needed to get out of that hell, not you. And I'm betting you brought the bugs down on us. All so you could sit comfy while you hatched your plans."

"Damn it, Trax. You're so naïve. I did what had to be done. It wasn't like I could ask your permission in front of Wagner."

"You couldn't find a way to do that, but you believed you'd escape, no problem? You're so damn sure of yourself."

That wasn't fair. And, damn it, he *had* pulled off the escape *and* the rescue. "No, I'm not. I wasn't. The situation was fluid. I had to create options."

"Without a fucking clue of what you were doing, you set up our grisly deaths and bet on what, making shit up? If my crew weren't the best this side of the galaxy, bugs would have skinned us alive. Think you're a hero? You're an agency spook through and through—everyone's a pawn."

She was twisting the circumstances. It had been a stroke of—if not genius, certainly clever desperation. And he'd done it for them, not himself. A wedge of doubt unbalanced his surety. He pushed it away, angered by the chilling discomfort inside as much as her attack.

"Let go of me."

"Or what? You'll drive us back to the bugs or your corporate buddies?"

"They are not my 'buddies'. If you knew what I discovered…"

She laughed in his face. "What you discovered? We saw—"

"Will the two of you give it a rest?" Crumpler walked around the nose of the APC, leaning against it when she stopped. "Hayden was stupid and full of himself. But, by luck, he was right. Save beating some sense into him until later. Staging needs to know what's going on, and you better let me see to your leg before you die of septicemia and I run out of energy to care."

Trax's surprise warmed Bill.

"You're alive?"

"Despite all best efforts. The spook here wheeled me out of the hospital."

"To save her life," Bill said. "Wagner's cutting and running. She won't take anyone who can discredit her."

Giving him one last shove, Trax stepped back. "Wagner running? Where the hell to? There's nowhere to go."

"She has a dropship. It's big—large enough for plenty of cargo, and if her crew is limited, she could stay in orbit for a while."

"Years?" Amy asked.

Bill glanced at the short woman. Like Trax, she had taken a dirt bath. Her suit had burn marks where lights and other equipment were located. Her expression was unreadable. He considered her question.

"I doubt long enough for the Phase 3 ships to arrive. I don't know what her game is, but the colonists are distractions. BILT4 won't come to our rescue—they're sending the bugs our way. And you saw how many of the damn things were crawling around that hill. We need to prepare Staging, or the colony won't last another day. How many attacked last time, a hundred? Imagine two hundred, three, four."

The crew laughed as one. Bill scowled at their cavalier attitude. They might have survived crawling through tunnels, but that was no reason for overconfidence. What was he missing?

Izy walked up and put a patronizing hand on Bill's shoulder. "You're thinking too small. Try thousands, and not just our little creepy crawlies. We've seen giant bugs that eat rock and shit it out. We've seen dragonflies with jaws that could cut you in two."

"And a bug city," Diver said, stretching his arms out vertically. "It was massive. You've never seen anything like it. Underground, the whole thing."

Bill looked away. Thousands. And different types. A city? This rabbit hole had turned into a full-blown chasm of insanity. "Did you get any footage?"

"Your friend, Karlo, burned out our gear," Trax said.

"What did you notice? Can you estimate the distances, the number of bugs? Were there other machines? Factories?"

"We should go," Harry said. "Talk while we move. If I was a bug, I wouldn't forget us."

She was right. They didn't have the luxury of time, and they could talk through a game plan while driving. Without evidence, they'd need a united front presented to Sturt and Ware. He reached out a hand toward Trax.

"I'm sorry I put you in a bad position. I'm sorry about the comm."

She hesitated. "You don't pull that shit again. I won't be told what to do at gunpoint. I won't be treated like a child. My crew won't either. We aren't drones. We matter."

"I won't pull that shit again. I promise."

They shook hands. She squeezed hard, very hard.

"When will the shooting start?" Izy asked. "I'm only here for the cheap thrills."

Bill glanced with a cocked eyebrow. Was the guy serious? On Izy's other side, Trax sat inside a foil blanket, her body hunched forward as she surveyed the outskirts of Staging. Her lack of reaction suggested he wasn't. And yet, it was a valid question.

Light bathed the ground, spreading from five points along the northern and eastern borders. The APC had crossed this diffuse threshold and traveled well past the point that Bill had expected to be challenged. They were hardly arriving with stealth, and the BILT4 guards assigned to watch the colony must have heard about the escape from Karlo. Did they fear the cannon?

Risking another percent, Bill brought the APC in a slow arc past the lights. As the glare faded, street lights and leakage from windows reassured him. The bugs hadn't returned. Yet.

His original plan had been to bypass the roads as long as possible in case there were guards or barricades, but he angled toward the northern road and the checkpoint he'd been waved through a day and an eon ago.

"This is too easy."

"Maybe they've taken a coffee break," Izy said.

Trax sniffed and leaned forward, her gaze searching. "You said BILT4 were mounting an expedition?"

"Yeah," Bill said.

"And the colony was red meat to distract the guard dogs."

"Guard bugs," Izy added.

"Something like that," Bill agreed.

"Then why bother stationing guards anymore? Wagner pulled them out to bolster her own defense or sent them with that expedition. Either way, the weaker the colony is, the more appealing a target it becomes."

A good point. Had they even collapsed the tunnels like they'd said? The APC bumped as it climbed the road edge and turned southward. They made it to the fab crew's facility without being spotted. It was past midnight, and the streets were clear. This was only a pit stop. Trax had Diver run in for a spare suit and water. She started dressing as they drove, shoving and elbowing Izy, who jostled Bill in turn.

As Bill brought the APC onto the main street, white beams jabbed at his eyes. Flashing red and blue lights switched on. A rover screeched to a halt, blocking his route. Bill braked hard and begged his heart to calm. So here it was. The whole in-the-ditches agent lifestyle was tarnishing fast.

"BILT4 or bugs?" Amy asked through the personnel hatch.

"Neither," Bill said, the markings on the rover clear to see.

Ware's voice came over a loudspeaker. "Hayden, power down and come out, hands high and empty."

There wasn't much choice. Besides, a resolution needed dialogue, not a standoff. Bill powered down the APC systems, one after the other.

"Wish me luck."

Trax leaned around Izy. "Wait till I've put on my jacket."

"He's after me. Let's not give him a reason to shoot us all. Give me a minute, and I'll get us that meeting." Bill opened his door, stepped out, and raised his arms while walking forward. Ware wasn't the kind to shoot first and ask questions later, but some of his deputies might not be so enlightened.

Ware sauntered from behind a rover, a rifle in his hands pointed down but not far from Bill. Judging by the number of other guns and heads poking up behind vehicles, the entirety of Eclipse's police force had turned out to subdue him. A compliment? One he didn't need.

They reached a position twenty paces from each other, some bizarre imitation of a duel. Except Bill was unarmed.

"On your knees."

"No," Bill said, as surprised by his words as Ware was. "We need to talk. The situation is dire. There's very little time."

"I don't want to hear it. BILT4 has been breathing down our necks like damn vampires. They're threatening to sue us over the damage you caused by attacking their compound. You could cost us everything, all of us. Years of our lives—torched for nothing. If they follow through, we'll be blacklisted from here to the other side of the League. Whatever your game is, it's over, and the agency can go kiss my ass. You're not taking us down with you."

"If I wanted to take you down, I have the pulse cannon to do it. You can't trust Wagner. They were the ones who put Staging at risk. Hell, they've compromised all of Eclipse, including every life on this rock."

"You promised me you weren't an agent. You said you'd stay out of the way. Instead, you're running around like a one-man army. Twenty-three dead, BILT4 say, and I've seen the footage."

Bill's eyes dropped as his brow creased. Twenty-three? No way. But it'd be an easy way to account for other losses while stacking the deck against him. "I didn't kill twenty-three. I was a prisoner—they'd put me to work. I'd have been dead if I didn't cooperate. You want to know what happened? A piece of alien technology exploded. I did what I had to do to escape. I'd expect no less from you."

Damn, the cutting of details, the emphasis on others, came back so easily.

Ware tightened his hand on the rifle grip. "Wagner said you'd lost it, that you were setting them up for the failure of your mission. They want you up on multiple murder charges, arson, espionage—the whole book. They're prepping a brief that'll fill half a dozen data slabs. Now, I don't trust them almost as much as I don't trust you, so I'm hoping not to have to shoot your sorry ass here and now. Get on your knees. If there's any truth to what you're saying, you'll have your chance to prove it."

The APC creaked. Trax stalked forward even while limping. Bill avoided looking her in the eye. At this stage, the only meeting he'd secured was with a cell. If she hit him this time, he'd cheer her on.

"You're wasting time, the both of you." She stood next to Bill with enough of a gap to show that she wasn't exactly with him. "The bugs are cutting up people, processing them like a damn summer harvest. If we don't act now, we're all dead. Everything you see here will be gone, carried away. It'll be like we never set foot."

Ware's angry expression took on a softer note of sadness. "Well, I'll be… Jane Trax. I heard Hayden left you for dead."

"It takes more than being stuffed down a bug tunnel to kill me and my crew." A hint of sorrow tinged her strident fury.

Bill had been there when Fitz had died. He should feel it too, even though he barely knew the man. But the horror of the piled bodies had inserted itself into his memory, a clot that allowed nothing else to flow by.

Trax continued, her crew joining her as she spoke, stoking further surprise in the police captain. "Hayden is a complete asshole. But he came back for us. It's the bugs we have to worry about. There are too many. We have to evacuate."

Her crew loudly agreed.

Ware glanced at the nearby admin building. Was he saying a prayer for Sturt to come and deal with the situation? When a miracle failed to eventuate, Ware straightened his shoulders. "We can deal with them. Every ground level is empty. Construction teams are digging a barrier of trenches that we'll fill with hardened ceramcrete. We're looking at sensors to pick up bug activity. Once the perimeter is up and running, we won't be relying on BILT4."

Bill gestured all around, his face hot with frustration. "Relying on them? Don't you realize they've abandoned you—the whole colony?

They're gone. Wagner's taking whatever tech they can, and they're lifting off. I've seen them filling their dropship."

"Damn it, Hayden. My hands are tied. I've got enough problems here and so do you. Whatever the corporates get up to doesn't affect the colony."

Ware's stubborn refusal to understand shattered Bill's patience with humanity. All the horror, the fear, the stress crumbled Bill's restraint. "Doesn't affect—Are you playing cops and robbers? Did you get your badge from a vending machine? Under your nose, BILT4 are violating every clause of the League Non-Terrestrial Archaeology Act. They've stoked up the bugs, and now they've set us all up as—"

"Enough!" Ware shouted, spittle flying from his lips. He aimed his rifle at Bill. "You're done."

"Excuse me." Amy marched up to Ware, a butterfly daring a frog to eat it. "Are you aware that BILT4 abandoned their posts at Staging's perimeter?"

"What?"

"They're gone. Which means that until the defenses are constructed, we have no warning system."

"What?"

"We saw it on the way in."

The pause Amy created gave Bill time to compose himself. "You said BILT4 told you I was coming. Did they tell you when I'd reached the city?"

Ware's face contorted. "No. One of Sturt's people called it in. A cannon gets attention."

"So pay attention," Trax said. "We have to evacuate. There's an underground city full of bugs, and they're digging and digging, expanding their territory. If we stay here, every single one of us will be dead. There won't be anyone left for you to police."

Ware called for one of his juniors to check in with the BILT4 guards. They all stood there in a circle of light under a dark sky, tired, angry, and with limited options. Bill tried to put himself in Ware's situation. An attack that couldn't be stopped, hundreds killed under his nose, and not much he could do about it. He was lashing out as much as Bill. They were hopelessly divided.

Though Bill was willing to concede one point. They could hardly raid BILT4 and arrest Wagner. Even if they did, the colony's precarious situation wouldn't change. Trax had it right. Evacuation was the only viable solution.

As they waited, Crumpler made an appearance, each of her steps a careful procedure to minimize pain. Harry assisted. Bill should have dropped the medic at the hospital first—Trax, too. Their wounds needed more than a medkit.

"Karen? The bugs had you," Ware managed, his balance shifting.

"They did, Robert. You have to listen. You can't let them take anyone else. You just can't."

"How did you escape?"

"I didn't. I was on a mound of bodies—the dying and the dead. The bugs would pick one and drag them away for slaughtering. Hayden, Trax, everyone—they freed me. When I woke up at BILT4, I was surrounded by injured corporates. They've been putting their own people through a meat grinder. I heard enough before a doc pumped me with sedatives. And then Hayden got me out. Again. I can't vouch for everything, but I trust these people, and so should you." Crumpler swayed, and Ware left his position to take some of her weight.

The deputy returned, his face pallid, too shocked to have called it over his comm.

"BILT4 is gone, Captain. They cleaned out their gear, took the sensors, everything."

Ware chuckled darkly. "I should have waited for the next planet. It was only a year behind this shit hole. Listen, Sturt ordered everyone back at night so we can protect them. That sounds impossible. Hayden, I'm taking that APC. If the bugs come—"

"It won't be enough, but you'll need it. Plug it in, though, it's low on charge."

"Aren't we all? I guess you're skipping jail again. Go see Sturt. Change his mind if you can, but don't count on it. He's already judged you. He's not giving up Staging, either. I suggested we move non-essentials until we're secure. He wouldn't have it. We're all essential for his damn schedule."

"And what are you going to do?" Trax demanded.

"Whatever I can. Post guards, cross my damn fingers, and in the morning, cobble together some sensors."

Bill nodded. Ware couldn't do much more without Sturt. "The survey shed has seismographs. You wouldn't need full geospikes."

"Noted. Sturt's in his office having another one of his damn management meetings."

To his credit, Ware quickly set his people moving. One took Crumpler to the hospital. Others drove off for the perimeter or to act as lookouts across the town. Bill walked past them, Trax accompanying him to the admin building without comment.

They took the elevator. The upward push accentuated his weariness, releasing flashes of his recent past. Horror, fear, excitement, loss of the person he had wanted to become after Marrick Prime. Perhaps it was all shock, a reaction to impossible pressures on his all-too-human mind.

Never thought it'd be so, but damn it, Dantalion, I miss you.

His mental walls were too weak for him to lock the thought away. For years, he'd never been alone, and that had stolen his sense of privacy. It had also given him a crutch—an inner world to retreat to, a coworker to debate with, a friend who never left.

Trax stood rigidly, her eyes boring into the elevator doors. If this crisis meeting didn't go well, and he had every reason to believe it wouldn't, he'd need to make a decision, perhaps the worst he'd ever considered. At least until all the flow-on effects wreaked havoc on an industrial scale. Could he get through to the prickly director? Could Sturt be convinced to embrace the lesser evil?

Without looking at Trax, he asked, "How far are you willing to go to ensure we evacuate Staging?"

She turned to him. "That's a stupid question. Whatever it takes. If Sturt doesn't listen, we'll go to the people. He's only in power as long as everyone listens to him. He can't go crying to the League for a larger pack of enforcers."

A rebellion. She wanted to start a rebellion. Was it any worse than his option? Was it any different? Was it any less realistic?

CHAPTER 25
COMMAND

The elevator doors opened onto a meeting already in progress. Trax frowned as she recognized the heads of department, everyone from Dale Jenkins in Mining to Katerina Zelen in Environment. Kotaro Honda, Trax's superior and the head of manufacturing, looked up with a quizzical expression. There were twelve of them in total, plus Sturt and a younger woman with jagged bright-yellow hair. Consoles and pads covered the table. Displays projected reports in front of the windows forming the nearest wall.

She scowled. Even when busy, a workshop should never become a dumpster fire. It sure was a far cry from the last time she'd been here with Kotaro to explain to the director why rapid manufacturing wasn't instant nor infinitely scalable. A small side table held glasses and carafes of water.

Other changes were evident as well. Crates stacked in neat piles bore labels: ration pack A, water, power pack (U3), and more. A cop sitting on one put down a mug of coffee, but Trax's gaze had already moved on. She sucked in air. A set of twin racks held a near twenty rifles. Why was the director amassing weapons that needed to be out there protecting Staging?

"What the hell are you doing here?" Sturt stood up from position at the head of the table, his gaze flicking back and forth from Trax to

Hayden, and his expression shifting from surprise, to what might have been fear, and then to anger.

Trax had dealt with assholes like Sturt before, the sort who skimped on safety margins, who made promises knowing the pain of delivery would fall on others. They hid behind artificial deadlines, jargon, and nebulous *concerns*, spinning the truth into wisps of nothing. There wasn't time for such nonsense.

She stomped over to the displays. They were filled with work orders, Gantt charts with nested task dependencies, and graphed projections. Everything needed for a project manager's wet dream. Even at a glance, she could see that none of it acknowledged the reality on the ground—or the danger beneath.

"This is all horseshit. Even without knowing what we know, you all had enough to go on."

"Jane—" Kotaro began.

"Don't you Jane me. Where's the concern? Great to have you back, Jane. Is the rest of the crew okay, Jane?"

"Enough," Sturt said, cutting the air with his hand.

Hayden approached the other side of the long table. "If I could—"

"Wait your turn." Trax spared him a brief glare. "Director Sturt, It's not enough. Not nearly. I've seen shit that would leave you standing in a puddle and freeze your balls so hard they'd fall off. You've not asked, but Fitz is dead. That's David Fitzsimmons. Have you taken him off the work roster? Are we all off it? You can burn all this. We're not facing a few drones constructed by a nutbar terrorist. There's an entire underground city. There are bugs of all different kinds. They have tunnels that go on endlessly. If we don't evacuate the hell away, we're all doomed. Your roster will be empty. No more shifts, no more output. Nothing. Not even dead bodies."

Sturt's face filled with false sincerity, like a backed-up toilet. "I appreciate that you have clearly gone through some kind of trauma, Ms. Trax, but you are beyond out of line. Go to the hospital and check yourself in. You're bleeding on the carpet. Rest assured, between our police and the security team from BILT4, you will be safe."

Hayden walked to the windows and slapped one. "From in here, you're blind. You need to give up on BILT4. Wagner is playing you.

Staging is a distraction. They're serving you up on a platter, so they can sneak alien technology off-planet."

That brought muttering from the department heads. The yellow-haired woman had been talking to Sturt while Hayden spoke, and that hushed conversation continued until Sturt picked up a pad and jabbed it like a finger.

"Given our existing morale problem, I didn't want this to become general knowledge, but I see there is no alternative." Sturt paused until he had every manager waiting attentively. "The LSA is attempting a hostile takeover. They want to kill Project Eclipse and claim the planet as League property. Think about it, if we fail, each land share becomes defunct. All that time and money poured into terraforming disappears with a failed license. We don't get a constitution protecting us until Phase 3. Bill Hayden is their way to ensure that never happens."

What was he talking about? Trax glanced at Hayden. The ex-agent sure appeared surprised, but then he'd also convinced Trax and her crew that he was leaving them to die. What if he had been, but later decided they'd be more useful alive?

Hayden crossed to stand in front of Sturt. "That is the most ridiculous flight of fancy I've ever heard. That's not what the agency is about. I'm not saying they're without faults, but this isn't one of them."

Which was exactly what he would say, no matter the truth. Acid burned in Trax's chest. They were losing precious minutes to dick-swinging. And yet, if that was Hayden's plan, everything he'd said to her was in question. The useless department heads kept silent as if engrossed by a game down to the last seconds with one play left. Well, it wasn't a game.

She stalked over to the pair, causing the yellow-haired woman to dodge out of the way. "I don't trust Hayden as far as he can throw me, but that's a hell of a thing to claim. Where's your proof?"

Sturt slapped his pad. "Right here."

He used the pad to throw data maps across the displays. "We all knew there were problems. Random faults and breakages escalating to damage that could not be explained away by storms or malfunctions. And then the bugs came. I stopped Ware from chasing the culprit because we had one. But look at this. See the time stamps from one rover. Compare them to the incidents. They don't all match up, but there's enough." Sturt walked around the table. "Hayden used his position as head of the survey team to sabotage our operations. His route went near, and then a day or two later, damage reports flowed in."

This caused an uproar as the managers poured through the data. Trax checked the map and recognized several dates. They were etched in her mind thanks to the reconstruction jobs she'd had to fit in.

She pointed at the little red glows that marked Hayden's rover signals. "Are these you? Are they accurate?"

A sheen of sweat on Hayden's brow matched his wide eyes. "They appear accurate, but they also mean nothing. You could put this kind of crap together for anyone who travels regularly."

Sturt snarled. "Like Charles Palao, the member of your team who was conveniently murdered? His rover was destroyed, and his body crushed, muddying the forensic evidence. Did he know too much? Was he your fall guy?"

"This is nuts," Hayden said. "If you believed that, you should have had Ware lock me up."

"Oh, we needed to know how deep this stink went. Remember this little escapade."

A display switched to a video feed. There was Hayden, stepping from an elevator to an office floor. He cleaned a mug excessively and set it aside. He talked to someone, and when they went out of view, he slipped into an office, looking around in a subtle, yet shifty manner.

"A little casual espionage using someone else's account," Sturt noted. "And this is one instance we caught. How many other times did he do it? What records did he alter? There are hash errors throughout the system."

Hayden sniffed. "I had to do the job you weren't. I needed to understand what was happening."

Trax clenched a fist. If Sturt was right, Hayden wanted Eclipse burned to the ground. Had the spook made an agreement with Wagner? Would he be willing to kill all ten thousand colonists to complete his mission? How many millions had died on Marrick Prime? *Abuk's heart.* A shiver ran through her.

"And then he waltzes in here," Sturt said, his lips curling as he made another gesture on his pad. "The butcher of BILT4."

Fresh video played—several feeds spliced sequentially. Hayden taking chemicals, mixing them. An explosion. Bodies. Some kind of large internal space, perhaps a warehouse. Hayden leaning over something. Another explosion. More bodies. The feeds jumped quickly, but Trax counted over twenty dead. And then there was the APC Hayden had boosted. It blasted this way and that, the footage switching to feeds showing BILT4 staff walking, then their agonized faces, their bodies, but staying on none. Only a time counter at the top pulled it all together. It was awful, just awful.

"It's doctored," Hayden growled. "That's not how it went. I've never even seen most of those people. That timestamp is pure fantasy. Yeah, I had to fight to escape with Crumpler, but this is sick. It's nothing more than an example of how far Wagner is willing to go."

"Erin," Sturt said to the yellow-haired woman. "Was the footage supplied by BILT4 doctored?"

"No, sir. It all passes tamper checks."

Hayden jerked as if electrocuted. A guilty conscience? She couldn't believe it.

She was nine. The house swirled with the odor of baking potatoes and the earthy undercurrent that accompanied any farm. The front door burst inward, falling to the ground with a thunderclap. Corporate soldiers charged through, shouting. One knocked Jane to the floor and hurried past, a rifle pointed at her mother. In seconds, they'd shoved both her parents to the ground and secured them with pain cuffs. It was the last she'd see of them for five years. The court case had been swift and confusing. Guilty of sedition against a rightful landowner. The evidence, her parents claimed, had been manufactured. Five years of hard labor and the farm confiscated. A childhood stolen.

The connection was there. But was that wishful thinking? Had he been working her, taking advantage of her past? Her gut said no.

She took a deep breath. "I'm alive because of Hayden. I'm not saying that I trust him, but I sure as hell don't trust BILT4. They marched my crew and me into a bug tunnel." She didn't say it was

Hayden's suggestion. He owed her big time. "You have to stop this pissing contest. Lock up Hayden or whatever, but listen to him, and listen to me. We. Have. To. Evacuate."

Sturt spread his hands wide. "Look at them, all cozied up. Privacy regs be damned. This woman's parents were both anti-corporate terrorists. What is her word worth?"

White hot fury burst inside Trax. She charged Sturt. The cop came from out of nowhere and got in the damn way.

"You don't speak about my parents, not one word."

"I'm docking you twenty-five percent of your land shares for that. If I didn't need you churning out parts…"

She reached for Sturt, advancing a step despite the cop holding her. "No one will give a fuck about shares when the bugs come."

"Get out of here or it'll be fifty percent."

She stopped fighting the cop and channeled the depth of her hatred for authority into a glare that should have cut through the director's skull like an axe. "I dare you."

"Done."

He still didn't get it. It was all a joke. She laughed.

"Now it's fifty percent—for your entire team."

The anger swept through her, causing her limbs to tremble. Her heart slammed in her chest. Heat radiated from her skin.

"Leave him." Hayden said it three times before she forced her eyes to his. "He doesn't feel in control, so he's lashing out. He wants you locked up or in submission. He can't see past his nose because what's beyond frightens him. The case made against me is pretty good, but you know it's wrong. It's all too damn neat. The rover times—they're close, but the days for some are off. That last video is the kicker, though. There's no way the timestamp is accurate. I know what happened. Even Crumpler might remember enough to prove it. And if those details are faked, then how could they be authenticated?"

What was he talking about? Who cared?

"Who's been working the director? The answer is simple. Erin Tyzen, hypernet engineer, and I'm guessing, a fairly decent hacker. She put the data together. She's vouched for it all. And someone accessed my sealed records early on. Who knows what else she's been sticking her fingers into? I'm guessing our hacker reports to Wagner."

Perplexed, Trax turned to the accused woman and widened her eyes.

Erin held a small gun. "Officer Weaver, carefully place your weapon on the ground and kick it away."

The room was silent apart from the susurration of the sliding pistol. Her aim shifted to Hayden.

"So much for the vaunted knowledge of the League Security Agency. I don't work for BILT4. I couldn't care less about them, though the relationship has been useful. They were only too happy to keep an eye on you. Bill Hayden, you think you're so clever. You arrogant monster. Director, he's moved on as if *it* never mattered. He doesn't understand because he doesn't care."

The skin of her face pulled tight with anger. "This is about Marrick Prime. It always was. My family: my father, my mother, my sisters, and my brother. All dead. Their bodies gone. Innocents slaughtered. LSA agent Bill Hayden spotted kidnapping a pilot and escaping once his work was done. He thought he could come out here and avoid punishment for his crimes. Well, he can't. If no one else will do it, I will."

Whereas Trax's anger boiled and bubbled, this woman wielded it like a scalpel. She'd pull the trigger when she was ready. That was obvious. And it was a sideshow, like everything that had come before. Another fool grandstanding while lives were at stake. Trax got the anger—Marrick Prime had sent ripples across all of humanity—but everyone needed to fight for the living, not the dead.

Trax tamed her impatience. "Can you shoot him later? Right now, we need to focus on Eclipse and the people here. Ten thousand of us are waiting to be served up as bug food."

Erin shrugged. "Justice has a cost. Like with the little accidents I had to arrange. Then our mechanical neighbors jumped in and did my job for me. I wanted Hayden tried and found guilty. I left the damn evidence, but Ware wouldn't listen. *Circumstantial* this and that. Hayden turned him, bribed him, blackmailed—it doesn't matter which. After the attack, I pointed Director Sturt to it all. He believed, but he was too worried about disruption to order a search for Hayden.

As if a schedule matters when punishment is due." She grew louder, her gestures jerky, her eyes wild as they switched to the spook. "Wagner screwed up, and he ran back here, arrogant as ever. No one else is willing to hold him accountable. I'll do it, here and now. Bill Hayden, I find you guilty of the mass murder of all the poor souls on Marrick Prime."

The cop put her hands out, palms down, in a calming gesture. "Let's not do anything we'll regret. Now—"

"Stay out of it," Hayden and Erin said simultaneously.

He turned to Trax as if the pistol trained on him no longer mattered. "Sorry, I couldn't be more help."

The urge to slap his whiny face had her hand halfway up before she realized what she was about to do. He was giving up. In her books, that was worse than almost any other failing. "Hayden, you asshole, say something."

The spook raised his hands, whether in submission to her or Erin, Trax couldn't tell.

"I was on Marrick Prime to find a path toward peace, and I failed as big as it gets. I didn't give the order, but I wrote the report that sealed the planet's fate. Make of that what you want. After, I didn't fight for change. I ran from the agency. And yet, here I am, caught up in its mess and failing just as hard."

He cocked his head and looked at Trax. "What would you have me do? Would you welcome the LSA to Eclipse if that's what it takes to start the evacuation? Would you bring on the control that you hate so much to save lives?"

What was he on about? He was genuinely asking her something. Was it permission, forgiveness? Trax scowled as Erin steadied her pistol. Hayden kept his eyes on Trax. He wasn't going to beg for his life. He wasn't going to ask for help. And yet, Trax was close enough to his executioner to tackle her. And probably get killed for the effort. Was Bill Hayden, accomplice to genocide, worth the risk?

Erin's finger caressed the trigger.

It wasn't the first time he'd had a gun pointed at him, but it was the first time Bill remained calm. He'd fled the agency to be someone different, a bitter solo explorer of the far reaches. Then a chance presented itself. A chance to be a better person and make better choices. Redemption. Was that taking responsibility for his actions? If this was justice delayed, it was still justice delivered. He'd never had the right to survive Marrick Prime. If only Erin Tyzen could see the truth—this wouldn't give her peace. She didn't understand yet that there would never be any.

You're taking the easy way out. The voice crawled across his scalp as if coming from an implant. But Dantalion had been excised from his flesh. It was his own thought. He didn't want to give up. He hadn't escaped Wagner's clutches to die here, the colony succumbing shortly after. His failures needed redressing, but not like this. People were counting on him, even if they didn't know it. Just like when he was in the agency. Damn it. Beth would be laughing. She had cast her net, and it was time for him to step forward and be tangled.

No more passing responsibility up the line. He would do what was necessary. He would give up his freedom and claim power he had never wanted. If he survived. Trax's frustrated stare bored into his mind, and he remembered his promises to her. What good could power bring without consent? He cocked his head and examined the engineer—her grim determination and forthright honesty were a beacon of integrity cutting through the murk of interstellar civilization.

"What would you have me do? Would you welcome the LSA to Eclipse if that's what it takes to start the evacuation? Would you bring on the control that you hate so much to save lives?"

Another question remained unasked. Would she save his? The answer to both would be the same. Erin ran a finger along the trigger. There it was. So be it. At least Eclipse had Trax and her crew. She may not trust him, but he trusted her.

Trax launched, a wall of determination that slammed into Erin. Plasma flashed. Heat bloomed. Shouts. The shattering of a window. Bill staggered backward, stumbling over the cop's pistol. Blinking against the afterimages, he reached down and retrieved it, checking its readiness out of habit. Managers dove beneath the table. Trax and Erin wrestled, the barrel twisting this way and that.

And then it was over. Trax had the gun, and Weaver rushed in, pinning Erin to the floor.

"Go ahead," the hypernet engineer screamed over the wind whistling through broken glass. "Kill me, too. Finish off what you started."

Bill checked the barrel of the pistol he held. It pointed at Erin. Slowly, he lowered it. "There have been too many deaths already."

Sturt backed away, disheveled and wearing an expression of horrified disbelief. "Hayden. I curse the day you joined the Eclipse roster. You've brought nothing but chaos. You're destroying the colony. Get out. You're no longer welcome here. Consider yourself exiled. You too, Trax. You're damaged goods."

Trax slammed him against the nearest wall and leaned in close. "You can't do that. You don't have the authority."

His features twisted into a sneer. "You think we're in a disaster? That grants me all the authority I need. The pair of you have an hour to get out of Staging before I issue a shoot-on-sight order."

Trax leaned on him, hard. "And then what? We'll be safer than the poor bastards you're trapping in Staging."

This was it. The moment he'd been avoiding. The moment Beth had somehow known would be thrust upon him. He needed to reclaim his place in the agency and more.

"Trax, let him go. I'm going to hurt him more than you can. Director Oliver Sturt, I'm relieving you of command. I'd appreciate your help organizing the evacuation, but I'll settle for you staying out of my way."

"YOU HAVE NO AUTHORITY!" Sturt pushed Trax away when she let up pressure. "I'll have you shot for this. Mutiny! I'll have you hung. I'll feed you to the bugs one limb at a time."

Bill wandered over to a console and confirmed its hypernet connection. He brought up the personnel section and requested an override. When the screen asked for authentication, he toggled the options using a little-known feature and brought up a command code request. The details spread across a display next to the broken window, shimmering in the disturbed air. The command code was long. Very long. It wasn't a problem. The agency had trained him to memorize details. The console accepted the code and ran through an ID check.

The display churned out line after line of data, before clearing and leaving a simple message:

WELCOME TO PROJECT ECLIPSE, DIRECTOR HAYDEN.

Gasps came thick and fast. A transfer notification spread across the hypernet. Every implant not blocked by interference would be vibrating with the update. Trax swore, long and loud. Sturt's mouth kept opening and closing, but no words came out. That was something.

"I have all the authority I need and more than I could want. Sturt, join the team or bench yourself."

"You—You won't get away with this."

Bill chuckled darkly. "I won't run from the consequences, not this time. But we are going to run from the bugs. Officer Weaver, please escort our previous director from the premises. Erin, too. Once you have, let Captain Ware know that I'll need to see him at his earliest convenience."

"Ah, I guess."

"I'm still director!" Sturt shouted. "You can't do this!"

Pain lanced through Bill's skull. He grimaced as it seemed to twist rather than diminish. This wasn't a moment to succumb to a headache. Placing the officer's pistol into her hand, Bill said. "I trust you. I need you to trust me, too. We have lives to save."

He turned his back, allowing the officer to make her choice.

"Ah, Mr. Sturt, Ms. Tyzen. This way, please."

The right choice. He cast his gaze across the room. "Everyone, you have five minutes to take a breath and settle yourselves back down. After that, we have an evacuation to plan."

He walked over to the water and poured himself a glass, ignoring all calls for his attention. Trax moved aside, her expression one of consideration. What, he didn't know. Nor did he have the capacity to wonder. The pain was spreading: needles of fire in his skull, joints that throbbed, flashes across his vision, high-pitched ringing in his ears. He clenched his teeth as his shaking hands spilled water. He knew this. Lines of code burst across his vision. Beth had played him once again. The agency hadn't removed his hardware at all. They'd never let him go. It was all an illusion. He'd never been free.

"Hello, Bill, it's been a while." The synthetic voice was in Bill's head.

"Dantalion, it's not been long enough."

Once again, Bill's mind was no longer his own.

"My, my, you have been busy, haven't you? Quite some journey."

"You don't know the half of it."

"Not yet. I'm downloading and reconstructing the updates pushed onto the hypernet by my clone, but given the timestamps, I'm sure you'll have more to tell." The sneaky bastard. Bill hadn't known the cloned copy could do that.

"You'll have to wait; there's work to be done."

He drank the water and focused on the cool sensation as it slid to his stomach. His body was calming now that the implanted network had come fully online. There was no longer any excuse to put off what had to be done. He returned to the table, taking Sturt's seat. None of the department heads had used the chance to leave.

"Here's how this will work. I'm going to give you a situation update. You're going to do the same for me, and then together, we're going to evacuate. Everyone goes before the sun sets. I don't have time for disagreement or to ask nicely. And I'm sure as hell not going to insult you by demanding loyalty or making threats. This is about doing our jobs and saving lives. Trax, can you start us off? You saw more of the bugs than I did."

The fab leader didn't move at first. She'd found a stronger drink from somewhere and took a swig of the amber fluid. He needed her for this. More than he'd thought. Yes, she'd saved his life. But she was one of these people. Bill had always been an outsider. No matter how much Sturt had tried to smear her reputation, Trax was a colonist through and through.

She emptied her drink and hobbled to the table. Damn, he was asking an awful lot. She really should be in the hospital. With a grunt, she sat on a corner and pointed to a map still hovering in the air.

"Right," she said. "Listen and listen good."

As she talked, Bill felt a measure of relief. She was with him. For now. While he did what she thought was right. Perhaps that was a good thing. Someone to keep him honest. Someone who'd stop him from instigating another a Marrick Prime. And she was an expert in her own right.

"This is nice," Dantalion said. "It's always useful to have a local team. It's just like old times."

Bill winced.

I hope not.

CHAPTER 26
FROM THE SKY

Trax winced as she took an awkward step through the wide-open doors of CF-S1, her main fab, and entered a hive of activity much later in the morning than she had bargained for. She should have refused the hospital stay—there wasn't time for weakness. They'd put her under, and, after poking, prodding, and stabbing, they'd gelled her enough to make each movement robotic. Some of the discomfort was her fault. One of her crew would have picked her up if she hadn't given them tasks instead of answers over the intermittent comms. But there was work to do and no budget for overtime.

The side of the building to her right was also open, funneling a gusty breeze and revealing the vehicle bays and her crew's role in the evacuation. You couldn't send ten thousand colonists into the wilderness on foot and expect them to survive. You couldn't even do it with rovers alone. They'd need shelter, food, water purification, and a thousand things not thought of. And what better way to ensure the right equipment would be available than to make it? As much as she'd wished they'd been on the move ten minutes after she'd finished with Hayden, fleeing without preparation would only be picking another way to die.

She scuffed the hard floor. Four faces twisted around, and her crew charged like they'd been offered a free drink. They hit her one after the other, rocking her this way and that. The pain was welcome.

Harry summed it up. "We were worried. Lots of rumors going round."

"All right, chip monkeys, the doc didn't fit me with an O_2 tank. I need to breathe."

As they gave her a nanometer of space, Izy asked, "What the hell happened? We heard you were shot."

"Shot?" Trax snorted. "I don't have time for that. Don't believe what's flying around on the hypernet."

"But someone shot at you, right?" Diver said. "And there was a coup."

Amy shook her head. "Not a coup. It was a lawful transition of power, or, as I see it, Hayden cut off Sturt's balls."

"But the boss was shot at. That ain't lawful."

Trax put a steadying hand on Diver's shoulder. "I saved Hayden's miserable ass and opened a few cuts, that's all. What you need to know is this: Management, as always, is a nest of vipers. Hayden arrived with baggage. That's old news. But he's also the one willing to order the evacuation, so whatever his motivation, he's doing what we need done. If that changes, we worry about it then. Understood?"

When they agreed, it was time for work. She walked deeper into the facility, assessing progress with a critical gaze. "Give me a status report."

Harry rubbed her hands on her thighs. "All vehicles are charged and lubed, but Bandit needs to stay. The brakes can't be trusted."

Leaving gear behind grated on Trax's soul, but seconds kept burning, forever lost. "No Bandit. Got it. Izy?"

The usually languid man straightened. "I've loaded spares: resins, bars, powders, reels. As much as Abfab can pull. I'm prioritizing like hell on Aunty Jo's load. Amy and I think we should dump the mechs to gain space for beams and the like that we're not equipped to churn out."

Capacity vs. construction. "No. Work with the space you've got. If we need structural materials, we can use the mechs to cannibalize everything from terraformers to tractors. There are plenty of sites out there. Amy?"

"I crated and stowed the most likely tools we'll need. Since then, I've been running the load calculations for Izy and helping Diver with a launcher."

Trax noted dozens of canisters across Diver's main bench. "What's cooking here?"

"More grenades." Diver hurried over to his toys. "Don't worry, I've loaded a whole slew of precursors. But I thought the grenades I made last time were shit. So, I've upped the bang and tossed in tungsten chips. I mounted pouches of insta-glue on the tips, yeah. Pull the tag, toss, and if you get a direct hit, it'll stick to the bastards."

She couldn't disagree with the necessity, and Diver was skilled, but rushing explosives was asking for trouble.

"Anyone thought about food and potable water?"

Her crew looked at each other blankly. She shook her head. "Medical supplies? Spare clothes? Of course not. Kiddies, we aren't coming back because you forgot your teddy bears. Time to put the dolls and crayons away and get to work. This is how it's going to go…"

She laid out the plans and peppered them with questions to confirm details. The sounds of industry, panicked voices, and increasing traffic from outside lent another layer of urgency. Her crew worked their asses off as the sun crossed the sky, and Trax did the same, limping this way and that, directing, storing cargo, and assisting as she could.

With half an hour to go, she was standing outside, having given a spare ultracapacitor to an agriscience team so they could get their mobile lab up and running. The vehicle could hold thirty once they'd dumped their beloved microscopes and other gadgets. Parts were in short supply at the main vehicle repair shop, and there was no time to make more—and Trax, as sure as shit after a good curry, wasn't going to horde. Too many were already behind. Staging should have been a ghost town.

A flyer swooped low, coming from the east and creating a deep shadow as it headed toward the afternoon sun. Its six thrusters with blue ion jets washed her in heat and dust. After coughing up her lungs, she wiped her eyes clear and uttered a few choice insults. There weren't many of those pricks around, and that was a damn good thing. Hayden was taking a risk, given the changeable weather. She couldn't fault him for using the flyer—but the pilot was another matter. What were they carrying? Cargo, people? Its path was heading toward Adeona, the dropship. Cargo, then. Hayden had said he wanted it to form the core of their refuge. Another risk. How many steps of the pre-flight checklists were they ignoring so it would be ready to skip a few hundred kilometers by sunset? The flyer went out of sight behind a building, and Trax headed back inside, considering her long list of last-minute necessities.

Boom!

The ground rocked.

"Diver, did you try adding numbers again?" Izy asked as he poked his head out of the hauler's third trailer.

"Don't blame me. Boss, what was that?"

A plume of smoke and flames licked the air, growing thicker and thicker, quickly reaching hundreds of meters into the sky. Dust blasted outward, a thick, roiling wall glowing thanks to Staging's many lights. Another explosion shook the ground, then a third. The sun dimmed more each time. Trax sighed.

"There was a flyer. The poor asshole must have crashed flying too damn low. If they hit the dropship, and I reckon they did, Abuk save us, because that's gonna sting. Everybody, back to work, double time. If fire spreads, we'll have to haul ass sooner than we'd like."

The fab atmosphere turned grim, with little talk and much swearing. Over the next few minutes, the ground kept rumbling, and Trax struggled with the desire to help the flyer's crew. She was no medic. Trusting others, especially management, didn't come easily, but downing tools to do someone else's job was foolish. If Hayden failed, she'd kick him from here to the bug city in one go. Until then, she had his back and would stick to her post.

A keening siren drove daggers into her ears. They all stopped.

"Bugs?" Harry asked from inside a short mech holding a black, rectangular pack heavy enough to turn a human to paste and loaded with enough juice for a good explosion of its own.

Bugs? It was too early. Trax tried her comm. Nothing. Dust must be jamming the signal. She glanced outside and scowled. It might as well be dusk. She turned away, reluctantly. The vehicles wouldn't ready themselves.

Vibrations came up through her boots. This was worth a moment. She walked one way, then another, feeling it change.

"Is it bugs? They can't come up through our foundation, can they?" Diver said as he stared down, concern twisting his mouth. "It's damn thick."

Izy kneeled at his position by the vehicle bay doors. "Don't go calling anything thick. Glass houses, remember. They're not coming up. Can you feel that? They're moving along."

Amy brushed her hands on her legs. "They're after a soft spot. They'll come out at the foundation's edge."

Damn. They were too early. Everyone was meant to be out hours before the bugs showed up. The crash had created a false dusk, and the raging fire must have masked the advance.

"Down tools and mount up." When she saw every member of her crew hesitate as they no doubt considered one last item to take, she added, "Now!"

Harry's mech lowered the battery, and the mechanic opened its cage. Izy gave an assist, and they all coalesced around Trax as she headed for the bays.

"I'll take Abfab. You're all in Aunty Jo. Amy, you're driving. Keep it tight. If you get separated, go as far away as you can. Assume I'm doing the same."

"I can drive better," Izy said. "Let me take Abfab."

"None of you are going alone. And you drive faster, not better."

They reached the long bays where the vehicles waited. Trax climbed into Abfab's Frankenstein cockpit, then turned to Aunty Jo's blister. "Stay safe. Stay smart. Stay alive."

Izy, hazy even at this distance, gave her a lazy salute as he boarded the hauler. "Only 'cause you ask, boss."

The soil between the vehicle bay and the road cracked.

Trax dragged herself up and into the cockpit. Once inside, she lowered the canopy and ran through the start-up cycle while wiping dust from her stinging eyes. When all the indicators flicked green, she directed the fab rover forward at a slow speed. Aunty Jo strained against its trailers, then slipped in behind, its powerful lights encasing them in a bright bubble that barely reached nearby buildings.

Ahead, the crack expanded. Chunks of soil collapsed into darkness. Bugs poured out, one, two, five, ten—so many. She steered Abfab hard to the left, gritting her teeth and hoping that Izy had secured the onboard machines. A glint of metal arced through the air, landing on the far side of the hole. It rolled for a meter, then blew up in a flash of light and white smoke. Small holes appeared in both sides of her canopy. Trax threw herself back into her seat, but the danger had gone before she'd seen it.

"Diver, you asshole, that was too close."

No comm signal. At least the blast had fragged two bugs and left another limping. As the Abfab rolled by, a bug leaped onto its canopy, struggling to find a purchase on the smooth surface. She slapped the clear polymer, but that only drew the bug's attention. The little tools near its front extended, and a small saw blade spun. Trax's heart squeezed. Her skin prickled with heat. It was going to cut its way through and pull her out. She yanked the rover left and right, but it was heavy and responded too slowly to dislodge her attacker. The saw pierced the canopy, sending an acrid stink into the enclosed space. Could she open the canopy? And then what, run away? Hell, no. It'd leap onto her from behind.

She fumbled for the cockpit's small storage locker by her left leg. If there were a tool, anything, she might be able to… Her hand found a cylinder. She glanced down as she steered the rover onto the street. One of Diver's grenades. Bless the kid. She urged the rover to its maximum speed, earning flashing warnings. She'd have to wait for just the right moment. The rover bucked as she went over a hard lump. It could have been anything from a rock to a small vehicle. Either way, it was crushed by the time she moved past.

The bug finished cutting a length creepily similar to her shoulder width and started another. The horrible whine of its progress set her teeth on edge and drowned out the useless siren blaring across Staging. Anyone who didn't already know the bugs had arrived was screwed. The third line of a square grew with inhuman patience as Trax dodged a group of colonists running across the road. She swore at their stupidity and regretted not stopping to pick them up. Though, with the bug hanging on, they would have refused.

After slipping thin appendages through the cut lines, the bug worked the flap it had created. When the transparent material proved too stiff, it started cutting a fourth line. Was it watching her with anticipation or smelling her fear? At least it didn't drip saliva. Trax gripped the grenade and waited. When the blade had almost reached the end of the fourth side, the flap flexed outward, and dust blew in. The edge lifted farther… farther. The bug's abdomen was clear, but if she stuck the grenade there, it'd blow them both to pieces. Up and up. The section of canopy snapped with a sharp report, and there was nothing between Trax and the killing machine. It leaned close.

She pulled the grenade's tag and thrust it between the bug's appendages, the force breaking the glue pouch on what she hoped were sensors. Only then did she hit the arming button. Two of the bug's legs let go of the cockpit as it tried to remove the obstruction. She pulled her arm back, and the bug's flailing appendages battered her. The saw cut into her suit, scoring a line of red agony down her forearm. Trax shrugged the pain off and slammed on the brakes. The bug went skittering along the cockpit and off, rolling forward, then dancing madly as it tried to remove the foreign object.

Trax ducked low. The deafening blast slammed air into the canopy's open wound. Shards cut further holes, and she counted herself lucky that none found her flesh.

Grinning savagely, she brought the rover back up to speed and enjoyed crushing the bug's remains. Her watering eyes stung as she steered into a patch of mostly clear air. The improved vision revealed chaos. Painted by a reddening sun, already rust-toned bugs scurried along the walls of buildings or chased those on foot. Others dragged victims into the ground. Where the fuck was Hayden?

A comms signal came through—a general alert from Ware. "Anyone remaining on the east side of staging must head west across the bridge. No playing heroes, no stupidity. Just move it!" The message repeated, so she killed it. Ware was going for the same game plan as last time. Hopefully, the bugs hadn't anticipated that.

A hundred meters ahead, bugs massed in front of two parked rovers that blocked the way. What idiot had done that? Didn't they know the bugs could climb? People moved on top of the rovers, and then Trax realized what they were up to. Blasts of plasma erupted from the rifles her crew had cooked up earlier. It was a steady attack, perhaps by those familiar with weapons. There were certainly a few ex-soldiers in the colony. They hit bugs repeatedly, spewing robotic death, but this wasn't some incursion of a dozen machines. They were everywhere, and the spirited defense only drew more bugs.

She turned hard right. "Amy, can you hear me?"

Amy's voice came over the comm. "Yes, boss, but who knows for how long?"

"Are you still following?"

"We are. Just a little farther back—your driving is erratic."

"I had a bug problem. Stay as close as you can and don't lose visual. We're still heading for the bridge, but I'll take whatever route gets us there in one piece."

"Understood."

Trax cut the connection and almost wet herself. A line of people strung across the road, carrying assorted crap that slowed them down. She worked the brakes and leaned forward, sticking her head out of the damaged canopy. Fear stained their expressions, so she swallowed her anger and made a quick decision.

"Get on wherever you can and hold tight. Dump whatever you're carrying. It's not worth your lives."

She counted wasted seconds as the truth broke through. They abandoned their possessions and swarmed aboard. It wasn't safe, but it was all she could offer. Once again, she set off.

Five turns kept her alive but brought her to Staging's northwest edge. At an empty junction, she headed south toward the bridge. Another pocket of resistance came into view on her left. Several crashed rovers had bled fire retardant over the road. At the edge of visibility, two people retreated toward another rover, one of them pulsing like a firefly as they shot at bugs dropping from an apartment block. Trax built up speed to crush a few on the way through. The colonist with the gun turned to her. It was Sturt, and he had Erin with him. Passengers screamed as Trax adjusted her direction. What had they expected? They'd wanted the express route; they were getting it.

Sturt pushed Erin into the nearby rover and spun to face a bug that was too close for Trax to knock down. He fired, but it wasn't enough. As Trax passed, she saw the bug leap on him, sharp limbs skewering his torso in a bloody attack. And then she was through without a chance to process the horror show.

Fuck!

A nimbus of light formed in the thick air ahead, revealing a stalled exodus stretched across the bridge. Only two police vehicles had arrived to defend the choke point, and there were as many vehicles as people on foot. Hayden had botched the evacuation.

A movement in the sky had Trax raising her hand to swat a bug— the small kind. It wasn't though. It was a flyer. It was the same flyer. The one that she'd thought had crashed. What was it doing? It dropped altitude and slipped across the top of buildings near the bridge, chased by blasts of plasma from below.

Boom! Boom! Boom!

Fire. Smoke. Heavy panels spinning at speeds that turned them into razor blades. They cut into nearby buildings and wobbled violently. Debris dropped from a decapitated building like ancient cannon balls on the line of those fleeing. She let Abfab slow. Had the flyer finally crashed? No. The sensation of falling gripped her guts. She thought of Diver and his grenades. The flyer was dropping bombs, ones far more potent than the chemist's homebrew. Were they trying to kill the bugs? What idiot would do that so close to a bridge filled with evacuees? Disgust rippled across her, souring her mouth and leaving her shaking. Who would do that?

BILT4.

The flyer turned back. It had missed. It hadn't aimed for the buildings.

Izy's voice came over a shared comm channel. "Boss. Why are we stopped?"

"See that flyer?"

Multiple voices agreed over her comm, and she was thankful for the sense of connection. This wasn't a time to be alone.

"It's going to blow the bridge."

"I think the angle's wrong," Amy said with a curious tone. "It's going farther south toward the power plant."

"Oh, shit," Diver said.

Izy sucked in air. "That would wipe the shit right out of you."

They were right. If the plant went up, nothing in Staging would survive. Not even the bugs. That wouldn't be the end of the bastards, Trax was sure, but they'd take a hit. "Why not leave the bugs to do their work?"

"No witnesses," Harry said. "It'd scrub all the evidence, every bit."

She was right. Some people—mostly corporates—were utter scum. Trax shook her head and opened a Staging-wide channel, the sort of action that got your comm privileges revoked. It wouldn't be enough, but was all she could do. That and get her crew out of the city limits.

She cleared her throat. "Everyone, listen up. Don't cross the bridge and get the fuck away from the western side. East, north, south, wherever, but get out."

CHAPTER 27
THE BIG PICTURE

S tifling a yawn, Bill forced his eyes to focus on a display filled with the growing cargo manifest of the Adeona. Sturt, the complete ass, had concentrated supplies in Staging on the assumption that one place would be easy to defend. More likely, he wanted to watch every work team like a hawk lest they waste time on unimportant things like meals and sleep. He'd already forced through a twelve-hour workday.

And along Bill had come, waking everyone up early and making twelve hours seem like luxury. They'd toiled most of the day, and he'd grown impatient despite the progress. Signs of bug activity had been reported far and wide. They were growing bolder, or Wagner had really stirred them up. Either way, he couldn't risk sending unprotected folk in dribs and drabs. He'd arranged for the upper management to operate from over the bridge to ensure a level of organizational redundancy. By now, the entire colony should have been there too, with the Adeona already in the air.

Should have—it so rarely became *was*. Around him, administrative staff marked up displays, shouted down comms links, and hurried in and out of the central restaurant where Bill had set up his command. The ground-level position gave quick access and brought Bill closer to those he was coordinating. Rectangular tables formed rows, and consoles, pads, and displays covered their surfaces. The cool tones of blues and greens gave the Seafarer's Lament its nautical theme, that and a dozen white and red circles hanging on the walls.

Beyond the windows, the hard-packed soil of Central Park had been transformed by steady deliveries of cargo to the dropship waiting on its far side. The Adeona's bulbous design and dusty skin didn't offer confidence. It had been critical as a ferry in the early days, then as a power source for longer. It should have finished its life as a museum piece, but its destiny lay elsewhere.

"Bill, you're being spoken to," Dantalion said through their bonded internal communications.

He looked up. A woman stood before him. Her suit had the dirt of someone who'd been outside for a while. Her curly hair was sweat-slicked against her scalp, and yet she appeared energized thanks to glinting eyes and an inability to stand still.

"Yes?"

"I'm Heather Wild, with the northwest scout team. I was on first relay."

With no time to burn waiting on comm interference, Bill had sent out two teams, each with instructions to leave rovers at forty-kilometer intervals. If that wasn't short enough to keep a link up, the information could be relayed physically. A low-tech solution that he'd first encountered as a foil to comm-traffic monitoring.

"Go on."

"Tran has completed the survey at site Beta as per your instructions. There are no signs of bugs or bug tunnels, and the tributary is flowing clean water."

Beta was four hundred kilometers away and perhaps a little close to the unpredictable seas. On the other hand, the bugs had avoided water last time, and a protected flank wasn't a bad thing. If he green-lit the site, the colonists wouldn't settle down. It was a pit stop on the journey to safety.

"Is there a suitable location for the dropship?"

"Yes, sir. Three potentials. I'll upload them now." Heather tapped her wrist. "Tran listed them in order of preference. The first isn't the largest, but it's the flattest and has the most stable soil strata."

"Is the route easy?"

"Mostly. We've got beacons dropped to—"

Bill's jaw tightened. "You put down beacons?"

"Yes—"

"Damn it. I want them off now. What's the point in escaping if we leave them breadcrumbs?"

Her cheeks brightened even though the error wouldn't have been hers. "Right away."

He watched her hurry out. They couldn't afford mistakes like that. Worse, the longer people remained at Staging, the more opportunities there were to make them. Perhaps he should have ordered everyone out last night.

Dantalion stirred. "In such chaos, half of the colonists would have been left behind, half of those who completed the journey would have died of starvation in days, and the rest soon after, thanks to the weather. You cannot move ten thousand people without preparation."

Yet, he had moved almost eight thousand across the river and set them up around the town's power plant. Every vehicle that could be spared from the preparation was getting juiced along with portable batteries. His instinct said go now even though he hadn't heard back from the site alpha team.

"Dantalion, what do you think? Should I get them moving?"

"Bill, you know the analysis as well as I do. The bugs are unlikely to come en masse until well after dark, and even then, we cannot be sure it will be this night. However, starting the convoy will be a slow process."

"Everything is a slow process. I should have ordered a thousand rifles or two."

"Requiring the allocation of every resource and dooming the colony if we lose Staging. Besides, these people are not soldiers, and the bugs don't line up like a shooting gallery. You've already made that choice. What about the convoy?"

"My instincts say to go. Yes. Issue the order packet to the dropship crew. I want them closed up, and the launch area cleared. They're to head to Beta as soon as they can. The convoy, too."

"As you wish."

"No, you rock-headed ass-hat!" Ware marched inside the restaurant, his eyes unfocused—a clear sign he was talking on his comm. "Standing around scratching your balls and shouting isn't good enough. You're meant to be checking every single apartment in that building. Move it, or I'll have you greasing rovers instead. Understood?"

Using ex-soldiers to fill out the small police force was a sound idea, but apparently, some of them were ex for a reason.

"Hey, Ware, we have a site. I'm sending the dropship now. I need you to—"

Boom!

The windows lit up like midday, and then they shattered. Pressure lifted Bill off his feet and tossed him backward. He hit a table and slid over its surface, landing on the floor in a heap. His ears rung, and his left cheek itched. Feeling for the cause, his fingers grasped a shard of window sticking out his flesh.

"I'm overriding your pain momentarily. Pull it out."

The shard caught on flesh. Bill tugged with slippery fingers. Warmth dribbled down his chin. When it came loose, the flow increased.

"Keep focused, Bill. You have to move."

"Oh, shut up."

Bill rolled over. One of the logistics team lay unmoving next to him. He checked for a pulse—present—then turned him onto his side. He was breathing, too. "Someone get a doc over here. I have one unconscious. How is everyone else?" He had to shout—the damn sirens were screaming blue murder.

There were plenty of cuts and bumps, but against the odds, no fatalities. Ware was up and about. He'd see to them. Bill retrieved a rifle he'd claimed earlier from the small stockpile, crunching unsteadily over crushed glass and optronic debris, then headed out to the street where human cries mingled with the siren's scream. Erin's pistol already rested in a borrowed holster on his leg, but he was learning not to underestimate the danger he faced.

The Adeona resembled a hard-boiled egg ready to eat. At least it would have if eggs could burn. The top half was gone, leaving only a few twisted struts. Thick black clouds billowed ever upward, shrouding the wreckage, and the air was laden with dust stirred up by the explosion. Crates of cargo lay scattered and broken or burning, their timid flames dancing in waves of heat pouring from the decapitated dropship. Colonists ran here and there, helping each other or seeking safety. Another blast shook the ground as a spray of molten alloy sprayed out the top. Bill stepped to the left and leaned against a rover as a murderous rain fell.

"At least there are no bugs."

"Can it, Dantalion."

Blue ion trails flickered above. Bill's brow creased as he searched the air. A flyer circled overhead, disappearing into the afternoon sun, then returning with golden glints. *Who the hell is that?* Wait, it was familiar. BILT4. He'd seen the flyer while escaping.

"Dantalion, can you get into the hypernet?"

"You want camera footage? Sorry, pal, the particulate count is interfering. And by the looks of it, the blast slagged the main hard-link comm relay."

A glance at the shattered remains of the low, domed hub confirmed the AI's assessment. It had been one of the first additional buildings, a vital nexus when techs confirmed the impact of endless interference on wireless signals. Nearby, a couple of traffic cameras stood intact. No good. They would have fed directly into the Staging datacore through the hard links. He needed access to a camera with local storage. He spotted an easy target in the growing haze and jogged over to an air filter dispenser. Vending machines like these, now almost forgotten, had been vital in the first year when breathing units were mandatory and filters clogged regularly. He put his left forefinger against the maintenance data port. A tingle confirmed a physical link. Had Beth been there as he lay in the hospital, being cut up so they could pretend to remove the tech?

"Dantalion, crack your optronic knuckles and get me the footage."

"Crack my knuckles? Bill, keep up—you're the director. I don't even need to knock."

A virtual display hovered in front of his vision. A blurry image of the dropship appeared with a flickering timestamp. He couldn't expect more from a camera with a short focus, and artificially increasing the image quality meant inventing details.

"Scrub back a few seconds."

"I'll slow it down, too."

The recorded flyer swooped low, then pulled, accelerating fast. A blurry object arced down toward the dropship. It penetrated the hull. A flash, and the recording garbled until settling on a scene of devastation.

"Make sure you keep a copy of that."

"Of course, Bill."

"The bastards blew up the Adeona. Why? To soften up Staging? To keep us here for the bugs? How did they know? They must be using satellite data to watch us, or we have a traitor. The agency can sort that out when they sift through the fallout. Right now, ready or not, we need to empty Staging."

Bill hurried back to the restaurant, all too aware of the flyer still circling above. Through the smoke, he spied Ware out front with six of his officers. Dark patches huddled beneath his eyes, scratches decorated his forehead, and ash drifted from his hair.

"Hayden, where the hell were you? I've had half the department heads screaming murder. I'm not your babysitter."

"Murder is right. That BILT4 flyer above us dropped a bomb on the Adeona. It may have more. I'm calling the evacuation now. We'll need cover. Get the APC's cannon warmed up and hunting." He'd stationed it by Staging's power plant, where it could guard most of the colony's personnel. The cannon should have a direct line of sight, even if the distance would make targeting tricky.

"Jesus Christ, Bill. Anything involving you is a shitshow. Didn't you see the update? The APC's a no-go. Something's wrong with the internals. The controls are locked out."

"Seriously, now?"

Dantalion brought up the relevant notice—it had come in a second before the blast. "They have it on a trailer. Forget about it."

Seething at losing his best chance to protect the evacuees, Bill considered his limited options. Damn, being in the hot seat burned. Yet, he wasn't going to turn that observation into an excuse.

"All right, Ware, I need you to get rifles up on roofs taking potshots."

"That's pointless." Ware shook his head. "Plasma rifles can't take down a flyer, and aiming through smoke is hopeless."

"There's a small chance. And if they don't, the pilot might panic. Either way, they'll buy us time. Make it so."

Leaving Ware to put the order into action, Bill rounded up the administrative staff and doled out tasks. The facilities that had been feeding the dropship its cargo were hopefully packing up and moving out thanks to the siren, but he had to be sure. Several rovers pulled out from the side of the road and raced off. Colonists loaded injured into the remaining vehicles and ferried them to the bridge, leaving Ware's patrol rover and a couple of quad bikes. Despite the siren and the roar of the burning dropship, it was oddly quiet. Sure, by the bridge, it must be chaos, but here, the start of a fresh human civilization may as well have been abandoned an eon ago.

Ware poked his head out his rover's window. He was alone. "You coming?"

"You have shooters on the roof?"

"They're going up now. Quit stalling."

"I feel like I'm forgetting something." Bill turned in a slow circle. Who had he left behind? He certainly didn't fear for Jane Trax. She'd proved she could take care of herself and her crew. A slight smile crossed his lips, then soured. "The monitoring stations. Damn. The people watching the sensors—they know they didn't trigger the siren. With no bugs, they won't move."

"I'll round them up."

"No. You've got enough on your plate. Get everyone over the bridge. I'll grab one of the quad bikes and give them a heads-up. Pull your shooters down once the bridge is clear. We won't be much of a target when we return."

"Hayden, you're the director. I can't believe I'm saying this: we can't afford to lose you."

"I don't plan on getting lost. And remember, the colony's got a spare."

Bill mounted a quad bike, waved to the scowling police captain, and headed east. The streets were busier than he expected. He had to dodge rovers and those on foot stuffing cargo into parked vehicles. They should have stopped and hauled ass. That's what he'd ordered. But even the couple of thousand left on this side couldn't leave instantly. He'd held them too long, put them under too much risk. What else could he have done? If the orbiter had survived... The enormity of its loss crushed his soul.

Two bulky rovers blocked an intersection, forcing him to detour. The shock absorbers rocked, and a pair of wheels rose off the ground. Bill twisted, throwing his weight until it steadied on all four wheels and tossed dust behind like a bird's tail. A passing shadow told him the flyer was overhead. Where was it going?

Bill reached the northeast edge of Staging, where grain silos took over from industrial structures. Was the flyer returning to the BILT4 compound? That was pure optimism. Potential targets rolled through his mind: grain, a few power relays, the agriscience HQ. All low value. The colony's main transmitter, its thin framework stretching high into the sky, secured by wires in an ancient yet dependable design—that could hurt. And past that... the sensors.

He knew it before he broke free of obstructions and saw the flyer bank, kicking up dust with its ion engines as it accelerated. Its target was clear. One, two, three bombs. One after the other, they dropped along the network of sensors, the second scoring an almost direct hit on the portable office. Bill brought his quad bike to a skidding halt. Horror and anger warred, prickling his skin and twitching his muscles. Each boom was a drumbeat on the road to hell. A breath later, the first of three shockwaves battered him, the others following with scant seconds between. Shaking, he reached a hand out as if he could grasp the dead and rip them from their fate. His fingers found only dust and smoke.

Why?

Dantalion projected a map of Staging in his vision. "The monitoring site watched the ground. It was no threat to the flyer." The damn AI had no sadness in its voice, only curiosity, and that sickened Bill. "So why bother? Bill, let's assume the pilot is a rational actor."

There was always a reason, no matter how foul. Bill ran a hand through his hair. "It took the orbiter out first to stop us from surviving long-term. Destroying the Adeona also sets up panic. It drives everyone west—but that's safe from the bugs. It trashes the sensors and slaughters the monitoring folk, leaving us blind to the damn bugs. So, Wagner wants the bugs to pick our carcasses? No. That's not enough reason."

He coughed. The smoke was damn thick. The sun was barely more than an angry spot. Whoever had made the bombs had no idea what they were doing.

The ground vibrated. Bill glanced down. "Oh, shit. It's too early—the sun hasn't set."

"The shock waves from the explosions could have roused them."

"Or Wagner has her goons prodding them. But too early? Oh, damn. The smoke. She's diabolical. The smoke is creating an artificial night. I have to warn people. Can you get a signal?"

"Not yet, but soon. The bombs stirred up more interference, but there are faint hints of the carrier waveform. I suspect that if we moved back into town, I could error-correct."

An ear-splitting crack had Bill shelve his concern. Ground collapsed near the edge of a weather monitoring station, a pole festooned with sensors. It leaned drunkenly, then fell. Like a stick of celery in a blender, it spun, slowly disappearing downward. Around it, bugs poured out. Six skittering legs with dagger-like ends, rust-toned alloy shells, and at their heads, blades, cutters, small welding flames—a mix of tools all ready to act as weapons. They headed for the heart of Staging, some splitting off to infest the structures they passed. Down the road he'd come, another opening released more of the... of the plague. A plague Bill had underestimated.

He turned the quad bike, and headed back into Staging, avoiding the bug holes. It wasn't like he could take them all out with his rifle and pistol. What could he do? What use could he be? *This can't be another Marrick Prime.*

Dodging a collapsed stack of pallets, he came face to ass with a bug grasping several pads. What the hell did it want with them? With no time to think of an answer, he leaned back, shifting the bike's balance, and hit the lowered rear. The bike's wheels caught on the segmented shell, throwing Bill up, along, and off. Gravity snapped it down, bottoming out the suspension, and punished his joints.

"Bill, comms are available. Captain Ware has already issued a warning for all personnel to cross the bridge."

The bug had turned the way Bill had come, no doubt confused by its use as a ramp. He left it behind but had to follow the city outskirts as more bugs blocked the route west.

"I'm hearing chatter from his people. Some are in a holding action near the center, and others are continuing to target the flyer without success."

"I've noticed."

Cutting back, he almost ran into the rear of a squat rover that was more building than vehicle. CS-241, he could make out on its side despite the four bugs that worried at its hull. A field science lab that shouldn't have been on this side of the river. People inside were screaming, at least four of them. What were they thinking? He could practically walk faster. Cursing, Bill zipped ahead, picked a spot near Staging's main antenna, and braked. He pulled the rifle from his back and switched off the safety. It was a simple design without the optronics to feed the sights directly to Dantalion. Thankfully, the bugs were occupied.

He stood, aimed, and fired, picking his angles carefully, and following up with burst after burst of plasma when the bugs fell to make sure they wouldn't get back up. It wasn't much, but damn, it felt good to put down some bugs and save a few lives. When he'd finished, the battered and smoking lab pulled up nearby.

The driver waved. "Need a lift?"

"Hell, no. Just get to the convoy. No stopping for snacks."

"Right you are... Director!"

The lab rumbled deeper into a colony of smoke. Burning cinders leaped across the road above, starting a new blaze. Bill slumped on his bike. His effort had been token—saving the few while his failures had doomed the many. Perhaps that was why Beth had saved him, a token victory on a mountain of failure. He should have anticipated Wagner. Her character had already revealed itself. He didn't deserve to join the exodus. He should wait here and suffer the consequences.

"Bill, don't think that. Not everything is a matter of deserving. You either survive or you don't."

"You're a machine, Dantalion. You don't get it."

"I am programmed to spot pointless, whiny self-flagellation. Though, honestly, I am calculating the probability that you are avoiding the challenge of continuing. There are seven open channel requests for you. It's time to get back on that quad bike, get your ass over the bridge, and lead nine thousand colonists to safety."

"Near ten thousand," Bill said as petty revenge. "Don't get sloppy."

"I am using a model of likely deaths. The longer you take, the more there will be."

Bill let his rifle dangle from its strap. "All right, all right. I'll go."

The ground shook again. Bill waited by his bike. "What now? I mean, what the hell is next?"

A warehouse corner subsided, groaning, popping panels, shrieking. An opening grew. Another bug hole, huge enough to swallow two rovers side by side. What was it going to be? His hand rested on the bike. The answer crawled out. Six of them. Bugs an easy four meters long, with stilt legs. These had much more defined heads than the common bugs. Stalks covered the top and two vertical cutting blades formed a mouth. Lights flashed along their bodies, red and white, reminding him of the way some animals used bright colors as a warning. As they reached open space, each bug stretched out twin wing pairs, the anatomy somehow familiar and yet disturbingly *other*.

"Dragonflies, Bill. They look like dragonflies, crossed with stag beetles and a guillotine."

When all six had their wings extended, they leaped, and jets of purple flame launched them upward, destroying the impression of nature gone mad. This was the work of intelligence—he'd known that —but where was that intelligence?

"Bill—"

"Not now."

"There's an all-hands comm from Trax you should hear."

"It can wait. I need to work out what to do about the dragonflies. They won't care about a river."

"I don't think it can wait."

Eying the struts of the nearby antenna, Bill said. "Play it."

Trax's voice came into his mind, loud and intense. "Everyone, listen up. Don't cross the bridge, and get the fuck away from the western side. East, north, south, wherever, but get out."

He shook his head, wanting to ignore her demand as panic-induced, but he couldn't bring himself to believe it. Jogging over to the antenna base, he said. "Get her for me."

"Link open."

"Trax, I'm hoping you have a good reason." He climbed the antenna struts, tracking the dragonflies. Dantalion boosted his muscle output, speeding his ascent with a cocktail of stimulants and boosted nerves. Tomorrow, if he lived, the payback would be a bitch.

"Hayden? BILT4 is bombing us from a flyer."

"I know. They took out the orbiter. That's why everyone has to cross the bridge. I don't need you—"

"It's the power plant, you overpaid snoop. They're going to blow it up. Anyone near will be vaporized."

Jesus fucking Christ. He switched to silent communication. "Dantalion, is that possible?"

"Unlikely. It's a Mack-Chen 7 series. They possess many layers of redundant safety systems."

What about the Adeona? Should the orbiter have blown up so easily? Bill's mind went to the APC. It should have worked. He reached the top of the antenna, gaining a clear view of Staging and its assailants. "Access the plant and confirm that the systems are active."

"Yes, that would be best. Accessing…"

"Hayden," Trax shouted. "Are you listening?"

After settling his legs around the antenna struts, Bill brought his rifle up and peered through the sights. The dragonflies were already dispersing, two heading east at great speed. He tracked one despite the swaying antenna, fired, and missed.

"Dantalion?"

"A terrible shot, but I can't help you. I'm having trouble accessing the plant's control system. The hypernet engineer has been tinkering. Do not assume any of the safety systems are active."

"Erin, not Wagner's people? How do you know?"

"There's a plain text message: Hayden, this is for Marrick Prime, Erin."

"That'd do it. Unless it's meant to frame her. How long do we have?"

"Footage from feeds nearby shows the flyer circling higher. It is likely the pilot is trying to balance accuracy with staying out of a potential blast radius. I cannot determine when they will act."

"And the shooters Ware had on the roof? Surely, they have enough range."

"The buildings are gone, Bill."

Closer by, three dragonflies dropped out of sight. He imagined screams floating on the air, flesh torn asunder, people ripped from their vehicles—or merely plucked as they ran, only to be dragged underground for eventual flaying, dismemberment, butchering.

"Give me an all-colony comm," Bill growled.

He steadied the rifle and fired again, scoring a shot on a dragonfly leg. The machine contorted in the air, shaking its buckled limb. Rather than going for a killing shot, he searched the buildings for signs of other dragonflies. He needed to keep them busy. And if they spotted him, they'd be an easier target as they closed.

"Speak, Bill, and be heard."

Smart-ass AI. "This is Bill Hayden. All personnel must move away from the power plant immediately. Dump anything that slows you down and get to site beta. If you're on the east of the river, head north if you can, but the priority is to clear the area. Go."

Dantalion broke the link and pushed a stream into Bill's vision, ruining his aim. Bill growled but focused on what he was seeing. Two of the dragonflies had reached the west bank. He laughed. The fuckers were chasing the flyer. For once, something was going right.

"Enjoy the karma, you bastard!"

The flyer jinked this way and that, but with two highly maneuverable opponents, it had no path out. One dragonfly caught the nose, grappling, and sending it into a spin. The second dived onto the flyer's tail. The sounds of cheers joined the feed. Those on the west bank were watching. He'd ream them out later. Right now, they all needed a hit of something positive.

The feed moved, the camera operator finding a cleaner shot between onlookers. As the flyer dropped, the dragonflies cut into its hull. Flames erupted from these wounds, and the combined mass jerked crazily. The feed bounced—the camera operator ran as cheers twisted into shouts of horror. The power plant took up the corner for an instant—right below the tumbling combatants.

"No, no, no!"

Flyer and dragonflies crashed into the northern edge of the primary power unit, ripping open the side and exploding. The feed cut out. Bill hoped with all his being. But the sky turned blue-white—bright enough that Dantalion cut his vision for harrowing seconds. When it came back, smoke shot upward and billowed out. A blast wave followed, its rapid advance marked by the shattering of buildings, buildings that could survive a hurricane. Would it reach him? He looked down at the ground far below the tip of the antenna he hung from.

A sledgehammer of over-pressured air smacked into him, launching him from the antenna. He flailed as behind him, the steel struts bent and stabilizing wires snapped, their ends whipping like a furious kraken. It was a hell of a way to go.

A rope of wire flicked toward his face. He wasn't even going to feel the landing. Dantalion overrode control of his nervous system. His back arched. The wire whistled past. His right arm jerked. His fingers clasped the strands of metal alloy, and the wire dragged him in a new direction, his heart thudding madly and his head giddy. A dragonfly zipped by, its wings hopelessly twisted.

"Thank you for flying Eclipse Air!" The shout was a mistake. Bill coughed and choked as dust stuck to his throat. The ground rocked in his vision. Giddiness shifted to vertigo. "Oh, fuck!"

"Don't be a wet blanket. I'm using our inertial guidance system to track where we are. More or less. Get ready."

"For what?"

His hand released the wire, and his legs stretched out, knees bent. Pain lanced through his feet, right up his knees, and into his hips, but he rolled forward, over and over, standing as the dust steadied and a sweltering heat dried his skin.

"Hmm." Dantalion sounded smug. "I'd give that landing a nine out of ten. You need to work out more."

Above, the antenna leaned. No, it was moving. It was falling. A metallic groan announced its death. Bill shouted and threw himself to the side, his AI content to let him try. The structure hit the ground, shaking it, and throwing up yet more dust. Gasping for breath, he felt for his legs. Still there. With no excuse to stay down, he forced himself to a wavering stand and peered through the haze.

Had he died and gone to hell? Which one? All of them. Staging was ablaze, its structures mere bones. All of it gone. Endless hours of toil. The hopes of thousands, of hundreds of thousands still to come. Heat weakened alloys, melted polymer, cooked optronics, charred food. That blast hadn't been directed. The convoy. There were no buildings to soak up the force on that side. It could have expanded on and on. How many were dead? How many were living? His body shook, and he slammed his fists down on his quad bike—it had ended up nearby, wheels up like a dead insect, yet improbably intact.

He'd allowed another Marrick Prime, smaller but no less grotesque. This time, the sole responsibility was his. He'd assumed command. In his arrogance, he'd believed he knew what was best. In his haste, he'd made faulty assumptions, built a failed model of possibilities, and burned the colonists on the pyre of his errors.

A few bugs dragged themselves back to their holes. They'd had enough. For Bill, fleeing to the edge of human civilization wasn't enough. He was exactly like the bugs, feeding on humanity, offering only death in return.

"We both made mistakes," Dantalion admitted. "But stop wallowing. There's work to be done."

"Work? There's nothing to be done. Everyone's dead."

"Bill, why did you join the agency?"

He spat out dust. "You know why."

"Why, Bill?"

The silhouette of a dragonfly formed as the machine dragged its busted body toward him. Its lights had failed and its cutting mandibles were out of alignment. It could still kill him if he waited.

"Bill, why?"

"I'm not answering."

"I do not run out of patience, Bill. Why... why?"

"Jesus, I wish they'd cut you out and recycled the parts into toasters."

"Bill, why?"

The dragonfly was close now.

"Because I was stupid and idealistic. I thought I could make a difference, make the League better. I was naïve. Humanity can't wash off its taint. Get enough of us together, and it all turns to shit."

"There aren't many colonists left. Wagner has almost won."

Bill leaned against the quad bike. "Thanks for rubbing it in."

"If you think about it, any colonist who survives puts her plans at risk. Witnesses could bring her down. You could still do that." The AI's intelligence matrix must have corrupted.

"After this, you think anyone's going to believe a word I say?"

"There may be other survivors who will die without your help. Together, your evidence might be enough."

The dragonfly reached out with a blackened, warped limb, not quite able to hook his flesh.

Damn it. Dantalion was right. He thought of Trax and her crew, who had never given up in the bug tunnels. What if they were out there, hurt, caught under a rover, only needing the slightest assistance? Could he leave them, and by extension, could he stand here waiting to be eviscerated? That was surely as contemptible as leading the colonists into the tunnels himself.

And, he admitted, Wagner had to pay. How smug was she in her shiny base, sitting on a throne of her own dead, crowned in glory, wielding an orb and scepter of alien tech? Karlo, at her side, blood thick on his hands. If Bill gave up, she'd win, and BILT4 would extend its tendrils throughout the League, knowing there were no checks on its power, no limitations to the actions it might take.

A fresh fire burned inside him. It was fury instead of the idealism that had brought him to the LSA. It came not with hope, but with determination.

Maybe humanity was beyond redemption, but it wasn't beyond payback.

CHAPTER 28
COUNTDOWN

Red lights blinked down the curved surface of the dropship, segmenting the craft like a mandarin. Its bulk rested in a depression hiding much of its thirty-meter diameter. Unlike the fruit, the center extended upward, finishing in a rounded cone. BILT4 was emblazoned on each segment. The base consisted of engine constellations, their golden barrel-shaped ends resting just above the heavy ceramcrete pad thanks to six retractable legs. Jose Karlo noted they rested a little lower than the previous day. Another twenty-four hours—forty-eight at most—and his job would switch to the little death of reports.

He rolled his shoulders, shifting his armored suit, and let his glare radiate his frustration. Ms. Wagner stood nearby, along with Amaruq, the dropship's pilot and stand-in captain. Bright lights washed the dropship's surroundings as the sun dipped near the horizon.

"With respect, ma'am," Amaruq began. "There needs to be a safety margin. All it takes is poor weather and we won't reach orbit—or maintain it. We've junked everything non-critical already."

Ms. Wagner had shucked her usual fancy attire for a high-end flight suit. Her boots were stitched with subtle patterns of flowers, but at least they had a level of practicality. She offered the pilot a tight smile. "Can't blame me for asking."

"No, ma'am."

A comm request came through to Karlo.

"What is it, Handley?" Karlo had put him in charge of the security desk for this shift. The ex-soldier hated being relegated to a chair, but Karlo had little choice given the number of his team that had bled for the corporation.

"Chief, we've got word from the expedition. They're not far off, but they've got near on ten bugs behind them."

Karlo moved away from Ms. Wagner. A final expedition was the most reckless, stupid idea he'd ever heard. He'd put his worst people on it, fearing he'd lose whoever went. The decision still left a foul taste in his mouth. "Tell them to put the bugs down, not bring them here."

"They can't, Chief. They used everything they had fighting their way out, and their ride's damaged. Its top speed isn't enough."

"Damn it, send the kamikaze drones, all that's left." He could take out the bugs on arrival, but he couldn't risk letting them close—Ms. Wagner had refused to hide in her office or on the dropship. He respected the hands-on approach while also hating it.

"Right away, chief. Drones away."

Another layer of defense depleted. Karlo rubbed a bruise on his forehead unconsciously. The secure enclave had decayed into a leaky bucket, more so thanks to that asshole, Hayden. Its gates had been cleared of debris after the spook's escape, but Karlo had ordered rovers moved to serve as barricades rather than beg for the resources to rebuild. The project was winding up. It was all about make-do until they launched and left this cursed land behind.

"Handley, take the perimeter to standby when the expedition is in visual range."

"Will do, chief."

Wagner joined the link. "What's happening?"

"The expedition is returning, ma'am," Handley said.

Wagner made a thoughtful hum. "So soon? Are they bringing anything?"

"I believe so, ma'am."

"Then, let them in. I want to see right away."

"Yes, ma'am."

Karlo frowned at the usurping of his job. "Handley, get Styles and Ito out to the gates. Make sure the expedition's clean."

"Right, chief."

The arrival didn't take long. The kamikazes took out the bugs, and the expedition, what was left of it, rolled on inside.

A single dented and scarred hauler squealed as it stopped, its one remaining headlamp sending a beam more to the left than in front. Three of the six guards Karlo had assigned rode on the open-tray back, hunched around a mammoth lump of alien tech, much of it covered by a tarpaulin. Beneath, black cables, tubes, and a long curve of rusted metal. Ragged, shiny edges showed how the expedition scrubs had cut it free. From what, though? Karlo let the curiosity leak away and strode to his people.

"Report."

The three guards leaped off the rover and lined up.

The shortest, Antonov, said, "It looked good at the start, Chief. The bugs had thinned out. The seismic sensors suggested they'd taken the bait and were headed to the colony."

Karlo scowled. The play was dirty. Antonov continued, oblivious. "We found a few bits and pieces but nothing good. The scrubs insisted on going deeper. And what we saw, damn, chief. You wouldn't believe it if I told you."

"Don't. I don't give a shit. What happened?"

"We retreated and circled a bit and found this. It's crazy big, but the scrubs insisted on taking it. They cut it out, and that brought the bugs. We rolled the thing for ages before we could winch it up the entry shaft. We had to shoot the whole damn way. Bugs kept coming out of these small openings. You'd think you were in the clear and one would drop right down on you. And when we reached the main shaft, the tech was too damn big. We had to blow it wider. That was when we lost Garibaldi and Baker. Even once we got this damn thing on the hauler, they kept chasing. One leaped on Keynes—I tried to keep hold, but it dragged him off. Poor bastard."

"This better be worth it." Karlo scowled at his assembled guards. "Good work. Get yourselves cleaned up and recharged. Weapons nearby at all times, understood?"

"Yes, Chief," the three said and staggered off, clearly in the grip of a post-adrenaline slump.

Ms. Wagner was interrogating the scrubs, and they were gesturing toward the dropship. That didn't look good. Karlo went up to the pair. "Ma'am, this hasn't been screened. You should keep your distance." If she were to die just before they reached safety, his career, and likely his life, would be over.

"Jose, the circumstances dictate cutting a few corners. Risk is part of business."

That worked well with Hayden, didn't it? "Ms. Wagner, small pieces have gone off like bombs. If this *thing* explodes, it might vaporize us." And they already had a weapon of their own with that power.

"You need to think of the bigger picture." She gestured to the scrub. "Explain."

The scrub was a woman with pale brown eyes and wiry hair. Her cheeks were chubby, but there was nothing soft about her expression. "We found a few new items." She held up a bag containing black spaghetti. "There are novel isotope signatures in this tube. That might be contamination, but the initial readings are solid, so we're thinking not. Now, the shit on the back of the hauler? That's *something else*. We think the bugs came from off-world, and this is proof. If we glean just one new advance, it'll be worth a fortune."

Was the scrub telling the truth? None of it made sense. He knew what the boss had told them—don't come back unless you have something big. Ms. Wagner hadn't meant it literally, but they'd followed through. She waved over the dropship pilot, igniting Karlo's concern. She couldn't be serious.

"Amaruq, I need your crew to load this right now. Nothing else happens first."

"Load it? I said before there isn't space—"

"Make the space. This is not a debate."

"Ma'am," the scrub said. "We haven't assessed the power situation."

"You'll have to do that later. Let's be blunt. Our metal friends are occupied with our neighbors. And when they are done, those that remain will turn their attention to our compound. We've poked the nest enough to guarantee it."

The pilot ducked his head apologetically. "I'm sorry, ma'am. I really can't allow something that potentially dangerous on board, even if I could find the space. It needs to be—"

Ms. Wagner's expression chilled. Her eyes narrowed, her body stiffened, and a great big Cheshire cat grin stretched across her face.

"There is an autopilot function that will fly me to orbit. Would you like to remain behind so you can stay *safe?* It would solve a small part of the capacity problem."

Amaruq took a half step back, wilting like a stale ration bar. "I'll find room, ma'am."

"See that you do. Well, off to it." She gestured to the scrub. "You, too."

When both were out of earshot, Ms. Wagner turned to Karlo. "With this as a nice little bonus, we can be sure of a welcome return. The unavoidable losses will be excused by the board as the price of business."

Karlo grunted. "They'll want to pin this on some asshole—pardon my language."

"And the dead will be ready to accept blame with open arms. The colony, our helpful Bill Hayden, the machines. It's so sad that there won't be tweezers small enough to find their remains."

"You can't be sure of that."

She put a hand on his armored chest. "Jose, you must know me better than that by now. I am beyond sure, trust me. Even now, one of our flyers is above Staging, loaded with custom munitions and ready to clean up."

Karlo tensed, his ears heated, and his brow creased. Which fucking weasel took to the air without telling him? And where had she found weapons? Had she raided his store of spare mines? He'd fought for a place in the manufacturing queue and laid hundreds to protect the compound. The one serious weapon BILT4 had supplied at the outset wasn't an answer for *anything*. Had she taken the nuke? No. She'd said munitions. That was plural. Still, she should have brought him into the loop. She knew nothing about combat operations. When the generals got their hands dirty, it was the troops who ended up covered in shit.

He crushed his anger mercilessly. "They have the APC. They can shoot a flyer down. If they do, they'll have evidence that we attacked them."

"Don't be so stony-faced. We have a friend—well, more of a partner —in the colony. She's been slowing their escape with a series of targeted hacks and sabotaging their defenses. The APC isn't a problem."

"You can't trust a colonist."

A dull bang came as if from all around. He knew that effect. A distant explosion, a large one.

She tilted her head, a gleam brightening her eyes. "I trust in her hate for Bill Hayden. I've promised to lay the blame squarely on his shoulders. She sees the death of the colony as a small price to pay for his eternal public damnation. Who am I to deny her heartfelt request? I've got a few last-minute things to do. Be a good boy and keep an eye on my cargo. Tell me as soon as it's secured."

He watched her walk away, not to the admin building. He should have been curious, but he couldn't shake what she'd said. *Death of the colony*. She said it so calmly, but it bit into Karlo like acid. The necessity was clear. The bugs were in the open, Hayden had seen too much, and any of the dirt farmers might know enough to implicate the corporation. Yet, it didn't sit right.

Ten thousand people. It was impersonal and cruel. He couldn't say why it mattered, but it did. How different were Ms. Wagner and Hayden? The asshole had suggested dumping his friends down a hole rather than letting them die a quick death. Impersonal and cruel. Maybe Ms. Wagner was doing the colonists a favor. A quick death from afar beat what the bugs offered. Yes, she was ruthless, but she wasn't cruel.

He looked to the west. Almost free of this shithole. He wouldn't let anything delay their flight.

"Work faster!" he shouted at the scrubs hovering around the alien payload. "Or we'll leave you behind."

CRATES LAY ABANDONED by the dropship's ramp. Scrubs had unloaded artifacts, dumped the protective padding, and repacked them tightly. The crew had also been busy, dropping padded seats, beds, even boxes of food pouches. The covered mass of alien tech rested on a low trailer tethered by two thick cables that dragged it millimeter by millimeter into the spaceship's maw. Scrubs had connected several pieces of equipment—also covered. Ms. Wagner should have told them to wait until orbit. Why do that instead of following the power draining procedure he'd previously seen? Why not take the time to ensure they weren't all blown to atoms?

He pressed his lips together. Why the rush? Working loading at night, even with lights, was a recipe for errors. He puffed air through his nose. There was only one answer. Ms. Wagner had pushed the departure forward. She wanted out before morning. Why hadn't she told him? Because she expected him to work it out. She was like that. But her growing habit of withholding decisions could bite them all on the ass.

Handley requested a comm link.

Karlo accepted. "Good timing. Call everyone in. We're shifting to standby mode for the exit strategy."

"Yes, chief. I mean, no, sorry, chief. It's the bugs. The sensors are going nuts. They're coming nor'-nor'-east, a click away, two tunnels at least. Hard to say how many, but it's not looking good. I thought they were all meant to be at the colony."

Extinguishing a flicker of fear by force of will, Karlo considered his options. They were fast diggers, but he had a few minutes. A tight smile formed. This is what he was born for. He linked in the rest of his team.

"Listen good. It's time to gear up. We have incoming bugs. Our priority is to get Ms. Wagner into the dropship and take off. I don't care if we leave the secret to eternal youth behind. If they don't drag that piece of alien shit in now, we'll dump it. Styles and Ito, collect our boss and escort her aboard. Antonov, Davison, Feist, take up positions around the dropship. Handley, activate all mines, set the turrets to auto, sound the general alert, and bring my helmet. Questions?"

"What about the scrubs from the southern camp?" Handley said quickly. "They're a few hours away."

"Do you want to wait for them?"

"I—I guess not."

"I don't hear you moving."

His guards dropped from the link, no doubt scrambling. If Ms. Wagner refused, he'd have to be the one to throw her over his shoulder, but right now, he needed to be here, ready to respond. Settling his rifle in his hands, he waited. Along the wall at regular intervals, pulse cannons popped out with mechanical whirrs. They were smaller than the unit on the APC that Hayden had stolen, making them easily concealable—a sensible tradeoff. A lot of things had changed since the compound was erected. Searchlights switched on, creating a moat of brightness in the bloody sunset.

The three guards he'd ordered around the dropship jogged toward their position, each acknowledging him when close. More footsteps announced Handley, juggling a rifle, a belt of grenades, a helmet, and a pad. The guard was more rounded than most, but he passed the physical each year, knew how a rifle worked, and didn't whine. That made him good people.

"Here's your helmet, chief. All defenses are active."

"Have you heard from Styles and Ito?"

"I think they're still looking. Wagner's implant isn't showing on the map."

God damn it. What was she up to?

A muffled thud sounded from beyond the wall, accompanied by a narrow column of dust. *Bug, meet mine.* More thuds. Screeches came from closer by. Karlo checked the dropship, raising his rifle. The cargo was almost aboard. They'd had to ditch the platform underneath and were now dragging it, metal on metal. Not his problem.

Where was she? He brought up a comm link. "Give me a status update."

"We're with Ms. Wagner, chief. We're heading toward the dropship now. Route is clear."

Karlo scowled. "No fuss?"

"I think she was waiting for us."

Another thud, closer than before. He killed the link. "Handley, bring up the external cameras."

"Yes, Chief." The guard swiped through options on his pad until the two most appropriate cameras displayed a bizarre scene. Karlo had ordered the mines placed with underground mesh triggers, an untested idea—until now. The results gave the impression of an invisible giant lumbering to crush a fantasy castle. Dust would blast up into the air, each time closer, the pattern matching the two tunnels that must be beneath. Thuds accompanied each explosion, the delay between visuals and sound shrinking as they closed.

He glanced above the pad. Scrubs hurried from the dropship. He saw movement elsewhere, too. The surviving employees, seventy-five in total, dashed toward buildings, shouting at each other. When one from the dropship came within reach, Karlo grabbed her.

"What's happening?"

"Didn't Wagner tell you? The remote wiping commands have failed. We've got to manually trash every console and server in the compound before we can take off." She shook herself free and ran.

Handley tilted his head. "Chief, there isn't time, is there?"

"Hell, no." His boss was a sneaky bitch. This wasn't about data cleansing. The dropship's ticket queue had just gotten shorter.

In counterpoint to this urgency, a measure of peace returned. The blasts had stopped, though a dust haze rose above the compound's walls. Had the bugs run out of metal bodies to throw at the mines? It would take pressure off but not change the situation—the exit was already in motion. He opened a link to his guards.

"When we pull out, it'll happen fast. Wait for my order, but as soon as you get it, retreat to the dropship ramp. I want to see calm the whole way. I want to see caution. Keep this link open."

What he did see was his boss walking steadily down the road, flanked by her assigned guards. She knew exactly what was happening, but damn, she was cool about it. Her eyes locked with his for a moment, and her eyebrows quirked. Was she enjoying this?

Handley raised his pad. "Chief, we've got something."

Shifting his gaze, Karlo studied the camera feeds. Soil shifted, the details stolen by the haze. Twin spots of darkness. They spread. Holes. Bugs surged out, barely fifty meters from the walls—a sea of them, reminding Karlo of a cockroach plague he'd endured on Erivani station. Pulse fire followed, the compound's cannons releasing streams of blue lightning that seared through segmented armor, turning machines into melted trash. For a moment, the situation appeared contained, and he let out a breath.

A disk rose from the leftmost tunnel entrance. It was as wide as the opening, rough and dirt-covered, and its similarity to a boring machine was uncanny. Energy spattered against the surface, shedding clods of dirt and rocks, but leaving little more than indents of glowing orange. From the second hole rose another disk. Shields? The feed angle revealed long legs and strange flat shapes at the edges.

A blur launched upward from behind the first shield. Five more followed with wings outspread and purple jets propelling them.

He took in the new enemy with his own eyes. "What the fuck is that?"

"They look like dragonflies, chief."

"That they fucking do. Everyone, it's time to go."

After gaining height quickly, the dragonflies swooped toward the compound, sharp movements confusing the few cannons that shifted to target them.

He brought another link up. "Ms. Wagner, you have to run!"

"We can't have chaos, Jose. I must show calm, or our people will get worried and stampede aboard."

"Fuck 'em. Run!"

"Very well, since you insist." She shifted into a jog.

The three guards around the dropship opened fire as dragonflies landed on the wall, tearing cannons from their mounts. Plasma rent holes in wings and fried chunks of the machines' torsos, but they swarmed inside with only one collapsing. Grimacing, Karlo aimed his rifle and laid down fire of his own, sidestepping as he did to close on the ramp and his boss's path. Beside him, Handley did the same. A second dragonfly went down. *How do you like that?*

"Watch out!" Antonov screamed.

"No—" Davison's outburst turned into a wrenching, agonized cry.

"What's happening?" Karlo demanded of his guards. Blinded by the bulk of the dropship, he could only wait.

"One of them got Davison. It cut him in half. Oh, god. Oh, god. Ah, it hurts. Mamma—" Antonov spoke no more.

Feist appeared around the right side of the dropship, just as Ms. Wagner reached Karlo.

"We don't have long," the guard said with a shaking voice while walking backward and firing. "The crawling ones are coming over the wall."

So fast. So many of them. Damn it. "Feist, keep laying down fire. The rest of us, form a circle around Ms. Wagner."

Ito took point, Styles on the boss's right and Handley on the left. Karlo held the rear, shifting to squeeze off shots as they presented. The combined clattering of bug legs created a soundscape of driving rain that overwhelmed all other noises. Two dragonflies hopped forward, their crawling brethren flowing into the depression where the dropship waited.

"Handley, clear some space out front, then we charge. No one stops."

"Frag out!" Handley tossed five grenades as far as he could manage, forming a line from left to right.

The little packages of furious energy exploded, sending a shockwave choked with shrapnel. The closest bugs writhed as if in pain.

"Go! Go! Go!"

They charged for the dropship, making good time until Ms. Wagner tripped over a smoldering bug and fell heavily. Only twenty meters to go.

"Get her up," Karlo demanded.

Ito let his weapon hang and hauled Ms. Wagner to her feet. The delay was swiftly punished. A dragonfly's legs clanked as it landed next to Styles. He poured fire into its head, causing it to twist violently, and one pair of wings smacked Ito edge-on, knocking him off his feet with a sickening crack.

Ms. Wagner sprinted for the ramp. Better late than never.

"Cover her," Karlo shouted, pausing to shred two bugs as they followed.

"Watch out!"

Handley shoved Karlo to the side as a rearing dragonfly stabbed glinting legs. One embedded into the packed soil. The other thrust right through Handley's armor as if it were foil. The leg rose, lifting the guard off his feet. The bastards couldn't have another of Karlo's people. He grabbed Handley's leg and crushed his rifle's trigger. Heat beat his flesh, and flashes of plasma strobed his vision. The dragonfly flailed with its free leg while bringing Handley to its terrible maw.

"Let go, chief. I've got this. I've got this. Get to the ramp."

The tips of his boots barely on the ground, Karlo looked up, blinking as blood dripped into his eyes. Handley held two grenades. The brave asshole had made his mind up. Waiting would only extend the pain. It was time to let go. Karlo ran, looking back, wishing there was something more to say.

The dragonfly tilted its head and snapped the blades of its maw together. Handley's legs tumbled down—so much useless flesh. His body writhed, and he let out a bellow that should have shaken the world. And then the grenades went off, obliterating both man and machine.

Stumbling, Karlo called out to his people. Where were they? Surely not all were gone. Not a single response on the comm. Fuck the bugs. He turned his attention to the dropship. The ramp was gone. The doors were closing. His universe shrank to the remaining sliver. His boots slapped the ground. Five meters away. So thin. Four.

He sent a broadcast comm. "I'm here; open it!"

Three meters. Barely a crack. Two. Karlo leaped.

The dropship's hull greeted him without forgiveness. He staggered back, then pounded on the sealed doors. "Let me in, damn you. I made it. I made it."

"Oh, poor Jose." Wagner's voice came over the comm. "You almost did. I think we might have had room for you, too. But we're already going to redline the engines, so it's probably for the best. I'll write up a very heroic report—no superlatives spared. You had better step back. It's going to get a little warm."

He shook his head. "You can't do this to me. I've kept you alive. You owe me."

"Come now, Jose, let's not get personal. Business is business. If it at all helps, I won't let you suffer."

The engines kicked in, spreading a vibrant blue along with intense heat. Without a choice, Karlo backed away. The compound was awash with bugs, some already dragging flailing scrubs toward the wall. He reached the top of the depression when the dropship hit full power, slamming the pad as it launched and tossing him down into the bug melee.

He'd worked hard for her. He'd saved her life. He'd expected something in return. Loyalty? How could he have been so stupid? *I won't let you suffer.* The bugs would eat him alive. She was so full of shit.

His eyes widened. There was always another angle with her. The nuke. Once she was clear of the blast radius, she'd set it off. All evidence of her mercenary actions wiped away. No one else to claim credit. She'd forget he ever existed. Bitch.

He laughed right from the belly. Damn, she had gotten him good.

What could he do? Dodge every damn bug, defuse the bomb, and escape alive? He roared his fury. It was damn impossible. He gripped his rifle. He'd been a marine once.

It was worth a shot.

CHAPTER 29
TRADE-OFFS

Sparkling water trickled in a shallow, wide creek, too new to have eroded a proper channel. At the edges, yellow-tinged reeds waved under the gentle ministrations of a morning breeze. Small shapes wiggled back and forth—catfish? Splotches of darkness in the brightening sky announced the ever-growing contingent of birds. Bill splashed through the creek, spreading unnoticed ripples that were quickly consumed by the current, and kneeled next to Trax. The engineer cradled a sodden colonist filthy with ash like the grass that spread to the horizon.

He waited, his body wavering, his eyes blinking heavily.

"Dead. I don't even know the guy, but I feel it." Trax lowered her chin, and her voice took on a harder edge. "He made it this far and ended up face down in the water. What killed him—concussion, exhaustion, drowning? Who killed him? Who's to fucking blame?"

Dantalion activated sensors in Bill's eyes. "I can hazard a guess."

"Don't."

Trax gave Bill a light glare. "What?"

"Talking to myself. The bugs, Wagner, Sturt, the board of BILT4, the LSA, the civilian planners… me? I don't know. I just don't know. Leave that for later. Right now, you need to do the next thing. I've seen you in action. Nothing stops you. You could make a dropship from a carrot and a bottle of beer if you thought it mattered. Hell, Trax, I envy your resolve. Let's take—" Bill peered at the suit. Cooley, said a bloody label.

"Paul Cooley," Dantalion offered. "Filtration expert. Fifty-one years old. No children. Played the trumpet. According to his diary, a fan of horror."

The poor bastard had seen enough horror firsthand. "Let's take Cooley to the pyre and give him what dignity we can."

They lifted the body onto a stretcher rigged to Bill's quad bike. After strapping him into place, Bill issued a few commands, and the little vehicle headed off. They walked stiffly in the same direction, toward the tail of a caravan of rovers, a line so small it was beyond heartbreaking. Silhouettes of colonists flickered among them, details bleeding in as the sun rose. A wooden framework marked the end of humanity. It was barbaric, and yet this ancient practice held a vital purpose. The bugs must not get the bodies. What they wanted meat for didn't matter. They must be denied.

A drone flew overhead, its four little ion trails like embers in the sky. Bill could sense a tickle through Dantalion as it connected with the peer-to-peer network.

"Bill, you're not going to like this."

How many billions spent on AI for that gem?

"Don't take it out on me. I'm the one that's looking through the footage. You can see for yourself if you want."

Bill sniffed and said silently, "Tell me."

"Staging's mostly flattened, and what isn't is burning. There are no signs of bugs or humans. On the west side... Bill, they didn't make it. With no buildings to soak up the blast, it spread far, catching those who were already moving. I can't even confirm the number of dead. The remains are too slagged."

Sighing, he wondered how long it would be before he forced himself to see the results of his inaction.

"What?" Trax said.

"The survey data from Staging has come in. The city, the people— all gone. You know, there's something that really gets me—yeah, beyond all this. Crumpler. We got her out of the tunnels. I got her away from BILT4. I had medical ready at the front of the convoy. So close. It was for nothing. Hell, she could be back on that pile."

Trax put a hand on his shoulder. "You're not thinking straight. The power plant stopped that. It would have been quick."

"But not merciful."

She squeezed his collarbone. "No, not that. None of us knows when we're finishing our shift. She patched me up, and she made Ware see reason. She used her time well. You can't ask for more than that."

By the time they reached the pyre, Cooley rested at one end. Ninety-three bodies in total, each documented as far as possible. It was the best that could be done, the best that he'd allow. As the stragglers had slowly congealed together under a night sky illuminated by the incineration of their home, they'd brought their dead. He'd wanted to send them away to safety as quickly as they appeared, but they'd refused to leave their fallen comrades. And, Bill had concluded, they refused to move on alone.

Ware had arrived with three wounded at the camp hours before dawn, his vehicle a mess of bug holes and heat-distorted panels. Dawn became the deadline, as dusk had been the day before. Was he repeating his mistake?

Colonists gathered around the pyre, stifling Bill with their close-ness. Diver pushed his way through and handed over a flaming gadget. The smell of accelerant and fresh sap merged with that of ash and blood and shit. They were all looking at him.

"You are terrible at public speaking. Shall I put together a speech?" Dantalion said. "I have some moving building blocks on file."

"No."

Bill took a step forward. There was no comfort to offer. They were fucked, and they all knew it. "I—I don't know what to say. I signed up to get away from plots and schemes and suffering. I think I brought them all with me. I kept myself apart. That was a mistake. I didn't make friends with them." He gestured to the pyre. "I didn't even meet most. I'm less for it. You've lost friends and colleagues. That pain is sacred ground that I will not tread. It would be wrong for me to claim to know what they would tell you to do next."

He walked up to the pyre and brought the flame to its base. As it caught, he moved along, igniting further patches. "I can't say they'd tell you to keep going. But I'm telling you to. We've seen the worst of humanity. And we've seen something that is not human at all. We aren't machines. We hurt. We grieve. We've seen the worst. Now, we're going to see the best of our species. We're going to pick up the pieces. We're going to survive. And then we're going to thrive. I can't order you to do it, but you're going to. I believe it. I believe in you. Take a moment to say your goodbyes. We move out in ten."

As Bill retreated to his quad bike to give the mourners their space, Dantalion said, "Not your worst."

"Someday, you're going to be turned into scrap."

"Yes, but your flesh will have rotted away long before. Speaking of rotten, are you sure we should head north?"

A whoomph and a flash brought a wave of heat. The pyre raged. Ninety-three dead accounted for, along with two hundred and eighteen survivors huddling close. Almost ten thousand gone. Still, they weren't the only ones alive.

"The team at beta must be alive. One of us will ford the river. We'll need every pair of hands we can get. No one is going to survive alone."

"It's more mouths to feed."

"And there's food to be had. How hard can it be to grind wheat into flour? Farms and the housing project—that's plenty of resources at our disposal."

"Is this what you want, a summer camp?"

"You know what I want." Bill glared at the sky. He'd seen that damn dropship leave a trail last night as it screamed toward orbit. She was up there, laughing.

"Wagner. You can't get everything you want."

"I've worked that out. She'll wait. I have other responsibilities. The living are more important than revenge. Even more important than justice—and ego. The League had that wrong."

Another straggler approached. Perhaps the delay was worth it after all. He came from the east, carrying a rifle, features lost in the sun's intensity, until he closed.

Karlo.

Bill's jaw tightened, his shoulders knotted, and he reached for the simpler rifle strapped to his quad bike. The mourners noticed, too. They stiffened, and anger spilled across them, threatening to reforge them into a mob. He considered feeding the asshole to the pyre. The cold truth of their precarious situation demanded he think deeper. The man had abandoned most of his armor. Where it had covered, his suit was intact. Elsewhere, he bore a mess of bloody cuts and punctures. He was alone, on foot. Bill strode between the thug and the colonists.

Karlo stopped twenty meters away. His rifle pointed to the side and away. "I see you're still alive, Hayden."

"I have a habit of that. I see you are, too."

"Dead men don't get paid."

Bill understood, and he laughed.

Trax strode to his side. The crew couldn't be far behind. "What's so damn funny?"

"She's gone."

Karlo nodded. "Yeah."

"She left you behind."

"That she did."

Bill glanced at Karlo's rifle. "You need to hand that over."

"Are you going to kill me if I do?"

"No. I'm no judge. I'm sure as hell not an executioner. Unless you give me a reason."

Trax approached Karlo, sensibly giving Bill a clear line of sight the whole way. Karlo put the safety on, removed the charge brick, shrugged the strap over his shoulder, and held both out as gingerly as if he were passing over a beloved childhood toy. She took the rifle with surprising calm. Then she belted him across the face. His jaw rocked to the side, and he stumbled back a step, grunting.

"Yeah, I deserved that."

She held the rifle tight. Was she going to use it as a club? Seconds passed. Finally, she leaned forward and demanded, "What the hell are you doing here?"

"He has nowhere else to go," Bill said.

Karlo took a bottle hanging from his belt, exaggerating each move when Bill raised his rifle, and swallowed the contents. "The bugs came for us. Wagner was greedy. She wanted more, always more. That meant our scrubs kept poking the bugs, looking for the good stuff. They went back one time too many. The dumb fucks brought them right to us. She prioritized the alien tech over people. There were never enough seats for all of us to pull out."

"You volunteered?" Bill asked, already knowing the answer.

"Yeah, right. She played me. She played everyone. Left us all to die. The bitch wanted to make sure we weren't around to poke holes in her story. She set the damn fusion bomb to blow once she was safe."

Diver made an odd squeak. "She blew up a nuke?"

"No, dipshit. You still have the skin on your flesh, so no. I diffused it."

Was he telling the truth? "I thought you said the bugs were attacking."

"They were."

"But you had time to disarm a bomb."

"I multitask well. I tried to save some scrubs, but I couldn't. The bugs kept coming and coming."

Trax growled, raising the unloaded rifle. "You fucking bombed our power plant, killing thousands, and want to pretend you would have risked yourself to save anyone else?"

"That wasn't me. Wagner arranged the flyer. It's not how I do things. If I have a problem with you, I'll be in your face, just like you."

Her eyes flashed. "Don't compare us. Just don't."

"I bought time, but we're all going to die soon enough. There are too many bugs, and we're stuck on this damn rock."

"We should leave him," Trax said, turning to Bill. "He's a murderer and a traitor to humanity."

"I'm a good shot, and I know all the BILT4 resource drops. You need me."

Trax spat on the ground. "Never."

"Look," Bill said, wondering yet again whether he was making a terrible mistake. "Leaving him here is as good as killing him."

"Good, then—"

"Remember, I said we have to be better. I don't trust him, either. We don't have to. I don't think he wants to die. He's not a fanatic. With no

294

way off the planet, our interests are aligned. We can use his help. I'm not going to waste him. We can't afford to."

"If he steps out of line once…"

"Then we'll deal with him."

Bill gave everyone another fifteen minutes, then ordered the colonists to their vehicles and led the way on his quad bike, alone and yet closer to people than he'd been in a long time.

WHY WOULD anyone travel so far to live in housing bunched up like grapes? Most of the dwellings were two-story courtyard designs, colored in a variety of pastels. Large windows were framed in black or white polymer. Roofs sloped at different angles created the illusion of individuality. Unfinished, wide roads were punctuated with offshoots for public transport and parking. Staging would have connected via road, rail, and air before the next set of colonists arrived. Weren't they going to be in for a rude shock?

Bubbles of dissolvable composite encased completed buildings, keeping them clean. This neighborhood was a spot for those with money. Staging would have kept going as more affordable accommodation, abandoned by many as new, distant territory was claimed. A capital would emerge. As years passed, Staging would have slipped into a refuge, and then a trap for those down on their luck. The first city's future was always going to be a graveyard. What did that make this place? Stillborn?

Bill had left the rest of the convoy a short distance away, refusing company while he reconnoitered on his quad bike. The silence and stillness suggested he was traveling through a photo, a moment imprisoned in eternity. Housing shifted to skeletons, then to barren roads until warehouses and assembly plants dominated his view. He believed shops and offices would have replaced the utilitarian buildings next year.

He stopped out front of a set of portable units—housing even plainer than that in staging. His skin tingled with the chill from riding, and his legs were shaky when he dismounted.

"Hello?" His voice echoed, fading, fading.

If Sturt hadn't pulled everyone back to Staging, colonists would be working, eating, drinking, living here.

"Is the local net up?"

"All systems are in standby mode," Dantalion said. "I can activate them if required."

"Any signs of life?"

"No."

"What about bugs?"

"Nothing obvious, but then you already know that. The convoy is waiting. Are you going to let them in?"

"When they see this, they'll want to stay."

"The bugs are too close."

Bill leaned against a unit's door and took in the unfinished town. "They'll still want to stay. They'll think they're safe here. It's human nature."

"Lucky they have you to stamp that out."

"Very funny." Where had his choices gone so wrong? How had he ended up on dirt and not in deep space? He really could have made a go of it. Leasing a ship and heading out beyond the oncoming wave of civilization. Maybe even rig the vessel so he could fly it entirely by himself.

"How far is far enough?"

"Eclipse possesses three continents. The further from the bugs, the better."

"I can't argue with that. Can you reach the convoy?"

"If I activate the local net."

"Do it, but keep the signal strength as low as you can."

"Paranoia?"

"Everyone *is* out to get us."

"True."

Within the hour, the convoy arrived. Bill directed them near the warehouses in an orderly fashion and placed Ware in charge of raiding the stores for food, water, clothing, and anything else useful for human needs. Trax did the same for equipment supplies. Relenting to constant demands, he opened a few showers but set someone in charge of keeping them short. Any suggestion of staying was met with his swift no and a new task to keep the speaker busy. They would be ready to go at a moment's notice.

His caution extended to the team at beta. Only once the convoy was ready to move on would he risk communicating. Even the drones he'd wrangled from the convoy for scouting were all pre-programmed to return before downloading data. And they weren't heading straight back. Wagner could have more surprises, or the bugs might be smart enough to follow.

He wandered as others worked, seeking to clear his mind for the tough decisions ahead. A lonely flyer encased in a protective covering sat on a launch pad, dirt piling against one side. It called to him, but he'd made his choice. He couldn't cut and run now.

Shadows flickered along the ground. Bill reached for his rifle but relaxed when he spied two of the drones he'd sent out.

"Dantalion, what have we got?"

"Patience. They're downloading at a glacial pace. It's like talking to you. Here we go. Staging."

Lowering himself to sit against one of the flyer's landing support, Bill accessed the footage. A virtual window opened, revealing the destruction. The fires were mostly out now. One drone had swept past the power plant. Nothing remained—its position was marked by a massive crater and the circle of black glass that ringed it for nearly a kilometer, at least on the west side of the river. Only farther away did the shape of destroyed vehicles rise up. Dust devils swirled on scorched soil, imitating life.

The east bank had a different story to tell. The nearest structures were rubble and slag. Farther out, they took on a surreal visage: broken, melted, alien. Movement! He leaned forward, then remembered to zoom in. Survivors? Among the shadows, bugs toiled. He licked his dry lips and absorbed the details. The bugs carried out different tasks. Some cut off panels and supports. Others hauled sections down into tunnels. One bug carried several consoles out of an office window and made its way to the ground, undulating as it went. They were stripping Staging like they'd stripped the people they'd captured. A shiver ran through him.

"Dantalion, do you think they'll break the tech down for raw materials or learn from it?"

"Why not both, or neither? Remember, we have no proof of intelligence, at least not here. Any conclusions must be tentative."

The view had moved on, and a scorched rover rested under a slab of building. A hole in one side was matched by debris lying on the road. A bug crawled out far enough to drop a lump before disappearing inside. The lump hit the road and rolled a short distance. It was a head, neatly severed at the neck, all the hair burned off. Bill closed his eyes, but the image remained.

"I've seen enough. Is it available to everyone?"

"I've held all data in case you had security concerns."

"Security? Throw in morale and mental health. Lock it up for the investigators. No one needs to see this any time soon."

"Very well. One of the drones we sent to BILT4 has returned."

"I don't want to see."

"And I don't want to risk your frail physical form, but the drone collected pertinent details on its return trip."

Great. "Show me."

An expanse of hill, mostly denuded of grass, filled his vision, the details blurring as the drone zoomed along. The view jerked back and forth in a nausea-inducing kaleidoscope. The paired drone he'd sent with it came into view, its little ion plumes darting as it followed a collision avoidance algorithm. A dragonfly swooped after it.

"Where is this?"

"Near where you recovered the fabrication team."

"Okay, so they're guarding their base."

"Wait for it."

The view shifted as the drone rose and banked. An impression of darkness and glints. And then ordinary ground.

"What was that? Take it back and slow it down."

"Yes, master. I live to obey."

On the second viewing, it became clear. Bugs worked to excavate dirt, stripping it down several meters. Rust-colored metal showed in a ring at the middle of their efforts, and in the center, a hole. The metal had gently curving lines. An iris. It was a domed iris, on a vast

298

scale, opening like a damned pupil. The structure filled him with dread.

"The Staging blast didn't even hurt them."

"That is one interpretation. They likely suffered significant losses. This activity, however, suggests—"

"That they can replace the losses, fast."

"A gold star for you, Bill. That or they had already pulled back enough resources to attack the BILT4 compound."

"They're opening up, too. In the daytime. They think they've won."

"Or they've entered the next step of a scripted routine."

"Karlo was right. We're fucked."

Bill got up. Another continent wouldn't be far enough away. He crossed to the warehouse where he'd last seen Trax, using a rear door to enter a narrow corridor. Inside felt no safer. He turned and took a door.

"Bill, surviving this far would qualify as a miracle according to a variety of statistical models."

"Are you trying to cheer me up?" He'd entered some kind of maintenance bay. Several large mechs waited in parking bays, covered with white and red stripes.

"Any day you're not shot, cut up, or blown up is a good day, Bill. It's a matter of perspective."

The anthropomorphic design of the mechs caught his attention. They couldn't be mistaken for bugs. These were the sort of machines to crush them. He sighed at the wishful thinking.

"Surviving for now isn't good enough. We've been pumping out metals, polymers—everything they need to expand. We couldn't have made the situation easier for them. Maybe it would have been better if Karlo had let that bomb go off."

"That is defeatist. Besides, it's only a tactical nuclear weapon."

"Remember Marrick Prime? I kept sending reports arguing that we needed more chances. I was so sure I could find a faction to reason with. I was still in denial as the agency pulled teams out, one after another. I wrote the final report too late, giving them time to set off nukes on three damn planets."

"Seeking change from within is a valid strategy. It has worked elsewhere."

"Yeah, but sometimes it lets things fester."

"You claim too much responsibility. Marrick's despotic government chose to attack. The League military chose how to respond."

"But I am responsible *here*. I can't make the same mistake."

The decision came, unbidden, enormous, final. Bill's skin flushed with heat. Damn, Beth was going to get her pound of flesh. "Karlo's nuke—if dropped into the bug city, it'd wipe them out, right?"

"It is a reasonable assumption. If their fabrication facilities are centralized, the threat would be greatly diminished. Another gold star today, Bill."

"That flyer. I could use it to drop the bomb right down their throat."

"Bill, you saw they are guarding it well. Even if you tried a suicide run, the odds of success are virtually nil. We do not own the skies."

He slammed a fist into a mech leg, earning pain. "God damn it. These people don't need me playing shepherd. If I take out the bugs, it's worth the risk." A quad bike wasn't large enough to haul the nuke. He looked up at the mech. "What if there's another route? Trax and her crew made it to the bug city via tunnels. If I use a mech, I'll be able to carry the bomb in."

Trax stomped from around a corner. "That's a stupid plan. You'd never make it."

Damn. He hadn't realized he'd been speaking out loud. How much had she heard? "You haven't seen what the bugs are up to. They're open for business. And I have this feeling we've only seen the start of what they can do."

Her crew wandered in behind her.

"What's up, boss?" Diver asked.

"This asshole thinks he can pilot a mech up to the bugs' front door and set a nuke off."

"Sounds like suicide," Harry said while wiping a rag on a hunk of machinery.

He needed their help, not their scorn. "I'll set it to go off on a timer. If you can do something to make a mech go faster, I might have a chance."

"Something to make a mech go faster," Izy said. "Looks like we have a new designer on the team."

A tiny smile bent Amy's lips. "It'd be an interesting project. There'd be trade-offs. And I think we'd want armor."

"And weapons," Diver added. "Stuff that would work in tunnels."

Trax turned on her crew, hands on her hips. "You lot are not coming. Two are enough."

"Wait," Bill said. "Two? I'm the only one going."

"Not if you want a mech." Trax's voice was firm, her eyes steady, her will clearly hard as granite. "We'll set up a pair. But Hayden, the plan is to get out, you included. That's how I operate."

"Sorry, boss," Amy said. "We're a crew."

Harry put a greasy hand on Amy's shoulder. "We work best together."

Karlo walked in. He'd changed into a colony suit with construction badges, but still had his weapons. "There you all are." He scowled. "What's up?"

"Be very, very quiet." Izy put a finger to his lips. "We're hunting bugs."

Bill walked over to Karlo. "I'm sending the bugs to hell. I need to know how to work your nuke."

Karlo's eyes widened. "You've got to be fucking with me?"

"Not coming with us?" Izy asked.

"Hell, no. You try that, I'm getting out of here as fast as I can."

Where did the man's moral compass stand? What did he perceive as beneficial? Bill put out a hand. "I'm going to put Ware in charge, but I'd like your help. Get the people as far away as possible and keep them safe."

Karlo grabbed his hand and squeezed. "Sure, if only because it'll piss off Wagner."

"Looks like you've got a little army," Dantalion said. "Beth would be proud."

Ensuring he was silent, Bill responded, "You don't seem worried. Don't you care about your optronics? You'll die as much as I."

"Worried? Bill, Bill, Bill. Don't be silly. This is what we were made for."

CHAPTER 30
LOAD UP

Terrain flickered above a workbench, projected by a portable display. The warehouse lighting cut between those standing around it: a tired Ware, Karlo the murdering scum, a lean, haunted Hayden, and of course, Trax and her crew. She'd pushed her people beyond what she had the right to ask of them. They deserved more overtime bonuses than the parents of triplets, and yet they asked for nothing. And here everyone was, pissing away seconds like used beer.

A humidity hung in the air, adding to her discomfort.

Ware slapped the workbench with both hands. "No. This is nuts. We took too long and lost almost everyone at Staging."

"I know that," Hayden said, a dark edge to his voice. "I know that damn well. That's why you can't stay."

"We have almost no one left. Heaven knows we aren't drinking pals, but we need you." Ware swept his gaze across the others. "You're all going to die, and we need you. There's not enough of us as it is. We have to outsmart the bugs and survive for years. We have to work out what the hell will happen when BILT4 rescues Wagner. If she doesn't have any nasty surprises for us, we still have the question of what to do when a hundred thousand new colonists arrive expecting homes and food. Ten thousand dead will be nothing. And you want to take the only fab crew we have?"

Trax leaned over the workbench. "He's not taking us. We're escorting him. I decided, and it's what's going down. There's no time for playing. We know mechs, and we'll know what we've built."

Hayden raised his hands. "You all have valid points. The situation is dire. We're all having to compromise. If we don't put an end to the bugs now, there's nowhere far enough to run to. We've left them all the building materials they need. It's a smorgasbord. Who's to say they won't build dropships? What do we do if they're in orbit when the Phase 3 ships arrive? They have the tech to jump systems. What if they reach a developed planet? Imagine the resources at their disposal. How many bugs could they make? How long would it be before they're right across the League? By rights, I should be pulling everyone into this op, but I'm not. If this doesn't work, you're the backup plan."

Images of farmers chased in fields flashed across Trax's mind. Cities, their towers covered in bugs like infested crops. Alien craft launching to orbit like spores.

Ware moved back from the workbench. "Do you even have a plan, a real one?"

"I'm working on it," Hayden said. "And that'll be easier once you've got everyone moving."

To Trax's surprise, Ware turned to Karlo. "What do you have to say?"

The question was greeted with a shrug. "If they're going to die trying to save me, I won't stop them. Even if they succeed, they'll die."

Screw that. "Not happening. We're going to whack the bugs and saunter out. You can kiss my ass when I return."

Hayden stared at her intently. She returned it with equal strength, and he broke first. He walked around the bench and stood before the police captain. "You're going to be in charge. Pick up the beta folk—the alphas, too, if you can make contact—and get the hell out of here. Don't stop. You're now deputy director. If I die, it's down to you."

"I don't want that." Ware poked Hayden's chest. "You wanted to run the colony, not me."

"I know you'll do what you need to. We all will."

"If I'm in charge, the convoy is bugging out now. We're not waiting around for you to change your mind. We won't help you. You're entirely on your own."

At least there'd be fewer distractions. Trax leaned over the workbench. "Better get moving. You keep everyone safe, got that?"

Ware gave her a nod. Bill put out a hand, and Ware studied it. They shook.

"Touching, isn't it?" Izy whispered from behind as Ware strode out of the warehouse without a backward look.

"Can it."

"Yes, boss."

Karlo worked his jaw, then tilted his head. "What is the plan?"

Hayden returned to the workbench and the hovering map. "You said the bomb is in the southwest corner of the compound. We'll circle around, grab it, and head over near the bug city. Once we've drilled down to a suitable tunnel, we'll deliver the nuke, set the timer, and hightail it out. Simple."

Karlo sneered. "That's the worst plan I've ever heard."

The asshole's attitude hit Trax's buttons, despite her agreement. "You can do better?"

"I'm getting as far away as I can. That's the best plan. But if you're stupid enough to try this, you need to think smarter."

Hayden bristled. "What can I do? I can't negotiate with them. I can't manipulate them—they're machines. Going in slow and quiet is all I've got."

"Jesus wept. You're all going to die. Treat them like a military force. They respond to attacks. You do feints to get their defenses elsewhere. You need to go in hard and fast. If you drill, they'll hear you. They're going to know you're coming. Use shaped charged and blast your way in. Don't stop. Don't let up. It's Close Quarters Battle."

Damn. He was right. She could see it in Hayden's face. The man's eyes had gone distant, like he was arguing with himself.

The spook pressed his fingers together. "Stay and help. I could do with your expertise."

"Not happening. I only fight when I'm getting paid."

"I could offer you land shares," Hayden said with little conviction.

Karlo headed for the exit. "This dirt is worthless. I'll leave you details on the location, the authentication codes, and how to arm the nuke. That's all you're getting. I'd say you can thank me later, but there won't be a later."

Trax wrinkled her nose, happy to see the back of the last of BILT4 on Eclipse. She couldn't help but wonder if he was setting them up as part of an elaborate plan by Wagner to clean up the last of her mess.

Hayden turned to her and the crew that had been as quiet as she'd ever known them. "You're not going to die. Karlo was right in one way. I've been reading the situation the wrong way. I need to treat the bugs like there's a mind behind it. They respond to what we do. I've seen it. We've seen it. I'll get a plan together, a good one. But first, we need to talk about the mech design. I've been thinking that—"

"No, no thinking." Trax pointed a cautionary finger. "That's not how it works. Use that spook brain of yours to come up with a list of tasks you need the mechs to do. We'll see what we've got to hand and what we can do with it to meet that. I don't want you interfering. You'll slow us down. Now, how much time do we have?"

Damn, it felt good to focus on the right things. This was what she lived for.

"Time? Less than none. Whatever you can do."

She laughed and turned to her crew. "Typical management work order. All right, oil monkeys and chip jockeys. Listen up for our scope and gird your gonads. There won't be time to ask questions later. Make them smart. Make them count."

Her crew waited for Hayden with steady eyes.

"Right," he said. "We can't get the nuke through the smallest tunnels, but…"

SIX FRAMES STOOD IN A SEMI-CIRCLE, their alloy struts threaded with cables, actuators, sensors—a thousand different components for utility or safety. Tethers hung from the ceiling like vines, securing the machines and obfuscating their true form. Mounds of discarded components lay behind, with sections of hydraulic pipes and old optic fiber bundles snaking through.

The air stank with the tang of hot metal and the sweetness of curing polymers. Small construction drones flew around them, sparking as they completed the full welds of tacked-together additions. Trax hated using them—if there was a design flaw, no human would know until it was time to put the mechs to use. But beggars couldn't be choosers, and she could have done with a crew of a hundred *if* the hundred knew what the hell they were doing.

She wasn't happy with the mech chassis either. For consistency and size, they'd left those on the haulers alone and used a set of construction units from the site. She didn't know these intimately and had little trust that their maintenance cycles were taken seriously.

"I could use an assist."

Trax put down a torque wrench and hurried over to Harry. The mechanic had lain on a raised cart, her powerful hands grasping a heavy gear resting out of place in a hydraulic unit.

"What can I do?"

"See that bundle run near the chassis coupling? Pull it up."

When Trax did as asked, Harry shifted the gear into place. "Pass me the housing."

The comradery of their work was like a filling meal. Their friendship had changed since coming to Eclipse, and Trax missed the old times. Together, they secured the housing.

"You don't have to come," Trax said. "You could take the fab and catch up with the convoy."

"No. I'll be carrying the bomb."

"Harry, you never wanted to be here. You wouldn't be if I hadn't suggested it."

"I make my own choices."

Chuckling, Trax stood back. "That you do. All good here?"

"All good."

Would it ever be again? Five years ago, Trax had run into that pub, unable to contain the good news. Selected for the first phase of a new colony. It'd be hard work, but the rewards were incredible. Harry had been quieter than usual, and it had taken a while to unearth her pain—

the mechanic's whole family wiped out financially in the graphene crash.

Too excited to consider the risks, and wanting to help for selfish validation, Trax had pushed Harry to sign up for Phase 2. Hell, she'd decided she'd defer, and they'd go together. What a team they'd make. They could fix Harry's money problems and get away from the corporations that had ruined them all. Hadn't that turned out peachy?

She left the mechanic and headed toward Amy, telling herself she wasn't fleeing—just making sure her crew was busy.

"Boss, can you pass me the fiber splicer?" The slightly built optronics expert was right inside the frame of a mech.

"Here. Why so many cables? We don't have time for improv."

"Everything we're doing is improv, and Stubby here is for Hayden."

"And that's important because?"

Amy spliced loose optic fibers to the main control runs. "It's obvious. He's more wired up than a starship's bridge. I'm giving him extra processing, sensors, and a few other minor adjustments. There's no point wasting him. You should think about that."

Across the warehouse, mechanical limbs waited, and components stood in stacks. Trax bit down on her frustration. "We don't have time for anything fancy. And no time for guesses."

"Nothing fancy, boss, just good sense. I've heard rumors, and he fits them. And it's giving me time to plan the control layout. Consider it therapeutic."

Trax stood back and took in the mech. Drones finished welding the cage around the head and moved onto struts that would help protect the hydraulics. Direct actuators would have avoided this, but replacing the lot was out of the question.

"Are you sure you want to come? This isn't what you signed up for."

Amy paused, one hand outstretched to return the splicer. "I'm loving it. Designing on the fly? A real practical purpose with no forms and assessments and management interference? This is magic. And I've got a couple of bug chips I packed to check out when we return. Always good to study the competition. Shame we have to blow them to atomic sludge, but I'll take what I can get. Nice talking, boss. Can you give me some peace? I need to think."

"I'll leave you to it."

Izy whistled while raising a panel to the farthest mech's side. They'd considered making this one into a quadruped for carrying the nuke, but there was already too much to do on the fly. Fitz would have locked down a solid design in no time. Wheels and tracks were out, too. Wheels for the likely damage, and tracks would have required churning out more virgin parts than they had time for. Besides, with all the alien bugs, humanoid shapes felt like a statement.

This is us. When we kick your ass, remember it.

She sniffed, pleased with the thought. Izy had fretted over reforming enough panels for armor. And they all knew that the polymer sheets, even the high-grade panels they'd scavenged, were a compromise. Tungsten carboceramics would have been best if they'd had days to fab the first samples and dial in the process over many more.

Close to the warehouse entrance, Diver danced between mixers, vats, and a seemingly endless set of cylinders. He was outfitted in a bulky hazard suit protecting himself from the reek that drifted in with each gust of wind. Behind, barrels rested on the ground or in stacks— enough ingredients for a cocktail that would end them all before they'd met a single bug. She winced at his exuberance.

She returned to her station and looked through the task list, sliding fingers into the roots of her frizzy hair. So much to be done. The responsibility was too heavy. She couldn't find joy. But maybe, just maybe, she could find satisfaction. She tapped an item: calibrating the voltage regulators on mech four. Not sexy, but vital. She rubbed her hands. These mechs weren't going to be pretty, they weren't going to be perfect, but they'd be the best-damned machines her crew had ever assembled.

Later—an amorphous concept when so engrossed—she was attaching Hayden's disassembled rifle to the mini turret on top of his mech when he called her name repeatedly.

"What?" she snapped.

"We need to talk."

She'd told him to stay out of the way. What the hell was he thinking? "Later. Busy."

"Now, please."

She leaned over and glared down from the mech's four-meter height. Blue tinged the sunlight sneaking in from the warehouse's open doors. A storm was coming down from the distant mountains. They hadn't had one like this for a while. Perfect.

"I told you to stay away until we're done. You interrupting is going to push that back."

He put a hand on the mech's arm, triggering a warm heat of territorial instinct from her chest, right down to her toes. "Remember that non-existent time limit only shaped by a vague looming doom?"

"Yeah, and?"

"It's pretty much here. You've got two hours, max."

"Two hours?" Classic management. Everything becomes urgent because they can't sit still twiddling their thumbs. That reminded them of how useless they were. "Not a chance. Even the software tuning will take that long, and we're hours away from having the hardware assembled."

Hayden surveyed the room as if only now noting the state of the machines. "I've been sending out drones for reconnaissance. Bugs are coming—right to us."

Trax slapped the rifle barrel, sending it tilting down. "What the hell do you mean, right to us? That doesn't make a lick of sense."

"I would have thought the same, but a rover's heading this way with three dragonflies on its tail."

"Someone else made it? We have to help."

"I don't think she'll want our help. The opposite, in fact. The rover's coming from the same direction as the bug city, and the drone caught a glimpse of the driver. Any guesses as to who?"

"There's no time for games."

"Erin Tyzen. I don't know how she broke out, or how she escaped Staging, but it was her. She knows where we are, and she's bringing along some friends."

"Damn." Trax tilted her neck, cracking her upper vertebrae. "Sturt.

I saw her with him at Staging. Hayden, you are shit at making friends."

"I've noticed. That's why the limit. I don't expect to talk Erin down, but there's a chance I can get through to Sturt and have him divert their path. If so, you get your time back."

"A bug killed him."

"Then two hours it is. We can't afford to skip town, either. If Erin doesn't find us, she'll follow the convoy tracks. We have to stop them here."

Izy strolled over. "There's another solution. Take a drone or two with some of Diver's grenades and blow up the rover. The bugs won't have anyone to follow. We can sip tea and eat scones."

Hayden's brow creased. He wasn't much of a killer, despite his reputation. He'd probably already thought of Izy's approach and dismissed it.

She could respect that, even if it was inconvenient. "We'll do it somehow."

"Is there anything I can do to help?"

Trax narrowed her eyes. Two hours. Only two hours. "I don't know. Is there anything you can do?"

"I have hands. They're good at holding things."

"That'll have to do."

Complete a woefully spec'd design with the wrong equipment, too few staff, and an amateur on a deadline as sharp as a razor? Yeah, they had this. They had to.

CHAPTER 31
MADE FOR COMBAT

The heavy panel shifted to the left, its grinding sending a shiver through Bill's spine.

"Oh, dear, Bill. You should pick up a hobby to improve your coordination. I've heard knitting is fun."

He shoved the triangular panel back into place with his left hand and fired the bolt gun repeatedly, securing the piece, then swapped to a UV light and cured the adhesive. "If you wanted to knit, you should have gotten yourself embedded in a factory."

"I prefer to be mobile. Or at least using my smarts. We should be analyzing the situation, not getting your hands dirty with manual labor."

"You were fine throwing me around before. I'm doing what needs to be done. The plan is sound." He replaced the tools on a cart and picked up a bracket to secure a length of cabling inside the mech's shoulder. Dantalion had highlighted the part in his vision and now did the same for where it fitted. The construction queue seemed out of order to his amateur understanding, but parts kept arriving, and questioning the fab crew had already proved pointless.

"The plan is a wisp of hair in a hurricane. The odds are not in our favor."

"Are you a military AI? Are you loaded with combat strategies and tactics? No? The agency didn't train me in them either. I won't over-think this time. So, you can get off my back."

The bracket snapped into place, an elegant design. He gently teased the cabling into its grip, defying the rough frustration he felt. Dantalion didn't get it. It was easy to advise when someone else had the responsibility. The lives of the survivors depended on Bill, not a lump of optronic ego.

The situation was spiraling, a familiar feeling, but it was all a far cry from his life in the LSA. There, everyone had an agenda hidden within paranoia and wrapped in need-to-know. You didn't get close. He'd spent too much time with Trax and her crew. They weren't friends, but they weren't strangers, either. He respected them, and perhaps something more. He was also going to get them killed. At least, that part he knew well.

"Would you like an update?"

Bill wiped sweat from his temple. "Hit me with it."

"I believe I lost another drone to the increasing winds. The final telemetry suggests it crashed rather than defaulting to auto return."

He grabbed a panel, this one set for the mech's lower forearm. "Screw the drones—what about Erin and the bugs?"

"Very close."

Harry appeared in Bill's unfocused vision. He startled, and she took the plate. "I'll help."

"Sure."

Glue. Activate. Place. Fasten. Set. He looked for more pieces, but there were none.

Harry held out a fist. "Not bad."

Nonplussed, Bill bumped it with his own.

Lightning flashed, strobing the interior of the warehouse, followed shortly by a crash of thunder that could have been the end of the world. He glanced outside at what might as well have been night, a faint blue tinge to the silhouettes of the unfamiliar town.

"What's next?"

"Nothing," Trax said from nearby as she slipped a rag into a pocket. "They're ready. Back up like a good boy."

When he did so, she tapped some controls on her left forearm, and a series of cracks, snaps, pops, and hisses announced the disconnection of the cables dangling from the ceiling. They retracted, and he imagined a mad puppeteer setting dangerous creations free. Only now did the true nature of the mechs brand itself into his mind.

They stood nearly four meters tall, thick-legged, long-armed, and with a palpable aura of menace. Clear polymer sections connected to form blisters with almost a full one hundred and eighty degrees of vision. Despite the rush and recycling of materials, the panels that formed the armor fit tightly, each coated in gloss black. Protuberances stuck out of each mech, formed of different parts, different shapes. Somewhere in the build schedule, the team had found time to attach bright yellow running lights, and a variety of powerful spotlights festooned the shoulders. They were angry giants, monsters from fairytales.

"What have we created?"

"Pure ass-kicking," Izy said while putting an arm around Bill's shoulders. "A better question is, what can't these babies do?"

"Teach you to be serious." Trax rubbed her hands. "Tape your mouth shut for a sec. Hayden, listen in. We had to go for a lighter chassis than I'd prefer because of the tunnel diameters. But it's not all bad news. These aren't standard mechs anymore. We've reduced their max lifting capacity to up the speed of movement. A crapload of sensors feed fluorosilicate fiber runs to a twin control board with 20k EFVA chiplets. They'll dance like my grandmother after downing her third whisky. Amy's proud of that, so smile and nod. It's a tricky balance, though. The mechs are not going in light. The polymer armor helps with the weight, but it won't take a hit like tungsten carboceramics. See these?" She pointed at dark antennae near the top of a mech. "We've added beefier comm repeaters for peer-to-peer—don't expect much, but it might help. Each hydraulic line has a leak kit, but if the bugs do enough damage, you'll bleed out fluid and become a meat statue. The actuators are all upgraded to VS-23's. Harry, you want to explain the batteries?"

"Sure, boss. Come 'round the back."

Bill and the rest of the crew followed the solid mechanic and inspected the chunky packs attached to a mech's back.

"The internal battery is under the armor, but these extenders will up our range. When they're low, you hit the eject and they'll drop. They'll be easy to damage, so don't show your back to the bugs. Got it?"

"Understood."

Izy clapped his hands. "Remember, be careful where you take a dump. Don't trip up anyone else. Two points to Izy. Boss, you have to let me do the armaments."

"Go ahead."

Izy stretched out his arms. "You are in for a treat. Each mech has a custom set of hardware perfect for your bug-squashing needs. Some might say that we picked whatever random junk we could bolt on, but I say we've created a spread that would make Marines jealous. Let's start with Harry's ride. Look at that hammer. One ton of super-dense pain—that's the hammer I'm talking about, not Harry. It's backed up with a net gun to hold the critters steady, and don't forget a suite of four micro-drones."

"With some of my grenades!" Diver added.

"That's right. This mech is also beefed up with additional armor, a crane from our mechs, and that little frame. Why? Harry's going to be carrying the nuke. Amy's mech mirrors the net gun while adding a big stick—an ultracapacitor. A warning: don't touch the conductive rods on the end. And to finish it off, a frickin flamethrower!"

Trax put her hands on her hips. "I said that was too dangerous."

"Sorry, boss. The idea couldn't be denied. And you trust Amy. It's not like I'm going to use it. You've got dangerous kit, too. Those impact shears are self-sharpening. And Billy-boy, you can't miss our forgiving leader's beautiful shield. Behind that, her left shoulder has shaped charges ready to deploy. I was going add another flamethrower, but we didn't have the parts, so her right shoulder has a paint sprayer."

"Paint?" Bill raised an eyebrow.

"Diver mixed a brew that soaks up most of the EM spectrum. Get it in the right spot, and it should blind the bugs' sensors. Or do nothing. Hard to say. But we might as well get on to the cream of the crop: mine. Quite simple really, twin plasma blades. I wanted them three meters long, but the boss said there wouldn't be room to swing. Halved—such a tragedy. Where was I? Yes. Wire grapples on the shoulders are launched electromagnetically. I can go up or down, like the wire effects in ancient movies. Not heard of that? Forget it. And to finish it off, that beauty on my mech's head is a foam cannon. It's fed by ten liters of high-expansion goop. The bugs can cut through it, but it might buy us time.

"And mine," Diver said as if he were waiting for a birthday present.

"Of course, buddy. Diver's our artillery. Quad grenade launchers, each fed by independent magazines of thirty homebrewed balls of mayhem. The smaller tubes there are flare guns. We ain't going in the dark no more. And for some up-close protection, his mech's chest has an array of fifteen plasma torches. Small range, but one hell of a bearhug."

Bill eyed the remaining mech, recognizing the remains of his plasma rifle on top.

"You see that beauty? We couldn't do much to up the punch, but the rifle now has high-flow liquid cooling, a direct feed into the main battery, and a turret offering a full 360° field of death-dealing. Toss in a single grenade launcher, and you'll have plenty of chances to splat bugs. Closer to home, you have a reinforced gripper, which is our nuke-carrying backup as well as a chance to pop some bug skulls. To finish it off, a polycrystalline doped carbide drill with more torque than your average hauler. I would have spec'd it even longer, but Amy said it would look like you were compensating."

Swallowing to give himself time to take it all in, he considered what they'd achieved. It was breathtaking. It was makeshift. It was desperate.

"These are completely absurd." He glanced at them all, finishing on Trax. "They're nuts. And I love them."

"Bill," Dantalion said. "It's time."

He nodded. "Thank you, everyone. I don't deserve your help, but I'm damn happy to have it all the same. The bugs are coming. There are only three of them. This is a chance to shake out the systems, but don't play heroes. We're not drop troopers."

"We're better," Izy said. "We're engineers. Nothing can stop us."

"I'm not." They needed to understand this was serious.

"You helped build them," Diver said to the rest of the crew. "He should be like an honorary one."

Bill chuckled. "I don't think it works that way. It's good that—"

Trax cut him off. "Great pep talk. Everybody, mount up."

The front of Bill's mech split open, a sign that Dantalion was already interfacing with the system. Inside were footrests, torso straps, and space for his arms to move gimbaled control sticks, reminding him of the imposing but impractical combat mech prototypes he'd seen in classified briefings.

He pulled himself up, strapped himself in, and told Dantalion to close up. The sides whirred quietly as they shut, reminding him of being sealed in for a long sleep. Slight pressure along his legs and torso came from inflating bags of air. They'd pick up the signals going to his muscles and provide limited shock protection. A slight hum announced the hydraulics coming online, and an interface appeared in his vision while the built-in HUD remained off. The running lights switched on, his mech first, then the others.

"Ready to go, Bill. The battery is feeding clean power, hydraulic pressure is nominal. Temperature is below optimal but warming steadily. Air filtration is functioning, and CO_2 levels are well within human tolerances. I am quite impressed with the datalink Amy installed, though I am rewriting the installed code. It's very off-the-shelf."

"Don't forget to add a game of Minesweeper."

"Very droll, Bill."

Beneath his hands, the control sticks vibrated as if hungry to be used. He tested the limbs tentatively, extending, retracting, rotating.

"We don't have time for this. I can easily pilot the mech for you with greater precision than you can manage."

"Damn it, Dantalion. I'm not your puppet. Burn that into your chips, will you? I don't need you to wipe my ass for me."

To prove his point, he shifted his leg slightly. The mech stomped forward, its balance handled by the onboard computer. He angled toward the front of the warehouse, gaining confidence with each heavy step. The smell of volatiles tickled his nose. He held back a sneeze and almost swung a mech arm right into his head. Dantalion wisely stayed silent.

The warehouse opened to elemental chaos. He stood at the precipice. This was it. The other mechs joined him.

"Out there, it gets real. Anyone want to stay inside?"

Trax said over the comm, "We're not being paid by the hour, Hayden. Where do we go?"

Bill switched his spotlights on, illuminating a cone of dust and the nearby portable factory the crew called Abfab. He guided the mech over the threshold and out into a blue-tinted storm. Where were they going? Straight to hell.

AT THE EDGE of the town, they formed a line with Trax and himself at the center. A bright blur on the horizon sprouted a blinking square in his vision—Erin's rover. Dantalion's overlay placed three triangles over flashing smudges in the sky. According to AI, they were dragon-flies. Arcs of lightning exploded across the heavens. Closely following thunder boomed again and again, breaking up the white noise of dust slapping against the mech's armor. Occasional drops of rain hit the blister, sliding off as the material broke surface tension.

"This planet ain't terraformed."

"Quiet, Diver," Trax growled, "If you'd wanted it easy, you should have waited a decade."

Izy coughed. "That's why my cousin used to go for the older—"

"Izy!"

"Just trying to guide the impressionable youth."

Bill snorted. These people were not spooks or soldiers, and he was okay with that.

The blur evolved details. A rover, less bulky than most, with hazard lights flashing on as well as its headlamps. Bill marched his mech a few steps forward, then lowered into a slight crouch and brought the rifle online. Sighting data coalesced in his vision, and he considered the grenade launcher. It wouldn't be killing in cold blood, but he couldn't do it. If it came to that, let it be face-to-face.

The rover closed.

"If that hits one of us, it will inflict significant damage," Amy said, her voice cutting in and out as the storm interfered with the signal.

"Hayden," Trax said. "Are you going to kill her?"

"I don't want to."

"That's not what I asked."

One hundred meters. Eighty.

Bill clenched his teeth. *Come on. See reason.*

Sixty. Forty.

The rover braked hard, the rear sliding until the vehicle was side-on. Rocks and dust sprayed, but the storm swallowed it all. In the blinding swath of mech lights, the rover's wounds were stark and raw. Gouges, cuts, dents—barely any surface remained untouched. The rover had been chewed up and spat back out. How it could keep going was beyond his understanding. How Erin did was all too comprehendible.

The rover's door opened, and she exited, wearing a respirator and rocking under the wind. Her comm joined the peer mesh. "Hayden, is that you?"

He raised a mech arm. "I'm here."

"You think you can escape your sins, but you can't, not in the end. I'll keep going until you pay. I'll never stop. You hear that? I'm your very own avenging angel."

"You're pretty good at escaping yourself." Coils of anger tightened. Why couldn't she see the cycle she was perpetuating? "I'd thought we'd lost you at Staging, along with all those people you murdered."

"Their deaths are on you! If you hadn't signed on to Eclipse, they'd be alive. I may be an avenging angel, but you're the angel of death. I know what you're doing. I know why you haven't taken me, too. You want me to suffer. You get off on it, don't you?"

Bill walked his mech closer. "No. I don't. I wish Marrick Prime hadn't happened. I wish I'd uncovered the nuke plot that led to it. I wish the League had found another way. I wish you and I had talked, that you'd found help before we reached this point. Wishes don't help.

They don't come true. But this has to stop. You can't keep hurting others to assuage your own pain."

Dantalion overrode her response. "Bill, the dragonflies are circling above."

Trax spoke next. "Hayden. You need to give up on therapy. We've got bigger problems."

"Oh, shit," Diver whispered. "Oh, shit. We're gonna die."

Izy laughed. "No way, no chance. You and me, we're going to die from sunstroke with iced tea in our hands and music in our ears."

Trax was right. And he hoped with all his might that Izy was. "I've got the only rifle. So, we need to get the bugs onto the ground where you can reach them. Keep moving and support each other. Remember, we outnumber them."

The first dragonfly dove, streaking down, its flashing abdomen leaving a line in his vision. The ground rumbled as the mechs scattered. Bill's mouth dried like he was in vacuum, and adrenaline shot through his veins, his shaking rapidly steadied by Dantalion. He wanted to clear out, but he was the idiot with a rifle. He brought up the target acquisition and fired several bolts of plasma in quick succession. Wind tossed the dragonfly in unpredictable fits, and the infernal interference played merry hell with Dantalion's attempt to lock on using the mech's civilian sensors.

Banking hard, the dragonfly dodged out of his view. Bill turned the mech as the crew shouted at each other.

"It's going low."

"On your left!"

"Who's left?"

Trax spoke over the comm. "Diver, get back. Izy, shut up. Amy, ready with the net gun."

Where were they? A thud forced him to look away from the sky and put a mental wall between the voices and his thoughts. Erin's face appeared in front of his. He jerked his head back, thumping into padding. What the fuck was she doing?

"I told you I'll never stop. I'm going shuck you like an oyster."

She had climbed him. She was completely nuts. He brought his mech's gripping arm around. "Dantalion, help me pick her up without crushing her ribcage."

"Now you want my help."

Together, they lifted her away, cursing and kicking as she went. He needed a roof to stick her on until they sorted the bugs.

"Hayden, watch out!" Amy shouted.

A huge clang shook his mech. It rocked forward, tipping dangerously before he took several steps. A dragonfly had landed on him. Its legs digging in. Bill frantically swung the arms up, saw Erin dangling, and stopped. The bug leaped forward and away, jolting him once more. He shook his head and peered out. Erin was gone. Just gone. Had she fallen?

An object dropped from the sky. Dantalion tracked it, as Bill sent the mech into an urgent reverse, but it hit his blister and tumbled down. Red spattered across his vision, only to be washed away. He looked down, continuing backward.

Erin's head. The body hit next, limbs flailing like tossed spaghetti. His heart rate spiked.

"Shit. Shit. Shit. Dantalion, where are the bugs? What's happening?"

"I believe it is called poetic justice. Live by the bug; die by the bug."

"Stop philosophizing. Give me the bugs' loc—"

Izy's mech charged into view on his left, swinging wildly as a dragonfly snapped toward him. When his twin blades jabbed forward, it jumped into the air, quad engines boosting its height. A net made of strapping and weights flew past and into Izy, tangling his mech.

"Hey! Do I look like a bug?"

Amy sniffed. "You bug me enough."

"You made a joke. Someday, you'll be a real girl."

The dragonfly, no doubt seeing weakness, dove onto Izy. Bill wasted seconds searching for a clear shot, but only managed to singe its rear. Trax reached them and bashed the dragonfly with her shield, then caught one of its legs in her shears.

They didn't need Bill. Following the markers Dantalion fed his view, he spotted a second bug in the air above Diver. Bill advanced, firing an almost continuous spread of plasma. The acrid stench of hot polymer filled the air as he pushed the weapon's limits. One of the dragonfly's rear wings buckled. A drive burned up. The bug dropped to the ground, scrabbling, flattening its wings against its body.

Diver had fled a short way. Now, the young chemist turned back. "Try some of this."

Three *whoomps* announced grenades. The first went wide, a ball of intense white, followed by a wave that rocked the dragonfly. Any damage was superficial. The second was an almost direct hit. The grenade slid on dirt, rolled under the dragonfly, and went off right behind it. Bill flinched as the machine flipped ass-over-head, fire belching from its abdomen. The third grenade fell short. Diver's mech stumbled back and fell.

"Diver, are you okay?" Bill shouted, bringing his mech close, fearing each thud of the heavy feet must be a foreshadowing drumbeat. "Diver, can you hear me?"

With its three remaining legs, the dragonfly crawled onto Diver's mech and opened its powerful vertical jaw. Bill shouted wordlessly, blasting the remaining wings until he reached the melee. Inside his mech, Diver twisted and shouted. The dragonfly grasped the blister and bit. The mech's torso lit up as fifteen plasma cutters burned. Uncaring, the jaws kept closing. Cracks spread across the clear polymer. The blister distorted further and further. Pieces of the bug superheated, creating tiny explosions that fired shrapnel.

Bringing his mech's left arm around, Bill latched onto the frill of sensor stalks and pulled. "Get off him!"

A panel shattered, bloodying Diver's face. His mech's arms flailed.

No way, you piece of shit.

Sensor stalks ripped free in a shower of sparks. Cursing, Bill raised his mech's right arm, spun up the drill, and brought it crashing down onto the dragonfly's head. Brown smoke poured into the swirling air. The jaws tightened. He drove the drill farther and farther into the machine's skull, squealing, grinding.

The dragonfly froze, a monument to what—destruction, mindless hunger, an uncaring universe?

"To survival, Bill, to survival."

Dantalion's comment brought Bill crashing back to the mess before him as gusting waves of blue haze rattled off mech and bug alike. A mess of buckled panels and the smoldering dragonfly head smothered the silent kid. Bill gripped a mandible and pulled.

"Diver, if you can hear me, don't move. I'm going to free you."

"How is he?" Trax demanded between grunts, clearly caught up in her own struggle.

"I'll tell you as soon as I know. What about you?"

"One down. Amy's chasing the other with her flamethrower. Don't worry about us."

Alloy groaned. Polymer cracked. The mandibles jerked back a short distance. More. The hydraulics of Bill's mech hummed, and an unpleasant heat cooked his lower back.

Come on. Come on.

With one last metallic, ear-grating scream, the dragonfly rolled away. Bill shuffled his mech. "Diver, it's gone."

A pale face, splattered red and with closed eyes, lay among a halo of polymer and that cursed rust-colored alloy.

"Dantalion, can you open up his mech?" Bill reached for the toggle that would open his own.

"You should remain inside until you've secured the location."

"Make yourself useful."

"Always."

Bill's mech opened. Thick, dirty air beat at his mouth and nose, choking and burning. He shoved his respirator on and secured it. Clear air played over his coated nostrils, and he shucked his straps and dropped to the ground. The blackened and distorted plates covering Diver opened, though the blister wobbled and stopped partway. His suit had two punctures, both red-edged.

Ducking beneath the blister, Bill reached for Diver's neck. If there was a pulse… The skin was cold and clammy.

"Hey, there, Diver. I know your real name. I won't say it. Not even now. But I need something from you. I need you to live. Can you do that for me?" Bill sniffed and his eyes, narrowed for protection, watered. "I mean, the forms would be terrible. And can you imagine what Trax would do to me?"

Was that a beat? Bill leaned in close.

"Come on!"

Another beat.

"Boo!"

Bill jerked back, his head slamming into the underneath of the blister.

Diver opened his eyes and grinned weakly. "I had to decide between that and you giving me mouth-to-mouth, but you're not my type."

The urge to strangle the kid faded, and Bill laughed. "All right, sleeping beauty, let's get you inside. Your bug hunt is over."

Behind them, flames erupted, reflecting off the mechs and brightening the nearest buildings. Izy leaped through the fire, chased by a burning dragonfly. He dropped his mech to one knee and spun around, his glowing plasma blades already in motion. Two slices, and the dragonfly collapsed.

The blades powered off, and Izy stomped close. "Is Diver okay?"

"I'm good." It didn't sound convincing.

"Fantastic. So, did you see me? Do we have it on camera?"

"Too busy bleeding."

Bill started extricating Diver as gently as possible. This wasn't a good start.

"Don't worry, it gets worse." Dantalion brought up a map. "I requested an ongoing trace from the satellite network. Three blips have come through from the nuclear device in the last hour. I have also interrogated the deceased's rover."

There was no time for Dantalion's games. "And?"

"After extrapolating from the partial coordinates and accounting for potential data corruption, I am convinced the device is in motion." Soft circles appeared on the map, connected by a line of blinking arrows. "Our prodigiously legged opposition has most likely taken it underground."

The bugs had the nuke? Bill's shoulders slumped. Did they understand what they had? How long before they dismantled it or set it off far from the bug city? Bill scowled at the horizon. Eclipse was one clusterfuck after another, and it had begun before he'd ever set foot on its soil. *Beth. Damn, you owe me. You owe everyone here.*

"That's as good as wishing, Bill. Move on and ask yourself this: how are you going to get it back?"

Even that question had to wait. He extracted Diver and carried him back to the warehouse. The crew brought their mechs to either side, acting as windbreaks and an honor guard. Once inside, they all worked together to clean wounds and otherwise make the kid comfortable in a small office. Bill found himself treated as one of the crew, part of the solution. When Diver raised a hand, Bill clasped it, reassurance passing both ways.

When they left the kid to rest, he hit the crew with the news. They took it pretty well. He had to duck Trax's thrown wrench, but that was understandable. Where she had gotten that wrench from, he had no idea.

Leaning over a workbench to the side of the warehouse, he studied the remaining engineers. "This won't be easy. That's okay. We're the best crew on the planet. No one here is an idiot. I don't think spycraft is that different from the design work you do. We're going to define the situation, look at our available resources, and develop a solution. And we're going to do it fast."

We're the best crew. Where had that come from? But as they worked, it felt more and more true.

CHAPTER 32
THIS BOY GOES BOOM

Yellow running lights kept them in a pool of visual warmth. Cold, white spotlights flared on the vaulted ceiling of an expansive terraforming tunnel, and Trax thanked Abuk that there was no bug big enough to have made it. She clenched her jaw. Underground again. Un-fucking believable. The layered stone would have been beautiful if polished. Someone else could do that—anyone else. Subsidiary tunnels branched out at irregular intervals like the veins of a living organism, the work of smaller boring drones long ago released by the main cutting unit. Those machines would have been a sight to see.

The echoing stomps of mechs did little to calm her raw nerves. They'd left the storm and rain on the surface along with Aunty Jo, and the tunnel's air had desiccated after a shallow rise had trapped the runoff. The imperfect seal of her mech passed through the ticklish smell of dry stone despite the filter's best effort. Her back itched with dried sweat, adding to her mood.

Hayden plodded alongside, and her crew were close behind. The remaining ones.

"This way," Hayden said when they reached another side tunnel.

She followed him in, scowling at the narrower confines that forced her to dim her lights, and corralled the mechs into single file. Why couldn't the bugs live in trees?

"We should have used a quadruped design," Amy said after a little while, her voice harsh in the confines of her mech. "It would have given us a lower center of mass and increased stability."

Izy chuckled. "Centaur mechs would have made my butt look big."

"Not enough parts. Not enough time," Harry added. "You know that."

Rush jobs were the bane of Trax's existence. They inevitably became messy, demonstrated by the fact they had already changed plans. A nuke on the run and bugs everywhere. The initial route—head down the way she and her crew had escaped, blasting tunnels wider when needed—proved no good with dragonflies patrolling the storm-tossed skies. And they'd run over a bug or ten on the ground, Aunty Jo's weight pancaking the metal scum. Hayden, to his credit, had been ready to adapt. He was growing on her like a cheap, poorly made tool that kept on proving useful.

She'd suggested the tunnels, remembering Margot's farm, and hated herself for it the moment the idea passed her lips. He'd taken her idea and run with it, his head apparently filled with an almost encyclo-pedic knowledge of their underground web, and surmising the rest from remembered geological survey data. There was something chilling about the way he froze as he considered as if he were an android prioritizing number crunching over maintaining a semblance of humanity.

That image took her mind back to Diver lying under shiny emer-gency blankets, assuring them he'd be fine. If anything happened to him… He'd promised to head north with Abfab if they didn't return in a day. He hadn't liked it, and she hadn't liked the delay. But the storm was no time to drive on autopilot.

"It's too damn quiet without Diver," Izy said, as if reading her mind. "Who am I going to make fun of? I bet he's sipping beer, eating reconstituted corn chips, and watching replays of the '38 football season."

Trax managed a maudlin smile that he couldn't see. "I wish he was here, too. He's a good kid. He's got a good future if he can get off

Eclipse. I know we could have done with him, but I feel better knowing he's safe."

"You're not his mother," Harry said, heat in her voice. "We all signed up to this. We're all in."

"I didn't mean it like that." Trax examined the curved ceiling that pressed unsettlingly close to the top of her mech. She'd thought they'd settled this. She was their boss. She didn't own them like some corporate assholes believed, but their safety was her responsibility. That hadn't changed just because some alien robot bugs added humanity to their diet. Why was Harry acting like she wasn't respecting her?

Hayden's mech slowed, then stopped near a hole far too small for them to fit through. "See here on the left, I think it's a bug tunnel. The acoustics suggest it leads to something bigger. Harry, you've got drones, right?"

"Yes."

"Great. Can you send one through? Let's see what's on the other side."

Plates opened on the left thigh of Harry's mech, and a small drone took flight. Its four ion drives pivoted as it dodged around mechs, bathing them with blue light. A camera feed started broadcasting, and Trax accepted it. The resolution was poor over the peer-to-peer network, but it was enough. The drone hovered at the entrance, and then a small light switched on, revealing a short tunnel. It flew a short distance, then entered a bug tunnel, the surface reflecting a glossy but uneven red. Above, cabling ran like a spine, secured by the translucent coating.

"We should fit," Hayden said.

"If not, we can suck our guts in," Izy added.

It was time for the shape charges. The thought sent chills through her. Explosions in a confined space were beyond merely dangerous—they were downright reckless. She'd be breaching safety regs by the dozen. Diver had copied the design from mining specs, but no one had time to read the manual on how to use them. If she got it wrong, really wrong, they would be entombed in their mechs, waiting for their oxygen to run out, one voice dropping silent at a time until the last died alone. She sighed. Make an educated guess and cross fingers. The life of an engineer.

"Give me space."

Hayden shifted out of the way, and she turned her mech awkwardly to face the hole. A few commands and the simple targeting system activated. She extended her mech's left arm to the side, shifting the shield out of the way. Another command, and panels opened from her mech's torso down to the legs, stopping with clangs that ran through the alloy frame. She licked her lips, then marked several points around the entrance. Two meters. That was a lot of stone. She rotated a digital representation of the tunnel and selected farther spots down its length.

"Setting charges."

She toggled the physical safety switch and hit the launch button. Her mech trembled as sixteen squat cylinders launched, each smacking into the assigned location—more or less. Gel glue released on impact, spreading out from their circumferences.

"Back up and cover your ears." Her adrenaline spiked as she retreated, sending her heart racing. It was hot in the mech. Why hadn't they added cooling? Her fingers jittered over the firing command.

"Activating!"

She hit the command, then wriggled her hands up to her ears while counting down from five. On zero, a sharp series of cracks, reminiscent of fireworks, sent sparks.

Is that all?

Bone-shaking booms rocked her backward. A high-pitched whine burrowed into her brain. Chunks of stone battered her mech. And the icing on the cake—thick dust choked the air, overwhelming her filters and setting off alarms.

"Everyone okay?"

Her crew sounded off.

Hayden said, "Good. We need to clear the debris fast. The bugs must be stretched thin between patrolling and plundering, but we knocked on their door."

They worked smart, employing Harry's crane to drag the largest pieces out of the way, spreading them thin in case they needed a path to retreat. When satisfied, Trax crouched her mech and went through, proximity alarms howling. The shield ground against stone, a fork across a plate. Jagged stone reached for her mech, hungry as if it could sense her life inside. She closed her eyes and kept the mech moving. And then the noise was gone, and she was in the bug tunnel. She maneuvered to clear the exit. Hayden followed, his spotlights reduced to night-club effects in the haze.

They were in. Izy complained as he joined them.

Amy went after Harry and asked for everyone to wait. "I'm seeing interesting seismic readings."

"Bugs," Hayden said. "We're close to them. That's good."

Good? They had screwed up mightily for that to be good. She checked the map on her mech's system, noting the detail on the route they had taken, and the complete lack ahead. Well, she was facing the right direction. She set the mech marching forward.

Hayden broke a growing silence. "I've had a blip from the nuke. We can't estimate the distance, but we're heading the right way."

"We?" Amy asked.

"I misspoke."

Ahead, the tunnel opened up. Trax slowed her mech, her right hand tensing on the controls. They'd reached a small chamber where another three tunnels terminated. A lump scuttled across the ground, pausing, then moving, pausing, then moving. She held her breath and strained her eyes. A bug.

It was different, taller than the woodlouse model. Maybe a meter and a half at its highest. Its legs were shorter and stubbier, and two long arms reached forward. They picked up an object, part of a compressor unit—perhaps a P130—and lifted it. One of its armored segments flipped open, and it dropped the junk inside.

"Bug ahead. It's alone."

"We don't want it alerting its friends," Hayden said.

"Thanks, Agent Obvious. I'll walk up all nice and quiet. You can take a potshot if it runs. Just don't shoot me in the back."

She brought her mech forward, powering up the cutting shears.

Nice, bug. I'm just coming to say hi.

When she reached the chamber, the bug halted. It turned to face her. Three ways for it to flee. She circled to the left, giving Hayden a clear line of sight. Closer. Closer. The bug turned to face her, then spun around and made for another exit. Hayden fired, and a blast of purple plasma cut a scoop out of its body. It changed direction and tried to dart past Trax. She bashed it with her shield, knocking it against the chamber wall, brought up her shears, and slammed them down. The rust-colored shell buckled. She slammed it again, then opened the shears, sticking one cutting blade into the damage. Hardened edges sliced through the bug as if it were butter. Sparks showered. She leaned her shield against the bug, holding it as she tore it apart piece by piece. This was for Diver. And for everyone else.

"Boss," Izy said, "Unless you're making sushi, I think we're done here."

He was right. The bug was dead. Broken. Whatever.

Amy brought her mech over. "Another model."

Trax gestured with her shears. "Even bugs need cleaners. Forget about it. We don't have time for curiosity."

"Curiosity is how we avoid mistakes. Wouldn't it be good to know what they are doing with the gear?"

"They could be planning a yard sale for all it matters right now. Hayden, which tunnel?"

"I'm working on it." His mech wandered back and forth between two options. "You won't like this, but I'm not sure. I'm getting signal echoes from both of these. Either's a good bet. And there's plenty of noise coming from both. I think we're talking a lot more bugs."

Amy poked the smoldering wreckage. "We should split up."

Izy brought his mech's hands to its hips. "Rule one, don't split the party. Everyone knows that."

"If you think it's a game," Amy said, "play to win."

Trax furrowed her brow. "Hayden?"

"We don't have much choice. If the nuke is this close to their city, it'll be out of our reach soon. It won't matter if we have two or two hundred mechs at that point. Amy's right. You can take as many of your crew as you want. I'll take this tunnel." He pointed with his mech's drill. "And you take the one on the left. It should be possible to pick up the signal with your kit pretty soon. Once you've got it, if it fades, you'll know you went the wrong way. If that happens to either of us, we head back and join the other."

Trax moved her mech so she could see her crew. "Who's going with Hayden?"

"I will," Harry said quickly, cutting into Trax's heart. Was their friendship over?

"I better go, too, boss," Amy said, an eagerness in her voice. She was clever but strange. "Someone will need to make conversation."

Izy piloted his mech close to Trax. "Road trip! I call shotgun."

Great.

Hayden's mech lumbered down his tunnel, stripping her of more of her crew. It felt more like he was cutting away her organs.

"Boss?"

"Yeah, we're going." She brought up the troubleshooting settings in her comm controls and set it searching. "Let's snatch the nuke before Hayden."

"Do we win a prize?"

"You can gloat."

Izy made his mech clap its hands. Thud, thud, thud. "Good enough for me."

THE STEPS of the mech no longer filled an otherwise silent passage. The distorted noise that bounced through its length reminded her of a factory, one running at full capacity. Motors whining, belts spinning, pallets slamming. It was different, though, like the music of an unfamiliar culture. As she advanced, her mind broke the details down into its constituent parts, the separation of guitar from piano, ukulele from a cat being strangled.

Legs. Bugs were walking; a lot of them. She checked for the nuke. The signal had grown stronger. No reason to head back. There was pumping, too. And grinding. What were the bugs up to? An unpleasant stink slipped inside as well. *Don't. Don't be.* She tensed her muscles and stepped her mech through an open ring, spying bug shadows elongated on the tunnel wall. The wall gave way to an opening and a downward-sloping ramp made of crushed rock and coated with more of the red gloss they loved. The odor of putrid meat hit her like an uppercut, souring her stomach.

Izy groaned without humor, without energy. "It had to be, didn't it? Why couldn't we have taken the other tunnel?"

The entrance had changed, but she knew this place, this charnel house. She swept her mech's spotlights across. It was truly cavernous now. The single pile of bodies had become two, both large enough that they joined at their bases. Many were burned beyond recognition, but she spotted suits from both the colony and BILT4. None could be saved this time. And there were other carcasses. Birds, small mammals, fish. Over all this, bugs scuttled, selecting flesh to drag away, or tending the piles like farmers hoping for a bumper crop. The butcher stations were still there, packed with more bugs that stripped, skinned, gutted, sorted, and binned.

A single tear slid down her cheek.

Cables, flexible pipes, and blocky paraphernalia covered much of the floor, a twisted mirror of the desecrated tendons, arteries, and bones that waited in piles on its haphazard surface. Beneath: bare stone, metal plates, and large grills, seemingly without rhyme or reason. Machinery coated the walls. Shining light on sections at a time, Trax identified patterns of components. They had the same segmented look as the bugs themselves. Bony plates from which vents pushed steam or thrumming circular protrusions.

The scene burned into her mind, yet it didn't weaken her resolve. It set it ablaze. "We're going to toast these bugs until their ashes blow on the wind."

"I'm thinking marshmallows on sticks."

"What?"

"Never mind."

More bugs entered, dragging limbs and parts beyond identification. They dropped these at the base of a pile and swiftly left, perhaps to retrieve more.

She shook her head in minute movements. "I just don't get it. It keeps pricking my mind. Why? Why are they doing this?"

"It can't be food—they're machines. Corrupted code?"

Thousands of years were liable to flip a few bits. "I hope so, Izy. I hope that's it. Abuk help us. If some mind is behind this evil…"

"Don't say that. We've been screwed enough by twisted-ass minds like Wagner and Sturt."

"Some board back on a core world sent us here with no warning. You're right. We have all the evil we need."

She checked the nuke signal. Ahead and down. There was an exit on the far side. All they had to do was cross this horror show.

"See that tunnel?" She pointed with her mech's shears.

"That's the bathroom?"

"That's where we're going to piss on them. But there's a crap-ton of bugs between. How do we get there?"

"We could put on bug costumes. I saw it in a movie, once."

Trax placed her shears on his mech's shoulder. "It's time to get serious. I can see three possibilities. One, we distract them. Two, we sneak around. Three, we run and pray."

"Well, I did borrow a few grenades from Diver. That's a distraction."

"Izy, think. You don't have a launcher. You can't reach enough of them to make a difference, and if we start running and throwing, you'll blow us up."

"Why not two and three, boss? Sneak until they react, then run like there's a two-for-one deal on fries."

"Good enough for me."

She started her mech down the ramp. So many bugs. One skittered by, climbing the wall, ignoring her passage. All too soon, she was on the ground, placing each step of her mech with precision. Tripping over the mess on the floor was out of the question. She kept to the right, following the wall, staying far from the dead.

A flicker of movement from above. She looked up. A dragonfly. It perched upside down on the cavern ceiling, wings partially extended. Had it noticed them?

"We've got company above."

"I see it, boss."

Her right mech leg snagged. She stopped. A tube had looped around its foot. She carefully raised the leg, hoping the balance algorithm could cope with the mech's modifications. A small shake. Another. A larger one.

"I'm snagged."

A bug wandered close and raised a cable. There were cracks in its covering. Age related, she guessed. It extended a small tube from its head and squeezed goop onto the section. Trax held her leg up, her muscles tingling. *Go away.* The bug waited. Sweat collected at Trax's temples. She counted the seconds. On twelve, the bug lowered the cable and left for a distant part of the cavern.

She lowered the leg.

Izy brought his mech close. "That tubing has caught between the ankle joint and the shin panel. It's compressed and gone right in. If you stay still, I can work it free."

"Do it."

She heard his mech actuators whine as he went down onto one knee with far too much grace.

"It's thoroughly wedged. I might need to get out to free you."

The bugs kept working. But how long could this last? "No. No way. You're not risking it." She lowered her shears. "Put the pipe in. I'll cut myself loose."

He pulled enough slack and fit in both ends of the loop. She activated the shears, cutting through with ease. Pink gelatinous fluid gushed out.

"Every day in your crew is a delight. You're free."

The dragonfly lit up, circles and lines of red flickering across its glowing white abdomen. It dropped, spreading its wings, lighting up its engines, arcing toward Trax like a missile. She brought up her shield and braced, swearing non-stop. An angry bell rang. The impact slid her back on the wet ground. The dragonfly's legs grabbed her shield's sides, and its weight forced the defense down.

A blue line of plasma flashed. "Hold on, boss!"

The dragonfly's maw loomed over her shield. Trax opened her shears, brought her arm back, then stabbed forward, aiming for a joint. The shear tips caught, and she closed them, cutting through the bug's armor. Sparks rained down on her blister. The dragonfly lunged, and she bent her mech back as it tried to return the favor. She'd been waiting. Blades closed, she rammed her shears into the machine's wound and set the shears to open. In this direction, they had little power and no edge, but the dragonfly's insides weren't protected. Smoke accompanied sharp cracks, and the dragonfly juddered.

More blue plasma. The dragonfly spasmed and dropped.

"I got it, boss."

Trax lowered her shield to glare at Izy. "I had it. You were on clean up."

They both smiled, but hers dropped as fast as it had come.

Segmented bodies stopped their tasks. They turned. And like a metal wave, they flowed over the cavern. She caught the first with her shears, not closing enough to sever, and swung her mech's arm, letting the bug's momentum carry it up into the wall.

"Option three. Run!"

"On it."

Chaos. She moved as quickly as she dared. Blocking, cutting, knocking aside. For every bug that she fought past, another two appeared. Behind her, Izy made his mech dance, his blades slicing and dicing. The bugs kept coming, bogging them down.

"Care package!" Izy shouted. From the edge of her vision, she saw he'd opened his blister. Two small objects flew out. A bug leaped at him. He swung, missing as it thudded into his mech's chest. The blister vibrated, caught on something.

"Do you—" she began.

Two grenades exploded. The pressure wave rocked her mech and pushed into her eardrums. Shrapnel cut through her blister, hot slivers burrowing into her skin. Bug limbs crashed off the ceiling. And still, they came. She advanced a few meters. A third blast.

"Izy?"

"That was my spare battery. I'm good." He was panting. "Not far behind."

What wasn't he saying? She used her shield to cut down on another bug. The grating beneath her bowed. "Izy. Do you need a hand? For once, don't be a show-off."

"Keep going, boss. Almost there."

She risked turning her mech enough to see what he was up to. Bugs were crawling all over him, cutting into his mech, grabbing the arms, weighing them down, rendering his plasma blades unusable.

"Damn it, Izy. Hold tight."

"No, boss. It's been a pleasure working for you. You need to go on. Nuke them for me."

She leaned her mech's weight onto the bug under her shield, earning a loud snap. The bug froze. "I won't let you die here."

"I'm bleeding out. One of the bastards got a leg in. My mech's screwed. I'm losing hydraulic pressure. Ha, the mech and me both." He was inching his mech across the floor, away from the exit and toward the butcher station. Cables launched from his mech, embedding into nearby machinery. They snapped taut and dragged him onward.

"Get out of the mech. I'll carry you."

"Come here and they'll have you, boss. Don't worry. They won't cut me up. I took more than two of Diver's grenades."

She scowled. "You what?"

"Ten of them. Eight left. I knew you'd get all safety conscious. I'll give the bugs something to eat. And if we're lucky, my tank of foam will slow them down and buy you time. But you have to go."

How could he ask that? If she ran, wasn't she as bad as every damn manager, every corporate scum that demanded worker's souls and skipped out when things turned bad?

A bug appeared at her mech's leg. She kicked it away, growling with a tiger's fury, her eyes wet and blurred. He'd fallen in that time and was now crawling.

"Boss—Jane—you have to go on. Diver's counting on us. So is the convoy. Don't ruin my moment."

"Ismail al-Jazar, you're almost as good as you think you are." She screwed up her face, fighting the sadness but embracing her admiration. She'd never forget him or his mix of bravado, humor, and talent. "You can't go without saying something cool."

"Ha," he laughed, then coughed wetly. "Good point."

"Well?"

"Hold on tight. Here it is. Tick tick—this boy goes boom."

Her brow creased.

Oh shit.

She jerked her controls, directing her mech toward the exit as fast as it would go. Bright light. Her mech flew off the ground and slammed into a wall. A hail of dirty orange metal scoured her mech. Her blister cracked in multiple spots as she rebounded. Gravity reached for her, snarling, tossing her down like a wrestler. She hit the floor. Grating buckled, bent, gave way.

Free fall.

Darkness.

CHAPTER 33
GESTATION

Irregular blips from the nuke's comm reached Bill as he continued down the tunnel past another ring that Amy had called an iris. The rock, the tunnels, and whatever lay ahead distorted the signal, but he was close. The lack of bugs grated on his mind. His breath echoed in the confines of the mech, and the air filter couldn't clear the growing stink of his sweat.

One chance. They had one chance to save the remnants of humanity clinging to this world. The red sheen coating the circular wall had him on edge as much as the insanity of the task. It suggested he'd climbed down the mouth of a beast and was actively working his way to its stomach.

"That is morbid, Bill."

"It's an organic thing. You wouldn't understand."

"I am encased in your flesh. I have some familiarity. It may surprise you, but we have an awful lot in common."

"Thanks for that picture."

"Oh, I have records of the operations, if you're curious."

Damn AI. Dantalion loved playing with him. It had been better when he was alone. No, that was a lie. And not because of Dantalion. Bill was grateful for Harry and Amy trudging behind in their mechs. Their presence grounded him—if you could call jumping at every damn shadow grounded. The spotlights played with the barest hints of irregularity, filling his mind with waiting terrors.

Keep calm. Use distraction. "How you are two holding up?"

"Fine," Harry said. She'd only come with him to piss off Trax, though he couldn't say why.

A pause, and then Amy answered. "I'm curious."

"What do you mean, curious?"

"What's it like being a spook?"

Bill tilted his head back, accidentally raising the arms of his mech. "We're not meant to talk about it. Secrecy goes with the territory."

"Must be hard for therapy. Is that why you have an embedded AI?"

His heart jumped.

"Bill, she is dangerous."

He swallowed and asked aloud. "What makes you say that?"

"Curiosity. But the reasons for the conclusion are straightforward: the pauses in your speech, the type of information you have access to, the systems you can connect to. I've been reading your mech's diagnostics, too. They underline the truth."

"What does she want, Bill? Ask yourself that. She thinks like an agent."

A backup planted by Beth? His gut said she wasn't. Dantalion was paranoid. An agent worthy of the job wouldn't be so obvious.

"My AI is called Dantalion."

"You shouldn't have told her that."

"And it thinks you'd make a good spook."

Amy made an amused snort. "No chance. I'll stick to circuits. They're much more interesting and logical than people. Can I speak to it?"

Dantalion wriggled in Bill's mind. "Absolutely not! I am more classified than this mission. And I am only designed for communication with you."

Except for all the networks the AI danced around. "Sorry, Dantalion's feeling shy."

"It has emotions? Aren't you the one in charge?"

Bill's skin tingled with heat. The one question that no agent could ever fully answer.

"Dantalion, say hello to her."

"No, Bill."

"That's an order."

"You are an asshole," Dantalion complained, but the capitulation gave Bill a reassurance he hadn't realized he needed. The AI connected to the peer-to-peer network, and spoke, its voice sounding slightly different, thinner, and more robotic. "Greetings, Amy Martin."

"I have a lot of questions for you."

"I will not answer them. Bill, the acoustic signature is changing. Something is ahead."

A diversion, if ever he'd heard one.

Darkness swallowed the mechs' lights, its veil punctuated with glints. The tunnel opened wide on both sides. He activated his rifle, and the turret shifted under his control. Rust-colored alloy. Bugs! Rows and rows of them, both left and right. His finger hovered over the trigger. They stood rigid, uncaring. He brought his mech to a stop and twisted around. These were different.

Long, thin bodies on six legs, and a pair of equally long arms finishing with eight multi-jointed spatula fingers. A neck-like structure connected to a wide head bristling with sensors. The effect was an unsettling amalgam of a praying mantis and a hammerhead shark. Their exteriors were segmented but without the overlap of the original bugs. And they were clean, unpitted, glossy, new. His eyes narrowed. How many were being churned out?

"Christ," Harry said, maneuvering her mech close to a row. "What do these ones do?"

"Nothing good," Dantalion said over the comm to Bill's surprise. It continued. "We should move on."

The mantis wasn't the only new design. Bill advanced slowly. On his right were long designs with eighteen stubby legs. Nozzles poked out of the back segments in concentric circles like hairs. It was on one of these caterpillar units that he noticed the silver-white of a familiar alloy. Then, knowing what to look for, he identified other abnormalities.

"Anyone seeing this?"

"The human-made components?" Amy sniffed. "Fascinating.

Aliens assimilating our technology. Usually, it's the reverse. I knew coming along was going to be worth it."

"They're just reusing parts," Harry said. "Nothing special."

"Nothing special?" Bill leaned forward, and Dantalion zoomed a section of his vision. One tube had a part number.

Harry leaned her mech over a mantis. "It's just mechanical. If it fits and does the same job, why not? Shoddy, though. I wouldn't. Too many variables with different alloys. Leads to faults."

"Meaning," Amy said, "it's not an ideal solution. If they needed raw materials, they could smelt, separate, and remix to their parameters."

Bill raised an eyebrow. "That sounds complicated."

"No," Harry said, her voice oddly strained. "Just time-consuming."

So the bugs had a time constraint. Why? Wagner poking in their home? Was all this self-defense? He pictured Charlie, vivisected without compassion. No, not self-defense. Yet, the bugs had landed on this planet, only to do nothing until humans showed up. He was missing a piece of the puzzle, and it itched in his brain like crazy.

"Bill," Dantalion said into his mind. "I'm detecting power emissions."

"Where?"

"Everywhere. Heat. EM."

He angled his mech down the tunnel and started walking. "Time to go."

Behind him, Amy and Harry bottled their curiosity and followed. The bugs waited, metal statues. He kept imagining heads swiveling toward him. The chamber reached an end with an open iris. This one was different. Deep purple patterns of circles and lines bloomed on the segments as he approached, reflecting on the dark surfaces of his mech.

"That doesn't look good." He stopped several meters away and checked the nuke's position. Ahead, of course.

Harry stomped her mech to his side. "An alarm?"

Amy's mech appeared at his right. "It's the first active iris we've seen, apart from the one Izy urinated on—don't ask—so let's assume the rest were inactive alarms. They didn't have enough power. Then why not focus on building a power plant? Because that's not what the bugs are programmed to do."

Bill pressed his lips together as he glared at the lights. Had they brightened a little when he'd brought his mech close? Amy's reasoning matched his experience surveilling bureaucracy. He scowled. Now was not the time to get lost in a mental exercise. Each second they wasted meant the nuke was getting farther away.

"I'm going through. Keep your distance in case I trigger something."

"*I* can't keep my distance," Dantalion said directly to Bill. "I'm stuck in you. You should have sent one of the others. They are expendable. You are not."

The symbols brightened. A meter out, he was squeezing his sphincter, wishing mechs could tiptoe. Half a meter out, the iris snapped closed. He halted his mech and pushed, feeling only a slight flex as he gave full power to the action. "If they don't want us through, we must be on the right track."

"Yes," Amy said, "but we're not on the right side."

The atmosphere changed. Background noise. A lot of it. Mechanical whining, clicks. "The bugs are awake, aren't they?"

"All of them," Harry said. "Get out of the way."

Bill did as the mechanic demanded, then wished he hadn't looked back. The bugs were performing strange dance-like motions, summoning a host of leaping, demonic shadows.

"Testing the joints as part of a startup sequence," Amy said, her words clipped. "Harry, you need help with the door?"

"I've got it. Won't be long."

Harry's giant hammer swung into Bill's view and then out. A colossal boom echoed. He gritted his teeth. "Shit! You're going to smash it open?"

"Works for a lot of things."

And then the bugs marched. It was the sound of a thousand hammers beating the ground. And it came with the sweet scent of lubricant. The nearest, three caterpillar bugs, were a mere ten meters away. Another boom announced the second of Harry's strikes.

Bill started blasting. Plasma spewed from his rifle. The first bug went down, smoke pouring out of five holes. He shifted aim to the next, wishing there weren't so many more. To his right, bright orange burst from Amy's mech, a stream of liquid fire that washed heat through his mech. He stopped firing, wondering what had gone wrong, but the flames engulfed the second caterpillar, then the third, and continued until a semicircle of hell surrounded the mechs. Clever. Amy was damn clever. He sucked in his breath, seeking the oxygen the flamethrower had consumed with glee. The line of fire roared to the beat of Harry's drumming. Bill dared hope it would keep the bugs at bay.

It didn't. The machines pressed through, flames lapping at their sides. He started shooting again, but the bugs pressed closer whenever his aim shifted elsewhere. Amy sprayed more fire, bringing a mantis down, and setting two others ablaze as they closed. They kept marching closer.

"Harry, are you through?"

"Do I sound like it? I need another minute."

His eyes flicked to the grenade launcher controls. An enclosed space, nearby targets—what could possibly go wrong?

"Easy, Bill. You could do a Diver and blow us up."

"I'll take the chance. Give me some ballistic projections."

Curved lines blinked into view. Damn, that ceiling was close. "Frag out!"

He pumped two grenades through the flames and into the midst of the bugs. The blast hammered his eardrums. Bugs tore apart, sparking, smoking, sizzling. Others were blown forward, and he stomped the head of a mantis before it could rise on skittering legs. Metal groaned as his mech's weight bludgeoned the surprisingly weak casing.

A pair of mantises hurried over the metal corpse with surprising grace and grabbed hold of his legs. The featureless heads twitched as he battered at them, but they embraced his mech with their legs and pulled at the armor plates on his mech's thighs. His mind drew a connection, and he shuddered, imagining his skin peeling back. A third mantis climbed one of its brethren and set to work on his blister. Memories of the slaughterhouse crawled out of his mind, dragging the stench of death and the horror of impotence in the face of uncaring malice.

"I got you," Amy shouted, and Bill conjured a fresh horror—being sautéed to death inside his mech.

Twin prongs thrust against a mantis. *Oh, shit!* He squeezed his eyes tight, but white still burned through to his retina, accompanied by a tremendous crack. Barely visible through chaotic afterimages, the bug dropped away, smoking, sparking, stinking.

"Thanks, Amy. I owe you."

"No, you don't. You're one of us now. Crew looks after crew."

Invigorated, Bill spun up his drill and stabbed it into the mantis on his mech's right leg, vibrations shaking his arm. In seconds, he slipped in deep and worked the bit from side to side while grasping the bug's head with his mech's grippers.

A loud hiss. The mantis bucked, releasing its hold. Bill tossed it into an approaching caterpillar, and another flash cooked his unprotected eyes.

"Amy, watch out with that thing." He blinked rapidly, tears dripping, seeing solid white wherever he looked. What if he was blind? All those bugs crawling over him, ripping his mech apart, dragging him out, filleting him, and he wouldn't be able to see them coming. He wouldn't be able to do a thing to resist.

"Bill, stop being so melodramatic. I'm resetting the breakers and bypassing a few singed short-wavelength filaments. You will have visuals back… now."

White bled into the fiery hell of moments before. His mech was clear, but twisted panels stuck out, revealing the machinery beneath. The bugs advanced, their bodies wreathed in flames.

"Way's clear," Harry announced.

"Go through. Amy, you're next."

Amy rested her mech's ultracapacitor over its right shoulder. "Want me to lay down covering fire?"

He really didn't want to be cooked. "Save it, just in case."

Harry called out when she was through, and Amy disappeared. He set his turreted rifle to work against the nearest bugs, retreating slowly.

Carnage followed, and so did the bugs. A thud. He'd backed into the wrecked iris.

Here goes.

Abusing the hydraulics, he threw his mech around and into the tunnel. Actuators whined, triggering alarms. The bugs scurried after. Once more, he demanded all the mech could give, spinning to catch a caterpillar with a left hook as it reared back, and following with a kick. A mass of bugs loomed as if he'd just lifted a rock lying in sodden soil. Revulsion struck the primitive core of his brain, and he retreated well beyond the mangled iris.

"Get back! Get back!"

Dantalion filled his vision with firing solutions. With no time for care, Bill aimed the grenade launcher as best he could and sent several anonymous cylinders ricocheting into the bugs. *Come on, glue.* The closer they stopped, the better. In theory. The explosion was like the hand of God—gods, an entire pantheon. Events blurred; details twisted. It all stopped, and calm enveloped him with a satin blanket of apathy.

Resting on his back, he noticed a bug lying on top, a spent lover. A comforting background hum, or more a throb, played pleasantly in his ears. Dust danced on the surface of his blister, obscuring the world beyond—if one still remained.

"Bill, you have to move. The bugs are digging."

Groaning, he stretched his back. Bands of fire squeezed his ribs.

Dantalion hissed in his mind, "Come on, stop being a lazy asshole. You accepted the deal. You took over the colony. You have to be a big boy now."

"Leave me alone."

"You tried that, didn't you? You shipped us out to the middle of nowhere, all by yourself, and look where that got us."

"It's not my fault. Beth—"

"Not your fault? You take responsibility for everything and nothing at the same time. You're a paradox, except you're easily solved. You told the agency that Marrick Prime couldn't be cracked. You said their minds couldn't be changed and there was no opposition to speak of. You tried harder than anyone else to prove yourself wrong, but you were right. We have to live with that. But did you ask for the bombard-ment? Did you get back up and learn from it? No. You ran from responsibility the first moment you could."

Bill rotated his head, testing the limits of his stiff muscles. "I made bad choices, Dantalion. They killed good people. I killed good people. It's what I do. I'm already doing it again. Ten thousand, Dantalion, ten thousand. How many left?"

"There'd be none if Sturt had stayed in charge. Sometimes there are no good choices."

He tried to find a position that didn't hurt, and his mech mirrored his actions, bringing nausea. "No good choices? That's what every manipulative, self-serving slime comforts themselves with. Trax had five good people in her crew. One is dead, another too damn close. For all I know, both Trax and Izy are gone, too—the latest in my long tally."

"You're going to give up? You're going to forget about Amy and Harry, forget about Ware and the convoy? Are you going to lie here and wait for the bugs, telling yourself that letting them die is for the best? If the bugs are capable of getting off planet, are you going to tell yourself it's someone else's problem, that you're not responsible?"

Anger flooded Bill's veins, hot and thick. Grinding took over from the hum in his ears. "How did you get to be such an asshole? I'm one guy. I can't fix everything."

"How? Ever thought to analyze yourself, hotshot? I'm you—part of you, anyway. My personality matrix is based on a scan of you. How else would it be compatible? I just didn't turn to mush. So, you're not one guy. You're two. And the two of us aren't alone."

Locked in his head with himself? What had the agency done to him? Bill shoved the bug aside, along with the disquiet. "Amy, Harry, are you there?"

"Here," Harry said, her voice groggy. "Damn boys and big bangs. Just fixing a loose connection. Amy?"

"I've completed a system check. I'm all ready to go. But, Hayden, your mech's legs are buried. Wait a moment."

It was good to hear them, so good. The two engineers worked quickly, Harry joining Amy's initial efforts. They dragged him to the end of the tunnel, then raised him until his mech stood. Smoke wafted from his back. He released the exterior battery, and it clanked to the ground. That was the least of his problems. The cave-in had mangled his mech's left leg, and black fluid dribbled down to its foot. The leak kit had saved his hydraulic pressure, but the reserve tank was low. He tried a few test steps. Limping. Great.

The bugs' efforts echoed from the tunnel, though the thuds and grinding faded as he moved away. Even his own mech's steps disappeared behind a background of pumping and bubbling, suggestive of an intensive care suite set up in a warehouse. Where the hell were they? He adjusted his spotlights and immediately felt crushed by insignificance.

"Anyone else seeing what I'm seeing?"

"Breathtaking," Amy said.

Harry followed with a question. "What are they?"

The curved ceiling was an easy fifteen meters tall at its lowest point. Black pipes and oil-sheened cables crisscrossed like jumbled spaghetti. Many were of human construction, connected by similar size, with no apparent regard to material or aesthetics. Soot still covered some. There had to be a hundred meters to the other side, and then the length—it just kept going beyond the strength of the combined beams of the three mechs. Vast, and yet in no way empty.

A discordant assortment of thuds and bangs drifted from the darkness of the ceiling, emphasizing the scale of the facility, that and how alone the small group of humanity was.

Cylinders stood on the ground in endless, imposing rows, each with a base of brown-red metal nearly three meters across and perhaps one high. Wobbling tubes stretched from the ceiling and plugged into chunky connectors. Extending above the curves of these bases were transparent tanks as tall as their diameter. Swirls of dirty pink and red goop circulated in a clear fluid and a grid of bubbles flowed upward. Bill piloted his damaged mech close to the nearest, his attention captured by this bizarre, almost organic juxtaposition to the bug technology. His hands tightened on the controls, his breaths came shallow and fast. What was the form floating inside?

Perhaps the size of an elephant with a white surface—a skin—slick and bulbous, patterned with pulsating lines. Twin raised gray cords stretched the skin starting at one end, continuing along its curved top, and down to the rear—a spine, spines? Hints of edges suggested segments and plates. Eight limbs protruded, each with two obvious joints. The three lower pairs were bunched up, but the pointed tips were visible along with darker shadows inside. The upper limbs were thicker, tapering down to eight fingers, if such long appendages could claim that name. They were positioned on two opposing sides that interlocked, then released, closed, then opened.

There was no obvious neck. Instead, the bloated body finished at a stubby end with a puckered opening half covered by eight arm-thick fangs that flexed on muscled stalks. Behind and above, a mass was visible through the translucent skin—long, pale sausages joined together at a single point. A brain? Perhaps, most disturbing of all were the four deep-purple spheres that pressed against the skin while remaining covered. Bill leaned closer. The spheres swiveled toward him. Eyes. They were eyes. But not human. Speckled, coppery edges traced cross-shaped pupils that narrowed into fine lines.

Heart thudding, Bill pulled back. Limbs struck the tank, shaking it.

"What is that?" Harry said, her voice filled with disgust. "It's no bug."

The answer clicked into place, filling dozens of holes in Bill's tapestry of reality. "These are the real bugs, the minds behind the machines. Or they will be."

"Birthing tanks," Amy said as she slowly circled the cylinder. "They've been ramping up production. Some of the other maggots are much less developed."

She was right. What were the implications? "They landed, ready to start a colony. But the planet wasn't what they were expecting or something went wrong."

Amy raised a tube with her mech's arms. "The machines that were meant to set up tanks and grow bug colonists couldn't complete their mission. Until we came along."

Harry leaned the head of her great hammer on the tank. "They had to steal our tech?"

"Yes"—Bill swallowed as the inevitable detail dried his throat—

"and no. They've made plenty without our gear. What they needed was organic material. They possess some kind of FTL, but if they're cloning, either it's not as good as ours or they are far from home. So, they land on this planet that isn't what they expected and go dormant. Our terraforming probably disturbs them, and then at some point they find chemicals—"

"Proteins," Amy said. "Pretty much everything else should be available in one form or another unless it was a trace element."

"Let's say proteins, then. Maybe from Charlie or some nameless BILT4 asshole, but the machines discover where to get what they need. This flips a switch, and they start growing their new bosses. Meanwhile, Wagner keeps poking them, and we're hamburgers in rovers, roaming meals."

He held his breath. Was there a chance to communicate, to find peace? The legs skittered off the tank, and the creature swam close, fangs pulled back like a viper ready to strike.

Dantalion brought up a circle in Bill's vision, adding a flashing light. "The signal is weakening, fast. We have to go."

"What if I can stop this?"

The fangs snapped forward, cracking the tank. Pink goop oozed down the outside. Bill's heart pounded.

Amy came to his side. "I don't think it wants to be friends. Think about it—did they code their robots to avoid harming existing life?"

The creature attacked the glass again, the bass thud accompanied by a series of ominous crackling as stress lines radiated across the surface. Damn it, why did it always come down to this? Annihilation. Us versus them. He looked at Amy and Harry, cocooned inside their mechs. Us or them.

Let the judgement of history fall where it may. The choice was clear, though the reason was surprising. This wasn't about Beth, the LSA, or the League. He simply cared too much for Trax and her crew—hell, for humanity. He knew where his loyalty lay.

Us.

A terrible *whoomp* sounded from above. The ground shook. Metal clattered. The tank exploded, sending shards flying and thousands upon thousands of liters of fluid gushing. He retreated, raising his mech's arms instinctively. The creature slammed into him, its legs locking around his mech's torso, its fangs stabbing. They hit his blister, cracking the polymer. A second strike added more impact scars before he could set his drill spinning. Flesh pulsated and those eyes—they were filled with hunger, determination. A third strike, all within a single breath. The blister disintegrated, leaving the circle of eight thick fangs a handspan from his face. Rotten meat. Sickly sweetness. Bright yellow fluid pooled at the tips. Venom?

His mech held him as tight as any restraints. The alien was so fast. Amy and Harry would never have time to help.

Us versus them?

Them had the lead.

CHAPTER 34
THE FULL SCALE

O ver and over, Trax fell, beaten and bruised inside her mech, her stomach contorting with every jerk. Groans, snaps, and cracks accompanied her descent as the mech tore through pipes and cabling. It all came as brief glimpses, flashes revealed by a circle of light spinning in a pool of darkness. The shield caught again and again, jerking her mech's left arm and wrenching her shoulder.

Sparks burst and liquid sprayed. *Abuk, where is this?* She reached out with the mech's right arm, slowing the spin one obstruction at a time. The mech slammed feet first into a flat surface, jolting her before bursting through. Her ears popped. The space opened up into a great chasm lit by a handful of beams. Chaotic flashes burned into her retinas—an endless array of circular fish tanks disappearing into endless night, statues, a revolting wet mass, a floor rapidly approaching.

Her trajectory shifted as tangled cables resisted, throwing her forward, a child on a swing. She screamed but refused to look away. Not statues—mechs—and she was hurtling into one covered in a pale lump that appeared a cross between a maggot, a spider, and a tardigrade.

Impact. Her head slammed back into thin padding, jolting her brain, and her blister filled with a deranged artist's blend of fangs and a dark, coppery orb. A putrid stench like a busted bathroom recycler burned her nostrils. Her mech touched ground. She twisted, fighting the cables and tubes that had been her lifeline when falling. Splatters of pinkish fluid slid slowly down her view.

"Boss!" Amy shouted.

Hayden came through her comm and ears at the same time. "Damn, am I happy to see you and those big mech feet of yours."

She scowled and worked to free herself with her shears. "What is all this?"

Hayden's trashed mech limped into view. "Say hello to Eclipse's first colonists and mass murderers."

"Boss," Harry said. "Where's Izy?"

Trax's spine locked; grief crushed her. "He… he didn't make it. He saved my life. You should have seen him cut the bugs down, and then he… he was magnificent."

"Almost as good as he thought he was?" Amy asked.

"Better."

The stomach-curdling white mass shifted. Trax screwed up her face. So many legs. And that maw—not even a mother could love it. It leaped straight for her. Shock slowed her reaction, her shield moving far too late, even as her heart pounded a fast tempo. The legs stretched out, pointed ends angled in, an action mirrored by the fangs.

Harry appeared to her right, swinging that massive hammer. It connected with the creature, sending ripples of force along its mass, forcing a strange hiss from its mouth, and driving its trajectory offline. The mechanic followed, bellowing, and was ready when it skittered on shaky legs. She brought the hammer down on one of two lines that could have been a spine, snapping it and earning another hiss as the creature's legs on one side failed.

Trax approached but dared not assist. Harry kept swinging her hammer over and over, battering the creature, the alien, long past its collapse. Pale, viscous fluid pooled around its body.

"I think it's dead, Harry."

"It's not enough. They ruined everything—everything. You know my family's broke. All of us. We've lost everything. Did you ever think of what they're doing while I'm out here? They're borrowing off the promise of me having land to sell. We're in hock, boss, to the fucking Delphin Mafia. If I don't have something to show… me, my parents, my cousins—we all die. And they'll make the bugs look like amateurs."

Shit. For someone growing up under the thumb of corporate injustice, she'd been far too blind to the state of her friend. Harry always had things together, money, chill. Nothing fazed her. Trax closed her eyes and dropped her chin. Getting Harry to sign up had been no favor. If Harry had stayed home, she would have worked something out. Or not. The League was a hard place to be in debt, legal or otherwise. What a mess. Should she apologize? To what end?

Harry had said she wasn't her crew's mother. But damn, she wanted to hug Harry, ruffle her hair, and promise her it would all be okay in the end. The mechs kept them apart, denied their humanity. She'd felt powerful strapping into her makeshift machine of war. Now she felt alone.

Her eyes strayed to her instrument display. The nav system was offline. The external battery was gone, and the primary was down to ten percent power, thanks to several damaged modules. Her body felt the same. She glanced up and caught Hayden's gaze. His blister had been ripped open, leaving him vulnerable. It wasn't fear she saw in his eyes, though. It was compassion. From a spook? Well, she'd kicked an alien and battled robots. Anything could happen.

"Trax," he said, "we need to go. The nuke is stationary. Now's our chance."

"I hear you. We're almost there. It's like any project—the last few tasks always seem the hardest. But Harry, nothing ever stops you from getting a job done. You have reserves of determination that could power a star. And, Amy—"

"Don't sweat me, boss. I wouldn't be anywhere else." She expanded her mech's arms. "I wish I had a chance to play with all the alien tech, but I'll settle for a nuke."

Trax angled her mech toward Hayden, who was peering among the tanks. "Playing with alien tech is what got us into this mess. Let's not repeat Wagner's mistake. Hayden, you got a direction?"

"Between the tanks."

Rattling sounded from above and a bug dropped, hitting the ground nearby with a harsh clatter, chunks of foam tumbling after. Trax gripped the bug's head with her shears and lifted its kicking body slowly off the ground. "There are more where this bastard came from. All right, crew, move out." She squeezed the shears control and enjoyed watching the bug twitch until she cut through something vital.

The tanks reached the height of her mech, leaving her feeling like she was walking through a forest of horrors. The aliens within, some small, some enormous, swam to watch them pass, and the thud of flesh on glass echoed, a deranged rhythm of pure malice.

"Boss," Amy said, "another one's dropped. Make that three. How many did you leave up there?"

"Too many."

A bass crash resounded. Trax paused, leaving Hayden to continue. "What was that?"

"That was the tunnel we collapsed," Amy said. "Bugs are coming, boss. More than three. I suggest we pick up our pace."

"Agreed." She started off again and tutted at Hayden's limping mech. "Spook, do you need a walking stick, or do you want me to carry you?"

His mech lurched into an ungainly, and all too slow, run. "Better?"

"Not much." She upped her mech's speed and ignored the power reserves as best she could. A bug darted at Trax's left side. It was thin with a long, sideways head. *No, you don't.* A quick bash from her shield sent it flying into a second.

"Boss, it's getting crowded."

"How many, Amy?"

"Approximately as many as can fit."

Trax flicked through her controls and brought up a rear camera feed for reversing. Behind her crew, bugs spread, a wall of merciless machinery. So many. The aliens must have been building up their servants' numbers, ready for when they hatched. A stream of bugs scuttled close from her right and she dismissed the view. She battered one bug, then dodged to the left around a tank. Brilliant blue plasma flew in all directions, and she ducked instinctively.

"Watch out on the right!"

"Cooking!" Amy said, and orange light flared.

Harry growled. "God damn it."

"What's up?" Trax asked, trying to spot her friend as she dodged another set of bugs.

"Nothing. Just bugs. More bugs. Bugs every-fucking-where."

The spotlights danced, blinding points reflecting off tanks, burning her vision, yet never filling in the shadows. A bug, a woodlouse, dropped from a tank onto her mech. Two of its legs skittered on her blister as it sought a hold. It took her back to the hospital basement. Grimacing, she bashed it with the edge of her shield but couldn't dislodge the machine.

A tank cracked in front, releasing a torrent of goop. Her mech lost grip, its screeching feet sliding into the tank and the fangs of an alien. Mouth open in horror, she punched with her shears, then grabbed a bug leg from above and dragged the machine down. The size was just right, her fizzing mind said, so she shoved the bug into the tank's hole. Bug and alien writhed, and she took the chance to move clear and pick up speed.

They needed to stick together. Where were the others? "Back to the center, if you can. Everyone got it?"

"Yes, boss," her crew said.

Her brow creased. "Hayden, what's your position?"

"Not good. I don't have the speed. But don't wait. Get to that nuke. That's what matters. I'll find a way to catch up."

No way was he going to catch up. He was sacrificing himself. Damn. He'd worked hard. He'd tried non-stop, even if he'd failed almost as often. He was arrogant, demanding, and self-absorbed. But he cared for folk. He had grit. And not a bad ass.

"Don't be a hero. Izy already took that spot."

Hayden grunted, pausing before saying, "Don't think I'll be going down a hero, no matter what. I'll see you soon. Keep moving and… be you."

She heard him fighting through his comm and imagined bugs over-whelming his mech, tearing him out through the broken blister. "Hayden, you're all right."

He screamed, and then his comm went silent. She nodded to his memory, the only sign of respect she could offer.

Amy came from around a tank, flames dripping from a nozzle at the center of her mech.

"Harry?"

"Right behind."

An open iris promised a way out. Purples and reds flashed on the edging, those damn alien markings—lines and circles, writing or art or warning—she didn't care.

"The last one closed on us," Amy warned.

"Still have charge enough to shock it?"

"Should do. Charging it now."

The blades of the iris flowed out of the ring, constricting the hole. They were too far.

"Amy!"

"I used to do javelin in college. I wasn't any good, but—"

The optronics expert raised her ultracapacitor, the long device held above her mech's shoulder. The arm swung forward, catapulting the ultracapacitor. It whistled through the air, then hit the left side of the ring, and a sharp electric crack sounded above the rumble of bugs and thuds of mechs. Blue lightning flared while segments of the ring shattered, tossing debris.

The iris blades had stopped, but the gap wasn't enough. Trax pushed her mech to its maximum speed. Her brain bounced inside her skull as it went. *Get the shield to the front.*

Impact. Her momentum battled physics. Her head jolted, sending a spike of pain down her spine. Polymer and alloy squealed, groaned, snapped. And then she was through, fighting the controls to maintain balance. Hydraulic fluid leaked from a dozen spots. The shield's edges had buckled. Several panels were missing from her mech's right side, and one hung loose.

The ground transitioned to black glass. Her mech slid until it transitioned again to smooth, dull metal. Momentum kept her mech going until she regained control, at the tunnel's end, and claustrophobic tightness gave way to an expanse of alien industry, of alien might. Bug city.

Ahead, a narrow stretch of rust-colored alloy plates crossed from one side of the immense inverted cone to the other. Pipes and cabling ran along either edge, all secured with the same red material that coated the tunnels. The city's curved wall went up and up and up, leaking patches and lines of dirty purple around a host of machinery with purposes she couldn't fathom. Bugs crawled along these, and along more bridges that crisscrossed the void in ever-increasing lengths. A deep, evolutionary-fueled horror gripped her chest. No human belonged here.

Far above, a bluer tinge slipped down, accompanied by a surprisingly welcome howl. Open air. She wasn't entombed. Not yet. If only she could see the stars. A hundred meters and more. A hard truth settled on her. There would be no grapes, no vines, no home built to take in the scenery, and no friends sitting around a genuine wooden table, eating and drinking. She blinked back tears as her comm system connected to the satellite network briefly. Should she send a message, a farewell, a plea?

"The nuke, boss. It's there, on the left."

She spotted it—down a drop to a platform that covered half of the level. The nuke's barrel-shaped form with a cubic middle rested near a section of curved wall with open panels. Connectors, fins, pinpricks of light, copper wrapping, a circular opening—and bugs, bugs crowding it all. Just like the nuke. A section of its exterior casing was missing, explaining a radiation warning from her mech. Damn it. If the bugs had dismantled the initiator, it was all over. Every second lost made that more likely. And an army of bugs was coming. Hayden wouldn't have slowed them down long.

"Harry, lower us down. We'll clear the bugs and set the nuke's timer. And then—"

"What?" Harry asked bitterly. "Flap our arms and fly out?"

"I'd settle for a ride on a dragonfly," Amy said. "But that's not happening either. Look at it this way, Harry, we've done more than most. And we won't have to do maintenance on the mechs."

The truth cut like a plasma torch. "I'm with my friends. If this is how it ends, I'll take that. You're also the best damn crew I've ever worked with. Every time, you've put in more than I asked, more than you owed. If it wasn't for the bugs, in a few years there'd be a thriving colony up there, and it'd be like that because of you. This crew—we make shit happen. So, if I'm going to punch out, I'm going to take the bugs with me. How about you?"

Harry's sweet voice became a growl. "I'd strangle them with my bare hands if I could."

"Let's be a little more efficient," Amy said as she brought her mech near Harry's and grasped the gently swaying hook. "Feed us some cable."

They set to work. Harry turned her back to them, lowered her mech to one knee, and grabbed the sides of the bridge to brace. Trax went first. When Amy attached the hook, Trax walked to the edge. There was no neat way to rappel down, so she stepped off, dropping fast. The cable pulled taut, and she swung back and forth, above flooring, over darkness, and above floor once again.

"Roll some cable."

The cable extended, and her mech's feet hit the floor. Vertigo gripped her, and she steered the mech forward with shut eyes until well clear of the edge. Thankfully, the hook came loose, and she remained safely inside her mech as it retracted. Five percent power. She cleared the space and waited. How many bugs? Twelve. And that was assuming no more leaped down. Ice chilled her nerves.

"What's the plan?" Amy said as she landed.

"Squash the bugs, hit go on the nuke. Harry, you joining us? There should be something to hook yourself on."

"No. The bugs will be here soon. I'll slow them down."

Trax closed her eyes and pressed her lips tight before drawing in a shuddering breath. "Thanks. You've always had my back."

"What's one more time?"

"Everything." Trax rolled her shoulders. "Amy, I don't need to tell you we're outnumbered. We go in fast. I'll throw them in the clear for you to toast when I can but don't cook the nuke. That won't make it go boom."

One more thing. Trax flicked through her controls until she found what she needed. A playlist she used for exercise. A guitar solo started off the first track, joined quickly by a pounding rhythm. She set it over the comm, then charged toward the bugs. In the periphery of her vision, the bug city walls appeared to shift, but she put it down to a stress-induced optical illusion. And then the fight began.

She caught the first bug unaware and sheared through its head. The second reared as she slammed the warped edge of her shield down on its back. Another working of the shears, and the bug flailed mindlessly. She kicked it aside as flames came far too close.

The remaining bugs turned to the mechs. The battle was swift and brutal. Sparks flew as a bug spun its saw and cut into the optic cables controlling her shears. She lifted it high and threw it down, stabbing her shears into another that appeared in its wake. Her limbs ached as she pushed for responses that her mech couldn't give. Sweat dripped freely, stinging her eyes. Events merged into a kaleidoscope of terror and fury. When a bug hung onto her shield, she screamed in frustration. Fire licked its surface. Heat warnings blared. The bug dropped. Trax spun around, searching for the next threat.

Bugs littered the floor. One rocked near the edge, then exploded, its parts disappearing in a burning rain. Panting, she checked her mech's condition. Two percent power. A line came to her, something from an ancient recording she'd stumbled along. *Running on the smell of an oily rag.* It was an odd saying, but it was all too appropriate.

Amy's mech opened. "I've got my tools. I better get to work."

Trax kept close. Amy knew what she was doing, and she needed protection more than anything else, but it was hard to see her so vulnerable. To keep from changing her mind, she watched the bugs crawling around the city. Many carried pieces of familiar materials. It reminded her of ants bringing back food to a nest. Except she was in the nest. And the walls were shifting. Tall gaps inched open without obvious reason, leading her eyes upward. A silhouette descended, switching from darkness to bright white and red. A dragonfly.

"Amy, I don't want to be the asshole looking over your shoulder, but you need to work fast."

"Doing what I can."

And that had to be enough. Trax raised her shield over Amy and waited with as much calm as she could muster.

CHAPTER 35
GROUND ZERO

A spike thrust by Bill's ear as he released the last strap. The leg's metal chilled his flesh and soul alike.

"Hurry."

"And here was I planning on taking in the scenery."

Bill pulled himself out of the hole where the blister used to be. His mech still flailed and fired plasma, the heat wash cooking his scalp. The bugs were all over, battling an empty shell remotely controlled by Dantalion. The link wouldn't reach far, but then again, the mech wasn't going to last—just like Bill. Metal bodies muffled the spotlights, casting shadows, ensnaring him in a writhing cage. Pointed legs thrashed. He crawled between them, a weak, soft bag of flesh ready to pop. Acrid odors scraped at the back of his nose, burning the tender tissue. Torches, saws, and blades came out of nowhere. Bill threw himself in one direction, then another, unable to process fear, only continue his desperate escape.

He pressed against a curved surface. A tank stretched upward. Grabbing a tube, he dragged himself into a small gap. A carpet of bugs spread until consumed by darkness. There was nowhere safe. Behind him, a pale mass moved. His body shook, sick with adrenaline. How easy would it be to give up? To let the bugs finish him off, to end it all, to end the fear and the guilt. But no, not this time. He swallowed it all, accepting the sweet agony of existence and the sharp edge of hope. If he could help Trax and her crew, if he could save the remaining colonists, he'd accept all that came.

"Dantalion, how high can you make me jump?"

"The tank? High enough."

A mantis turned and darted toward him. Bill's legs tingled, and he jumped, reaching the top of the tank with his elbows propping him up while his legs dangled. The mantis grabbed his boot. His body slid, and the force on his elbows ground his bones. He kicked out, missing, and felt his balancing giving. He screamed and kicked again, connecting with the bug's head. Shock ran up right to his thigh, but he lashed out a third time and caught the bug's arm. It slid, pinching his skin before losing hold.

He scrambled onto the tank's flat top, chest heaving, feeling the thin covering flex under his weight. Better than nothing. A grasping robotic hand reached up. He couldn't stay, and yet, where could he go? His mech's spotlights were gone, leaving faint outlines and a fuzziness thanks to Dantalion boosting his vision. The rest of the bugs would soon join this one.

"The mech is no longer responding," Dantalion confirmed. "We're on our own."

A caterpillar flowed over the top of the tank, accompanied by the mantis. They sure as hell weren't alone. Swearing, Bill turned and sprinted. "You know what to do."

His boots slapped the ground with incredible speed, and his hip joints threatened to shatter. At the edge, he kicked, soaring forward over bug after bug. They leaped, torches and blades and grippers searching. The next tank was a world away. Air whistled, chilling his sweat-soaked hair. And then he was skidding across the top of another tank, the bugs swarming its sides. An instant later, he was in the air again, screaming in pain and sheer animalistic pleasure.

You can't catch me.

From tank to tank he went, a midge followed by a ravenous flock. Except, they didn't want to eat him. They wanted to chop him up and feed him to their masters.

Don't think that. Don't look for an excuse. Just do what has to be done.

On and on, leap after leap, bugs pouring up tanks, scrabbling along the ground, each without the weakness of flesh, of humanity. And then he landed on the last tank, his momentum carrying him forward past a circle of blackened and torn floor. Ahead, a shattered iris promised escape. He laughed at the lie but jumped anyway, hitting the ground and rolling before coming to his feet. A bug followed right on his heels.

He kept going, following a faint path of light bleeding from the iris. Behind, the bug clattered. Its vocal silence was almost worse than being chased by a tiger. The sheer impersonal nature of its aggression was an affront to the natural order. As he closed, the iris grew brighter, and the cavernous hatchery dimmed. Fire burned in his shins. His lungs sucked in sandpaper. A shadow blocked the iris.

Not now. Not another damn bug.

"Hayden, that you?" It came over a satellite link.

What did that mean? "Harry?"

"Oh, shit. You're a hardy bastard."

"That's up for debate."

The bug was gaining millimeter by millimeter, as his exhausted body ignored the demands Dantalion was issuing. Endless bugs swarmed around the last tanks and followed.

"Keep coming. Don't dodge."

Hard metal clipped Bill's boot. He stumbled but regained his footing.

"I said, don't dodge." Smudges erupted from Harry's mech.

"Doing my best."

Drones. Their pale blue flames sent them careening forward, leaving the thinnest gap for him to slip between. A blast threw him forward, and he skidded along the ground, his ears ringing and his vision blurred. He pulled himself up a column—no, it was Harry's mech. The bug was on its back, rolling, its head missing. She'd set off the drones. Damn, these people were good.

"Hayden, you functional?"

"Yeah, thanks."

"They're with the nuke. Can you help them?"

He nodded, then realized she wouldn't be able to see. "Yeah. Let's go." He hurried around her, giving her space to turn.

"No. We're all dying soon. I have a job to do, and I finish what I start." Her mech took a step forward, a step toward the mass of bugs.

"Wait!" He could tell Dantalion to control the mech remotely. She didn't have to die. Not yet.

"Bill, I can't. Amy rigged our mech differently. I have no access to Harry's."

Damn it. "Harry—"

"Shut up, Hayden." Harry's mech shifted into a loping run. "My family needs you. If you live, you have to get the League to help them."

He clenched his fists, desolation on his face. "I can't. They won't listen to me after this."

As she closed on the bugs, her spotlights painted a scene of machine versus machine, but Harry was inside. She wasn't blindly following orders. She was making a choice and paying the price willingly.

"Curse you, Bill Hayden, just promise me."

His eyes stung. "I promise. Whatever it takes, I'll do it."

She barreled into the bugs, breaking their charge.

"Bill, don't waste her sacrifice."

He turned and hurried down the corridor, hearing Harry's screams of fury, refusing to cut her off even when fury melted into anguish. The corridor gave way, and he was inside a mechanical hell. It was exactly as the crew had described and yet infinitely worse in person. Metal everywhere with that rust tone he wished he could scrub from his memory. Bugs climbed, oblivious to his presence. The far side of the city was different. Long vertical sections had opened, and an enormous mass of machinery slowly extended outward. Further up, bridges crossed an ever-increasing gap, and right at the top, a murky blue. The storm was clearing.

A dragonfly zipped down. His gaze followed it to Trax. The bug bounced off her raised shield. Beneath, Amy worked on the nuke next to a broken bug. One last jump then. He stumbled onto the bridge, entering the bug city fully, then dodged to the side and threw himself forward into open air.

Trax had kept her shield up, and he landed on its scarred and buckled surface, grabbing the edge as his legs slid off. Shears thrust forward.

"Stop. It's me," he shouted. "Trax, it's me."

"Hayden?"

"No, I'm the tooth fairy." He dropped to the ground. "What's the situation?"

"Harry?"

"She held them off to give us time."

"I—I see." Her voice was rough, her pain obvious. "Time. We're pretty much out of it."

The nuke was a mess. Whole sections of its exterior were open. Wires and fibers sprouted like disheveled hair. Lights blinked, and an insistent beep went right to his brain.

"Bill, the shielding is compromised. Avoid prolonged exposure."

He laughed. They both knew that wouldn't be an issue. Amy sat, leaning against the nuke. The innards of a bug spread across her lap, and her shaking fingers cut a length of wire with a small tool. Blood stained her left, starting just below the shoulder. It was wet and a hole steadily dripped more like a depraved hourglass.

They were all going to die, that much was obvious, but damn it, they should go out together. He'd finally found people worth knowing, and he was losing them. It was a selfish thought, and he embraced it all the same.

He kneeled by Amy as a tremendous crash announced another attack by the dragonfly. "How are you doing?"

"I've almost got it."

"I meant how hurt?"

"Doesn't matter." She paused, shook, then continued. "They were after the fuel. To fix their mess, I had to reposition the charges and the inner shielding. I'm so dosed, I'm glowing. Not that it matters. I just need to jump a broken circuit, and I'm ready to go. But my stupid fingers won't do what I want."

"Here, tell me what to do."

He followed her instructions, and a small device dangling on wires came to life with data scrolling on an embedded display. He entered the codes Karlo had handed over, and twin red lights flashed.

"Trax," he said, surprised by the steadiness of his voice. "It's ready."

"Let me get out." Trax's mech groaned and opened. She landed on unsteady legs. "Amy? You said you were only scratched."

"Work to be done, boss. You know how it is. It's funny, but I don't want to die. There's still so much I want to do. I have so many designs to try."

Bill placed a hand on Amy's, hoping she would accept him in this moment of intimacy.

She turned hers slightly and held his as Trax kneeled and gave her a gentle hug.

"The bugs are here, boss. You two better go."

He looked back. They were pouring out of the tunnel. It was time. And the responsibility was his. He raised the nuke's control unit. *Sorry, Harry.*

"You're the best I've ever worked with. And Harry and Izy and Fitz. You've shown me so much. Thank you—for all your help, and for being… who you are."

Trax slapped his shoulder. "You don't suck, either."

He lost himself in her gaze and pressed the detonator.

He held his breath.

Five minutes appeared, quickly counting down.

Amy giggled, her face tight from pain. "I couldn't risk changing the programming. You have five minutes to get away. You should have seen your faces. Izy would have loved it."

"Stop laughing," Trax growled. "We're taking you with us."

"You can't. You have to keep the bugs distracted or they might break it again." The effort of those words seemed to sap the last of her energy. She closed her eyes. "Boss, put me down, gently, please."

Bill shuddered. It wasn't over. It hurt so much, but it wasn't over. He gave Amy's hand one last squeeze as Trax laid her flat.

Amy's eyes flickered. "Dantalion says he's coming." She stopped breathing.

Bugs leaped down from the bridge. Bill let Amy's last cryptic words slip away. Five minutes to keep the bugs busy. Five minutes to pretend he and Trax could escape. He looked up. They'd never climb out. *Screw it.* No giving up. Right to the end. "Get up your mech."

"Batteries dead. It's going nowhere."

"That's fine. It's our ladder. Job's not done, right?"

Trax nodded. "I never turn in anything below spec."

They grabbed hold of the mech's legs and climbed, reaching the raised shield as the bugs started up.

Bill held his hands together. "Step here and grab the ledge."

She placed her foot, and he boosted her toward the nearby ledge. In a blink, she was on a lip of the wall, reaching down. A mantis climbed onto the shield. Bill jumped, clasping Trax's hand. The mantis shot forward, but she yanked Bill up like he was made of aerogel. The bug hit the wall and fell to the ground. More would come. He scanned the wall above. There were plenty of handholds. If only he could convince his body to try.

"Hayden, you're not paid by the hour. Move that flat ass of yours." She shoved one of his hands onto a metal protrusion.

He hauled himself up, and Trax did the same.

"That's better."

Meter by meter, he rose, delirious with exhaustion, with emotions he'd spent so long fleeing. "My ass isn't flat. It's the suit." The words popped out, without any of his usual consideration, his scheming.

"Sure, white boy. Keep telling yourself that."

He frowned as she pulled ahead.

"And don't look at my ass to compare," she said. "You don't know me that well."

His head tipped back as he chuckled. "I'll buy you a drink later."

"If I'm not washing my hair."

The bugs had crowded around a spot on the far side, those that weren't dragging Amy away. They followed an unseen route, the leaders doubling back toward the two climbers.

"Bill, there's a flyer overhead. I'm picking up its transponder. It's descending, fast."

"Don't toy with me."

"It's coming, Bill. Get ready."

A comm link opened. "Hayden, you still alive?"

Shock slapped Bill as real as a physical blow. "Karlo?"

"Couldn't let you have all the fun. What's the nuke status?"

"A few minutes, tops. We're climbing to keep the bugs busy until then. I'll send you all the data I have. Take it and get out. Give it to the LSA when you can."

"And make you look good? No chance. I'm coming down hard. Who's with you?"

"Just Trax."

"Be ready to jump."

Bill groaned at the thought and said to Trax, "We're getting a ride."

"What?"

"Karlo. He's flying down."

"Give me some of what you're on."

Shadows shifted. The flyer appeared above, jinking crazily as it dodged bridges and a massive rusty lump that had grown like a tumor on the side of the bug city. Below, the bugs flowed across and up the wall.

The flyer flared its engines. Bill blinked against the light and heat, spying an open side and a short, flexible ladder dangling like a dog's tongue.

"Get in," Karlo said, his voice audible through the comm as the roaring flyer drowned out all else.

"You first," Bill shouted.

Trax looked down.

"Go!"

She jumped, catching the ladder, her momentum swinging her back and forth. "Your turn."

He looked down at the bugs. They were ignoring the nuke. Perhaps they weren't programmed to care, or they saw the humans as their biggest threat. If he boarded the flyer, would that change?

Trax leaned toward him, one hand outstretched. "Hey, Spook. You owe me a drink."

A bug spun its saw and jabbed with a dagger-sharp leg. Bill threw himself away from the wall. A beautiful sensation of flying enveloped him in a cloud of peace. Trax grabbed his arm. They clasped hands, and his feet found a rung.

The flyer shot upward, tossing them in all directions. Bugs jumped like fleas, legs outward, seeking flesh, only to fall unfulfilled.

"Enough sightseeing, Hayden."

He followed her up, lucky to avoid being smashed against walls and bridges. Bugs threw themselves at the flyer, bouncing off the hull. A dragonfly with two faulty engines dove, but Karlo ducked beneath a bridge, then brought the flyer out, climbing nose up. Bill sought the door controls, hanging on to a handle and gaining bruises with each change in direction. On the third try, he hit the right one. It swished shut, but the beating continued.

Trax, who had strapped herself in, grabbed him and pulled him into the next seat. "Safety first."

He secured himself. "I'd hate to break a regulation."

"I want to break them all," Karlo said, from the pilot's seat, his broad shoulders and solid head blocking little of the view thanks to a clear roof canopy. He twitched as he dodged. "I'm sick of cleaning up someone else's shit."

"Ain't that the truth," Trax said. "Hey, what's that up ahead?"

"No back seat flying."

Bill's eyes widened. Now he understood. The gaps in the wall. The lump of metal. It wasn't part of the bug city... it was a bug. Thirty meters tall, maybe more. Eight legs. A large central mass covered with irises. The legs stretched across the city, and the irises opened.

"I think we've really pissed off the bugs."

Tendrils extended from the irises, each one tipped with a glowing point. Bill gripped his seat tight with his left hand. His right found Trax's. They carefully avoided each other's gaze. Balls of yellow flared, and the tips launched, gaining speed at a tremendous rate. Karlo spun the flyer, losing altitude. Missiles! Explosions tore holes in the city walls, spraying clouds of debris. The flyer tipped up again, shaking violently as Karlo pushed it to its limits. He darted toward the barrage, slipping between missiles with a barrel roll, then heading up between the legs.

The attack didn't stop. The giant bug had a full complement of launchers around its body. A blast sent shrapnel through the hull, perforating the floor close to Bill's boots.

The edge of the city came and went, and they shot into the night sky. The brightest moon watched them, and the horizon quivered with the passing storm. Bugs worked on the surface, erecting structures with uncaring efficiency. The giant bug kept hurling death as two of its legs reached the surface.

"Hold on to your balls," Karlo shouted, and the flyer shot forward, shaking, dropping, rising.

Bill gritted his teeth as the acceleration crushed him against his seat. Dantalion linked into the flyer and brought up a rear camera view. The bug reached the surface, hunching over the city, firing salvos. Thankfully, the missiles were unguided, and their aim grew worse as the distance increased.

"Ten seconds, Bill."

He turned to Trax. Serenity lay across her face, though her grip on his hand was tight. He couldn't think of anything to say, but perhaps he didn't need to. She quirked an eyebrow and smiled. And then the nuke went off.

Crimson filled the sky, so intense it became white. The canopy dimmed before drifting back to a shade reminiscent of a wood fire. The rear camera feed showed a dome, like a small sun resting at ground level. It faded slowly, a false comfort.

The flyer bucked, and heat radiated from all directions. A fist of air slammed them into a spin. Over and over they went, the sky and the soil dancing with no regard for human frailty.

He smiled. It had been worth it.

CHAPTER 36
FALLOUT

"Brace. We're coming in for landing!"

Landing? They were being rattled like dice in an almighty fist. Flames licked the canopy, and the now-gleaming foam in the hole between his feet wobbled as if it were a bubble about to burst.

The flyer's nose tilted up. The rear hit the ground with incredible force, slamming Bill's vertebrae together. Sudden snaps followed a continuous grinding. Thick smoke crawled down into his lungs. The flyer tilted to the right, followed by a bang that rattled his brain. Everything went dark.

A HAND RESTED on his cheek, firm but gentle.

"Hey, wake up."

Bill groaned but chose to stay still and enjoy the sensation. A slap brought stinging pain. He squinted. Trax leaned over, undoing his strapping.

"What was that for?"

"For looking dead." She offered a hand.

His wobbly legs held his weight. The entire left side of the flyer was gone, so they clambered out. His head cleared rapidly. A trail of debris and flaming grass marked their route and illuminated the crash site. The flyer's rear engines were missing, along with most of its body-work. What remained of the vehicle was blackened, blistered, warped, or on fire.

He glanced at the empty cockpit. "Karlo?"

"Here."

A line of crushed grass led to a dark patch a dozen meters away.

"You, okay?"

"A few broken ribs. You two?"

Trax stretched, her bones audibly clicking. "Nothing to write home about. Hayden?"

Bill spoke directly to Dantalion, "You've been quiet. Care to give a diagnosis?"

"I'd say you were beyond saving, but you've shown promise."

"What's the damage?"

"Bill, you take away all the fun when you make it too easy. Very well, you've got a nasty concussion and substantial soft tissue damage throughout your body. I'm limiting your pain as little as I can. Don't attempt anything stupid. Your radiation dosage is well above recom-mended levels, but nothing that can't be managed with medical care. You'll die of thirst well before that."

"I think," Bill said out loud, "I think I'm good."

Trax gave him a gentle shove. "Then we better get walking."

They made slow progress. A huge mushroom cloud loomed sullenly in the distance, though it was far too close for comfort. They had crashed to the southeast of Staging, in a spot that was mostly hills with tall grass and the occasional tree that had found its home without human intervention. The stalks all leaned to the west, and the trees had lost their foliage. Patches of blue dust remained from the storm, but they'd be washed away with the next rain. Insects hummed, unconcerned by the life and death struggle between two species.

Satellite connectivity was patchy. Bill tried to comm Ware several times to no avail and shared his frustration on the last attempt. Karlo explained that the convoy had deactivated their comm devices in case the bugs were using them for tracking. It wasn't a problem—Bill knew where they were headed—but a ride would have been nice.

Not too far ahead, according to Trax, there should be a small maintenance station. Food, water, and basic medical supplies would set them up for the hike. Occasionally, a bug or two wandered near, and Bill would drop low, waiting with his companions for the machines to pass.

"Can they rebuild?" Karlo asked one such time.

"Each bug has tools," Trax said. "If there are enough of the right kind intact and they have the materials, it's technically possible. With our fab setup, we could rebuild Staging given enough time."

Bill raised his head to check on the bugs' progress. "Their behaviors were geared to kick-start the alien colony, and they're all out of embryos to grow. Yes, we need to be cautious—anything can go wrong at a colony. However, our list of immediate problems is long, and our metal friends aren't at the top."

The bugs disappeared over a hill, so they continued their trek north.

Dantalion made a surprised sound. "Bill, you have another message from Beth. It just unlocked. I hate it when they hide things inside me. If we meet her again, I'm going to tell her a thing or two."

Bill chuckled. He could sympathize.

Trax gave him a look.

Bill shrugged and said to her, "Ever feel like you have a voice in your head telling you do to things?"

"Yeah, it's called a conscience." She punched his arm. "You'll get used to it."

Dantalion laughed. "Apparently, I'm the angel sitting on your shoulder."

"What does that make Beth? Let's hear what she has to say."

A small figure appeared in his vision—Beth. She sat behind her desk in an unremarkable office. Her shoulders were slumped and the skin beneath her eyes was bruised. The league flag, a diamond pattern of yellow stars on a black background with a green circle at the center, hung on the wall behind her.

"Hello again, Bill. This is the seventh, no eighth, variation I've recorded for just this part, so apologies if I appear less than enthused. It's no judgment on you. I could have left the alternatives to AI, but if I have asked a lot of you, then it is only fair that I also make some token effort. If you're listening, it means BILT4 has carried out serious transgressions, you have taken over the colony, and you have contained any immediate threat. I am sure you have maintained appropriate records to aid in any prosecution or covert punishment. Thank you for your service. The League owes you a debt. I will keep my word as previously discussed, though we'd welcome you back into service if you so choose. We need people like you. People with a conscience. We always have."

She looked off-camera for a moment. "This version also means there are ongoing serious issues on Eclipse. I can't give you orders or advice. Anything I say would be pure guesswork. All I can do is remind you that unless you have been able to send word, a hundred thousand new colonists will arrive on schedule. They will also bring another courier craft. If the situation allows, make sure you are on it. When you reach the Dorad shipyards, I'd like to be there personally to give you your ship."

Remind me? She was dumping their safety right on his shoulders. A hundred thousand people. What did she have against him?

"Who says she has anything against you?"

"She throws me into the worst situations."

"I'd take that as a compliment."

Bill kicked a small rock and watched it roll.

"What if I don't want to do what she wants?"

"She can't make you, can she?"

"That's the question."

"What's biting your ass?" Trax asked.

They had reached the top of a hill, and in the east, the true nuclear power in the system painted an orange hue across the horizon. Trax had found a straight branch and tidied it into a walking pole—or a rudimentary spear. She cut an impressive figure, strong, determined, and dangerous.

"We were Phase 2."

She nodded. "Yeah, I know. We have a big job ahead of us. It's not just about our survival. We have to take what we can and get far from the fallout. Resow crops and rebuild the manufacturing base. It's impossible, but we'll have to do it or a lot more people die."

"You're screwed," Karlo said. The tightness in his face could have come from the pain of his injuries... or not. "You had ten thousand people. Now you don't even have a tenth of that."

Anger bubbled inside Bill, fueled by indignation. Had Karlo forgotten his part? All the loss slammed into Bill at once. Amy. Harry. His survey crew that he had ignored until they were all gone. Crumpler. The cops he'd worked with. Even that asshole, Sturt. Bill stared at the BILT4 guard, teetering on the edge of violence. What would it achieve? Lashing out wasn't justice.

"Why did you come for us?" he demanded. "You were safe enough with the convoy."

Karlo shrugged. "I was a marine pilot once. Flew fifty-three combat missions in the Grayson FMA-1132. Made a few mistakes. Did things I shouldn't have. But I'm no coward. I was sitting there in a shitty rover, ignoring whining dickheads who ignored me, thinking about you dirt farmers going in to set off the nuke—*my* goddamn nuke. I have some fucking pride, so I went back and found that kid, Diver, bleeding everywhere. He'd tried to fix his mech."

Trax grabbed Karlo. "Is he alive?"

"I sorted him. He'll live. Made me feel worse, though. So I took the flyer. Thought I'd see what I could do. The storm made flying a real bitch. That and the damned bugs. When I spotted their base, I decided to go right down the bugs' throat. I figured it'd buy you time."

And maybe buy him some redemption. Bill looked into Karlo's fierce eyes when Trax released him. The guy wasn't asking for anything. He was too proud.

"Maybe we *are* screwed. That doesn't mean it's not worth trying. Are you going to help?"

Why do I feel like I'm asking myself the same question?

"I've got nothing better to do."

Until the courier ship came, Bill could say the same thing. It would be just as dishonest. Yes, there was the sensation of a looming catastrophe like an iceberg headed for a yacht. That wasn't the reason. It was Trax and Diver and Ware, and maybe a tiny bit Karlo. He'd found his crew.

A glint in the distance caught Bill's attention. He watched for movement that didn't come. It wasn't a bug.

"That should be the maintenance station," Dantalion said. "Try not to get lost."

It took them half an hour to reach a single squat building with an attached vehicle shelter. A battered rover sat inside. Trax started running as soon as she saw it. Bill followed, and even Karlo hurried as best as his injuries allowed.

"I don't care if every motor's burned out. I'm going to fix this baby up and get us moving!"

The station door opened. Bill reached for a pistol he didn't have. His mouth dropped.

Crumpler stepped out, holding a large knife.

"You're alive?" Bill said, dumbly.

"Don't look so happy."

"How?"

"Comm came through. An agronomist had broken his leg. He'd reached the station, but the ride was killing him. I was on my way when everything went to hell. It's only gotten worse since. There are three inside. Are you all that's left?"

"No," Trax said. "A convoy's heading north. A small one. Can you move your patient?"

"In another day if we go slow."

Karlo joined them. "The longer we wait, the more radiation there'll be."

Crumpler's eyes narrowed. "You set off the bomb?"

"That was more me," Bill admitted. His reputation wasn't going to improve.

"And me," Trax said, putting a proprietary hand on Bill's shoulder. "And my crew. The bug city is gone. We nuked it, and I'm not going to apologize for that."

Tension released from Crumpler's stance. "All of it?"

Bill raised his hands. "If the bugs could survive that nuke, they'd deserve to win. It's gone. Their damn horror show is over."

"Come inside." Crumpler gestured to the open door. "I'll check you over, and you can have something to eat and drink."

They stayed in the cramped space for the day, sharing stories with Crumpler and the agronomists. The medic checked each of them over, admonishing them for their no doubt foolishly received injuries. Toward dusk, Bill went outside and found enough wood to make a fire. It was good to be with people, but it was also good to have some space. A short while later, an agronomist broke open a case of beer.

Trax brought one to him.

"I thought I was meant to get you the beer."

She clinked her flask against his. "I always get my crew a drink after the job's done."

"I'm your crew?" He took a sip.

"You're still in the probationary period."

"I'll bear that in mind." He raised his drink. "To absent friends."

She repeated the phrase and took a long pull. They stood in silence as the fire cracked and popped. "I'm going to find one of the seed-banks and plant vines. The first vintage will be ready by the time the Phase 3 ships arrive. I'm done with waiting."

"I've got access to the survey records. I'll help you find a spot with good soil."

"I said, I'm done with waiting." She grabbed his suit and pulled him close for a kiss, a long one.

His lips tingled, and a smile spread across his face when they parted. "Is this how you treat your crew?"

"They should be so lucky. So, Spook—"

"Bill, call me Bill."

"So, Bill, are you going to stay?"

That was a loaded question. "I don't know. The fallout—the political fallout—is going to be huge. I don't think I'll have a choice. I'll have to go for a debrief. For a lot of them. And I've got some people to look after."

"Will you come back?"

He looked into the flames, trying to imagine himself by a fire burning next to a large house overlooking an endless vineyard. "When I came, I planned on seeing the stars. What I was actually doing was running away. That's over. I still want to travel, but I'll do it for the right reasons. And I'd like to come back to Eclipse. I don't know if I'd stay, but I'd like to return. It's a rough planet, but it has beautiful views."

He leaned down, and they kissed again. They held each other for some time. High above, pinpricks moved in the clear sky, satellites zooming by in a field of stars. Elyse Wagner's dropship would be among them. He forced his grip to remain light. Somehow, she'd receive the justice she deserved.

A streak flashed across the sky.

"A shooting star," he said. "Time to make a wish."

Trax raised an eyebrow. "Wishes? A waste of time. As long as I've got my hands, I'll make what I need."

He took her hands in his. "If the rest of us can find half of your determination, Phase 3 will be all right."

"You better believe it."

He'd wanted to believe in the League, in the LSA, in the dubious missions he'd carried out for a theoretical better future. It had all been shades of smokey gray. Eclipse was real, tangible, something he could believe in. Here, he could make a difference and know it. It might not be enough forever, and he might fail worse than ever before, but he'd know he was trying for the right reasons with the right people. That was an opportunity worth more than any land share, and he'd take it with both hands.

CHAPTER 37
ORBIT

From orbit, the mushroom cloud matched its name perfectly—a little growth on the surface, puffy and pretty. Elyse Wagner took one last moment to savor the view and dismissed the recording. Late was better than never. There would be plenty of time to revisit the capstone to her success over the coming weeks and months.

Her small office with its plain bulkheads was only relieved by a display with a live feed of the spinning planet below. Eclipse. Well, it certainly had been a blotch on her career until she dragged herself back into the sun. She stepped outside her office into the dropship's bridge, her gait cautious in the artificial gravity.

Only two of the twelve seats were occupied. Captain Amaruq sat, his gaze hovering between two large displays filled with graphs and numbers. One of his juniors worked at a console, frowning.

"Ms. Wagner," Amaruq said, standing quickly. "Can I help you?"

There was a haunted, fearful look in his eyes. She didn't appreciate the accusations they made. His attitude might become a problem. Loose ends would not do. She added it to her checklist. "No. I'm merely stretching my legs." She arched an eyebrow toward the junior. "Is there a problem?"

"No, ma'am. A few sensor anomalies. That's all. We'll track them down soon."

"Your dedication is appreciated."

Elyse went to the bridge elevator and punched in the code for the largest cargo level and waited. The BILT4 automated courier that had been hiding on the far side of the largest moon was now among the stars, taking home her message. A retrieval mission would take time, even if the board understood the urgency and the opportunity.

The doors opened to level C3, and her stilettos tapped pleasingly as she walked across the alloy floors. Crates filled much of the space, each held in place by bright orange straps. She moved between them, enjoying the maze of artifacts. This route was well worn with good reason—at its center lay her true prize. A cylinder of metal almost three meters across and one high. Above that, a tank of liquid. Several blocky, white medical units had been bolted to the floor, each modified by techs to support the life of the creature within. Unfortunately, none of them lived long enough to shepherd the equipment. The maggot swished in its prison. It had grown quickly, its mass now substantially larger than her own. That must be a sign of health. The dark, coppery eyes swiveled toward her.

"Hello. I see you're awake," she said, running a hand along the tank. "I do hope you don't outgrow your home. A live sample would be so much more valuable than a frozen corpse."

Its eight fangs retracted.

Clearly, it couldn't understand her, but she still found her lips quirking. This was going to be fun. "Do show some manners. I can turn off your food supply at any point. If only you could talk. For all the technology that you have to share, there's one question that I am most anxious to find an answer to—where do you come from?"

The floor jerked, and Elyse stumbled, breaking a heel and twisting her ankle. A high-pitched warbling sounded. Red lights flashed across the ceiling. She discarded her shoes and pulled herself up, using the tank to maintain her balance as the dropship trembled. A scowl creased her brow as she waited for her heart rate to steady. When she was satisfied with her composure, she opened a comm.

"Amaruq, kindly explain what happened to our rather expensive vessel."

"I can't be sure, ma'am." Tension hardened his words. "We might have been hit by a micrometeorite or had a pressure blowout. There are hull breaches on levels P1 and C2, and there may be small leaks elsewhere. I've sent someone to investigate. I think it's going to be ugly. The primary oxygen recycler on P1 is non-responsive, and we already had the secondary open to clear the filter blockage. That damn planet's dust gets everywhere. We needed a higher maintenance tempo."

Definitely a whiner. When deadlines were tight or numbers stretched, workers needed to rise to the occasion, not fish for excuses. "Did you say ugly?"

"Yes, ma'am. No new oxygen is being generated, and the CO_2 levels will soon rise. I'm taking us into a lower orbit. If we don't get the systems back online, we'll have to land."

Land? Over her dead body. "Captain, that is not an option. Activate the autopilot and go fix it. Do you understand?"

"Yes, ma'am." He didn't sound pleased.

She didn't care. She closed the channel and considered returning to her quarters. Soon. Not right away. It wouldn't do to look afraid.

A loud bang made her jump. Howling wind followed, sucking her across the floor until her feet hooked a tube from the tank. The pressure scraped her ankles, and it took all the strength from countless gym sessions to keep her feet anchored. The creature slammed against the tank, and she flinched in surprise, losing her hold. Air whipped her across the floor and slammed her into a crate. She grabbed the strapping and held on tight. No. She wasn't going to be sucked into space because her hopeless pilot hit every single rock, despite the vastness of space.

A series of thuds came from out of sight, and the air calmed, dropping Elyse to the floor. The dropship jerked. She stumbled away from the crate, her face hot with fury. Incompetence. It surrounded her. She scowled. What was that sound? Footsteps? A savage grin twisted her lips. She smoothed her dress and strolled toward the source, a location near the hull, the freight elevator most likely.

The crates became a maze in truth, as she had to backtrack and find another route. When she left them behind, she faced an empty cargo elevator. It was wide enough to hold a good-sized rover, but its flat surface was empty. Bright yellow guard rails were down, and there was no sign of any crew. Flashing emergency lighting continued, constantly suggesting movement as shadows flickered in and out of existence.

"Whoever is here, report to me immediately." She stalked to the controls, a set up resembling a lectern, and placed a hand casually on its edge. "Don't keep me waiting."

Skittering followed. She held her place. She wouldn't sacrifice her dignity. The fewer people there were, the more important it was to show that you were in charge. A crack echoed, and a little ice dribbled along her spine. She clamped down on the childish fear. More strange noises followed: clattering like long fingernails drummed on a hard surface, bangs of metal on metal, an awful scraping.

Enough. She was going back to her quarters. She padded across the floor and between the crates. *Thud. Thud.* She picked up her pace. The drumming sped up as she did, growing louder, growing closer. She turned left when a crate blocked her way and switched to a sprint. A short distance, and she had to turn right. Fighting her momentum, she pushed off another crate, caught her arm on a strap, and spun out of control.

"Whoever is there, stop it! Stop it right now!" Her chest heaved, and she backed away. "I won't stand for it. I'm not someone to be messed with. Others have made that mistake."

A black mass towered over a stack of crates. Her eyes dissected its form. A bulbous head with a frill of charred sensor stalks, multi-jointed legs, burned stubs of what would have been wings, and a dull, smoldering body wafting the sharp, cloying unpleasantness of fried circuitry. It looked like a dragonfly after a cruel child had held it under a flame. How the hell did it get inside?

It had been on the dropship when they launched. The damn thing must have held on all the way up to orbit. They hadn't hit a meteorite; this damn bug had torn its way inside.

The dragonfly's jaws opened. She shivered, then ran. It leaped from crate to crate, chasing, its legs grinding, puncturing. Directions lost all meaning. The crates offered no way to navigate. Fear narrowed her vision, lightening her limbs, and added a sense of the unreal to her body. She stumbled, dropping hard on her knees, but leaped back up.

The crates slipped away, and she found herself back at the tank. She ran to a piece of medical equipment and tore the casing free, revealing the tubing that flowed out like intestines. She turned and grinned viciously as her fingers intertwined in the soft, pulsating tubes.

"You're fucking with the wrong human. I'm the damn queen bee, here."

The dragonfly approached, its legs stretched between two stacks of crates, lending it a spider-like appearance.

She leaned against the tank. "That's enough. Come closer, and I'll rip this out. Your precious maggot will die. Do not mistake me for someone merciful."

The bug's body swung slightly from left to right, but it didn't advance. She had it right where she wanted. She'd get Amaruq to come down with a rifle and put it down. Another sample. Perhaps it was worth this little inconvenience.

A loud crack came from behind. She dared a glance. Lines riddled the tank's surface. Inside, the alien pulled back, its coppery eyes staring at her. It launched forward, breaching the tank.

Crystalline polymers shattered. Fluid burst out, washing Elyse onto her back. She tried to scrabble away, but the slick floor offered no grip. The alien tested its weight on its legs, then made its way down the tank and across the floor.

"We can do a deal," she said, hating the tremor in her voice. "I can get you anything you want."

The alien stepped over her legs and peered down, its eight long fangs pulled back around its puckered mouth.

"You're intelligent. You must be able to communicate. Listen to me. I can get you anything. Food, resources, technology—entire planets filled with humans."

The cross-shaped pupils thinned.

"That's right. We can work together."

The alien struck. The fangs thrust deep into her flesh.

It couldn't end like this.

It wasn't fair.

Finally, the pain stopped. The wants, the needs; it all drifted to nothing.

Her body flopped as she was consumed.

THE LEAGUE NEEDS
YOU!

Write a review or click some stars and entice others to dare tread the treacherous surface of Eclipse

https://mybook.to/projecteclipse

Sign up to my newsletter for info on new releases, current projects, and my medieval escapades!

https://www.tillsley.com/newsletter

ABOUT THE AUTHOR

Robert writes gripping science fiction, urban fantasy, and epic fantasy for adults and children. When he's not writing, he's swinging swords for fun and bruises. He has previously written works for adults and children under the name R Max Tillsley.

facebook.com/rmaxtillsley
twitter.com/rmaxtillsley
instagram.com/rmaxtillsley

ACKNOWLEDGMENTS

This novel is a love letter to science fiction movies of the eighties and nineties. I miss the tech—the switches, the dials, the blocky guns, and the chunky vehicles that exuded power and promised adventure.

The following beta readers have dared the terrors of my drafts, seeking gold amongst the swamp of spelling errors and erroneous punctuation. You rock!

- Aaron Holding
- Nathan Heinrich
- Bree Polden

Authors J. R. Handley and Paul E. Cooley were kind enough to let me kill them. Go read their books! Noah, Heath, Eli, Terry, and Paul kept me entertained on various podcasts.

Imagine Dragons created earworms that haunted me as I wrote. Bones is still going through my head. So, thanks? I give no thanks at all to commas. You little bastards suck. I tip my hat to the marvelous Katie from Kaye Kemp Book Polishing for bringing them to heel.

Finally, a special thank you to my wife, Monika, for her encouragement, her keen mind, and her endless patience.

Printed in Great Britain
by Amazon

58860318R00227